DEFIANCE

DEFIANCE

AN AMERICAN NOVEL

OLIVER LANGE

Foreword by Sol Stein

STEIN AND DAY/*Publishers*/New York

This edition published 1984.
Defiance: An American Novel was first published
in 1971 by Stein and Day/*Publishers* as *Vandenberg*.
Copyright © 1971 by Oliver Lange
Foreword © 1984 by Sol Stein
All rights reserved, Stein and Day, Incorporated
Designed by David Miller
Manufactured in the United States of America
STEIN AND DAY/Publishers
Scarborough House
Briarcliff Manor, N.Y. 10510

Library of Congress Cataloging in Publication Data

Lange, Oliver.
  Defiance: an American novel.

  "Previously published as Vandenberg."
  I. Title.
[PS3562.A485V3 1984]   813'.54   84-45211
ISBN 0-8128-2993-X

For B.A.B.
with love

Foreword

The Hunt for the Great White Novel

by Sol Stein

It began with a strange telephone call from a young literary agent named Philip Spitzer, who had recently broken off from a larger firm to fly alone. "Sol," he said, "I've got a novel here that I'll let you have first look at under two conditions." I liked Spitzer; the softness of his voice made him sound like a writer; many agents don't sound like writers, they sound like people representing hermits or legends.

I asked for the conditions.

Spitzer said, "I'd like you to read the manuscript yourself, and I'd like you to read it tonight." Strong words from a soft voice. I had no objection to condition one. With fiction it's possible to tell within five minutes whether you've got a real writer on your hands. "However, if it's good," I told Spitzer, "I can't promise to finish it tonight. I've got guests coming for dinner. I might need two nights."

It was a deal. Spitzer sent the manuscript of *Vandenberg* over by an important messenger. Himself.

I knew by the end of the first page that I was in the hammerlock of a writer with strength. Pretty soon the protagonist, Gene Vandenberg, a semirecluse widower with a slightly retarded 21-year-old son, proved to be a character who, like the Ancient Mariner, had got me by the lapels of my imagination and wasn't about to let me go.

You are into the story a way before you are certain that this writer—I turned back to the title page to catch his name—Oliver Lange, could not only create characters as alive as your neighbors and have you achingly turning the pages but had something to say about the future that hummed with a resonance of reality that even George Orwell had not achieved in his *1984*. Orwell is, of course, one of the important writers of the century, a honer of truth who performed best in nonfiction.* But this fellow Lange was working through character. The plot idea of *Vandenberg*—the novel was named after its protagonist—in lesser hands might have come across as a fantasy. The fact is that Lange's novel, unlike Orwell's *1984*, doesn't seem like a parable at all; it speaks to the actual year 1984 with more strength than it did back in 1971, when I agreed to Spitzer's conditions.

I phoned Spitzer and asked him why the conditions. He said his instinct told him he had something that might be good or great, but he wanted confirmation. I was to be his litmus test. He sounded overjoyed that I was as enthusiastic about the book as he was.

I asked who Oliver Lange was. Spitzer said the name was a pseudonym. I didn't take that to be good news. Most writers use their own names; of those who opt not to, some are covering up disreputable pasts. Moreover, Spitzer went on, Lange himself was a recluse who'd holed up with his wife and three young children somewhere in the remote mountains around Santa Fe, in a rambling adobe house he'd built with his own hands. There was no electricity, and the family hauled their water from town. When I asked how I could talk to the author, Spitzer laughed. Lange was eight miles from the nearest telephone. In an emergency, it was possible to get a message to him within a day or so by leaving word with a neighboring rancher who had a phone and who would try to make the trip to Lange's distant abode, weather and time permitting. This would alert Lange to the fact that somebody was trying to get in touch with him. Lange would then have to make a 16-mile round trip to return the call.

Months later, I realized that this sort of lifestyle was no great inconvenience for Lange. He preferred pre-twentieth-century communication. He proved to be a formidable letter writer. When we did speak by phone, his message was clear. No, he wasn't interested in coming East to do publicity for his book. Lange didn't sound like a man with a message for the world, the way Orwell had, except for the thunder that boomed out of his pages as it does in Rip Van Winkle country in the Hudson highlands, where America, if you believed *Vandenberg*, lay fast asleep.

I asked Phil Spitzer what he wanted as an advance for the novel. He

*I published Orwell's *Homage to Catalonia* in paperback in the mid-'50s; its original publisher thought I was throwing money away. Orwell's most important work is probably an essay entitled "Politics and the English Language."

named a sum and I said "Okay." It was one of the briefest transactions of my career.

Unlike most novels, *Vandenberg* didn't need a lot of editing. I recall that some of the interrogation sequences were out of proportion and needed cutting, and there was one missing scene that seemed essential. I wrote to Lange. He wrote back, letters of substance, but I was getting nowhere with the changes I had suggested. I needed to be able to talk to the man face to face. My publishing company was a smallish one at the time, and I couldn't be spared long enough to fly out to Sante Fe, rent a car, follow a map that would have to be hand-drawn, and hope for the best. Even if I would have spared the travel time, I had the impression that Lange would not welcome visiting trespassers.

I began a campaign of suasion to nudge Lange into his battered Volkswagon for the long drive to New York, where, I now knew, he had been born. The fact is that this authentic southwestern novel had been written by a former citydweller, an ivy-league graduate (Columbia), who'd started his professional life working for *The New Yorker*. He'd had three children by an earlier marriage; something had gone wrong; he'd remarried and now there were three new children. I learned that he'd worked at a variety of jobs—plumber, carpenter, night watchman, disc jockey, psychiatric social worker—off and on to make enough to feed himself and his family, but that his focus was on writing. In the meantime, from that isolated adobe house, the kids were driven to school by Lange or his wife. Life wasn't primitive. Lange had rigged a TV set to run off a Volkswagon battery, and in his house, illuminated at night by butane and kerosene lamps, there was even a battery-operated stereo that played the classical music he refused to do without.

It was a little like getting together for the SALT talks, but the day finally arrived when Oliver Lange showed up on the doorstep of my home in Scarborough (he wasn't about to participate in anything smelling of business, like coming to the office). The locus of our meeting was my study, a small stone-walled room that had once been a sculptor's workshop. Its walls are two-and-a-half feet thick Manhattan schist, a strong stone from the bedrock of Manhattan Island, that glints like mica. The study has four large windows. Outside, the branches of huge hemlocks seemed to be barred only by the glass from reaching into the room. It's a great, isolated place to work. The only writer I had shared it with was Elia Kazan when we worked daily, line by line, page by page, on the novels with which he made his successful transformation from stage and film to words without actors. Kazan and I were friends. Oliver Lange and I were strangers except for the binding strength of his book.

Lange looks as powerful as his language. Many writers have a shy exterior. Their strength shows when they talk shop. Lange is a very large man whose physical presence was as impressive as his book (the touch of shyness showed later). He was built like a lumberjack, a stevadore, a brewery-truck driver. The palms of his hands were heavily calloused. His vocabulary was precise, rich, broad-ranging, thick with reverberation. He used words not to theorize but to sculpt his rock-hard thoughts.

In my study, crowded with its ancient L-shaped desk on which the veneer was pretty well gone, Lange sat himself on the typewriter chair, which seemed much too small for him, and I got the comfort of the one armchair. We went over the cuts in the interrogation sequences. A very strong unspoken message kept coming through. Though Lange had only one novel and a self-published book of essays to his credit, the man was a pro. I have little patience with amateurs who remember only the words being replaced instead of focusing on the intent.

I was warming to him because of his formidable concentration on the work at hand. Then we got to the nub: the missing scene, the crevasse in which the novel lost its life. I laid out my thoughts and then paused, expecting something like a verbal shoot-out—a sort of literary O.K. Corral. He would draw, I would draw, blood on the floor, and the victor (Lange, of course) would stomp out, slamming the door so hard the glass in it would shatter.

Lange sat there listening, scowling, silent.

I started to add something, but he cut me short. "Yes. Of course. You're entirely right," he said, and with that he turned his chair to face the typewriter, rolled a blank page in, and began typing rapidly.

During his brief visit with us (my wife, Patricia Day, got involved in the conversation when we retreated from the study to the living quarters below), I learned a few more facts about Lange. He hoarded his privacy—this was the main reason for the pen name. At that time he was forty-two and had published nothing in New York since that early hardcover novel, written when he was twenty-nine. With the pen name, he hoped to launch a second career. Satisfied with his life, he had no intention of letting anyone tamper with it.

When he was ready to drive off, he politely asked Pat for a bottle of cheap red wine, and would she uncork it, please? "For the road, you know," he added. Armed with the bottle, one hand free for driving, he headed the Volkswagon toward Santa Fe. The police didn't catch up to him.

A publisher's job is to broadcast a book out into the world, to compete with 40,000 other books being published the same year. He becomes known by the books he crusades for under these adverse circumstances. The *Vandenberg* crusade labored under several difficulties. The title, as we learned later, was misleading. Many bookstores and customers assumed it was a biography of the late Senator Vandenberg. Others thought it had something to do with Vandenberg Air Force Base. That is why in its third incarnation in 1978 it was retitled *Defiance: An American Novel,* the name it goes by today.

There was also an unusual reservation about describing much of the plot. If we revealed what the reader would discover in the early pages of the book, it would sound like science fiction, which it definitely was not. *Defiance* is a novel about the present, and what it says is as true in 1984 as it was in 1971. It seemed prudent to say next to nothing in the catalogue copy and on the flaps of the jacket about what it was that happened in Gene Vandenberg's America.

On the plus side, the Book-of-the-Month Club, to its credit, selected the book with alacrity, and one of the best known paperback publishers in the United States outbid the competition for the paperback rights and later, it is said, told a great many people it was the best novel his firm had ever bought. Perhaps most of all, we pitched hard to get the attention of the book reviewing community, which must of necessity inure itself to the din that is each year generated by hundreds of publishing houses on behalf of thousands of books.

That was a time when there were more serious book review media in the country, and *Vandenberg* made it on the shoulders of very strong reviews, helped along by word-of-mouth from knowledgeable independent booksellers. Though name-brand authors then as now dominated bestseller lists, it was easier at the time for a novel of durable merit by a pseudonymous unknown to make the lists, which it did. It was translated into seventeen languages.

After its first success, *Vandenberg* settled down to become something of a cult book among the young. They, whose blood leaps to the possibility of revolution against established systems, found themselves passing the word to each other about a novel that dramatized a revolution against the revolution. *Vandenberg* had the particular appeal of that early American flag, before the stars and stripes, the one that had a snake on it and said "Don't tread on me."

There is no Great American Novel because if one were so recognized it would kill hope and usurp the future. Certainly one would find widespread agreement that, among nineteenth-century American novels, *Huckleberry Finn* and *Moby Dick*, in their very different ways, are both American and durable, and perhaps even deserve to be called great. But each is missing an element. An *American* novel, to deserve that particularity, ought to reflect at least some of the profoundly political essence that distinguishes the United States from a great many other countries.

Most nations are homogeneous collections of humanity. The United States is a collection of the most unlike heritages to have ever assembled themselves by will in one place out of political impulse, the desire not to be oppressed elsewhere, the fervor to live undisturbed by government. As much as possible. In as many ways as possible. History is littered with authoritarian societies. But totalitarianism is the name given in this century to societies in which governments are co-extensive with all important activities in life, where the state, in contest with the individual, has ritual, law, belief, education, and control on its side. Asians, by and large, are used to being pushed around from without and within. In Europe, homogeneous communities have evolved some societies that hold a finger up to government. But all of these societies have lost some of their populations in the last three centuries—more so in the last century—to the North American continent, to the United States, which, unpopular as it sometimes is in the imaginations of those European nations, is populated by those who fled from there to here, the majority for political reasons. In the most important form of election men can make, they have voted with their feet.

While in decibels of political noise some of the nations of Europe and the Third World continue to make louder sounds than Americans, I suggest that the *soundlessness* of American political feeling is still the chief characteristic of this nation. Any country as populous and diverse as the United States is likely to have its share of toadies and sycophants and natural bureaucrats, but in what other country of the world are you as likely to find so many people who will put up *to a degree* with the restrictions of government but, when push comes to real shove, don't want to be messed with, won't allow it, and will take to the hills if necessary in order to fight back. The United States is the largest potential guerrilla base in the world. And *Vandenberg*, now called *Defiance*, is the novel that speaks to that essential character more than any other that has yet seen print.

Scarborough, New York
May 1, 1984

DEFIANCE

1

The Forest

. . . the deeper shock, then, was not that we lost, but that we lost with such ease, with an effortlessness that approached divine imperturbability. In terms of image, the world was presented with the Statue of Liberty, not as an inviolate emblem but as a vacuously grinning old whore, who after a token assault was debauched and then rolled docilely in the hay.

We proved the lie, were served up with a gagging portion of our own vintage distillation of apocalyptic horseshit—all the narcissistic swill about indomitable spirit, invincibility, courage and nobility of purpose —and demonstrated once and for all to those who looked on with interest a fact long suspected: that this nation, through a self-administered indoctrination of spurious righteousness, larded with the false rewards of superfluous luxury, had at last achieved the most tractable, malleable—let's face it, spineless—people to walk the face of the earth.

—Vandenberg, The Journals

EARLIER, THE SUN had risen above a dark ridge east of where he and his son had their camp, but the long, winding valley below was still in shadow.

This valley belonged to the uppermost part of what had been the old Martin Ranch, and now, from where he squatted on the lip of a rocky escarpment, he could see meandering streams down in the valley. These would be the headwaters of Cow Creek, and farther along still, where the valley opened into sloping, fir-bordered parks, there was a pond with a few black dots that were cattle, Hereford stock, two, maybe three miles off, but perfectly visible in the hazy dawn light.

He watched the cattle, the collar of his shirt turned up against the chill. He had been there for an hour, leaving his son wrapped in a quilted bag near the fire, scanning the valley with binoculars, waiting for the sun to rise higher.

The escarpment, or *peña*, was a natural lookout, and for him it was familiar. Years ago, they'd hunted here—Abilene, and the Deagueros, and the rest—dressed in red fluorescent vests and jackets then, pockets sagging with sandwiches, cans of beer, and loose cartridges, hunting the easy way, hunkered down among the rotting boulders, talking, but rarely above a murmur, because in fact a trail led down the slope beneath the lookout—a deer run, a *jornado del muerto,* Abilene used to call it, a little journey of death.

Finally, satisfied, he slipped the glasses into their case and stood up. His boot scraped against rubble. Looking down, he saw an encrustation of fossilized shells; he paused, and squatted again, and with his belt knife pried a few loose, stashing them in a pocket. Then he clambered off the point and walked slowly up to the camp, stopping a moment to check the horses.

At five, while stars still shone, a young black bear had ambled out of the scrub oak to stop and stare around stupidly, pig eyes blinking, snout swinging back and forth, trying to pinpoint his scent, and Vandenberg, up and dressed already and rekindling a morning fire, heard the horses snort, and, seeing the bear, rose from the still hot smoking ashes and strode down the slope flapping his arms and hissing furiously, "Hey! You get your ass out of here—"

Not loud enough, he'd thought, to rouse the boy—and the bear, finally spotting him, braked to a halt, then with a guttural *whoof* wheeled and trotted back into the scrub oak, moving despite the clumsy gait with marvelous grace and swiftness—but when he got back to the fire Kevin was up, propped on one elbow: "Daddy?"

"Wasn't anything," he said, getting down on all fours and blowing on the ashes. "Little bear—he was riling the horses."

Kevin sat up. "A bear?"

"You've seen bear a thousand times. Go back to sleep."

His son considered this. "What time's it?"

"Five—five fifteen. Tuck in for another hour."

"You want I should help you get that fire going?"

"Stay warm, darling."

"I can get dressed and get you some wood."

"That's okay. I've got plenty here."

"All right." His son lay down again and moved around in the bag; then, drowsily, "But if he comes back, wake me up."

"I will. Go back to sleep."

After a cup of coffee, he had left the camp, taking the binoculars with him, stopping among his horses. He disliked them and admitted that they frightened him, but up here they were needed, and now he stood in their midst, talking softly: "It's all right now . . . just take it easy," and the big chestnut, in a delicate and loving fashion, thrust its head forward, the upper lip curled, to snap at his shoulder. He slapped the muzzle hard with the back of his hand. "Quit that." For a moment, he and the chestnut had stared at each other, and then he went on down to the lookout. He moved slowly, stepping carefully, a large heavy-set man, gray-haired, fiftyish, dressed in filthy jeans, a wool shirt, and a decrepit Stetson whose crown was stiff with sweat. Except for the horn-rimmed spectacles, to which even now, in the breaking dawn light, a pair of clip-on sunglasses had been mounted, he could have passed for a local rancher.

COMMUNICATIONS

. . . America should not be called the "New World" any more; it should be called the "Old World." Its time is over.

—Nguyen Cao Ky

WHEN HE GOT BACK Kevin was up and almost finished washing. In the coals two cans of pork and beans were heating, lids peeled back. He waited for the boy to finish, and then they sat down by the fire and gingerly edged the cans to one side, poured coffee, and ate. "Thanks for putting the beans on," he said, after the first mouthful. "Could have stayed in the sack a while longer, though."

"I didn't mind," Kevin said. "I was awake anyway."

"Damned good," he said, and his son smiled. This was a routine. Whether it was beans or a piece of venison to fry, the son made breakfast because he knew Vandenberg liked him to, just as he knew his father would usually remark on the excellence of whatever it was he cooked.

The beans gone, Vandenberg tossed his can into the underbrush and rolled a cigarette. "Sleep okay?"

"Fine."

"Turning cold up here, nights," he remarked, looking at the sky. "I've been wondering—you warm enough in that bag? We'll have snow before long."

"I'm plenty warm."

"About time to start getting ready for winter."

"Will we use the cabin again?"

"I suppose so."

"I sure had fun this summer," the boy said.

His father nodded, then thought of the shells. "Hey, you'll never guess what I found for you, down at the lookout." And, as the boy showed interest, he reached into his shirt pocket, took out the shells, and gave them to him. "How about these?"

Kevin handled them, not recognizing the encrusted lumps, and then he understood, and he grinned. "Why, they're sea shells."

He said, "Maybe you can't remember—you were only about four—but one time, your mother and you and I went to the ocean. One day we had a picnic down by the beach in Mazatlán, and you

15

had on your swimming trunks, and you gathered up a mess of shells—like these, only these are old. We brought them all the way back here to New Mexico, and for a long time afterward you kept them in a jar in your room, and sometimes you'd play with them. I don't know what happened to them finally. That was a long time ago."

Kevin thought, then nodded. "Yes—I remember that. I remember our house. There was a big window in my room. In the morning the sun shone in. The cat liked to sit in the sunshine. I had an airplane . . . it hung down on a cord. We had good times then, didn't we?"

His father looked at him with pleasure. "We sure did."

Kevin examined the shells more closely, intrigued by the delicate flutings, puzzled now; he glanced slyly at his father. "You found these on the slope?"

"That's right."

"You're kidding."

"Nope."

"You find shells by the ocean—you just said so—not on mountains."

"Sometimes you do."

"Quit messing around," Kevin said. He grinned. "I'll bet you bought these in town one time, and you been keeping them, so's to fool me."

"No, I'm not fooling," he said, enjoying himself. "But you were right when you said you find shells by the ocean." He motioned with his arm. "All around us—right here where we're sitting—there was once an ocean." The boy gave him an unbelieving glance. "No, I mean it—that's why I brought the shells, to show you," he insisted.

He thought to himself, will he remember any of this? Or will it go, like everything else? But his mind's so damned amazing sometimes—remembering about that picture window in his room, when I myself hadn't thought about the place in—how long? Without haste, he explained, "A long time ago, maybe a million years—"

It was like a story to Kevin, but his mind stumbled at the length of time. "That long?"

"More or less," he said. "Anyway, the country here was under water, see? The ocean covered all this, and there were no mountains such as we have now—it was pretty flat, and everything was covered with water, and there were fish, and of course lots of shells—crustaceans—just as we have in the seas now."

"Did the water dry up?"

"No. What happened was that the land rose. There were stresses and strains going on in the crust of the earth then—still are, and now we have earthquakes and landslides only this was lots bigger—sort of like when you take a smooth sheet of paper, and if you lay it flat on a table and put both hands on it, the fingers spread out, and scrunch them together, why, the paper'll crumple, and that's what these stresses did, and the land had to go somewhere, and the only place it could go was up, so that's what happened. The crust of the earth buckled and rose up, and the ocean drained off, and that's why we have all these big old mountains and ridges you see around us—they're like that piece of paper, only they're made out of rock and earth. That's why, even today, if you look closely you'll find shells, even this high." He kicked at the dirt. "Not this—you have to find big rocks, outcroppings—old rock. Like the lookout."

"Could you sell these?"

"Not likely," he said. "Maybe if you came across one that was rare—"

"These aren't?"

"I doubt it."

"I'll save them anyway," Kevin said, slipping them into his pocket. "You can never tell. They might be worth lots."

He knew this was the boy's way of saying he treasured the shells, in the same way he valued other fool things that caught his attention—grouse feathers, porcupine quills, the bleached skull of a hawk—just as he knew Kevin, though he prized the fossils, would without hesitation give them to the first person who admired them, never questioning that the recipient would find delight in the gift. What need to explain about the Precambian Age, or Permian shale and Middle Pennsylvanian limestone? Kevin would not have caught any of it, and it would have robbed him of the dazzlingly simple notion that you can after all find sea shells on mountain tops.

He tossed his cigarette into the fire. "Getting late."

"You really mean it when you said we'd get beef today?"

"Sure. Sirloin tonight—how's that hit you?"

"Pretty good."

He poured the last of the coffee, and then reached over to the transistor radio he'd set on a rock and turned it on. The batteries were almost gone, but there was enough in them to pull in KGGM, ninety miles to the south, and they caught the last of the 6 A.M. newscast: "China's rocket potential," the announcer was saying, "is greater than experts had suspected, according to Dr. Fred Sundberg, Assistant Director of UCLA's nuclear physics department. His statement was part of a closing address delivered yesterday at an international seminar in Washington, D.C., attended by visiting scientists from thirty-six countries. Doctor Sundberg emphasized the strides made by the Chinese during the past two years. He said—(the physicist's voice, a flat, pedagogical tenor, came on)— Despite their rigid censorship, we can say that China possesses the means to deliver major ballistic offensives east and west. Though their strike capacity is, of course, nowhere near ours, either in inventory or sophistication, it is sufficient to destroy life on this planet. Monitoring stations in the free world have recorded the testing of as many as eight nuclear devices a month. At this rate, microcurie counts in the atmosphere could easily reach a critical point in six to eight years.'" The newscaster's voice came back on, and after a commercial for a used car lot in Albuquerque, went on, "Florida. Preparations for the forthcoming American-Russian manned deep space probe are continuing, and no major problems are expected that might delay the blast-off, scheduled for early March, a spokesman at Cape Kennedy said today. Optimism in scientific circles is running high since an entirely new computer package for the space vehicle was put through its paces—"

He turned the radio off.

Kevin said, "Gosh, ain't that something?"

"It sure is."

Kevin glanced at him. "You think that guy on the radio was lying?"

"It's hard to tell."

"I remember you used to cuss the television—you said it was all lies."

"So I did," he replied. "And so they were. Most of them, anyway."

"Do you think they're still lies?"

18

"Probably, Kev. I don't know for sure." He got up. "Let's go."

They broke camp. While the boy put away the eating utensils and rolled the sleeping bags, Vandenberg folded the tarp they used for a lean-to and put out the fire, kicking dirt over the ashes, making sure the embers were dead. Together they went down to the horses and led them back to the camp and saddled them, the pack rig going on the smaller chestnut.

It was warming now and you could hear birds calling back and forth, and once there was the anguished cry of a lone crow from somewhere down in the valley below, but mostly it was quiet except for the sounds they themselves made as they worked, the slap and jingle of harness, and once a grunt and a muttered curse from Vandenberg as he cinched tight the McClellan on Kevin's horse, the gelding rolling its eyes and finally farting in outrage at the cinch. The gelding was spirited, much younger than the gray he rode, and he had let Kevin have it because the boy could ride. Before bringing his son up here, he had used the gelding as an extra packhorse, disliking its temperament and tender mouth. The older gray was more to his taste. There was nothing fancy about the gray, but it could walk the high trails all day without tiring, provided he didn't push it too hard, and Vandenberg, a heavy man, appreciated this. It was his theory that the gray had spent its life above nine thousand feet, and that its heart and lungs had been conditioned to the thin air.

When they were ready, he strapped the rifle in its scabbard to the gray's saddle. Kevin, already mounted and waiting, was holding the lead rope of the packhorse. Vandenberg glanced once more at their camp and then hoisted himself into the saddle. They moved off, heading for the deer trail beneath the escarpment where he had watched earlier, riding loose-reined, letting the animals pick their way down the steep slope. The valley spread below them for miles, brightly lit now by the morning sun.

COMMUNICATIONS

Our peril was not the Bomb, or Communism, or the population explosion, but the state to which our life-style had progressed. By some sequence still not entirely clear, the American psyche curdled

*badly by the seventies. The improvement of our human condition,
individually and nationally, our raison d'être, became perfunctorily
mechanical. There was no spirit anywhere.*

*What I thought I could see though, from my vantage point, was
fear. The kind you find on a national scale. The sort that lasts
decades. The variety that absolutely blows the mind, boggles the
brain, and leaves in its wake listlessness. The excitement was gone.
All this became perfectly clear once the Occupation commenced.
The degree of obedience demonstrated—after the Soviets satisfactorily revealed that they were not the ogres we had been led to
believe them to be—proved that U.S. citizens, including the Great
Silent Majority, did not, after all, especially care who led them.
What counted was that they did not want to lead themselves. Supplied with the prerequisites of material symbolism (it was, perhaps,
the first time a subjugated country was permitted to retain nearly
all the hedonistic bric-a-brac that contributed to its downfall), who,
after all, cared to tackle the messy problem of self-determination,
a philosophical Gordian knot we were not equipped to unravel?
(For that matter, were our Russian guests correct in their persuasive
suggestion that free choice was extinguished on the American scene
by 1800?) Granted, ethical marzipan of this sort is unimportant—
what is, though, is the post-Invasion spirit of cooperation that
infected the country. Which is another way of saying that Americans were suddenly terribly glad they were not being punished for
the sin of being American.*

*You must therefore admit that when I chose my particular
course of action I was not out to set myself up as a spokesman, for
certainly no one who held such a poor opinion of his countrymen
would trouble himself with the futile task of improving their lot.
The idea of anyone looking to me for insight or advice was absurd;
and, too, years before, I had fallen into the habit of having as little
as possible to do with my fellow Americans, having decided for
myself, long before the present debacle, that if I maintained a
judicious distance between them and me my life could not help but
be richer.*

*As time passed, however, I was increasingly troubled by an
argument, inherently existential, that confounded me. By doing
nothing, I was no better than they. . . . Yet conceit if nothing else*

barred me from identifying with all those broader spectrums of American society, whose every action and thought was odious.

—The Journals

BY MIDMORNING, they reached the pond on the flats. It was shallow and weed-filled, and on the far shore corkbark spruce grew to the water's edge. The Herefords—four cows and three calves— looked up as they walked their horses toward them, then returned to grazing.

He checked the gray, and his son moved up alongside him. "Daddy, what if somebody's here?"

"Quit fretting. I watched this morning."

Miles overhead a swallow-winged jet, so high the barely visible fuselage looked translucent, ghosted across the sky, leaving a white contrail, followed a minute later by a distant roar that descended over the valley, the sound coming from far behind the plane. Before it died away, he dismounted, pulling the rifle from its scabbard. "You take the horses off a way."

He handed over the gray's reins, stepped toward the cattle, then stopped and sat, working a cartridge into the chamber, feeling anger and resentment as he sighted on the best calf, one that would dress out at a hundred and fifty, and as he began squeezing the trigger he thought, how stupid can you be, telling him we need beef instead of wild game, when the truth is that they've finally got you boxed— so good, in fact, that for months now they haven't bothered to patrol. That's what's eating you. They know you can't move. You can rot up here, for all they give a damn. And to show them you haven't given in, you've ridden half a day to rustle a calf you don't need. Anyone but Kev would tumble in a second. And if they come up here, you'll be running through the mountains all winter.

And then, with the cross hairs centered behind the calf's shoulder, an easy shot at seventy yards, the Springfield fired, silencing the birds in the meadow, and he heard the smack of the slug. The calf sank to its knees momentarily before staggering up again to trot off a way and then stop, staring around foolishly, its heart burst, wondering what had happened, already dead without knowing it, forelegs spread wide; with a plaintive bellow it fell over in the grass, legs kicking. He worked the bolt, slipped the safety on, walked over to the calf, and opened the jugular. His son watched, some distance off, and Vandenberg called, "I won't be long."

In twenty minutes he had rough-dressed the carcass, beheading it first, and then getting rid of the guts and sexual organs, leaving the hide on, but using his belt axe to split the breastbone. When he was done, he went to the pond and washed his hands and arms, and cleaned the axe and knife. Then he called the boy. Together they wrapped the carcass in the tarp, and then there was the job of getting the meat onto the pack rig, and they had to blindfold the chestnut before it would tolerate the smell. Once they were moving, the horse settled down. Already, above the grassy park they had left, crows wheeled in circles.

COMMUNICATIONS

One of the little freedoms left to us in this era of traffic lights, income taxes, no-smoking signs, diet consciousness, the draft, and anti-smog ordinances, is the freedom to tune our color sets any darned way we please.
—TV Guide, Vol. 17, No. 1, Issue #823

They had control of radio and television within, it must be presumed, eighteen hours or so. I always thought they had it sooner than that. The newspapers relied heavily on the wire services, and these were sending out canned releases that for all anybody knew had been composed months before. So, there it was. The word, then, for the first paralyzing day or two, was to remain calm and listen for further reports. Work stopped. No one went out much. People spent their time staring at the tube. The Soviets used imagination there, not releasing a single account of what had happened. Instead there were a dozen quasi-official versions, so that presently not even the most expert news analysts could tell which side was up. And of course there was the fear. (I found the dry detachment of my old friend von Clausewitz cast in a particularly evil gloom, doubly pernicious because the barb was inward-turned: "Public opinion is ultimately gained by great victories.") Interestingly, U.S.-Soviet relations had never been better, and only a month before the Invasion, the Secretary of State himself announced smilingly on Meet the Press, *". . . we [and the Russians] are getting along famously."*

The Russians bet heavily that the decades of cold war we'd functioned under had preconditioned our entire life mode to fragment when certain stresses were applied. Winner take all.

The fear I could understand, but what repelled me was seeing how, very shortly, the population regarded the Occupation with little more concern than it would have shown over the changing from a Democratic to a Republican administration. There, too, Soviet reasoning was more sophisticated than we might have once imagined it to be, for everything went on as before, and all the cherished Zeitgeist *regarded as essentially American, from Thanksgiving to the World Series, was conspicuously present in our red-white-and-blue calendar of celebrations.*

Also present were over two million Soviet troops, from Bar Harbor to Sauselito. Military Government did what it could to make this a palatable condition, verging on the apologetic when it exercised provisional power. Housing for troops was requisitioned in as friendly a fashion as possible. "Temporary measures," "for the time being," "in the near future," was all you heard. I suppose they must rank as the kindest and most magnanimous conquerors in history, and you had to listen with care to catch their subtlest implication: "Cooperate . . . it could have been worse." Americans themselves were the first to pick up on this.

C. M. Fair said it as clearly as anybody in The Dying Self: *"In the decades since World War II there has been little to suggest that the 'crisis of rational humane expectation' ended with the Nazis. On the contrary, the Germans, with their usual odd mixture of literalness and virtuosity, may have anticipated us."*

Life changed. There was gas and food rationing. The legal machinery of the draft was reenacted when it was revealed that China was preparing, and we were faced with the notion, difficult to digest, of young American and Russian conscripts fighting together on soil alien to both, five thousand miles away. This time around, there were no cardburners, no C.O.'s sweating it out in Montreal, no S.D.S. and campus insurrections, nor any of the other privileged-class high jinks that got by in the old days of befuddled benevolence —no one had money or time for such small adventures, or for the longhairs, either. Life changed—and it's been changing steadily ever since.

—The Journals

BY NOON THEY WERE camped several miles north of where he had killed the calf, at an abandoned mica mine on Elk Mountain. A year ago he had repaired a wrecked shack at one side of the mine tailings, not rebuilding it to the point where it would look habitable from, say, a cruising helicopter, but getting it tight enough so that it was dry.

A primitive road led to the mine, and farther down he had dropped trees across it that would stop a jeep or truck, but anyone on horseback or on foot could make it all the way. Because of this he never liked to spend more than a few days at the shack. A Forest Service watchtower was only a mile to the south, so that they had to be careful about smoke. During the old days, in the summer, the mine would have been visited every weekend by campers, but now that the forests were sealed off, no one came up.

Rarely, a helicopter patrolled this area, usually one of their Mil-4 mediums, with light machine guns mounted in the discharge ports on each flank, but they were afraid to fly at this altitude except at dawn, when the air was still and heavy. He knew this and camped high. He had an ominous feeling about helicopters; he believed that he could elude mounted men or vehicles, but there was something about the ugly, hovering craft that unnerved him. This was why he seldom went into the lower valleys, although occasionally he would make a foray into them, as he had today, or even, when the mood took him, ignore all the precepts of wariness and common sense and ride to San Sebastian to see Terry. This last was the most dangerous of all, because he was convinced her house was still under surveillance. Most of the time, though, he and his son stayed far back in the wilderness.

He had no illusions about the miserable conditions under which he survived, and during his first winter he had come so close to living on a subhuman level that it had affected his mind. That spring, he had emerged from the shack he'd holed up in, bearded, filthy, and half-crazed with loneliness. He knew he could never do

24

it that way again, and it was during the second winter, with Kevin for company, that he had begun borrowing books on history and philosophy from Terry's library; it was then that he had begun the journals, writing slowly in the thin winter's daylight in the notebooks she had gotten for him. This helped, but even so, the second winter had affected him still more. The life, he admitted, was too much for anyone used to civilization: the necessary feral qualities had been bred out of him.

He'd thought about this before going to Santa Fe for his son, but when he had actually seen for himself the way the boy was living, he had not hesitated. Much later, he began to piece together the bitterness that had corroded his mind. For Kevin was not merely companionship; he was the past. In that mind, stopped— magically suspended—so that as long as the boy lived he would have a child to care for, Vandenberg found absolution and a sanity that refuted the stories about him.

And having the boy with him made him even warier. He was not free in the mountains, and he knew it. He was no freer than the people in the cities and towns, no freer than any beast in a zoo, except that in his case the cage measured sixty by eighty miles.

COMMUNICATIONS

Disposition Summary   *#3251*

VANDENBERG, KEVIN TERENCE

D.O.B.: *12/14/51, Santa Fe, N.M.*

PARENTS: *Vandenberg, Eugene R. (Whereabouts Unknown)*
                 "   *Cora (Bancroft) (Deceased, 8/4/55)*

SIBLINGS: *Two half-sisters, paternal. No deviations.*

PHYSICAL: *No gross abnormalities. Mild spastic diplegia, age three, lessening by age six, extinct at age nine. Severe strabismus, left eye, corrected surgically, age four.*

MENTAL: *WISC given, ages 6, 12, 16, 21, indicate discrepant scores (verbal & performance) ranging from 10 to 50 pts. Bender-Gestalt and Goodenough Draw-A-Man given concurrently show comparable results. See appended scores.*

MINIMAL BRAIN DAMAGE SYNDROME

Visual Agnosia: varying, mild to advanced. Age/int. responses: 5-7 yrs.

Inhibition/Volition Reflexes: Excellent: 18-yr. level.

Coordination/Interdependence: Poor/Fair: 4-9 yr. level.

Speech/Vocal: 5-9 yr. level.   Attention Span: varying.

Mongolism: No abnormalities. Normally spaced great and second toes, no epicanthic fold, palms creased normally.

DIAGNOSIS & RECOMMENDATIONS

Moderate/severe retardation, varying age-intelligence responses. The patient's general level ranges from 5-9 yrs. Emotional responses: 4-7 yrs. No hysteria or hallucinations elicited, and there is a reasonably good attention span. Patient is obedient, trusting, and reacts excellently to placation. Generally speaking, this man is gentle, tractable, and affectionate. Inhibition-volition reflexes indicate excellent coordination, and there is no reason why the patient, with suitable training, should not be able to perform useful manipulative tasks. Physically, this is a tall, slender, well-muscled Caucasian male in excellent health. Interestingly, there is a distinct Lincolnesque Marfan's syndrome.

Patient requires minimal care. The recommendation is that he be discharged from this facility. Since our records indicate that one parent is dead and the other has deserted, he would probably function satisfactorily in a foster-home situation, where there would be familial ties, and where he could take on a limited role.

—James R. Forbes, M.D., Psychiatrist
La Madera State Hospital
La Madera, N.M. 87501

THAT AFTERNOON they butchered the calf, working slowly in the sun outside the shack, saving a dozen steaks, because that would be all they could eat before the meat turned, slicing the rest into thin strips for *carne seca*—jerky. Kevin strung wire along the south wall of the shack, and from this they hung the strips, after they had been soaked in brine. A few days in the sun would reduce them to brittle pieces of almost pure protein. It was tedious work, and *carne seca* quickly became the most tiresome diet imaginable, but it would keep them in meat for weeks. They were nearly done, and he was thinking of the dinner they would have that night, steaks and the last of the potatoes, when he heard a horse whinny. He listened, then said, "You hear that?"

His son nodded. "It was a horse."

He glanced around. Soaking in a pot near the cabin door was the last of the salted meat. Alongside it were stacked saddles and cooking gear. Their horses, hobbled now, were grazing a hundred yards off. They could have been ready in five minutes maybe, if the animals stayed docile and if they left the meat, but he knew they were not going to get that much time, and as he ran toward the cabin door he realized they would probably lose everything.

Kevin, sensing his fear, stayed close. Inside, they grabbed sleeping bags, the rifle and binoculars, and a canvas carryall, and then they were outside and running. More than anything he hated leaving the horses. Panting, he and Kevin trotted, stumbling at times, up the slope behind the cabin, waist-high in scrub oak, making for a stand of fir sixty yards off, and he had that terrible awareness that their backs presented a clear target.

Finally, a minute later, he and the boy made it to the trees, wriggling under the lowermost branches of a huge spruce until they were behind the base of the trunk. Sprawled on the thick bed of needles and fallen cones, they tried to control their breathing. He gasped, "We ought to see them soon, unless they're in among the trees."

"You all right, Daddy?"

"Christ, it's enough to kill you, trying to run at this altitude."

"Who do you think it is?"

"Hard to tell. Might be a stray—I doubt that. Animal on the loose would stay lower. A ranger—maybe troopers. At least we didn't start a fire. There's a chance they'll pass the shack and ride up to the main buildings. We'll see."

A quarter of a mile off, silhouetted against the skyline where the road crossed a ridge, a rider came into view, then a second, and a third. He put the binoculars on them, shoving his spectacles up on his forehead. He was still panting, so that the binoculars trembled, and finally he took in a deep breath and held it, which helped steady his hands. He watched for several minutes this way, breathing for a while and then taking in a lungful and holding it.

They were not in uniform, he could see that, but they were riding toward the shack.

"Are they soldiers?" Kevin whispered.

"No—*pero*, because they're not in uniform doesn't mean they're friends." There were local people, he knew, who, given a chance, would have shot them both, would have done it unfeelingly, not for the reward but to ingratiate themselves with M.G.

Then, lying on the needles, he recognized the big, rakishly cocked Stetson on the lead rider, and he put down the binoculars and said disgustedly, "Oh, shit." Even at that distance, there was no mistaking Tixier's ten-gallon hat and dude-ranch western shirt.

He raised the glasses again, and watched them as they rode closer. He recognized Willie Deaguero, fat-bellied, almost as dark as a Negro. For a while he could not identify the third man, and then he saw that it was Reuben Archuleta. Calmer now, and breathing normally, he kept the glasses on them, thinking, Reuben's dumb, but he idolizes Abilene, and if Abilene's acting all right then Reuben will, too, but you can't tell about Abilene. Tixier was intelligent and untrustworthy. He was like that big gelding, hobbled now down in the pasture—the minute you relaxed around that animal or started depending on it, it spooked. He glanced at Kevin. "You remember Abilene Tixier?"

"Is that Abilene?" his son said, raising his head. "Sure. We used to go fishing. Why, if that's Abilene, let's go down and see him."

"Take it easy, honey."

In no hurry, the three men walked their mounts up to the cabin and dismounted, their voices carrying easily; he heard Deaguero: "Abilene, you think this might be his camp?"

"It's somebody's camp," Tixier said. He walked over to the potful of brine-soaking meat. "Get a load of this." Then he went into the cabin. When he came out, he had the sack of potatoes and, falling into that *coyote* Spanish of his, called out, *"Aquí, Willie, cebollas es lost fritos, me gusto, sí?"*

Vandenberg watched them awhile longer and then said, "Kev, you stay here—I'm going down to talk with them."

"Can't I come, too?"

"Wait here," he said. "Don't come down until I tell you to. You understand? Don't let them see you until I tell you to come out, and if I don't call you, then you get the hell out of here." His son didn't like it, but he would do as he was told. Vandenberg had instructed him a number of times, and he said now, "I'm leaving the rifle with you. There's a shell in the chamber, but the safety's on. If I yell at you to shoot, fire over their heads—understand?"

"Yes."

"And if I don't tell you to come out, you know what to do, don't you?"

"Yes."

"Tell me."

"Go to Terry's," the boy said. He was alarmed now. "Wait till it's dark before I go near her house. And look around first. But, Daddy, isn't Abilene our friend?"

"He used to be. Let's see if he still is," he said, rising. "Now, stay put, like I told you." He began moving down the slope toward the shack, keeping low in the scrub oak.

Below, near the door of the shack, Abilene yelled, "Hey, Gene! You got company. You can come out now, Gene."

Vandenberg heard Deaguero say, "Maybe it ain't his camp."

And Tixier replied, "It's his, all right."

Moving closer, he saw Abilene walk over to the packhorse, untie a foam-plastic ice chest, and take out a six-pack of beer. "I'll lay odds he's up there in those trees right now," Tixier said. Then, in a louder voice, "How about a brew?" He squatted on a deadfall and began opening cans, passing them around. "If that don't fetch him, by God, nothing will."

Vandenberg's expression hardened. There was a time when he would have tolerated Abilene's cozening ways. Making a production out of a cold beer, this far from town. The multi-print shirt with the pearl snap-down buttons, and the hundred-dollar Stetson. The twangy drawl, and the homey style that would have been ludicrous if you didn't know that Abilene was, in a manner of speaking, observing his own act and relishing the image he presented: the tight, faded jeans, the expensive boots, the powerful, rawboned frame, the face weathered and seamed with sixty years of riotous living but still handsome, the eyes shale-gray. He had the kind of wind-seamed, burned-brown features you used to find in only two places—this part of the Southwest or among the hundreds of western types who haunted the corridors of the Screen Actors Guild in Hollywood—and Abilene had done that trick, too, relishing every bit of it, but never so much as when he was joshing some dude into actually believing he was nothing more than a simple, old-fashioned, cow-poke-shitstomper who'd never been east of Tucumcari.

Vandenberg stepped out from where he had been standing behind the shack. "Hello, Abilene. *Com' está*, Reuben, Willie?"

COMMUNICATIONS

VANDENBERG, EUGENE R. *Case Record #4076*
Progress Note
The patient is well-oriented, although susceptible to fantasying. He does not appear to be anxious, and his affect is appropriate. He is also capable of presenting a plausible case for his present circumstances.

As the interview progressed, however, it became clear that his values were essentially those of the typical sociopath, that he indulged in a blanket rejection of all he did not approve of, that he was not motivated to work (except "what came easiest"), that his description of his drinking pattern was highly unreliable, and that he tended to be manipulative in an extremely intelligent though not profound fashion and hostile when his manipulations did not succeed. At this time there is no clear evidence of psychotic thinking or neurotic distortion. Diagnosis: Acute sociopathic personality disturbance, with alcohol addiction. Social and vocational rehabilitation questionable.

—P. W. Ulanowski, M.D.
Cowles Rehabilitation Center
USSRAOOUSA

D-32

TIXIER, SQUATTED on the log, looked up, pretending astonishment. "Gene, how the hell are you? *Comó te cuelga el martillo?*" Deaguero and Archuleta came over.

"All right, Abilene. Yourself?"

"About the same. You're looking okay. Older."

"Time passes," he said.

"It does that," Abilene agreed. "Hell, it's good to see you. How about a beer?" He had not moved from the log. Vandenberg nodded, and Tixier opened a can. "I was saying to Deaguero this morning, 'Willie,' I said, 'if we ever locate that fool Gene, first thing he'll want is a beer.' Drink up—we've got one more six-pack in the chest." Vandenberg stood there, listening to the easygoing voice. "Gene, how'd you know we were coming? Ain't nothing in the world I love more'n steaks and home fries." Abilene stared at him. "Or were you expecting somebody else?"

"No," he said, "nor you, either. You scared hell out of me, coming up that way. I thought you were a patrol. One of these days you'll get shot."

"Me? Shot?" Tixier grinned. "Gene, this is my country." He turned to Archuleta. "Hey, *hombre,* rustle up some wood. Let's get these spuds to cooking."

Archuleta drank his beer and went off. Vandenberg said, "You alone?"

"Sure."

"Anyone follow you?"

Tixier caught the tone in his voice and laughed. "There's only us. We been all over these mountains, trying to scout you out. Up past Beatty's Cabin almost to Truchas Peak, over to Santa Fe Baldy, then down here to check Bull Creek. My assbones are plumb wore out. We knew you were up here, though. We kept finding sign. Actually, we started out Tuesday from Willie's dad's place, at Cañada de los Alamos."

He knew Abilene would not give a straight answer, but he asked anyway. "Why're you looking for me?"

"No special reason," Abilene said, lighting a cigarette. "We felt like getting out of town for a spell."

"A vacation?"

Tixier inhaled, then blew a cloud of smoke. "Gene, that's it exactly. I had to get out for a while. So I said to the boys, 'Let's see if we can dig up old Gene . . . camp high for a week.' So we promoted a little black-market bourbon and some chow and took off."

Vandenberg did not believe any of it.

Deaguero said, "That's the truth, Gene."

He said, "If they catch you up here, it's the pen."

"They got to find us first," Abilene said scornfully. "Hell, if they haven't been able to spot a dude like you, how're they going to get us?"

"Easy," he said. "All they have to do is park in front of your house."

Abilene pretended to consider this. Then: "If we go back, that is."

So, there's more to it than boozing around up here, he thought: something's on his mind, but he didn't want to come up here alone— and he talked them into coming. He said, "A few weeks here, and you'd be fed up with it."

"Gene, you don't sound especially tickled to see us," Abilene said, standing and brushing the flaky bark from the seat of his jeans.

"I'm not," he said coldly, watching the older man.

Tixier took off his Stetson and ran his fingers through his white hair. Then he put the Stetson back on, carefully adjusting the tilt, and grinned at Vandenberg, showing ivory-white dentures. "Supposing I was to tell you Willie's dad lost some cows last week—and that the old man was too sick with his ulcers—so we got permission from the District Office, all legal, to go find them. He gave us three days—the Occupation Man—but we'll take five, maybe six, and tell him we got lost. What would you think of that?"

"I'd think it was a lot of crap," he said.

"Want to see our travel permits?"

"I don't care about travel permits."

Deaguero said, "Gene, you don't have to worry about us."

But Tixier was already off on another tangent, shaking his head and staring down at the ground. "You've gotten mean, Gene—you been up here too long. You know, sometimes I'd get to worrying about you. I'd be sitting around at the house with Olga, and we'd just get to wondering about you, and what you were up to. You've had a hard time. No one'd argue that."

Vandenberg did not answer.

"We thought you might need a few things besides liquor," Tixier continued. "We brought soap, clothes, some coffee, flour— stuff like that."

"Keep it," he said. "From what I hear, rationing's bad."

"Figured you were low," Abilene said. "Hasn't been a single burglary around Pecos for a long time. But if you'd rather we kept moving, okay. Couldn't blame you much, I reckon."

Vandenberg said nothing, thinking, a year of waiting, and now

32

it's come. He knew I couldn't do it alone, and now he's finally gotten his nerve up.

Standing there, he felt no elation. Once he would have felt vindicated. He glanced at their horses, again noting the scabbarded rifles. Like being in the forests, the weapons meant a prison term. It was a five-year sentence with M.G. There was no appeal. A man who had not turned in his firearms to the Ministry for Public Order kept them hidden.

Archuleta returned with an armload of deadwood, and began breaking it into pieces. Watching the olive-skinned youth, Tixier remarked, "I know you're pissed off, Gene. But we'd like to spend the evening with you, though—be like old times.

He was sure by then that what had brought them up here had nothing to do with the wanted circulars, and he realized, too, how tense he was. He knew they would leave if he told them to. Finally, he said, "Suit yourself."

COMMUNICATIONS

The Arabs can be swung on an idea as on a cord.
—T. E. Lawrence, The Seven Pillars of Wisdom

Since a wise man may be wrong, or a hundred men, or several nations, and since even human nature, as we think, goes wrong for several centuries on this matter or on that, how can we be certain that it occasionally stops going wrong, and that in this century it is not mistaken?
—Montaigne, The Essays

THEY RELAXED IMMEDIATELY. Reuben, breaking his firewood, began humming a tune. Deaguero said, "I'll unsaddle the horses."

Vandenberg watched him walk off. The Jicarilla in him comes out more every year, he thought, the fat stomach, and that round, flat face. Expressionless. Except when he laughs, and then he comes alive. I'd like to paint him, but not laughing. Catch that mixture—

Indian, Spanish, Irish—God knows what. See if I could get that little fold at the corner of each eye. Mongoloid—epicanthic. Part Geronimo . . . part Sumo wrestler. That's what gives him the mean look. Reptilian. A fat lizard.

And Reuben, he thought, glancing at the young man, him and Tixier. You'd think that would have ended years ago, but maybe something like that goes on forever. These damned Spanish. Narrow-minded. But sometimes they pay no mind at all. He said, "Reuben, how's the family?"

Archuleta looked at him. "Pretty good, Gene."

The way he said it told Vandenberg that there had been trouble, but this was no surprise, because Reuben and his wife had, in the years Vandenberg had known them, separated innumerable times. Then he remembered Kevin. He turned to Tixier: "I've got someone up here."

This time Tixier's surprise was real. "You're not alone?"

He called up the slope, "Kev—it's okay. Come on down."

"He's up here?" Abilene's voice cracked with delight. "Shit, Gene, you mean to tell me you got that boy with you?"

They stood together, watching Kevin come down the slope, carrying the rifle and one of the bedrolls, walking quickly through the scrub oak, finally breaking into a trot. Then he raised the rifle overhead and waved a greeting, and even at that distance they could see him grinning.

"Hey, Abilene. It's me. Kevin! Hi!"

He glanced at Tixier and saw that the old man was immensely pleased, standing there with his weight on one leg, smiling, shaking his head in wonderment, looking tolerantly bemused, but not really, because his emotions could be touched. While the boy was still some distance up the slope, Abilene, without looking at Vandenberg, asked quietly, "Is he still the same, Gene?"

"The same," he said.

Then Kevin was before them, his face flushed from running, grinning with delight at Tixier, adoration in his eyes, waiting for the old rancher to speak, and Vandenberg knew that the boy's memories were good: tangled recollections, perhaps, of long-ago fishing and hunting trips, when Vandenberg and Tixier had been friends, and the long, lazy days on the high lakes with plenty to eat and drink, and the pack trips into the back country they'd made, to fish streams no one but Tixier knew about, the memories going back maybe twelve, fourteen years, and he knew that no matter what you said against Tixier, he was a hero to Kevin. The cocked Stetson, the drawl, the weatherbeaten movie-star face—these were perfectly real to his son, and to give Tixier credit, he was gentle with kids, had always been good with them. Now there was confusion in the pale gray eyes, and that was something you didn't often see. Ten years earlier, Abilene might have grabbed Kevin up in his arms and hugged him, but now Vandenberg's son stood inches taller.

Tixier stood a moment, grinning, looking him over, and then he said, "Why, you've gone and growed up on me, haven't you?"

Kevin smiled shyly.

"By God, you're a man. A real man. You're all growed up!" Then, to Vandenberg, as though the boy were not present, as though he were sizing up a horse he was considering trading off, "Too big to keep in a house, that's for sure. Lookit those shoulders. Lookit those arms, and the size of those hands. . . . Lord, I'd hate to have him hit *me*."

Kevin went red with pleasure, and Tixier stepped up to him and held out a hand. "Well, now, you're too big for me to kiss, that's for sure, so I guess we'll have to shake." Kevin set down the rifle and bedroll quickly, and grabbed Abilene's hand, pumping it, and Tixier put an arm around his shoulder and hugged him. "Son, it does me good to see you again. I missed you. We all been missing you." And to Vandenberg, "It's like old times, except he's gotten so goddamn big. Gene, you remember the old days?" Vandenberg nodded. "We sure had us some rare old times."

"Yes, we did."

"We'll have them again," Abilene said.

No we won't, he thought.

Abilene, his arm still around the boy's shoulders, was saying, "How about us going fishing for a week . . . for a whole everlovin' month?"

"I'd like that fine."

"By God, then, we'll just do it."

It sounds so easy, the way he's telling it, Vandenberg thought, and most of it is for Kevin, but he's saving some of it for me, to see if he can still lay it on. He said, "How'd you know we were up here, Abilene?"

Tixier let his arm drop from Kevin's shoulder and went over to the deadfall and got another beer. "Why, Gene, this may come as a shock to you, but there are a certain number of people around Santa Fe who still remember you and talk about you. Besides Occupation, that is. And not everything they say about you is bad, either. M.G. has clamped the lid on you, but folks remember. After your name stopped coming up on television, there was talk you'd split for Mexico, but I never believed any of that. Then, maybe a month ago, I saw Cip Griego—you remember him?"

Vandenberg shook his head, and Tixier said, "He used to hunt with us, years ago. Little old fart, used to work at the fish hatchery, and up at the Rolling R. Grumpy-looking *viejo,* acts like his teeth hurt all the time—he knows you from way back. Anyway, I was talking with him, and he was saying how they'd let him ride into the mountains twice this year for stray beefs, and how he'd found traces of enough deer guts by the streams to know somebody was still living up here, and the only one it could be was you."

"I remember him now," Vandenberg said. "But I doubt I'm the only one up here."

"Sure, a few other idiots are wandering around these hills," Tixier said. "M.G. calls them harmless eccentrics, if it mentions them at all. There was a rumor going around this summer about a guerrilla outfit, a big one, up near Tellerude."

He's trying, Vandenberg decided, he's poking around, to see if he can hit on something. He thinks nothing's changed, that I'm the same, and that's where he's wrong. He said, "That's just talk. That many men couldn't stay hidden from the copters."

Abruptly, bored with Tixier's chatter, he changed the subject. "They still have a reward on me?"

Abilene nodded. "A measly fifteen hundred—Occupation script. They're keeping you small-time, Gene. . . . They're smart. You're the only honest-to-God *comanchero*-type *hombre* we got hereabouts. You can't blame 'em for not wanting to let you get big again. Hell, if it was fifteen thousand, I'd blow the whistle on you myself—so'd Reubenito here, or Willie."

"Speak for yourself, *cuate,*" Deaguero said; Reuben was silent.

Tixier sighed, and adjusted his hat. "Ah, balls. What's money, anyway?" He went over to the saddles Deaguero had removed from

36

the horses and began untying his bedroll. "I'd say it's about ninety-eight per cent of everything, but that's all, *que no, amigo?*"

COMMUNICATIONS

The Achaians, says Polybius, abhorred all manner of double-dealing in war, not reputing it a victory unless where the courage of the enemy was fairly subdued.

—Montaigne, *The Essays*

Paralysis occurs when the obstacles to resistance, to alleviation attempts, and to flight are just as formidable as the difficulties of cooperation.

R. Hilberg, *The Destruction of the European Jews*

The question of the decade, if not of modern times, which remains unanswered and perhaps never will be answered is, How did it happen so quickly? (The formal declaration of war by the U.S.S.R. on the 27th November was a gesture—we know this much—by then, it was over. It was already ended on the morning of the 22nd, when the initial hysterical news flashes about what was happening in Washington, D.C., came over the air.) Embracing the long-term view, it is easy to imagine how in one hundred, two hundred years from now, history primers will refer to November 22nd as that exact moment when a vast shift in the balance of power took place, and, too, very likely as the departure point that marked the inevitable extinction of individual national government everywhere. As a contemporary event, however, especially when viewed by an observer whose vision has been sharpened by the knowledge that he was on the losing side, let me report that the climate was so drenched with sadness that one could scarcely help empathizing with those other nonwinning groups of the 1917 Revolution and the French rebellion, who in easier times would have been characters in a historical charade.

And, too, we would like to know what *happened. It is a matter of record that an adequate official version has never been published. They referred, with simpering coyness, to an ultimate weapon, but what is that? The rumors that circulated—and still go the rounds—*

37

favored a bacteriological or virus contamination of Washington's municipal water system. We knew afterward that the capital was cordoned off, and that it remained quarantined for over six months. Nonetheless, the idea of bacteriological warfare remains conjecture. The questions are still unanswered. It may be worth noting that even S.M.G.—Soviet Military Government—much of which is in contact with American civilians, does not know the exact method used to obliterate the population of Washington. Russian brass is to this day understandably jubilant, but their triumph is apparently as much of a mystery to most of them as it is to us.

Presuming some sort of germ or virus contamination, one would have thought that in a complex as strategically vital as Washington the water system would have been monitored with elaborate safeguards, for surely it would seem obvious that if several million people might be expected to drink at least one glass of water during the course of an ordinary working day, then so might the President, the Vice-President, and the members of Congress.

With regard to national defense—and here I am speaking in the broadest possible terms—one would assume that if, as the Soviets claimed, better than ninety per cent of those directly involved with national policy-making perished within, say, five or six hours, other safeguards ought to have automatically gone into operation. With the virtually magical retaliatory deterrents at our disposal—the redline phones, the silo-based ICBMs, the manned bombers, SAC, NAADC, and the like—why was not the final authority handed over to the Air Force generals in Colorado or Omaha? Or did a massive volley of ICBMs, as a few obstinately maintain to this day, get through to their assigned target zones inside continental Russia?

Is it possible that at top levels we were too predisposed to the idea that nuclear attack and subsequent nuclear retaliation were the next obvious steps in modern warfare? Whatever happened, the fact remains that our countermeasures, however sophisticated, and fail-safe were childishly inadequate. The Soviets speculated on surprise and time. They got the first immediately and won the second in the days that followed. The scope of their foray, one must ruefully admit, was Olympian: in comparison, the Normandy invasion was a rudimentary five-finger exercise.

In a few states, National Guard units were mobilized, but nothing significant came of their frenetic display of military hard-

ware. Perhaps not so oddly, our megalopolitan loci—New York, Chicago, Los Angeles—whose inhabitants of necessity had long since accepted a highly organized and regimented system of habit patterns, gave the least trouble. The painful emancipation of the Negro, so long in the coming, was effectively proscribed by universal military law (a stringent taskmaster), which stated in quite simple English that any individual or group who hampered, harassed or otherwise deterred Military Government from its appointed task would be summarily executed. In a sense the race problem was solved, since all men were, finally, equal, and like it or not the black militant had to make room in the same boat for the white brahmin, the Georgia cracker, and the well-wishing WASP: disparate shipmates, to say the least!

We know that some seven months later the first Soviet administrative cadres moved into the capital; by then, the mobile crematoriums stationed along the shores of the Potomac had departed. The wealth of statistical information that had accumulated in Washington and in other administrative centers—the files, the archives, the tens of millions of computerized records of the Social Security Administration, the FBI, the Bureau of Internal Revenue, the Veterans Administration—was theirs. With these data, plus their newly proven insights, they could judge the pulse of the nation and could plot their course of action accordingly, to their own best interests.

That sham conclave, the First American Provisional People's Congress, took its oath the following spring; heading the assembly's agenda was the drawing up of a working charter designed to lead to a more amenable rapport between Americans and the U.S.S.R. The Russian attitude, which heretofore had had a reputation for intractability (the adamant stand on the abolishment of private property alone very nearly did the American mentality in), now began showing encouraging signs of flexibility in granting some of the Congress's petitions, and this in itself provided an enormous boost to national morale, which, to put it mildly, had been moribund; with the formal ratification of the charter, at Dumbarton Oaks, people everywhere began to take hope.

By then, of course, it was over: England had been subjugated after a brief thermonuclear flurry; Western Europe went under; Canada capitulated; Japan was invited to join the new international Duma, *and wisely did so. It was a time of change, and in this*

country the prevailing mood was that we must make the best of it.
Personally, I encountered lasting difficulties in condoning this atti-
tude, as I had in accepting the first official press releases, published
in the Santa Fe Journal-News, *on the 27th of November, with their*
accompanying headline: WAR DECLARED. U.S.S.R. STRIKES
BACK AT U.S. PLOT.

I'd never believed much of what was printed in the old news-
papers, and when the Vietnam debacle, Black Militancy, and Yip-
piedom were at their heights, I believed even less, but it was not
until I saw that headline that I understood the difference between
a communications media that is bossed, cajoled, intimidated, and
wooed by its government, and one that is, quite simply, an exten-
sion of the government itself.

—The Journals

TOWARD EVENING, Reuben built a parapet of rocks around the
fire, and Kevin spread out bedrolls and sleeping bags with their
bottoms pointed toward the flames, and as it darkened and the first
stars appeared, the men drank bourbon and water from battered
metal cups that showed black rust spots where the blue enamel
had chipped. Vandenberg, mellowed by the whiskey, sat with his
back against the deadfall, near the fire, drinking quietly and
smoking.

Later they got to feeling hungry, and Tixier, by then a long
way from sober, declared himself cook and unpacked skillets and
pans from his gear. After larding one, he sliced potatoes and onions
into it for home fries, propping the skillet on the embers to one
side of the fire, dousing everything with salt, pepper, and chili
powder, so that, immediately, there was the smell of cooking. When
the potatoes were nearly done, he started the steaks, not guarantee-
ing any success, since, to his way of thinking, the meat should have
aged at least a week. Within minutes, the charred steaks and potatoes were forked into mess kits, and they began eating; the last
six-pack was opened and passed around. Afterward they drank
coffee, and Reuben offered cigarettes, and then they had another
bourbon, and Tixier, stretched beside the fire, propped on one elbow,
the big, carved-silver buckle and top button of his jeans opened,

looked around contentedly, let off a loud fart, and said, "Now, that was passable."

Deauguero agreed. "For an amateur, you don't cook bad."

"Never talk down my chow," Tixier said mildly. Kevin sat beside his father, elbows resting on his knees, listening to Abilene brag about how he'd run camps for as many as thirty hunters, finding delight in the spiel Vandenberg had heard a dozen times. Simplicity: everything into one pot—deer liver, grouse, beans, squirrel. And truthfully the old man really was pretty good, with a penchant for fussing over a sheepherder's stove, turning out one hot meal after another for his kids, as he called them, but it was not until Vandenberg had hunted with him for several seasons that he understood why Abilene relished the role of camp cook so much, why he never showed much interest in getting a deer or an elk, preferring instead the evenings when there was drink and talk, because this was, for him (or had been, in past years) the only available world without women.

It was when all the kids, the young men, the ones in their twenties and thirties, left their wives or girls and with big-game permits in their wallets made it to the high country for the fall hunt, taking vacation time or leave without pay or sometimes simply telling the boss to shove it, grinding in first gear up switchback logging trails to alpine camps in battered pickups loaded with food and gear and liquor, dragging horse trailers, for a week, two weeks, a month. And what better camp operator could you find than Abilene, who, esthetically and with marvelously suppressed sexuality, reveled in playing the housekeeper to a dozen or more boozing, profane hunters? That was when he would drop a hundred a week keeping everybody supplied with beer and whiskey and shells for their rifles.

Abilene was aware of what a couple of weeks up there meant— for them, it was the temporary recapturing of that childish fantasy of carefree leisure, and if, as it sometimes happened, he had a fourteen- or fifteen-year-old in tow, then that was his business; more often than not, a number of the older ones present (like Reuben, family men now) had themselves been escorted through the uncertainties of adolescence by Tixier, although they did not speak of it. Behind his back they called him Old Sudden Death, this being a reference to the kind of whirlwind courtship he was capable of indulging in when smitten. They drank his liquor and took advantage of him in a hundred small ways, but, paradoxically, they admired and respected him, because there was still the incongruity: you knew what he was, yet he was still the personification of manliness, the tall, lean, leathery old cowboy (a genuine Owen Wister mythic folk-hero-in-the-flesh) who knew these mountains as well as and probably better than any of the local Spanish—taciturn when sober, genially euphoric when stoned, imbued with his own charm and debonair dishonesty, mostly good-humored but possessing a brooding, bitchy, vindictive side too. He could, for a fact, despite his age turn combative so that the Spanish—his beloved boys—meant it when they said, "That Abilene, better don't fuck aroun' with him!" —while he, in turn, spoke of them as his people.

It was only Olga and Vandenberg and a few others who caught a notion of how much the old man had to drink in order to keep from going to pieces; who'd seen him on the month-long benders, the floor of his room littered with empties while he sprawled among urine-soaked sheets, liver-swollen, fingers wandering aimlessly in pubic fleece, too drunk to speak; who knew the fears that ate at him: age, mainly, the horror of growing old, the vanishing of the Hollywood good looks—or, worse, that someday, someplace, while drunk and careless, he would slip and cozy the wrong punk and be hit by some vice cop to the tune of a couple of years in the state pen. That, Abilene himself was the first to admit, was a trick he might have survived when younger, but now it would kill him— they'd truck him out in a coffin, and dump him at the National Cemetery, on Rosario.

If you knew any of it you could see in the brooding gray eyes something of fear and sorrow, and a kind of ineffably fatalistic bravery and suffering that was nearly great—hell, heroic—that had been paraphrased by Tixier himself once, in the Montana Bar, when, transcendentally smashed on Metaxa and in a moment of maudlin confidence, he bellowed at Vandenberg, "I've knowed I was different since I was fourteen, knowed it, and fought it, and lost it, so fuck it, and I can't understand why a man of your education and brains would even speak to a no-account hom'sexual like me, but I'm honored, and I won't forget it."

But he had forgotten it, Vandenberg thought, just as he forgot everything when it suited his style, including Olga, who'd put up with him for nearly forty years, following him around the country— the rodeo circuit in the early days, then a cyanide-blues dude ranch high in Idaho's Bitterroots, all the way to Alaska, where he'd gotten in on the King Crab boom—fronting for his psychotic irresponsibility, hating herself for her weakness, which was Abilene himself, super-handsome, Abilene who at sixty-two could still make women's heads turn when he stalked into a restaurant. Women were partial to him; they melted, fluttered, batted their eyes—no argument there—while he, smiling sadly, accepted their adulation with a judiciously contained show of old-time manners and shy country-boy courtliness, which they never knew was only a cover for an appalling disinterest in their gender.

Olga had loved seeing the envy in their eyes, but she had not loved it eight years ago when she had gone into the hospital for the first of the cancer operations, and Tixier, after barely seeing her through surgery, had gone and gotten stoned at Nikos' and had then taken off with some *pistolero* for a week's fishing on the upper Brazos, returning to her bedside red-eyed, hung-over, jowls white with stubble, contrite but not too contrite, to listen to her searing indictment of him until, having heard enough, he said abruptly, "Bullshit," and went down to the hospital's business office. Glancing at the bill, he laid down (so the story went) eleven hundred-dollar bills and told the clerk, "Write me out a discharge slip because I'm taking her home. She's getting cranky in this goddamned place, and I can change dressings and feed her as good as any of these nuns. You hurry up."

Now, thinking of the old woman, Vandenberg asked, "How's Olga?"

Tixier must have gone to some trouble coaching Reuben and Deaguero or they would have made a slip during the afternoon, and this, too, was very much Tixier's style—he could not resist deviousness.

Drunk, turning now to gaze at Vandenberg, the grief, real or pretended, was heavy in his voice: "Gene, she died, last Monday. We buried her at the ranch, like she always wanted. Dug the grave ourselves, on the slope back of the ranch house. That's how come we got permission from the District Officer to leave town. It wasn't Willie's dad's cows. I know how you felt about her, that's why I didn't tell you before. I didn't want to upset you. It happened in her sleep, and so far as the doctors could tell, she never knew a thing—that's something we can be thankful for, anyway."

COMMUNICATIONS

. . . you know, he was a fine-looking son of a bitch. One time, he got the idea of fighting. We'd been together for about a year. He fought light-heavyweight. He got some bouts up in the Dakotas and Montana, but he never won any. He never even took a decision. After a match, I'd rub him down with Cornhusker's. He'd stretch out on a wood bench, groaning from where they'd beat on him, with nothing on but the bandages around his hands. Yes, even with those welts all over him, I'd say he was about the finest-looking man I ever come across. Hair black as Indians', softer than silk. Everybody loved him. He was happy-go-lucky, and people, they liked being near him. . . . One minute he'd be laughing at you, the next at himself. It was all the same to Abilene. The year he quit rodeoing they introduced us both over the loudspeakers at the Calgary Stampede, and you should have heard the applause. People just liked him. It was no different in Hollywood when he started stunt work in pictures. Abilene'd get right down on his knees and throw dice with those Beverly Hills jewboys, and he'd come out ahead. Not bad for a man never got out of fourth grade.
—Olga Tixier, Santa Fe Conversations

OFFICE OF THE DISTRICT ATTORNEY
SANTA FE COUNTY, SANTA FE, N.M.
$1500.00 REWARD

NAME: EUGENE R. VANDENBERG *(No known alias)*

WANTED FOR: *Murder, Felonious assault, Sedition*

DESCRIPTION: *White, male, date of birth: 1/4/20. Height: 6'4".*
  Weight: 220 lbs. Hair: gray. Eyes: brown. Husky build, ruddy complexion. Scar on left temple. Wears spectacles.

OCCUPATION: *Artist.*

Wanted on charges including murder, felonious assault, sedition, and escape from confinement. The U.S. Marshal at Santa Fe, N.M.,

44

and the office of the Sheriff, Sante Fe County, N.M., hold warrants for his arrest. Subject is armed and is considered dangerous. If this man is located, please cause his immediate arrest and notify the undersigned at once, COLLECT, by telephone, telegram, or teletypewriter.

—Donald R. Hobb
Assistant District Attorney
Santa Fe, N.M.

THE NEWS of her death shook him. In a way he was surprised that she had lasted this long, but with the feelings of regret that rose in him there was something else. The trip up here, and their search for him. He thought, that's it—she's dead. There's no one to hold him back anymore, no one to front for him. He's alone for the first time in years, but why this? What has he got to gain by it? Or Deaguero? The big gesture? Coming up here, for how long? A week, a month? Not much longer than that, for sure, with winter practically here—they'll walk out on me two weeks after first snow. Him and his talk—guerrillas. Is that what he's thinking of? Or is it the last of the manhood bit? Showing us that he's still tough. Is that what he's out to prove—that he can go on the wanted list too?

He began growing angry, and then he nearly smiled. Now I know. And if I sit here long enough and let him take his time, it'll be like hearing my own words come back to me. And he'll take the credit. It has to be Cowles. Otherwise he wouldn't need me at all. He wouldn't have come up here at all.

COMMUNICATIONS

You doubt that the career of your great country is in eclipse— is on the wane? I say only this—look around you.

—Saint-Griseus

I know now that I have not the least talent for this isolated life, and that my choice to remain in the forests was a mistake. Once away from Cowles I ought to have headed straight for civilization, where, by exercising circumspection, I might have accomplished much more than I have here and would have had the additional luxury of an occasional hot bath. An alias, an attempt to somehow obtain identity papers—I might have evaded their security people for some time. Such a move would have been clever. I could have tried to make it to California, where I might have retained anonymity in the dense population. Actually, had the choice been mine, I would have returned to my ranch, but this was out of the question. There, I had found some adjustment in a sort of life most of my countrymen would have regarded as needlessly primitive; however, it satisfied me, and I felt it was a perfectly sensible way to live; indeed, on the infrequent trips I made to town, I often felt as if I were in another country.

—The Journals

THAT NIGHT, almost two years ago, he had gone into Santa Fe, walking the whole way, not even daring to stop at a pay phone to call Tixier. It had snowed, and it was nearly midnight before he reached the house on Cerro Gordo. There was no traffic, and for the last mile he had simply walked down the middle of the unpaved road, his shoulders hunched against the wet flakes.

When he got there, he went around to the back door and knocked until Abilene let him in. They went into the kitchen quietly, so as not to waken Olga, who slept in the front of the house, and Tixier had fried eggs, and there was a pot of black coffee. Abilene sat at the table under the kitchen light, dressed in jeans and a T-shirt, feet bare, the curtains drawn against the night, and Vandenberg stated his case, trying to convince the old man that now was the time to begin, and that he had to have help.

Abilene sat there and listened—*muy simpático*—from time to time nodding his head, and when Vandenberg was done he had refused to involve himself, still *simpático*, but it was a kiss-off nonetheless. He still remembered the words: "Gene, you're a middle-aged juvenile delinquent, that's what. You're a romantic. It's a grand notion, trying to take action against Military Government, but it won't work. Besides, I'm too damned old to live that sort of life anymore. I like my comfort. What would you have to show for it? A bullet from one of those little squirt guns they all carry? I like my comfort, like I said. I've got no more ideals—who in hell needs 'em? You try that kind of harassment, and they'll label you an outlaw. You're a criminal already. We've picked up your name on television half a dozen times since you broke out."

"You don't believe any of that, do you?" Vandenberg demanded.

"You're no criminal," Abilene said. "I know that. You don't have any real criminal tendencies. I know what criminal tendencies are, because *I've* got them."

"Then, why not?"

"Because you're bad news," Abilene went on. "They say you're a criminal, and if enough people in this law-abiding, chickenshit country say you're a criminal, then you are. Why, there're some in this town, who, if you told them Gene Vandenberg was sitting in this house, would get on the phone and dial city police without feeling anything except civic pride. So, there you have it." Vandenberg listened, without speaking.

"What I'd do, I'd turn myself in. Play it smart. Tell 'em you thought it over and realized what a mistake you'd made. Plead manslaughter or insanity, and ask for clemency. Hell, they won't hit you with more than five years or so. But if you don't turn yourself in, you ain't got much to look forward to."

He knew the old man was partly right.

"Gene, you think you can bluff them, but you can't. They've got every card. You pester 'em too much, they'll grind your ass plumb into the ground. They'll bury you. And all this about Cowles —I think you're making it out bigger than it is."

Vandenberg had told him about the compound earlier. He said now, "I wasn't putting you on about Cowles."

Tixier frowned. "I know a guy did a stretch up there this spring —fellow named Fleming. He's on parole now. Listen, don't think I haven't wondered about Cowles. Sure, it's not what they say it is, but it's not what you say it is, either. A guy does his time and gets out. You'd have too, if you hadn't gotten a wild hair up your ass. You're too damned set in your ways, Gene. You been looking down your nose and sneering at the world for too many years." Abilene paused, then added, "Why, you been begging for trouble."

He listened to this angrily, and thought, is it only me who's completely crazy? Have I drifted that far? He knew Tixier was wrong about the sentence M.G. would hand him. It wouldn't be any five years.

"What about your ranch?" the old man asked.

"Gone. I was out there today. They wrecked it."

"And Kevin? Who's taking care of him?"

"I don't know. They picked him up. I don't know where he is."

"I'm sorry about that," Tixier said, but his tone was relentless, and he knew the old man blamed him for the loss of his son. He knew then that it had been a waste of time coming here.

They had talked awhile longer. Tixier insisted that he was always welcome, that he could always come in for a feed when it got too bad in the mountains, so long as he came at night, but it was talk, nothing more. He had sat there for another half-hour, drinking Heaven Hill and drying out, waiting for the snow to let up, and when it did he said good-bye and left.

Even then, though, he had not been entirely cut off. It was Terry who had given him the transistor, who kept him supplied with newspapers and books. From these, and from talking with her, he had learned how bad it had become, so that finally it had not been the odds against him that made him abandon his plans but instead a total disenchantment. By the end of the second summer in the forest all the wild schemes had burned out; he was not so much resigned as resolved to survive—by then, all he wanted was to keep himself and the boy alive for as long as possible. By then, he had accepted the fact that he could do nothing alone. Now, here was Tixier again.

COMMUNICATIONS

Treason never doth prosper; what's the reason?
Why, if it prosper, none dare call it treason.
—John Harrington, 1723

That, too, was another self-deception, you know (during the superabundant years preceding the Invasion), on the part of those who thought they could get by without toeing the line. I mean the idiocy about the guerrilla business. That's about all it turned out to be: business—big business American-style, with endless promotion on all the junk, ranging from Geiger counters and do-it-yourself fallout shelters with revolving periscopes to James Bond folding

rifles. Distilled water, fancy food concentrates, snakebite kits, vita-
mins, machetes, sunglasses. Goosedown sleeping bags, alpine ruck-
sacks, Anzac campaign hats, with accompanying literature on how
to assemble your own neighborhood Maquis. *Batman in the Boon-*
docks. To listen to some, if the day ever came, five hundred thou-
sand citizens, all appropriate Rogue Male *types, would melt into*
the hills, and when they weren't creating havoc among the brutal
Occupation forces, they would be practicing the fine art of sur-
vival. Figure-four snares for rabbits and never mind the tularemia
and bubonic plague that's endemic in the Southwest. A length of
string and a fishhook and you could always snake a mess of pan
trout out of any stream. Of course, you stood a better chance with
the proper equipment.

Why, if a survival-and-guerrilla nut bought all the stuff the
sporting-goods stores and catalogs said he needed, it would have
taken a twenty-five-foot U-Haul trailer and two weeks of packing
to get him out of his damned carport. None of it having anything
at all to do with what they so knowledgeably and blithely referred
to as the art of survival. All of it tying in again with our inde-
fatigably American spirit.

There were the gadgets, then, enough to keep Christ knows
how many men alive and operational, but there was one thing no-
body considered—or maybe it was too grim to contemplate and
so we conveniently wiped it out of our minds—one thing that had
simply gone away from us.

Not spirit or bravery, nor was it anything like the will to win.
All that was merely good press, aimed not at the world but at
ourselves, on the theory that if you tell a man he's unbeatable he
just may perform a shade better. What I'm referring to was the
actual collective climate of temperament that existed at any given
moment in this country: the real, as opposed to the fancied, state
of mind.

To cite an example. If Congress had approved and the President
had signed a bill for eleven billion dollars slated for the harassment
and discouragement of foreign troops on United States soil, then in
six or eight months the esprit *would have filtered down to state and*
local levels, duly disbursed by appointed federal consultants, and
in neighborhood areas around the country you'd have witnessed the
birth throes of something like an organized home-guard movement.

The clod next door and the folks down the street, popping away on a rifle range that would probably have cost a half-million in federally matched funds. They'd have had appropriate identifying decals pasted in the rear windows of their cars to show that they were legally approved Minute Men, with maybe an easily translatable motto, such as Aufgeschoben ist nicht auf gehoben" *("Forbearance is not acquittance")* or "Videntum dicere ferum quid retot?" *("Why truth cannot be gay, I cannot see"), and there would have been I.D. cards and perhaps some sort of appealingly rakish beret to wear for the flacks, because anything big enough to cost eleven billion dollars would warrant fancy press coverage. But the rifles they carried would have been registered and, of course, like the ammunition burned in practice, entirely tax deductible. But no one would have stolen a gun and sent a bullet into some luckless Soviet GI. Why? The answer is simple. It would have been* illegal. *Not only would it have been illegal, it would have marked such an assassin for a dreary future, and as individuals we had learned to cherish comfort.*

Barring a few million in the armed forces who were coerced into at least perfunctorily practicing bravery in order to gain peer-group approval, Americans, as it turned out, were not tough. For us to leave comfortable homes and camp outdoors for longer than a week was a major adventure planned far in advance, and then the idea was to make a wilderness camp as much like home as possible—tents, portable generators, folding chairs, tables, collapsible crappers, radio, television, the works. Ché would have flipped. Battery-powered fluorescent lights. The trade literature ascribed the sudden popularization of transistorized, two-way walkie-talkies for hunters to the American's innate love of gadgetry, but there was a deeper significance in this pocket-sized gimmick that enabled a sportsman to keep in touch with a rifle-toting pal a couple of miles off: the average American male was scared to be alone.

There was something in all this involving more than a mere liking for convenience. The outdoors was lovely, but it had become alien. The only way to endure it for even a weekend was to surround oneself with the accoutrements of Sears, Roebuck. True, some could rough it—ranching people, sheepherders, Sierra Club mysties—but not many. You'd have to spend a winter alone above timberline to know about this. We've come a long way, in terms of survival, from the nineteenth-century Tierra del Fuegan, who took as a matter of course the fact that he would at times sleep naked on the ground in a snowstorm. It wasn't only the below-zero temperatures, or the prisonlike confinement of a small shack. The deep snows, which would have made a ski buff swoon with delight, were, as far as I was concerned, a lot of white shit. I often slept for days at a stretch, or, like Spenser, spent long nights in pensive discontent. After three months of this, I realized that nothing mattered very much. Not Soviet Military Government, nor the potential threat of the Chinese, nor even what I was doing. For the first time in my life I experienced real existential absurdity, and the shock nearly did me in.

I found I wasn't the least interested in the massive shift in the balance of power we are now experiencing.

What difference did it make to me if we were on the brink of something good? If the Far East was under control? If we got World Government?

What the devil did I care if we became one amorphous world family, wherein the hairy Ainu could greet the Hottentot as "Comrade Citizen"?

Personally, I couldn't have cared less about becoming a world citizen. The fact that I am an American citizen has never exactly held me spellbound with delight.

Moreover, let me take the trouble to assure you that the destinies of two or three billion souls are of no interest to me whatever. The figure alone blows my mind. What interests me is Gene Vandenberg, both free and trapped in a mountain wilderness, with winter coming on and no clear route to Mazatlán's sun-drenched beaches.

I've said this before, and I don't mind repeating it: I wanted to be left alone. Offhand, I know of nothing more deleterious to my liver than being the useful, contributing member of society the Occupation seems bent on making of us all.

I was, of course, corrupt. Heavy-handedly I went after one of the last options around: the privilege to make mistakes, to foul up one's life-style beyond repair. I demanded the right to be utterly useless, unsalvageable, a freakout clown and drunken buffoon, self-supporting to the point of being viable (but no further, friend), beyond redemption, if you will, a bona fide, guaranteed, full-blown fuckup.

I find the notion of Gene Vandenberg metaphorically putting his shoulder to the wheel of world progress along with three billion other souls, to put it mildly, very funny. Unfortunately, M.G. failed to be amused by my brand of finger-snapping levity.

The fault or lack of cleverness is mine. My ranch, as confiscatable property, was useless—it wouldn't have supported two cow units. Primitive indeed, it was miles from the nearest road and inaccessible in bad weather. No one could have raised any sort of crop on it, but there was the house that provided my son and me with shelter and privacy. Perhaps that was what they resented: privacy Unless we turned on the radio or came in to town for food, we were untouchable. And one way or another they had to be in contact. So they arrested me, and took the boy and placed him in an institution, and confiscated the ranch.

It's probably true, as they claimed, that I ran off at the mouth too much in bars. For that they brainwashed me. How stupid, really, when they could have easily fobbed me off as an irresponsible old fart. They ought to have let me go on boozing and painting, selling a picture here and there. I'd have died in another ten or fifteen years. By then an entire post-Soviet-Occupation generation of kids would have been in high school. Fertile ground.

To go back again: We needed something that wasn't there—the country was like a cake that had risen in the oven. Then somebody slammed the door.

We needed a messiah, someone out of Dylan Thomas's Welsh towns, where speakers stood on boxes at the edge of the sea, shouting speeches to the waves, someone who could have delivered a line like Churchill's charismatic blitz-time spiel about the English fighting on the beaches, in the fields, etc. I've always wondered if the run-of-the-mill Englishman would have actually fought. He might very easily have run like a son of a bitch at the sound of the first shot. But it sounded all right, you see. At the time, it helped foster an image of true grit and toughness, which, perhaps happily, was never tested.

But now we were tested, and all our vacuous, sentimental images turned out flawed. The image of the hardy pioneer. The myth and brag of American technology, self-confidence, and know-how. Edible Church and a G.N.P. that was cornucopian. We had the Rand Corporation, and fluoridated toothpaste, and so many cars our cities were being smogged out of business. We had produced *the All-American Tom Swift of the twenty-first century, and for want of a better name, called him Astronaut. America went on forever, but when the entire social complex fell apart—when a few small containers of virus, perhaps carried in a suitcase, took out the whole country—we were suddenly not defenders of freedom or anything else. We'd been taken on our own turf.*

I would say again that something had left us. It was not toughness, or that we had forgotten how to use our hands. Nor could you, sociologically speaking, lay the blame on the fragmentation or atomization of the family unit. Nor was it Johnson's employment of consensus politics, although it should have been obvious that a leader who is all things to all men is also, should everyone turn to him at once, nothing. Neither was it Nixon's indefatigable zeal and relentless West Coast optimism, though in giving credit to his era one might do well to note that only those who reach the heights of power are able to indulge fully in the heights of self-deception.

A big part of it had to do with what for want of a better term I called peripheral involvement, wherein the real interest or activity is shunted in favor of an image. This was a natural result of the boredom that arose out of material overabundance. True, we had never in our history had such a lively economy, but look at the people it produced.

I have always had a succinct reply to the theory that extremely accelerated and competitive progress creates only discrimination in the consumer market, which in turn creates a climate for even more vigorous competition: balls.

*Of what true significance, let me ask, was Lenin's original radical platform—*Land . . . Peace . . . Bread—*to a sulky, spoiled hippie of the late sixties?*

I am not speaking here of the silos bursting with wheat, or bargeloads of potatoes dumped at sea, or the farmers paid not to plant crops, but of the fundamental economy that was based on three words: newer, bigger, better.

At what point does progress and sophistication cease to be beneficial?

Or was it that we didn't use our intellectual and inventive capabilities wisely? Who, after all, really needed an electric carving knife? *Take Detroit, for years a target for every malcontent who drove. Most Detroit clunkers, given decent maintenance and driving, would have lasted two hundred thousand miles, calculated obso-lescence notwithstanding. But we had the seductive myth, promul-gated by endless advertisements in all media, of the sporty, well-groomed, successful young cat, who always somehow managed to look a shade acid-headed and faggotty, barreling down the pike at one-oh-five in his Bazazz-368 two-seater, with an equally joyful-looking young fish lolling in the adjoining bucket seat. Our accident rates attested to the fact that too many middle-aged fatties identified with the young acid-head, and perhaps the divorce courts gave a parallel indication that no small segment of American womanhood saw itself in the bucket seat. Our girl, the American girl—the fa-vorite pop-art, penvy bull's-eye of all time: ironed Nu-Glo hair, Max Factor epidermis, panties by Playtex, dugs slung in Maiden-form cups—given a Tampax phallus, she could do anything except pee standing up. Never in history was there a breed of broad so categorically dedicated not only to being a jet-propelled piece of ass but to being "fun." Unfortunately, the obsession with giving and getting a good lay was also, too often, peripheral.*

I'd thought years ago of leaving, but where? Mexico? Europe? Africa? The choice is unimportant. In any case, I would have merely been running ahead of an ever-widening spread of periph-eralism. I'd also have had the problem of getting a work visa. A physicist, an engineer—these sorts had no trouble immigrating, because they were needed. But there was scarcely a country in the world that had set up a program to encourage worn-out artists to open shop. That was where the old ranch came in. In a way, it was like having my own country. We had some bad times out there, but mostly I had a good feeling about the place.

—The Journals

HE SAID, "ABILENE, I'm sorry about Olga."

"It was bound to come," Abilene said.

"You say you buried her at the ranch?"

Tixier nodded. "She always said that's what she wanted. I went over to County Health and filled out the forms, and then got per-mission to bring her up. Said I needed help digging the grave. Had them by the nuts, there." Tixier grinned. "They've dreamed up regu-lations on just about everything, but they haven't changed the

54

law that says you can be buried on your own land. Willie and I built the coffin back in the garage, out of cedar. Two-by-eights, copper screws—it'll last. We put her in the pickup, and got Reuben. And after we'd finished, we got our horses and gear and took off."

"So you got the idea to come messing around up here, looking for me?"

"Kind of about that time, now that you mention it," Abilene said. "It was Willie's idea, really." He looked at Deaguero. "Ain't that so, *amigo?*"

Vandenberg knew it had never been anyone but Tixier's idea. Deaguero was not an originator. The big half-breed was not stupid, but he was not a leader.

Deaguero told about it anyway, smiling and looking from Vandenberg to Kevin, his English not good, talking low and quick, the Apache inflection coming through clearly, the words truncated, glottalized, but mellifluous. "I guess Abilene and me, we been thinking about it for some time, Gene. He told me about that time you came down to his house and wanted him to raise hell with you, only he had Olga to take care of. Gene, the way things are in town—you can't understand, you and your boy, what it's getting like, down there. They come on with all this horseshit about 'bolishing taxes, but then they bring in new taxes, and it's this and that and a hundred other things until, by God, it ain't worth a man's time to go out and work at his trade, and, son of a bitch, you say you won't work, why, they *fine* you! So, anyway, I was thinking about it. I got no family except my dad, and I could always make good money in heavy equipment, but no more. I was sort of figuring on cutting out anyway, and then Abilene and Reuben and me were talking, and they felt the same, so we said let's get old Vandenberg, because he's the man who knows all about it."

"Knows about what?" he asked.

Deaguero's round, dark face grinned. He said simply, "Why, we fixin' to dynamite the hell out of Cowles, where they put you."

He took a moment before going on. "Why?"

Deaguero groped for the proper word: "To *show* them."

"So? Cowles? After that?"

"After that, maybe play it by ear, head up to Colorado for the winter. Manassa, or the Conejos country—I know all that."

"You're nuts," Vandenberg said.

"No, Gene," Deaguero argued, "listen, I can walk away with a couple of cases of dynamite tonight. It's on the new four-lane where I been working, between Rowe and San Jose. Plenty of wire and caps, two electric detonators, locked in the superintendent's shack. No alarms, no watchmen, all you got to watch for is the Highway Patrol. In ten minutes I could get enough to blow up half of Pecos."

"You need more than dynamite," he said.

"That's why we want you," Deaguero said; he leaned forward. "You know the place."

"I know enough about it to know it won't work."

"He's worried about not having enough men," Tixier said: "Is that it, Gene?"

"I'm worried about staying alive."

"It can be done," Abilene insisted.

Vandenberg looked at him. "You have over fifty Russians in that place. There must be thirty security guards alone. Enough to man five watchtowers and the gate. There are four or five officers, not counting the commandant, plus the technical staff of instructors, psychologists, doctors, cooks, Christ knows who else."

They listened.

"There's a recoilless rifle set up at the gate—the only gate, really, though they call it the main gate. Each of the guards in the towers has a submachine gun. Within eighty yards of the gate there isn't a clump of grass to hide behind. They've got trucks, a scout car, a sedan, and the courier's motorcycle. The inner compound, where the prisoners' dorms are, has a double fence around it, topped with barbed wire, twelve feet high. The outer fence is electrified. There's a walkway between the two fences. That's a tight camp."

Willie Deaguero listened, his face expressionless, as Vandenberg went on. "Actually, they don't need that kind of security, not after they've had a guy in there a week."

Abilene looked up. "You still claim they use drugs?"

"Hell, yes."

Abilene said, "That guy I knew who'd been there—he never mentioned drugs."

"They do their time without even knowing it," he insisted.

"Gene, you mean they're high all the time?" Archuleta asked.

"Not LSD high, Reuben. They're walking on their heels."

Tixier said, "You mean, if you somehow opened up that camp, some of them might not break for it?"

"None of them would. That's why I gave up. I told you that almost two years ago."

But even as he spoke, his mind was working, and he knew it was possible. It could be done.

COMMUNICATIONS

MESSAGEGRAM

TO: L. A. INGRAM, CHIEF, SANTA FE CITY POLICE DEPT.
FROM: R. K. BARONOWSKI, COL., COMMANDING, DISTRICT THIRTY-
      TWO, USSRAOOSA
SUBJECT: TIXIER, HOWARD R. (AKA "ABILENE"), 3956 CERRO GORDO,
      SANTA FE
      DEAGUERO, WM. F., 839 ALTO VISTA, SANTA FE
      ARCHULETA, REUBEN P., 1432 CHAMISA DR., SANTA FE
THE ABOVE OBTAINED PERMISSION TO DEPART CITY LIMITS TO AT-
TEND BURIAL OF OLGA (NEE BENTON) TIXIER ON 10/11. TRAVEL
PERMIT TM-1340 ISSUED 10/10. NO CONTACT WITH THESE SUB-
JECTS SINCE 10/11. TIXIER IS CATEGORY IV. REQUEST CITY-
WIDE ALERT ON ABOVE CITIZENS. NO WARRANT BEING ISSUED AT
THIS TIME. NM STATE POLICE ALSO NOTIFIED. WHEN CONTACT VERI-
FIED CONTACT THIS OFFICE. DO NOT ARREST.

*There is no freedom on this earth, only varying degrees of bond-
age. Whenever men out of necessity band together, freedom is qualified. Moreover, man alone is never free. Consciousness in itself re-
futes freedom, and death offers the closest approximation to true
release, for then there is neither freedom nor bondage, but, one can
only presume, nothing.*

—*The Journals*

HE THOUGHT, but why the compound? Do they really understand that Cowles is the only site in the area? Or had Abilene finally
accepted his own two-year-old obsession with the camp?

57

Cowles more than anything else had committed him. It was the idea of the place, the calculated intent, the awareness that years of thought had gone into the evolvement of something like the Rehab Center, to which nobody paid attention, neither knowing nor caring that such a place existed. Or places. He wondered how many more there were, spotted around the country in similarly isolated areas.

Now, talking about it, the arguments and counterarguments locking automatically in a mental framework, he told Deaguero, "If you want to try it, I can tell you what to do. But you're asking for trouble."

Deaguero shrugged.

"You detonate a charge near that camp, and they'll have a manhunt going, *muy pronto*," Vandenberg said. "Not small-time. With the garrison they have at Glorieta Assembly, they can put two or three hundred men in these mountains in a few hours."

Deaguero looked at him. "They got to catch me. I know this country."

"So do the guys they'd be trucking up here," he said. "I'm not arguing that, Willie—I know you could probably keep out of their way. But you couldn't go back home in a couple of weeks. You couldn't ever go back."

It wasn't completely true about not going back. Tixier wouldn't be able to, but Deaguero had a chance of slipping back into civilization. Reuben, too. They were Spanish, and in this part of the country the Spanish stuck together.

"Gene, we need you," Tixier said.

"You need more than me," he replied. "There's not enough of us."

Abilene said, "I'll raise as many as we need. How many? Thirty? Forty?"

"Not that many," he said. "There aren't forty *primos* in the state I'd trust. That many couldn't move—they'd be spotted from the air. Trying to round up that many would alert M.G. And all you'd need was one spook, somebody who maybe felt both ways about it, and he could disappear on you, and you'd never know it until a dozen jets buzzed you."

"Gene, you have to trust people sometimes," Abilene said.

"No. You have to trust them. I don't."

"Well, damn it, then, how many?"

"A dozen. Maybe less," he said. "If you had eight or ten you were sure of, who wouldn't disappear when a gun went off, you might do it."

"So few?" Archuleta said doubtfully.

Vandenberg said again, "I'd try it with ten I was sure of. That many men and horses can hide. Not as easily as three or four, but you could hide them."

"They all need horses?" Tixier asked.

He finished the whiskey in his cup. "Abilene, you better listen. You get it clear in your head. Try something like this, and you're not going back to that nice warm house you and Olga had. You'll be on the run. You'd have to break into small groups and get way the hell back in the wilderness. They'll have air support, understand? And they'll have roadblocks across every logging lane leading out of here, from Albuquerque to Colorado."

"Wouldn't it be better to stick together?" Tixier asked.

"No. Keeping together means nothing unless you meet up with a large force, which won't happen. Two or three together they won't find, but if you bunch up, there's a chance a plane will spot you, and that would do it."

"I still don't see how it could be done with that few," Tixier argued.

He would have to tell them now, and he knew it. "Willie's dynamite is no good—you can't get near the gate at Cowles. At night, the place is lit up like a baseball park. But it could be used, all right."

"How?"

He said, "The tough part about the compound isn't the recoilless. It's the guard detachment, at Terrero." Terrero was a small settlement seven miles below Cowles. It flanked the winding dirt road that eventually ended, at ten thousand feet, at the compound. "A Soviet cavalry squad's billeted in a house at the side of the road," he went on. "There's a chain link fence around their stables and motor pool, but the house itself is outside. I'd thought of gasoline. A lot of it, working at night, around the base of the building. You see, it's all wood—a tar-paper roof. It'd burn. Two men with Winchesters could hold everyone inside."

He talked to them in an easy voice, but he could see that they were uneasy. Their idea of dynamiting the camp was just that: an idea. They hadn't really thought about it. Abilene said, "Why Terrero, Gene?"

"Because there's a phone line going up to Cowles. Start anything at the compound, and they give Terrero a buzz—in ten minutes, they've got a trailer-van loaded with horses and troopers on the way."

"So what? Drop a few trees across the road, above Terrero, and then go on up to the camp," Abilene said.

"What happens then, Abilene? You going to play shooting gallery? Snipe them off one at a time?"

"That's what the dynamite's for."

"You can't get close enough to use it," he said again. "What I'd do, though, if I had explosive, is use it at Terrero."

"The cavalry squad?"

He nodded. "I'd set a charge big enough to flatten the whole building."

"Something that big, they'd hear all the way to Cowles."

"Let them."

Abilene was thinking. "Is there a radio up there?"

"Yes."

"What's to stop them from radioing Santa Fe for help?"

"Because you knock out the power at the same time you take the cavalry detachment," he said. "Listen, quit arguing for a minute. The power line runs right past Terrero. Take out that line and everything above Terrero is without power or telephone. They have auxiliary power at the camp—a big motor generator, mounted on a two-wheeled trailer. You'd have to put a couple of thirty-thirty slugs into the generator, before they could crank it up and get enough emergency power to use the radio, understand?"

"I still don't see Terrero," Abilene said. "It means splitting up. Why not drop a tree across the road, then go on up and do it all at the camp—dynamite the power poles, shoot up their generating plant?"

But he was shaking his head. "At Terrero, inside, where they have their motor pool and stables, there are vehicles—scout cars, a semitrailer for hauling their horses. But best of all there's a half-track weapons carrier—a Russian job—and mounted on it is the biggest damned howitzer I've ever seen. I've had the glasses on it a hundred times."

Abilene nodded, finally understanding. "Sure 'nuff."

He continued. "Two men could do Terrero, with Willie's explosives. Then go in and get the weapons carrier. At the camp the rest would be holding down the security detachment. That's all you could do—delay them. Knock out the power, the telephones, and the auxiliary plant. Now do you see?" Abilene did not speak, and he said, "They're sealed off—but it's no sweat. They can't get out, but with rifles, you can't get in. They'll know that if they wait, help'll come. You can pin them down for half an hour—an hour—however long it takes to drive that half-track from Terrero to Cowles."

"And then?" Tixier asked.

"With the howitzer, the camp is yours."

"Gene, why not do it all from Terrero—all of us?" Abilene argued. "I hate splitting up. Blow the billets, the power line, get the weapons carrier, and go on up."

"There's still the emergency power supply for the camp's radio."

Tixier nodded. "Air support?"

"Yes. Also, I always thought they must have some sort of fail-safe plan, in case the camp went under attack," he said. "For all you know, they might have some kind of crazy order to go in and machine-gun everyone in the dorms."

"They'd go that far?" Deaguero asked.

Vandenberg nodded, and Tixier said, "Hell, for that matter, they could have the place mined."

"They could," he agreed. "I used to wonder, when I was in there, if I wasn't living over a ton of high explosive. If that's the case, and if the detonator is wired to a battery rather than the regular power system, there's nothing to be done. No one will get out."

"How many are in there?"

"Census was about two hundred when I was there," he said. "It's probably more, now."

Abilene stared at him. "Gene, if that place isn't mined, and if we can set them free—d'you realize what we could do with that many men?"

He caught Tixier's eagerness, half realizing that the plan was bigger and had been longer in the planning than Abilene admitted. "If you're thinking of a guerrilla force, forget it. Fifteen years ago

Kevin here could find his way around the woods better than any of them. They'd be worse than useless."

"Yet you wanted to turn them loose," Abilene said, still staring at him. "You thought about it long ago. And you been thinking about it since."

"Yes."

"Why?"

"Because they could be put to use."

COMMUNICATIONS

The cleverest method of operation lay in aping their own techniques. Somewhere, sometime, a start, however insignificant, would have to be made, if not by me by someone else. I was utterly convinced of this.

At one time, I would have worked with anyone—ultraconservative, ultraradical, Beatnik, bum, or motorcycle bandit—but they'd all been muzzled, along with the Birchers, the Rubins and Cleavers, Barry's Boys, and the Lincoln Brigade, as well as the Kiwanians, Lions, Elks, and Optimists and the others who hankered for a slice of R. Milhous' pie-in-the-sky bliss.

I was out to make trouble . . . real trouble. And I had no affiliations whatever. I would have used anyone available, would have cheerfully adapted any platform, would have gladly and hypocritically waved any flag, including that of the patriots, to achieve my purpose.

—The Journals

TIXIER HAD BEEN watching him. "Gene, you haven't told us yet—will you come in?"

He had too many feelings. There was Terry—and the possibility that maybe in a year, five years, life would change, or at least reach a point where he and she could live like humans again. Though this was a fantasy, and he knew it, the hope stayed alive. Still another part of him hated being manipulated in the way Tixier was using him this evening.

But it came again to him that this was a chance, surely the

only opportunity he was going to get. He thought, it won't happen again, not like this, and if I turn him down, Kevin and I will stay up here. It's not perfect. Abilene is the trickiest. You could let him run it, if he really knew what the hell he was doing, but he doesn't. But you can't let it slide by. He can get the men. They'll come up for him, but they won't for you. He'll sweet-talk them.

He said, "All right, I'm in."

Tixier, resting against the deadfall, remarked idly, "I was starting to wonder if you'd ever make up your mind." Deaguero and Archuleta, their dark faces lit by the flames, said nothing. "Hell, Gene, with you, it's a cinch," Tixier added.

He looked at the old man bleakly. "I'm running it."

"Sure, Gene," Tixier said. "I was figuring it that way."

"I'll bet," he said.

"That's the truth."

"I want the say-so on who comes up."

"You're the boss."

"I want to know who I'm with," he insisted. "With luck, we can open that camp and walk away without a scratch. But I'm not taking a chance on some juicehead *chicano*. That's the way it's going to be, or else we can forget it."

" *'stá bueno*. Have a drink," Tixier said. He reached for Vandenberg's cup and poured bourbon into it.

Even as he spoke, Vandenberg felt it was wrong. He could not understand, really, why they were up here. He was worried about his son, and how he was going to get him out of this.

Then he realized that he was thinking as though he and the others were slated to fail, that he was planning ahead for Kevin as if he, Vandenberg, would be leaving the picture completely, and he thought, listen, you've got to quit this. He wondered what the odds actually were. How dangerous was it really? Terrero and the Rehab Center? The odds were about three to one, he decided: three to one we fail. That's not too bad. If you can get the weapons carrier. And if you get more men. And if the guards stay put in the barracks and don't break out. But if even a couple of them get into the woods with those submachine guns, then you'll have a hell of a time doing anything. What you need most though is a few who won't blow it. A few who will follow it right through, until someone tells them to pull out. Abilene plays it cool, but it's hard to tell. He might fall apart completely. Reuben—he isn't worth a shit. You won't be able to leave him alone.

And in thinking about these and other things, he saw that Kevin would have to stay with him. He hated putting the boy in danger. He thought, but if he stays I'll spot him someplace where it's safe, where he won't be hurt. With the horses, maybe, off in the woods. If they don't like it, that's too goddamned bad. He drank some bourbon and said to Tixier, "Who else is there?"

"How many do you want?"

"The fewer the better. There are five of us now."

"Counting Kevin?" Tixier asked. "You want him in this?"

"I'm not sure," he lied. "If he stays, I'll give him a job he can handle."

"How about Ben Deaguero?" Abilene asked.

"Willie's father?" he said, surprised. "You said he was sick."

"His ulcers hurt some, but not that bad," Willie explained. "Matter of fact, he was set to come up with us."

"You talked to him about this?"

"Just a little."

"How much, exactly?"

"Only that we'd had it to the teeth and that we were going to demonstrate, and then maybe cut for Mexico," Abilene said.

"And he wanted to come?"

"That's one old man don't like Russians at all," Deaguero said.

Ben Deaguero must have been sixty-five, a huge wreck of a man with a long, ugly face, ebullient and outward-going, a long-time employee of the Game and Fish Department, until the Russians came. He had grown up in this part of the country. "He has a rifle?" Vandenberg asked.

"Ben? Sure."

"All right, then."

Tixier nominated two others. Vandenberg did not know the first, and he said no on this account; the second had a large family, and again he shook his head.

"I was thinking of Cipriano," Tixier said. Cip Griego was the ranch hand he had mentioned earlier, the one who had found sign in the mountains. Like Ben Deaguero, Cip was old, even older. Vandenberg figured he must be past seventy—he'd drawn Social Security for years—and he had a reputation from Rowe to Upper

Colonias for being ill-tempered. Griego had a house in Pecos that he shared with a grandson, but he was a roamer—he was at home in the forests. He was an incurable poacher, too, Vandenberg knew, and this was the sort he wanted, the ones who lived on the fringes of the law.

In spite of Griego's age, he again said, "All right."

"How about Nat Gabaldon?" Deaguero said, glancing at him, and Vandenberg was not surprised, because Natividad, too, was one of the old hunting crowd, not so much a buddy of Tixier but of Deaguero, a barroom brawler who drifted in and out of marriages, an ex-con, superficially easygoing and basically stupid, a sullenly dissolute cattle-truck driver who was quick to grin, but bad when he finally lost his temper, berserk and paranoid. Gabaldon, he remembered, had been in Korea, and he sensed that Willie would feel better with Nat around, and Willie, who said he could get explosives, was important.

He said, "How much does Nat know?"

"*Nada.*"

"Why do you think he'd want to get into this?"

"I just know," Deaguero explained. "He's my friend. He ain't afraid."

"Then go ask him." Tixier named others, and for one reason or another he felt wrong about them all, so that after an hour they were still left with Willie's father, Cipriano, and Gabaldon. Eight, with Kevin. That's not enough, he thought. There should be twelve or thirteen. If anything went wrong, they'd walk over us. Two for Terrero, and one will have to be Willie—he has to handle the explosive. Deaguero and maybe Abilene. They'd work all right together. Willie can drive anything. He and Tixier ought to be able to figure out that weapons carrier pretty quick. We'll be taking a chance that it'll be gassed and ready to go, and that there'll be ammunition. He said to Abilene, "Ben, Gabaldon, and Cipriano."

Deaguero and Reuben Archuleta stared at each other. After a moment, Abilene said flatly, "We need more than that."

"There's no one else," said Vandenberg.

Tixier's mouth set in an obstinate line, and Vandenberg said, "Abilene, a year ago I'd of tried it with five."

The old rancher did not like it, and he let Vandenberg see how he felt. Vandenberg sat there, waiting to see how far it would go, knowing that if he said the wrong thing he'd lose them, and finally Tixier said, "It's no good, if you want my opinion. I ain't that tired of living."

He said, "It won't be easy." Casually, he turned to Deaguero. "When can you get the dynamite?"

"Tomorrow night."

"Good," he said, and thought, if they sit around for a couple of days, drinking and telling stories, they'll cool. Abilene's spooked already. By tomorrow he'll start feeling sorry he ever rode up here. He said to Deaguero, "Can you do it alone?"

"I think so," Willie said. "The road crew is working about twelve miles east of San Jose, where the four-lane ends. They keep the dynamite in a steel shed, back off the highway. The caps and detonators are in the superintendent's desk. I can get in with a pry bar in a couple of minutes. Yale lock on the super's shack. Padlock on the steel shed."

"No alarm?"

"No," Deaguero said. "I check that place every morning while my Cat's warming up. The engineers have keys to the office, and at night they just lock 'er up. I've been inside, and I know where everything is. There's a chance I could be flagged by a prowl car, but that's all."

Vandenberg said, "Get two cases. What's in a case—twenty-four sticks? And the caps—and wire. Don't forget the wire. You say nobody's there at night, but don't take a chance. Bring blankets with you in the truck, folded. Put the dynamite up front on the seat beside you and the caps in the back. You'll be on dirt roads, and if those caps go, you want them in back, where they won't hurt you. Get a cardboard box, and pad the bottom of it with another blanket, and put the caps on that. Now Gabaldon—where is he?"

"At Rowe," Deaguero said. "He has a house there."

Rowe was a ranching community off the highway, east of Glorieta Assembly.

"Has he a weapon?"

"Nat? Hell, yes," Deaguero said. "And he has a horse."

"All right. You talk to him," Vandenberg said. "But for Christ's sake, don't tell him too much. Don't give the whole thing away."

Deaguero nodded.

"Tell him the truth," he said. "Say that a couple of us have

66

something planned, and that it'll be dangerous. But that's all. And that goes for you, Abilene, when you see Cip and Ben. Tell them where they can meet us. How about where the bridge crosses at Holy Ghost Canyon? That's a good place. Reuben can wait there with the horses. You'll all have to meet together. Either they come in with us, or they don't. If they don't, tell them to keep their mouths shut. Willie, you sure Gabaldon'll be home?"

Deaguero shrugged. *"Quién sabe?* He ain't worked much this year."

"Reuben can ride down with you to where you left your pickup. Tell Gabaldon to bring warm clothes, sleeping gear, a sack of food, and all the ammunition he has. Abilene, how long do you think it will take you?"

"Ben will have to ride from Cañada de los Alamos, and Cip from Pecos," Tixier said. "We'll have to wait on them. Figure a day. Day and a half would be better."

"Sunset, then? Day after tomorrow?" he asked.

It would also give any of them the chance to drop out. Let them think it over, he decided. The three of them will be split up. If one wants to run, better to have it happen while they're in town and away from Kevin and me, but if they come back up, we'll know they mean it.

COMMUNICATIONS

The world is absolutely out of control now, and it's not going to be saved by reason or unreason.

—*R. Lowell*

Somewhere, something incredible happened in history—the wrong guys won.

—*N. Mailer*

THAT FIRST NIGHT, they sat by the fire until past nine, drinking bourbon and water, and Vandenberg, still resentful and suspicious, got drunk. Tixier started on a meandering eulogy from which he would not veer until they tumbled him into his bedroll, an old theme—Abilene's—having to do with love, of the marvelous bonds of love that could exist among grown men, all the atrocious, sublimated tripe having to do with hunting and fishing and boozing, all of it so banal that no one except Tixier would have dared dwell on the topic.

Vandenberg frowned as he listened to the bleary monologue, but he knew it was halfway sincere, knew that if anyone so much as murmured a suitably sympathetic word the old rancher would simply collapse, be swept off by a crying jag, too overcome with happiness to hold back the tears—this was the gentle side of Tixier, who could snap a two-by-four across one knee. So he and the others kept silent, not that they had a chance to say much anyway, as Abilene guzzled bourbon and crooned, "Gene! Reubenito! Willie! You old bastards. I love you. You know that, boys? I really love you. I love all my boys, and I don't give a royal fuck who knows it. I missed you, Gene, we all missed you, and I want you to know this is one of the best nights of my whole life, all of us being up here together like this again, just like old times, why, if I live to be a hundred I ain't ever going to forget this night. We're all happy and together again, and that's the way it ought to be, the way it always ought to be. Yessir, I sure got some good feelings about this."

And, to Vandenberg, "Gene, I know I let you down that time when you came in to see me, and I know you're sore at me about that other time, and I'm sorry, and that's why we're up here now, to make it all up to you. I'm going to show you what it means when Tixier calls you friend. You mean, lowdown son of a bitch. I've always loved and admired you. Hard-nosed or not. You got independence. Isn't that right, Reuben? Isn't he the goddamnedest muleheaded, independent bastard you ever set eyes on? That's what I love about him. Don't take shit from nobody. That, and the way he takes care of that boy of his. He's bitched off at me, old Gene is, because he thinks I let him down, but I haven't really. We're up here, ain't we, and that's what counts. I want to tell you, I understand how you are with that boy, Gene, and how much you think of him, and that for all your meanness and hard-nosed ways, you love him. Gene, I can forgive you a lot for that. So don' be mad at me."

Vandenberg got to his feet and walked twenty feet away from the fire to piss into a pine clump; he said over his shoulder, "Abi-

lene, it isn't that I'm mad at you—I don't want you thinking that."
As he finished, he thought, that's true, I'm not mad. I don't trust
you, that's all.

COMMUNICATIONS

*Every government has, directly or indirectly, the power of life and
death over any and all of its citizens. By legislation, discrimination,
and police action, it can make them rich or make them poor. By
education it can make them loving or destructive toward their
fellow-citizens or toward the citizens of other nations.*
    Eric Berne, *Transactional Analysis Bulletin, Vol. 8, #29*

*. . . I believe that every human being is potentially capable,
within his "limits," of fully "realizing" his potentialities; that is, his
being cheated of it is infinitely the ghastliest, commonest and most
inclusive of all crimes of which the human world can acuse itself. . . .*
    —*J. Agee, Let Us Now Praise Famous Men*

AND NOW KEVIN, who stood so straight and tall, brown-haired,
with the wounded eyes of a startled deer, who bore no mark or sign
to indicate his limitation, neither shambling gait nor slack mouth,
nor the apathetic stare you sometimes encountered, who used to sit
and play with pebbles for half a sunny morning under the portal
at the ranch, who at sixteen could without straining hoist a sack of
Portland, but who would, if spoken to in a harsh manner, stand
before you swallowing painfully as tears trickled down his cheeks.
    Once—and only once—had Abilene, some seven years back,
made a pass, not even a real pass, but it was enough. He'd wandered out to the ranch in his pickup, and they had done some
drinking, so that by late afternoon he and Vandenberg were riding
a red-wine high, sitting in the kitchen, at the big, planked table,
with the boy beside Tixier. And Abilene, maybe drunk, maybe not
even thinking, had let one hand sink in a caress, half pat, half
squeeze, against the boy's thigh, and Vandenberg cooled. He had
stared hard at Tixier, whose hand by now was back on the table,
raging at himself for being so stupid as to let it happen, furious for

letting himself believe that Tixier, despite his weakness, was his best friend. He'd said, quite matter-of-factly, "Don't ever do anything like that again . . . you understand?" The old rancher had apologized, and they'd had another couple of shots of wine, but after that it was not the same. He and Tixier would still run into one another in Santa Fe bars, and then they would almost ceremoniously buy each other a beer and then talk, but still, it was not the same.

2

In the Compound

VANDENBERG HAD BEEN arrested on a Tuesday afternoon in July on a shopping trip in town.

At the local Piggly Wiggly, he filled a grocery cart with canned goods, vegetables, fryer chickens, hamburger, staples, some sweet rolls for Kevin, and a carton of smokes. After the checker had totaled his purchases and torn out the pages of coupons from his ration book, he stacked everything in the front seat of the truck, walked over to a package store, and bought two gallons of wine. After that, he drove to the post office.

There was nothing in his box except several bills, which he threw away, and a notice that the quarterly rental fee on the box was due. From the post office he went to the Red Top Chevron station, where he left the truck for a lube job, and then walked to the library, but a sign on the glass doors stated that the place was closed for inventory.

He came back across the sun-drenched plaza to the Montana Bar. In the old days this had been a hangout for the town's drinking crowd, and on weekends the place still came alive, but now it was quiet and nearly deserted. The owner, Nikos, a wiry, dark-haired man in his forties, was on duty behind the bar. Vandenberg had drunk here for fifteen years, in the beginning because the drinks were large and cheap, but later because it had become a custom. He and the Greek were friendly without being close. Out of perversity, he ran a bar bill, knowing Nikos' morale did a nose dive at the mention of credit. He customarily paid ten or twenty a month on it, and then charged about the same in beer and wine, so that it stayed around fifty dollars. Nikos, with glum humor, had observed a number of times that this impasse was going to continue until one of them died—Vandenberg, probably—in which case the Greek would be stuck.

Now, Vandenberg placed a twenty-five-cent piece on the bar and got a stein of beer in return. "Gene, how've you been?"

"Pretty good."

"Ain't seen you for a while."

"Nothing to come in for," he said. He drank some of the beer, and glanced around. "How's it going?"

"Real slow," the Greek said. With Nikos, it was always slow. Vandenberg had seen nights when the Montana was jammed—maybe ninety or a hundred Anglos and Spanish, old and young, with Bill Benavidez' Apodaca Hill Mariachis blowing their brains out in competition with the Wurlitzer—a lot of youngsters with their girls, but plenty of old-timers, too, who had settled down to serious drinking, so that eighty dollars an hour was going into the till, but still if you asked Nikos how it was going, he would look discouraged: "Slow."

They talked for a few minutes, and then Nikos went off to refill someone else's glass. Vandenberg finished his beer and got another, deliberating whether to phone Terry at school and see if she was busy. He watched, without much interest, a sports feature on the color set over the bar that showed Russian and American weight-lifting teams. He was on his third drink when a city detective named Gilbert Serna walked in. Most of the newer men on the force were strangers to Vandenberg, but years ago, when he'd had to drive Kevin in every day to special classes at Acequia Madre School, he and Serna had struck up a casual friendship at Fraser's Drug Store where they both stopped for morning coffee.

Serna walked over to him now and touched his arm. Vandenberg looked away from the television screen. "Hello, Gil. How've you been?"

"Hi, Gene. Where you been keeping yourself?" Serna was a broad, powerful man, no longer young, with a square, expressionless face, small-eyed, with gray, crinkly hair and a heavy paunch.

Vandenberg said, "I don't get in often. Gas rationing."

Serna interrupted, staring at him with interest, to-the-point. "Gene, there's a warrant on you. I'm going to have to bring you in."

For a moment he was too surprised to speak. Then, "What're you talking about?"

"It was filed last month," Serna said. "The sheriff has it, since you're out of city limits. I guess they couldn't figure out where that ranch of yours is."

"What's the charge?"

"Political."

"Oh, for Christ's sake," Vandenberg snapped.

"It's not for me to argue."

"Jesus, Gil, I haven't even *voted* for twenty years."

"Maybe so," Serna said. "But your name is on a list the D.A. received last month." He looked at Vandenberg. "We better go, Gene."

Nikos watched, from behind the bar.

"Listen, I've got my truck and all my supplies over at the Red Top," he argued.

"I'll have it taken care of for you."

"Take care of it, hell. You'll impound it. There's over thirty dollars' worth of groceries in it."

"Come on, Gene."

He knew it was senseless to keep on. He left his half-finished beer and went with Serna.

AT HEADQUARTERS a young girl in departmental blues made out a charge sheet, typing slowly on an Underwood. Obediently he handed over his wallet, belt, clasp knife, cigarettes, and then turned his pockets inside out. His belongings were placed in a cotton sack and tagged, and then Serna took him by the arm and led him down the hall to another room, where he was fingerprinted and photographed. From there they went to the bullpen, and it was then that he felt fear. He stopped at the entrance to the pen. "Is there bail? I want to use the phone."

Serna shook his head. "No calls, no bail. Not on political charges, Gene. We can only deliver you. After that, it's in their hands."

"But my kid's out at the place, alone."

Serna was silent a moment, and then he said, "If you want some advice, Gene, don't give them any static. Understand? A little cooperation. . . ." He shrugged. "Shit, they don't give a damn, one way or another."

Vandenberg nodded, and stepped into the bullpen: a large, square concrete room, unfurnished—not a cot or a chair—lit by a grille-shielded overhead bulb and deserted except for three drunks. At the base of one wall a shallow trough had been hollowed in the

75

floor, and this served as a urinal. One of the drunks, unshaven and looking sick, ambled over. *"Compadre*—cigarette?"

"No tengo tabac," he said. The drunk went back to his pals, and the three of them began talking in Spanish. Angry and frightened, Vandenberg looked around once more at the room, and then hunkered down, his back propped against the wall.

HE WAITED all the rest of that day and night, and by then he was frantic about his son. At six that evening the drunks were removed to the cellblock. He was given a plate of beans and bread and a cup of thin coffee. Later, he curled up on the floor and tried to sleep, but the glare of the electric light overhead kept him awake. Sometime during the night five more winos were herded into the pen. One of them had a bloodied mouth. The concrete floor was cold, and it stank of creosote, and Vandenberg, furious now, cursed the police for not providing blankets. A drunk, still far out, launched an off-key version of a mariachi tune. Several of the others joined in.

The next morning they came for him. The iron door opened, and a young patrolman beckoned. They went down the hall together, back to the room where he had been booked. Sunlight shone through the barred windows. A duty sergeant sat at a desk, talking to an Occupation officer. When Vandenberg entered, the Russian stopped talking and reached for several sheets of paper lying on the desk between him and the duty sergeant. He glanced at them, then got up and shook hands with the sergeant. He motioned for Vandenberg to follow him, and accompanied by the young patrolman, they went down the stairs and out into the narrow side street adjoining headquarters, where a prowl car was being washed and chamoised by a thirty-dayer. Parked at the curb was a gray Chevrolet panel truck. An enlisted man waited behind the wheel. The Russian officer unlocked the rear doors and told him to get in.

He balked, and the patrolman reached out and grabbed him by the shoulder. "Just a minute—where are you taking me?"

"Shut up," the Russian officer said: "Get in."

He hesitated. The patrolman gave him a shove, and he stumbled onto the steel floor of the truck's interior. The back doors slammed shut. A key turned in a lock. By the time he got to his feet, partially crouched under the low ceiling, the panel truck was under way.

He moved forward to the grilled window that separated the rear compartment from the cab. They were driving through town, headed west, and then north as they turned a corner at the hospital. The driver braked to a halt at a stop sign, waited, and then shifted into first, heading up Canyon Road.

It was hot under the steel roof. He hooked his fingers onto the grilled mesh and stared past the shoulders of the two men up front, and now, still frightened, he thought. it could be as simple as this. They could—if they wanted—get you up into the hills and fire a bullet into you and bury you. Who'd give it a second thought? Gil Serna? Nikos? None of them. Terry would ask questions if you didn't show up. But they could tell her anything. How would she know?

Crouched there, his face pale with fear, he half understood that what was gnawing at him had to do with what he called the "intolerable shock" of the past year. The Occupation had been in effect almost that long, and now for him, privately, it had culminated in this arrest.

The rationing, the coupons, the thousands of new laws set in motion by Military Government, the sight of off-duty Occupation soldiers shopping in local stores, the curfew—all these affected everyone. Now, however, a personal event had occurred that set him apart. He knew he'd been treated gently. What frightened him about the past twenty-four hours was the meaninglessness of it. Silently, he repeated the question for which there was no answer. Why? Why this?

HE KNEW almost immediately that the panel truck was headed for the Thirty-second Military District's Headquarters. The District comprised all of the state of New Mexico. Each of the other states had its own district. In Santa Fe, the capital, Occupation Headquarters was billeted in what had been St. John's College. This was an expensive complex, completed less than ten years ago, located deep in a picturesque cleft near a hill named Del Monte Sol. Begun as an extension of St. John's at Annapolis, the school had catered to precocious youngsters who'd encountered difficulties in more conventionally oriented schools. For a small college, the campus was elegant—so many Santa Feans said—and the same thought must have occurred to Military Government, for it had commandeered the brand-new buildings shortly after the signing of the provisional armistice, and now the low, broad administration buildings and study halls, with their terrazzo floors and high picture windows, housed better than six hundred Russian civilian and military personnel, into whose hands the governing of the Thirty-Second District had been entrusted. Only a few minutes from the state capitol, it was secluded enough to ensure that quasi-Olympian aloofness that USSRAOOUSA was partial to.

From his observation post behind the grille, Vandenberg saw the campus come into view. A concrete guardhouse had been erected at the entrance, and a sentry with a submachine gun slung across his back came out and saluted the officer riding beside the driver. The candy-striped gate was raised, and the truck drove through. Flying above the main building were the flags of the U.S.S.R. and USSRAOOUSA, and the new American flag.

They parked at the rear of the main building, and he was taken out and escorted through a side entrance to a small waiting room. A Soviet guard stood at the door, at parade rest.

Wooden benches had been placed against the walls on three sides of the room, and on one of them sat a man, a civilian, with receding gray hair. At first, Vandenberg thought he was ill. Then he saw that the man was near collapse. Unshaven, his shoulders hunched, he kept staring around distractedly—his hands hung loosely between his legs. Vandenberg had seen him around town, but he could not immediately place him.

The guard motioned for Vandenberg to sit. He and the gray-haired man waited together for half an hour, without speaking. Then another guard came in and took them down the hall to a small office.

Inside, a short, balding officer wearing gold-rimmed spectacles sat at a highly polished table piled with papers. He stared up at them as they entered, first at Vandenberg and then at his companion, and his speech, when he finally addressed them, was accented: "Which of you is Eugene R. Vandenberg?"

"I am."

The officer looked at the other man. "Jerome Fein?"

Vandenberg remembered his companion then. Fein, the insurance broker. He'd run for mayor once and had been on the City Council. Successful, with community spirit. A descendant of that nineteenth-century trickle of enterprising Jews, Armenians, and

Greeks who, laden with backpacks of sewing materials and gim-cracks, had made some truly adventurous solo expeditions into the then still wild West, staying, in many instances, to set up small general stores in backwater communities. (It had startled Vandenberg, years ago, to find in isolated villages like Watrous and Media such oddities as Findlebaum's General and Dry Goods, and Il-pagian's Feed and Grain.)

The bespectacled officer went on, "I am Major Grunot, judge advocate of the Thirty-Second Military District."

Vandenberg wondered if Grunot had been in the academic world. Behind the long table, the Russian looked very much like a middle-aged schoolteacher.

Grunot glanced at several sheets, and continued, the voice courteous, impersonal, "You have both been detained under charges filed against you by Military Government, including, specifically, the circulation of seditious and criminal propaganda."

Fein interrupted, his hands moving in the air, "Major—that's impossible."

Grunot shook his head. "Comrade Fein, you are here not to present your case, but merely to hear the charges brought against you."

"But my lawyer—"

"Yes," interjected Vandenberg, "can we call a lawyer?"

"No," Grunot said.

"Why not?"

"Because—you can't."

"Can I call a friend then?" he insisted.

"No."

"Listen, Major, I have a son who's mentally retarded. He's been alone since yesterday afternoon," Vandenberg said. "Let me at least have someone go out and get him—I live outside town. There are no neighbors."

"Impossible."

"Goddamn it, I can't just leave him out there."

Grunot stared at him. "Where is your home?"

As briefly as possible, he described the ranch's location. "Can you at least send a message for me? I have a friend who's a teacher —she could get him."

"I'm afraid not," Major Grunot said, "but the boy will be taken care of." He paused. "Your home—this ranch—is isolated, I take it?"

"Yes."

"Why is that? It seems curious to me that a man would live so . . . alone. Do you raise cattle?"

"No."

"Horses? Sheep?"

"No."

"What do you do there?"

"I'm a painter."

"This location was chosen out of necessity, perhaps?" Grunot asked. He seemed genuinely interested. "Or did you prefer it?"

"I prefer it."

Grunot considered this and then nodded. "Interesting."

Jerome Fein interrupted: "What about my family? You can't just come into a man's home at seven in the morning and arrest him. My wife—she'll be frantic."

"She will be informed of the expected length of your detainment."

"When?"

"In time."

Fein said, "Major, I want an exact breakdown on these charges you have."

"In time," Grunot said again. "As I explained, your case is not being tried here—you serve no purpose in presenting your arguments to me."

"When will a trial be set?"

"Your cases have been scheduled on the calendar of the Military Government's People's Court," Grunot explained. "You will be assigned a defense counsel."

"But how long will it take?" Fein insisted.

"From three to four months," Grunot said. "The calendar, unfortunately, is filled at this time."

"For God's sake, Major, I have a business to run," Fein argued. "I don't know what your charges are, but I'm sure there's been a mistake, there's a reasonable explanation. I can't let things slide for three months." Fein's demoralization was complete now. He stared at the major, then at Vandenberg, then back again. "I can't!"

"Comrade, you are going to have to," Grunot said. "There are no alternatives. Until your case comes up, I have no choice but to remand you and your companion to the Rehabilitation Training Center at Cowles."

Fein paused, then looked at Vandenberg. "What do you mean, companion? Listen, I don't know this guy. Are you trying to tie me in. . . . What's this all about?"

"You are not being tied in with anything," Grunot said, without interest. "Each of you is charged individually." He said something in Russian, and the guard stepped forward and escorted Vandenberg and Fein out of the room.

They went back up the corridor, the heels of the guard's boots clacking on the terrazzo floors, and out into the parking lot at the rear of the building. The panel truck that had brought Vandenberg was still parked in the same place. They waited until the driver and the same officer came out and unlocked the rear doors for them to enter. Once they were inside, the doors were again locked.

He heard the guard and the officer talking outside. In a minute, the cab doors opened and slammed shut, the motor started, and they drove off. The truck stopped at the sentry building out front and then moved forward again. Vandenberg went to the grilled window and watched as they drove out the four-lane highway, past the First Baptist Church, headed east.

FEIN DID NOT speak for some time. Vandenberg was sure the broker was suspicious, but then, as they sped past the old Bobcat Bite Cafe, Fein said, "Where are we?"

"Heading toward Vegas," he said.

Fein was sitting on the floor: "Why'd they arrest you?"

"I don't know."

"You haven't any idea?"

"No. I was in a bar, having a beer. The next thing I knew I was at police headquarters."

Fein was silent. Then he said, "They got me out of bed at seven. I mean, they walked right into my *house*. Right into the goddamned bedroom! My wife was in the kitchen, fixing cereal for the kids, when they rang the bell. She opened the door, and they walked right past her." He thought about this. "My God, are they crazy? What do they think they're doing?"

"Why did they arrest you?" Vandenberg asked.

"I told you, I don't know," Fein said plaintively. "I haven't done anything."

Vandenberg did not reply, and presently Fein glanced at him: "I remember you now. You're Vandenberg. The painter. Didn't I meet you at a party once?"

"Years ago."

"Sure. It was right after you came to Santa Fe, wasn't it?"

"I'd already been here quite a while."

"You were making a bundle with those paintings," Fein went on. 'Landscapes."

"I never made a bundle," he said. "I got by, that was all."

"You take this so calmly," Fein said. He got up and crouched beside Vandenberg, who moved over to share the window. "You realize what this means?"

"Nobody's calm," he said, "and I don't know what the hell any of it means."

"You don't know about Cowles?" Fein's face was close to his.

"I've heard talk."

"They say it's a prison."

"So I've heard. I've also heard it's a training center," he said. "There was a story in the paper about it, four or five months ago." He changed the subject. "I wish I could get word to some friends. . . ."

"You shouldn't have told them about your place," Fein said. "You don't have anything there—do you?"

Vandenberg glanced at him. "Like what?"

"Papers. I don't know. They'll search, you know."

"I have about seventy dollars' worth of drawing paper," he said. "Gesso panels. A few hundred back copies of *The New Yorker* and five or six thousand books, mostly paperbacks. Nothing wrong with that."

"I wouldn't have thought so," Fein said. "Until today, I swear, I wouldn't have thought so."

"Listen, we may only be at Cowles a few days. They may release us until the trial date is set."

Fein shook his head. "That's not a place for transients."

"Rumors."

"Maybe. But why have a place like that in the first place?"

"I don't know," Vandenberg said. "Maybe we'll find out."

"They call it a rehabilitation center," the broker said. "What kind of two-bit propaganda terminology is that? Why do they think they're kidding? Do they think we're fools? I'll tell you what it is. It's a detention center for political radicals and nonconformists. And in Germany in the thirties they had the same thing, and they called them concentration camps. Why else is it way up there in the mountains, hidden away? Are they ashamed of it, or something, that nobody can get without twenty miles of it since they built it? Who are they kidding? Are you a political nonconformist? Am I? Hell, no." He shook his head angrily. "I did my utmost to cooperate. I'm telling you that sincerely. But I'm not a guy who likes being taken for a fool. I majored in economics, and I have a pretty good idea of what they're doing to what they call our old capitalistic economy. If they want to do it, that's fine by me. I can't stop them. They can methodically wreck this country if they want. But let them save their breath and not tell me they're building a newer and better United States, because I know better. I'll cooperate, and I'll get by, but they're mistaken if they think I'm a blind fool."

HE HAD DRIVEN this route scores of times on hunting and fishing trips. Highway 85 travels in an easterly direction among the foothills of a spur of the Sangre de Cristos, crossing, some fifteen miles from Santa Fe, Apache Canyon and the village of Cañoncito. A few miles beyond is the Glorieta Baptist Assembly, a neo-Grecian collection of improbable-looking buildings interspersed with colonnaded and entablatured meditation walks and an only partially successful attempt at La Jolla landscaping, the overall effect being marred somewhat by the towering presence of a steel water tower. The Assembly had been erected as a place of instruction and solace for Baptists throughout the Southwest, but here too Military Government had stepped in, and now it served as a billet for a Soviet cavalry squadron.

Beyond Glorieta, a spur road leaves the four-lane highway, leading north to Pecos. In years past the village had served as a jumping-off place for the wilderness area. The town itself is poverty-ridden. There is a little ranching, a sawmill, and a fish hatchery, as well as the Forked Lightning Ranch, once owned by a wealthy Texan named Fogelson, the husband of the cinema actress Greer Garson. North, past the fish hatchery, is the Benedictine Monastery, where friars baked bread. Several miles beyond this the hardtop ends. A dirt road continues, and subsequently enters Pecos Wilderness, the road becoming narrower and increasingly difficult to travel, rising always in elevation, clinging to the sides of Pecos Canyon (a geological freak, a deep, ancient, tree-studded cleft in the forest), arriving ultimately at Cowles, twenty-four miles away and several thousand feet higher than the village of Pecos. Along this last stretch had been located a number of dude ranches, summer camps for boys and girls, and dozens of rustic cabins built during pre-Occupation days by moneyed Texans seeking relief from the scorching summers of such metropolises as Dallas, Houston, and Fort Worth.

The Chevrolet panel truck passed the entrance to Holy Ghost Canyon and then, several miles farther on, a cluster of buildings and a general store: this was Terrero. From behind the grille, Vandenberg saw that there was an Occupation unit stationed in a building on the left. The road was barricaded here by an aluminum stock gate, and the Russian officer up front handed orders to a sentry who came out of the building. The gate was unlocked, and they drove through. The stumpy piñons of the lower foothills gave way to taller pines. Farther on, they came to the slag heap of an old lead mine at Willow Creek. Here the road grew precipitous, and in several places the driver had to shift into first. Finally, the truck topped a rise and from the window he and Fein could see a series of peaks that stretched north, almost to Colorado, hundreds of square miles of forest.

Fein said, "Jesus, where are they taking us?"

"Cowles."

"It must be in the middle of nowhere," Fein said. "Have you been up here before?"

"Many times."

"Really?"

"My first wife and I used to picnic up here," he said, "and years ago I did a lot of hunting here."

Fein looked through the grilled window again. "Funny—I've lived in Santa Fe all my life, and I've never been up here."

"You missed a lot. This is good country."

He could remember fishing the Pecos in the late fall when the water was low and clear and the summer people had left. He'd found an old second-hand bamboo rod with a stiff action and had rebuilt it, laboriously shaving the sections down and shortening them until the rod weighed two and a quarter ounces on a postal scale and was only six and a half feet long, with a soft, whippy action. Using a tapered line and a two-pound leader, he could lay out fifteen-yard casts all day without tiring his wrist, although you did not need that much distance on the Pecos. He'd had a cheap assortment of nymphs and hackles, small ones on fourteens and sixteens, and with this setup he'd caught trout all along the upper Pecos and Cow and Bull Creeks, no lunkers, for they never ran over ten or eleven inches, but taken on the featherweight rig, they were sporty.

There had been other days on the upper slopes when he and Tixier and Spanish friends had hunted deer and elk, and still other times when, wanting a break from the ranch, he and Kevin had backpacked in for ten and twelve days, and they had found bear and mountain lion and grouse and herds of elk. He had hunted and fished the Chama and the Brazos and Red River areas, but the Pecos Wilderness was close. Terry used to tease him about living in this part of New Mexico, pointing out that he despised the town and its citizens as well as the art colony, and he had replied by saying that he did, in fact, think Santa Fe added up to a large zero, but that there was still the climate and the privacy and the feeling of being in the country. These were important to him, and he knew he could never find the same combination anywhere else.

Cowles came into view. They were still perhaps a mile from it, but he could see that it was not the same.

It was here, at over eight thousand feet, that the dirt road ended. Beyond, he knew, were a few jeep trails that probed a mile or two farther into the woods.

The privately stocked trout pond was still there, along with the guest ranch and the general store, but behind the main ranch house, where there had been fields and corrals, a series of Quonset huts had been erected, enclosed by a high double fence which was electrified. Surmounting the chain link fences were strings of barbed wire, their tops canted inward. Watchtowers, low ones built of heavy timber, not more than fifteen feet high, were spaced around the perimeter of the fences. Both Occupation and Soviet Army flags had been raised on peeled aspen poles. It reminded him of photographs he'd seen of German *stalags*.

Fein obviously felt the same; he said now, "My God, in 1945,

I was in the army, and we went into Munich. I drove up to Dachau with some buddies—you know, we figured we ought to see something like that firsthand. This was a couple of months after they'd liberated the camp, but the smell was still terrible. They'd cleaned it up a lot, but even so you got a pretty good idea of what it must have been like. I swear, Vandenberg, I think this is going to be the same thing. They've tricked us. We're not going to get out of this place. They're not civilized. There's no decency here. A civilized country would have no need for that." The broker poked a finger through the window grille.

Curiously, Vandenberg, except for his worry about Kevin, was for the first time almost calm. The fear that had been working at him—of being taken into an arroyo and shot—was gone. He knew he was safe, for a while at least.

COMMUNICATIONS

VANDENBERG, EUGENE R.
#4076   FBI 896 472

ADMISSION SUMMARY

This forty-nine-year-old Caucasian divorced male, no religion listed, B.S. and M.A. degrees, Un. Chi., Ill., was admitted to this institution on July 7, on an involuntary basis. Admittance authorized via orders from Judge Advocate's Office, Santa Fe, N.M.

IDENTIFICATION: *Social & political disorientation, chronic alcoholism.*

EXAMINATION DATA:

1. Physical: Within normal limits.
2. Lab/X-ray: Blood morphology & urinalysis satisfactory.
3. Mental: Patient obedient, coherent, relevant, rational, and with an intact memory. Has never had DT's, denies hallucinations. Judgment unimpaired and he has an insight into his condition.

Course in Center: Intensive. Category III.

Diagnosis: Sociopathic personality disturbance, alcohol addiction.

Prognosis: Fair   Competency: Full

Recommendations: 90-day-probationary status, to observe behavioral patterns. The following sedations, treated for consumption

with regular diet, are prescribed: AVT-21-R 10 mg T.I.D.; Libra-
trol 10 mg. B.I.D.

cc: Research & Statistics   *—C. P. Ulanowski, M.D.*
     JA Office, 32nd Dist.   *Chief Psychiatrist*
     Commanding Officer,   *32nd Dist Trng & Rehab.*
     32nd Dist.   *Cowles, N.M.*

AT THE MAIN BUILDING, the officer in the cab showed his orders. The rear doors were unlocked, and the two men were brought inside.

Admission took several hours. Forms were filled out for each of them, the answers to the questions being typed in by a military clerk.

They were brought to a bare room and told to strip. X-rays and blood samples were taken, their teeth examined. He and Fein were separated. An elderly medical officer in a white tunic who, Vandenberg guessed, was a psychiatrist asked him questions, touching at one point on his immediate situation, "Do you know why you are here?"

"No."

"No idea?"

He shook his head. The medical officer stared at him, and said finally, "You have been charged with suspicion of seditious activity."

"Yes—they told me that in Santa Fe."

"Well?"

"Well, what?"

"You have nothing to say about this?"

"What do you want me to say? That I've been wrecking your precious Military Government?" he demanded. "Blowing up bridges? Come on!"

"You're being cynical," the doctor said.

Vandenberg feigned astonishment. "I'm sorry."

"Please be serious."

"All right, doctor. I'll be serious."

"This is a grave charge, you know."

"I can believe it," he said.

"In our country it could mean life imprisonment."

"Is that all?"

"You would plead not guilty then?"

"Yes."

"Unequivocally?"

"Hell, yes."

"And you do not know why such charges have been made?"

"No."

"But there must be a reason," the doctor said. "So grave a charge would not be brought against a man without ample reason. At home, sedition is a serious matter. We think twice before bringing such a charge against a man."

"Listen, doctor," he said, "I've lived a quiet life, and I've obeyed all your laws. Most of them. I may not have liked them, but neither do millions of other Americans."

"I see." The doctor paused, and then changed the subject. "Did you serve in the armed forces?"

"Yes."

"When?"

"From 1942—August, I think—to 1945."

"Where did you enlist?"

"Chicago."

"What branch?"

"Army. The infantry."

"Where did you serve?"

"Europe."

"Do you recall your serial number?" Oddly enough, Vandenberg, who was absentminded about many things, did: "32223653."

"Honorably discharged?"

"Yes."

"Were you wounded?"

"Yes."

"Where?"

"Heurtgen Forest."

"No, no—I mean what portion of your anatomy."

"The left leg. Also, this scar on my forehead."

The doctor glanced up from his writing pad. "What caused that?"

"Shell fragment."

"You were lucky," the doctor said. "During your service, did you at any time receive medical treatment of a psychiatric nature?"

"Yes."

"What sort?"

"I cracked up," he said. "The war was over already. I guess it was around November of '45. We were at Le Havre, waiting to ship out. I was only in the hospital a few days."

"What they call battle fatigue?"

"Sort of. It was more of a case of nerves. We'd gone over to a sports arena to watch some boxing matches between outfits. I'd been drinking. I started tearing things up—throwing benches around—that sort of thing. A couple of buddies held me down."

"I see." The doctor made a notation. "Any psychiatric treatment since?"

"No."

"Veterans hospital? Private treatment?"

"No."

The questions went on. He wondered if another doctor was asking Fein the same things. Despite the warmth of the day, he felt chilled and uncomfortable, standing there naked. He could understand the psychology of interrogating a man who was nude, and he did not like it.

When the medical officer was finished, Vandenberg was brought down to another room. Fein was waiting there. They were told to sit in wooden chairs. Electric shears were applied to their skulls. The discomfort he'd felt over being naked was mild compared to his feelings when he saw himself in a wall mirror, his ears protruding from either side of a glistening, grayish-white poll. Fein complained bitterly as the noisy clippers ploughed across his skull.

They were next sent into a tier of shower stalls and told to wash. After that they went through the rest of the physical: heart, respiratory, blood pressure; the interiors of their mouths were again examined carefully, fillings tapped; then they were told to bend over and grab their ankles—a difficult position for Fein to assume, as he apparently had a hernia—while an orderly with a rubber-sheathed finger probed their rectums. Eyes squinted shut, grimacing with discomfort, Vandenberg guessed that this was a routine part of the admissions procedure. Hidden capsules? A ten-inch mill file? Face flushed from the stooped position, he said ill-humoredly, "Listen, friend, I realize you have a job to do, but I'd take it as a favor if you'd hurry up and remove your Bolshevik finger from my ass." The orderly said something in Russian, and chuckled.

When the medical examination was finished, they were taken

to a supply room, where they were issued faded but clean coveralls, heavy work shoes of an approximate fit, underwear, two woolen blankets, and a towel, soap, and Gillette safety razor kit. They were told to dress.

Vandenberg noticed the work shoes. At the rear of each rubber heel, a cut had been made—a V-shaped wedge. Ignoring the guard nearby, he said to Fein, "See?"

Fein looked at his own shoes: "Mine have them, too."

"They use the same trick at the pen," he said. "If anybody breaks out and they're searching for him and come across footprints, they can tell from the heel mark if they're after the right man."

"It doesn't surprise me," Fein said. "It doesn't surprise me a bit."

When they had dressed, they gathered their blankets and toilet articles and were taken to the commandant's office, off what had been the foyer of the main ranch building. The commandant was at his desk when they were ushered in, a tall, wiry man in his late fifties, with a thick shock of dark hair. He had a square face and a grayish complexion, the face, perhaps, of a peasant, and he had an immediately noticeable habit, when not actually speaking, of keeping his teeth clenched so that the jaw muscles stood out prominently, the mouth an austere line. His English, though accented, was excellent. Looking them over, he delivered himself of a speech in a quiet, diffident fashion.

"Good morning. I am Colonel Brushnevesko. It is my custom to address new arrivals in person and explain the regulations and methods by which we operate. If you do as you are told, you will probably never have to come to this office again. I hope so." He paused to let this sink in.

Fein interrupted: "Colonel, if I—"

The Colonel looked up at him with such a frown that Fein stopped. Brushnevesko said, "Please. No one gave you permission to speak. Under no circumstances are you ever to speak to me unless a question is asked of you. Do you understand that?"

Fein did not reply, and the colonel went on. "You are here because political charges have been brought against you. Every inmate here is a political offender. The charges against you are not my concern. In time, you will be informed of them. My task here is to provide food and adequate shelter. You will, I believe, discover for yourself that conditions at Cowles are quite good, better in some respects than many people experience outside. I am also here to see to it that you do not leave the area. Although you may have heard otherwise, this training center has been classified as a maximum security detention camp. This, of course, is perfectly obvious to anybody who has had an opportunity to see what we have."

Colonel Brushnevesko paused again, then continued, his voice dry, leisurely: "Let me explain the camp. I want you to understand fully. We have no secrets here. The inner compound, which is fenced in, has four dormitories, a cafeteria, a lecture hall, and three study halls. Our census, as of this morning, is one hundred and ninety-three. Soviet personnel are quartered outside, in this and the other two buildings you may have noticed. Meals are served at six in the morning, noon, and six in the evening. The food is good, and we all eat the same—my lunch today will be precisely the same as yours. Morning census is at six forty-five. The infirmary is in this building, if you report sick. After breakfast, there is an hour and a half of calisthenics, followed by four hours of lectures and interviews. One hour off for lunch, then four more hours of instruction. Aside from work details—cleaning, maintenance, cutting firewood—this will be your schedule. You do not leave the inner compound unless ordered to do so, and then you will be accompanied. At times, after the evening meal, there are additional lectures and sometimes films. If there are not, lights-out is at seven thirty. I might add that for the first three days, you will be kept in solitary confinement. This is not a punishment. It serves as a period of readjustment. You will be furnished with required reading material, at no cost. At the end of the three days, you will be assigned to a dormitory. You will meet your fellow trainees. You will also meet your lecturers and the interviewers to whom your names have been assigned. A question commonly asked has to do with letters. There are no letters. No telephone calls. No visits. Absolutely none."

He looked at them, perhaps hoping to find some signs of rebellion. Vandenberg stared down at the floor. The commandant went on: "To return to the compound. There are two fences, the inner and an outer. Each is four meters high, of woven steel mesh, topped by barbed wire. The outer fence has seventy-two hundred volts. The space between these two fences is forbidden. My orders, comrades, are that anyone caught in this space be shot. The sentries in the watchtowers understand very clearly that they are to shoot to kill, not wound. There are five watchtowers, seventy-five meters apart. The sentries are armed with submachine guns and shotguns. Every man in my security detachment is certified as an expert marksman. They are very good men. Exceptional soldiers. Dependable. Older than our average soldier. I know, because I picked them myself. They have a good life here, and they like the assignment—and you may believe me when I tell you that none of them has any affection at all for Americans. To them, you political troublemakers represent a threat to everything we are trying to accomplish. Let me put it this way—the compound has been in operation almost a year, under my command. During that time, no one has escaped. No one, for that matter, has even tried. I intend to maintain this record."

He paused again, and then said, "Your rehabilitation is entirely in the hands of the political department here, but the everyday side of your detention is my responsibility. Do as you are told. Avoid trouble. Personally, that will be enough to satisfy me. You will be here for a certain period. What you gain from the experience depends largely on yourselves. With your instructors and interviewers, you can argue and debate all you want. But with me, you will be obedient. I have rules, and I will not tolerate their being abused. There is nothing here but the camp. It is my camp. Troublemakers do not impress or intimidate me. We know exactly what to do with troublemakers here."

Almost in the same breath, Colonel Brushnevesko ended it: "You may go."

HE SPENT the next three days alone, his greatest worry still for Kevin. He knew the boy would eventually walk to town, searching for him, and would probably be picked up. There had been enough food in the house for several days, and in many ways Kevin could take care of himself, but he knew his son would become frightened and finally terrified when he did not return.

The cell was small but fairly comfortable. As in the bullpen, a grilled overhead light burned night and day. At one end of the cell, a small, narrow-barred window looked out on an empty field. At the other end there was a planked door with a hinged slot at the bottom, through which a food tray was slid three times daily. The door remained closed for the three days, and during this time he spoke to no one.

He either slept or read. Pamphlets had been stacked neatly in the center of a small wooden table. By the end of the second day, he had gone through the material in the pamphlets several times. The thickest booklet was entitled *The Role of the U.S.S.R. in the United States of America,* and Vandenberg read:

. . . the ultimate goal of Soviet Military Government, as a helping hand, is self-extinction.

The U.S.S.R. has no intention or wish to maintain a substantial Occupational Army on foreign soil, since it is far too costly, in terms of both manpower and logistical supply, and the effort would be better directed toward more useful fields.

Based on present information, it is hoped that the Occupational Forces can be entirely withdrawn from U.S. territories by the early eighties at the latest. By that time the United States will again be functioning as a totally autonomous body. Already there has been substantial progress. The old system of electoral representation, which was in effect a myth that existed via deceit and outright prevarication, has been abolished, and the citizens of the United States are beginning to accept the new system of choosing representatives, which, although it seemed strange at first, has proven an effective countermeasure to the old democratic method, which relied on huckstering and sham to achieve its ends. The national economy, which understandably suffered a massive setback during the first year of the Occupation, is now showing signs of a slow but steady recuperation. In terms of national defense, which had been oriented toward aggressive-weapons stockpiling rather than actual defense, industry is being regeared. Unavoidably, during this interim period of readjustment the production of consumer goods will be curtailed, but barring the occurrence of unforeseen emergencies, it is expected that consumer-goods production will gradually regain its old level; to cite but one example, the automobile industry is expected to go into partial production within the next eighteen to twenty-four months, and, best of all, with Soviet technological assistance, heavy manufacturing and industry will be 98.2 per cent pollution-free, thereby insuring an ecological upgrading far beyond the reach of the old capitalistic production-systems, which for two hundred years raped and plundered this once beautiful land.

It is understandable that this is a most difficult transition for the citizens of the United States. But now, more than ever before in history, is the time for optimism. This is not the time to look back. . . .

Another pamphlet, mimeographed and stapled, was entitled *Trainees Handbook* and repeated in detail much of what the colonel had said in his welcoming talk.

The isolation period passed quickly for him, and except for his concern about his son he felt curiously relaxed and unworried. He had, by now, formed the opinion that all this—the unexplained arrest, the incarceration without writ of *habeas corpus*, the isolation, and the shaving off of hair—was treatment given all new prisoners, with the purpose of putting them off balance.

AGAIN THE QUESTION: "Do you know why you are here?" This time the questioner was a psychiatrist named Orlov, a heavyset, friendly Russian with an extraordinarily resonant bass voice.

"No."

"How about the man who was brought up here with you—Fein?"

"I don't know anything about him."

"Why do you think you might have been brought here?"

He shrugged. "Political? Sedition—whatever they mean by that."

"But you are not guilty of that, are you? Sedition?"

"No."

"Do you miss having liquor here?"

"No. Yes," he said.

"What do you like to drink?"

"Wine, mostly. And beer."

"Umn. Wine. How much wine?"

"Roughly—about a quart a day."

"Sometimes more?"

"Yes. Sometimes much less."

"How long have you drunk like this?"

"Years. When I was younger I drank more. Whiskey then."

"Do you have dreams—nightmares?"

"No."

"Never?"

"That's right."

"Nonsense. Everyone dreams."

"I don't," he said. "Maybe once a year, at the most."

"What do you dream, when you have this once-a-year occurrence?"

"I can't remember. Different things. It's never the same thing."

"Do you daydream?"

"Very rarely."

"Really? That's very interesting. Most people daydream a lot."

"I don't. Probably because I keep myself busy."

"What do you do? I mean, during a conventional day? Tell me."

"Work around my ranch," he replied. "There're always chores when you live in the country. Chopping wood. Hauling water. I have no water supply—no well—I haul drinking water from town and have a cistern to catch rainwater. Repairs. Carpentry. Roof springs a leak. Chimney stops up or the road washes out. Always one thing or another. When I'm not busy with chores, I paint."

"Yes, of course—you are an artist, I see. What sort of painting?"

"Mostly landscapes. I work in tempera."

"What is that?"

"Egg yolk, mixed with glycerin or walnut oil, and dry pigments. They sometimes call it casein, but casein isn't the same."

"You enjoy this?"

"Yes, very much. But it's a difficult medium."

"Do you make money with your painting?"

"No. Enough to live on, that's all," he said.

"Do you think you are a good painter?"

"Yes."

"A great painter?"

"No."

"Do you think you could be a better painter than you are?"

"Yes."

"Why don't you try and become a better painter then?"

"It doesn't interest me."

"Wouldn't it improve your circumstances if you were a better painter?"

"Perhaps."

"You don't want to improve your circumstances then?"

"Not especially."

"That seems curious."

"Why?" he asked. "I have enough of what I need. I'm reasonably happy. Or I was, until I was arrested."

Dr. Orlov changed the subject. "You like people?"

"No. Not especially."

"What don't you like about them?"

"Different things. Mostly, though, I'd say lack of intelligence."

"You mean you don't like stupid people?"

"Yes. I don't care for stupidity."

"Do you think most people are stupid?"

"Yes."

"What else don't you like about people?"

"Many things. Hypocrisy. Pretentiousness. Insecurity. The veneers in which they envelop themselves. Unfeelingness—the lack of feeling for others. Cruelty. Shallow ideals, phony goals. Dishonesty —within themselves and in their relations with others. It's a dishonest world. Topping the list, though, would be lack of intelligence. You can forgive anything, but not lack of intelligence."

"But that's not a person's fault," Orlov argued, "being stupid."

"Include laziness then. Lack of trying to upgrade your stupidity —lack of trying to think for oneself."

"But 'lack of trying to upgrade your stupidity' . . . if you substitute 'situation' for 'stupidity,' then wouldn't the statement come, full circle, right back to yourself?"

"Perhaps."

"All these stupid people, what would you do about them? If you could, that is, theoretically do something about them?"

"Nothing. Ignore them."

"Pretend they don't exist?"

"No. I'd simply stay out of their way."

"What would you like to do with the rest of your life?"

"Exactly what I was doing before I was arrested."

"What was that?"

"Paint. Take care of my son, my ranch. Read. Drink a little booze."

"And ignore all the stupid people?"

"As much as possible."

"Are you afraid?"

"Of what?"

"Your situation here?"

"Yes. No. Not too much," he said.

"What does that mean?"

"I think I can handle it—a couple of months here," he explained. "I'm worried about my son, that's all. Nobody will tell me anything about him."

"But you're not too apprehensive?"

"No. I think there's been a mistake in the charges they have on me, a mix-up someplace. I think if I'm given a fair hearing, everything will be cleared up."

"Do you think your position here is serious?"

"Right now, yes."

"How serious?"

"Pretty serious," Vandenberg said. "This is a maximum security prison, or camp—whatever you want to call it. I don't think they'd bring someone here on a trivial charge. Am I right?"

"Who knows?" Dr. Orlov said with a shrug.

Vandenberg looked at him. "Have you any idea how long I'll be here?"

"No, I haven't," the doctor replied. He paused, then said, "Do you think you will profit from your stay here?"

"Profit?"

"Learn. Do you think it may be beneficial?"

"How can I say, when I don't know what this is all about?"

"Let me put it this way—will you attempt to cooperate with the compound?"

"Cooperate? What has that got to do with it?" he asked.

"You will not cooperate then?"

"Cooperation doesn't enter into it," Vandenburg insisted. "I'm a prisoner. They can make me cooperate, whether I want to or not. It's a senseless question."

"Have you thought of escape?"

"No. It's out of the question."

"Why do you say that?"

"We're too well guarded," he said. "Besides, where would I go if I got out?"

"Do you have anyone besides your son?"

"An older brother. He lives in Chicago. We aren't close."

"Your wife is dead?"

"My first wife died in 1954. I married again, but we were divorced."

"Can you tell me what the basis of the divorce was?"

"Incompatibility."

"In what sense?"

"She couldn't live the sort of life I wanted, nor could I live hers."

"Do you see her?"

"No. I haven't heard from her in many years."

"You aren't lonely?"

"Lonely?"

"Were there children by this second marriage?"

"Two girls."

"Do you miss them?"

"Of course."

"But you don't visit or see them?"

"No. They're in Connecticut."

"This doesn't bother you?"

"Of course it does."

"It doesn't seem to. You appear quite matter of fact about it."

"What do you want me to do, pull out my hair—of which there isn't any?" he said. "Something like that, you put out of your mind."

"Put what out of your mind?"

"Thoughts about kids," he said. "The girls were three and five when the divorce became final. The oldest is sixteen now. If I met her on the street today I wouldn't recognize her. I remember a five-year-old with blond hair, chubby, who used to curl up in my lap. I remember two children, not two young women. Because they're strangers doesn't mean I don't care about them. I simply don't know them. But the two children—them I loved."

"You have centered your attention on your son then?"

"Yes, I suppose I have."

"The problem he presents—the retardation—did this disappoint you?"

"You mean in the sense of the hopes most fathers are supposed to entertain for their sons? No, there was nothing like that. I was sad when we learned the full extent of the brain damage, but sad for him—not for my own hopes, but for what he'd miss in life, do you understand?"

"Yes. Do you have any other close relationships?"

"No."

"No friend?"

"Friend?"

"You are celibate?"

"No. I have a girl."

"Could you identify her?"

"I'd as soon leave her name out of this."

"As you wish." Dr. Orlov paused, and then said, "I would like to discuss with you only one other point, briefly, and then we can stop. How much resentment have you against the United States being occupied by Soviet forces?"

"How much? I can't say."

"A great deal? Comparatively little?"

"All that's relative, doctor, and it isn't easy to be objective. Every American feels resentment over what happened—it would be idiotic to deny that. I'm resentful, yes."

"Hostile?"

"Yes. But who can say whether I'm more hostile than the next guy?"

"Actively hostile?"

"What do you mean?"

"Overtly hostile?" the doctor insisted.

"No. I wouldn't say that."

HE WAS ASSIGNED to Dorm Three. A guard brought him in through the main gate. While the soldier was checking his weapon at the sentry box, Vandenberg inspected the big recoilless rifle. It was a large-bore weapon mounted on a concrete platform, and he saw that it had not been set up merely for show—canisters of rounds were stored in alcoves set into the concrete. The cardboard canisters were almost three feet long and about six inches in diameter, and he knew that a shell like that could take out a heavy tank easily. He also saw that it could traverse a full three hundred and sixty degrees, so that, if needed, it could be turned on the inner compound he was about to enter.

Once inside, the guard brought him directly to his Quonset hut. Under one arm he carried his rolled blankets and toilet gear. The compound was curiously quiet and deserted-looking, except for a few inmates who worked at various chores. He and his guard passed a large frame building with a pitched roof and unpainted sides. From its open windows, Vandenberg could hear someone speaking in good but accented English; he took this to be one of the study halls.

Two more men in coveralls were hosing down one of the wooden catwalks that linked the buildings together. At Dorm Three the guard opened the door and motioned for him to enter. He stood there without speaking until Vandenberg stepped across the threshold, and then shut the door.

The interior of the hut was as orderly as a military barracks. A row of neatly made bunks were spaced along the length of each curving wall, with an open walkway running the length of the building. Footlockers had been placed in front of each bed, and clothes racks had been installed behind the heads of the beds. At the far end of the building, partitions had been built for a washroom, showers, and latrines. The door leading to them was open, and he heard voices. Setting down his blankets, he went into the washroom.

Two men were mopping the floor. They looked up when he appeared in the doorway, and the older of the two set down his mop, wiped his hands against his coveralls, and grinned. "Hi. You'd be the new man." He came over and shook hands with Vandenberg.

"My name is Harris. Emil Harris. This is Bill MacGruder."

MacGruder, too, offered his hand, and Vandenberg shook it. He was about thirty, very stocky, with a swarthy complexion and a crew cut. Harris' brown hair was longer, and Vandenberg wondered how long he'd been in the compound—his own shorn hair would take several months to grow out.

"My name's Vandenberg."

"We heard this morning we were getting a new one," Harris said.

"Oh?"

"Mel Finney, the dorm captain, got the word. He's already assigned you a bunk. There's stacks of room. Only forty-six of us here. Mac and I have cleanup duty today, and Mel told us to give you the scoop when you came in, but he'll talk to you, of course, at lunchtime."

They went out to the main part of the dormitory, and Harris showed him the bunk assigned by Finney. MacGruder helped him make up his bed, using hospital folds, and Vandenberg said, "It's not much different from the Army, is it?"

Harris gave him a cigarette, the first smoke he'd had in three days, and he said, "What's the setup here?"

"Everybody's the same—political nonconformity."

"Very interesting, ethnically," MacGruder added. "We're all Anglo here—there's not a single Spanish-American."

"Maybe the Spanish know enough to keep their mouths shut," Vandenberg said. "Are there any women?"

"No—no women."

"What do you mean, political nonconformity?"

"A multitude of sins," Harris replied. There was no rancor in his voice, and his expression was amiable. "I'd say it covered everything from pamphleteering to rolling a passed-out Russian dogface in an alley."

"And yourself?" he asked, looking at Harris. "Have they told you what you're charged with?"

"Me? Certainly," Harris replied. "I've been here four months. I was one of the first. They tell me I'm due for discharge soon." He paused and struck a match for Vandenberg's cigarette. "I'm a physicist. I'm at the lab—Los Alamos. I went there in '61, then took two years off to finish my Ph.D. at Cruces. When the Soviets took over, I couldn't see any reason for them to continue developing tapes on packaged weapons. I tried to convince some of my colleagues. I was in Weaponry. Mac here is on the hill, too, but he's in a different section. Anyway, they gave me a choice. Continue research, or be given a Category IV designation."

"A Ph.D. on latrine duty?"

"We all take turns."

"Have you heard anything about another new man—his name is Fein?"

"No. He's probably been assigned to another dorm."

"Listen," Vandenberg said suddenly, "what goes on here?"

"Mel will tell you more about it," Harris said. "Rehabilitation. They'll go into you, Vandenberg, same as the rest of us. Listen, I had four years of analysis, but it was nothing compared to this. They don't fool around. They're not looking for excuses, but an answer. Give them credit. In-depth analysis. I mean, scopolamine, sodium amytal, hypnotism—the whole bag. Harsh. But some of the staff are bright, real bright. Offbeat, yes, but worth talking to. No mollycoddling. But maybe that's what this country's needed for years."

"But—you go along with it?"

"I surely do," Harris grinned. *"Número uno,* we're in here. This is your basic premise. You can argue with your personal interviewer until you're blue in the face, that's expected. But you're still in here, and it's their show, and there's not one of us doesn't want to get that discharge slip and get the hell out of here *pronto,* because the discharge is your passport. With that, you can walk into a People's Court, hear the charge, show your discharge, plead guilty, hear that suspended sentence, and walk out and down to the bus depot, and catch a ride back to your wife and family."

"They do release people from here then?"

"All the time. Don't let the concentration camp props bother you," Harris said. "That's only old Brushnevesko up front, acting out some weird little fantasy of his own. I'd guess about forty have been released since I've been here. The average stay is maybe three months."

"How come you've been here longer?"

Harris shrugged. "It may sound crazy, but I sort of enjoy arguing with them. Hell, on the hill, except for two trips to Pacific test sites, all I did for years was work, come home, eat, argue with my wife or fool with my amateur rig—I'm a ham. The work I did was not conducive to speculative conversation. Up here, I've done more talking than I have in ten years. But I think I've about used up my welcome. They tell me I'm due for review in another two weeks."

"He actually enjoys Cowles," MacGruder said. "There're a couple like him."

"A facet of a really civilized man is the ability to extract something worthwhile from the unlikeliest of situations," the physicist said. There was no arrogance in the statement. Vandenberg found it difficult to think of Harris as a troublemaker, scientific or otherwise. Barring his advanced degrees, he seemed an ordinary sort, and if Vandenberg had been introduced to him under different circumstances, say, at a cocktail party, he would probably have paid little attention to him, taking him for what he appeared to be, a bright young man with middle-class aspirations and values, with little to single him out from the rest of those around him except the specialized occupation toward which his natural talents—in this case, probably an inclination for mathematics—had led him.

AT NOON a siren sounded briefly, and shortly afterward the dorm filled with men in gray-green coveralls. Vandenberg was reminded of a barracks full of GIs in basic training. The men here, however, were older, some in their fifties and sixties. Like Harris, they gave an impression of affability. There was a lack of the constant griping Vandenberg had heard as a soldier, and this struck him as curious. Most of these men were obviously well educated, the sort who in civilian life would have achieved success. Among them he recognized a few whose photographs he'd seen in local papers: a well-known thoracic surgeon, an architect, two professors from the University of New Mexico, and a newspaper columnist. A few greeted him with a wave of a hand, or came over and introduced themselves. One of the last to enter was a very tall young man who immediately came up to him.

"Hello. I'm Mel Finney, the dorm captain. I see you found your bunk."

"My name is Vandenberg."

"Yes, I was told. Want a washup before chow? We fall out in five minutes."

"No, but you go ahead if you want to."

Finney sat down on his bunk. "Did you get through solitary okay?"

"It wasn't bad."

"Some new men can't take isolation," Finney said. "We all wish they'd do away with it. It's unnecessary. I imagine you're up in the air about it all."

"Pretty much."

"They didn't tell you anything?"

"Nothing."

"That's S.O.P.," Finny said. "You'll probably meet your interviewer this afternoon or tomorrow. He'll brief you."

"Do I just sit here until he sends for me?"

Finney motioned to a loudspeaker over the door. "The bitch box is our contact with administration. They'll call you when they want you. It's a two-way system—you can talk back. There's also a bulletin board in the main study hall, where they list extra assignments, special classes, and work details."

"Is it really as tough here as it looks?"

"It's not that bad," Finney said. "That's the truth. Of course, it's pretty scary to a new man. The high-voltage fence, the watchtowers—you wonder what the devil you've done to deserve all this. It's understandable. The shaved heads. You wonder why. It's needless—all of it. None of us is a fool. No one's about to take on that electrified fence. I've been here since April, and during that time not one guard has had to raise a weapon. What we do is ignore the guns and towers—we pretend they're not there. It's easier to live with, that way. In a way, it drives the guards nuts. As though they were invisible, or didn't exist."

"But they do."

"That's all right," Finney said. "They don't bother us, we don't bother them. I'm only trying to make it easier for you. The rest of it, the lectures, interviews—they're tough enough."

At that moment, the loudspeaker announced lunch, and they joined the others, assembling in a loose column, four abreast. They moved off, by no means in step, the men talking and joking. Vandenberg was left with the impression that whatever the compound was supposed to be instilling in its trainees, it was not military discipline. The neatly mown plots of grass, the tidiness and arrangement of the dorms—these smacked of the military—but the men themselves were completely informal.

The cafeteria too was modeled after a mess hall, with a serving counter, bins full of knives, forks, and spoons, stacked racks of metal trays. The food was good, as Colonel Brushnevesko had claimed, and Vandenberg passed along the counter, holding out his tray for generous helpings of pork chops, boiled potatoes, gravy, bread, butter, squash, and a large mug of coffee.

Everyone talked as they ate, but even so the meal was quickly finished, so that most had deposited their trays in the wash racks by twenty to one. Going out, he saw Jerome Fein eating with another group at the far end of the cafeteria.

Finney said, "We don't usually spend much time on lunch. If you eat fast, you can sack out for a quarter of an hour."

"They're not skimpy with their food."

"Food's okay. You get plenty of fresh air up here—you're always hungry."

"What did you do before you came here?" Vandenberg asked.

"Salesman," Finney replied. "I was with Van Ness-Lincoln-Mercury for nine years. I was also in the National Guard, a major. When Detroit's production was frozen, I was dead, of course. Tried other lines, but it was slow. My wife went back to work, too, but it was pretty tough."

"Why were you sent up here?"

"Pigheadedness, I guess." Finney lit a cigarette. "Some of us in our neighborhood—we have a Stamm house, over in the Casa Alegre addition—got together. A lot of us were in the same boat. Heavy mortgage payments, insurance, payments on cars. All of it, you know. Some were like myself, either out of a job or scraping by in any sort of work they could rustle. I helped draft a petition to Military Government requesting that in cases of dire need citizens be excused from the ten per cent Occupation levy."

THIS WAS, VANDENBERG knew, a mandatory tax intended to help defray the cost of maintaining Occupation troops. From its inception it had been unpopular. He had never registered for it and had never filed a statement, and he wondered now if that could be one of the reasons they'd arrested him.

"I still argue that it was logical," Finney was saying. "After all, the employment potential in this part of the Southwest has always been a terrible problem. It wasn't too many years ago that Santa Fe County was designated a poverty-stricken area, under both the Kennedy and Johnson administrations. Add to it the upheaval brought about by changes in government. . . . After the Armistice, a lot of us were in a bad way. Myself, as I said.

"We stood a chance of losing everything we had—our savings, all the equity we'd been able to build up. Hell, we'd already been hit with the voiding of securities and stocks, and then when they did away with credit buying, that was the end. I mean, you simply *have* to have some credit in a modern economy—if you don't, everything collapses. I didn't want to lose out. In pleading hardship I asked if there was any way M.G. could at least temporarily excuse certain people who could show they were having a bad time of it."

"But you were making a living?"

"I was driving a delivery van for a bakery," Finney said. "Less deductions, that netted me around forty, take-home. Why, shit, I have three kids in school, the house, two cars. I'd been a salesman all my life. For three years I led the whole regional area. I loved my job, and worked hard at it. You simply can't take that kind of man and put him in a delivery truck."

"They locked you up for that?"

"No. I petitioned the People's Court. They said such a petition would constitute a precedent, and we'd have the entire country lining up at every M.G. office, pleading hardship. When I refused to pay the levy, they picked me up."

"And you don't mind?"

"I did at first," Finney said. "But I don't think Cowles has hurt me. Sure, a lot of what they say comes under the heading of propaganda, but some of it hits home, too. Some of their thinking is pretty sound—they're trying to get a lot done in a short time."

Walking back to the dorm, Finney asked, "How is it out there?"

"Where?"

"Outside."

"About the same," he said. "I wouldn't say it's gotten any better."

"How's the rationing?"

"Stiffer. There's less to choose from, especially in the supermarkets. There are whole sections of shelves completely bare. Gas has tightened, too," he said. "They cut me from twenty-four to twelve gallons a month, because I couldn't show I was farming. You don't come in often on twelve gallons a month."

"You have your own place?"

"Yes, outside town."

"Ranch?"

"Sort of. Mostly fenced-in piñon and shagbark cedar."

The loudspeaker on the wall hummed, and a voice announced, "Dorm Three will assemble in five minutes, in Building Seven. Dorm Three, as scheduled, in Building Seven." There was a pause, then, "Vandenberg, Eugene R., to Building Nine. Vandenberg, Eugene R., to Building Nine, Room Two. Room Two."

The trainees stirred, got up from their bunks, smoothed their blankets, ditched cigarettes, and moved toward the door. Finney walked along beside Vandenberg. "Nine is the last building, next to the mess hall. They use it for testing and interviewing. See you later."

Vandenberg moved off alone down the catwalks, while the rest of the men formed up and ambled away in another direction. It was a hot, clear, cloudless day, and he felt content after the heavy lunch.

He found Building Nine and went in. The doors to all the rooms were numbered and shut; he could hear several men talking. He found Room Two and knocked. The door opened and a Soviet medical orderly told him to come in.

"You can sit at one of these tables. My name is Constantine."

His English was good, and except for the cut of his white smock, he might have been a male nurse in an American hospital. "You're here to take some tests, Comrade Vandenberg, five altogether. You have three hours to complete them. They're aptitude and intelligence tests. If one section is more difficult for you than others, don't waste time on it—go on to another, and come back to it later. You're probably familiar with this kind of examination. Any questions?"

"No."

"I'll remain here with you," Constantine said. "You can smoke, but I can't permit you to leave the room. Do you have to use the latrine? No? We can begin then. When you are satisfied that you have done all you can with one section, you can hand it to me. I will grade it. I have other work to do, so I hope my presence will not trouble you. Here is a ball-point. Good luck, Comrade."

HE FINISHED the last test a quarter of an hour before his allotted time was up. Constantine had already scored the first four sections, using cardboard master sheets perforated to show the correct answers that should have been marked in the multiple-choice slots. When he was done, he jotted the score down on a sheet of paper labeled with Vandenberg's name and identification number, and then looked up. "You did not do badly, Comrade. Not the best I have tested here, but by no means the worst."

Vandenberg said nothing.

"Wait here, please," the orderly said, rising. He left the room with the tests, and returned shortly. "I wanted to see if your interviewer was busy. He isn't—he'll see you."

"Lucky me," he remarked.

"Lucky? Why do you say that?"

"Nothing."

Constantine stared at him, then said, "Room Five, Comrade. I have already given him your tests."

"Thanks," he said. He went out and shut the door behind him, and walked down the corridor. He found Room Five and knocked.

A voice inside—he was immediately sure the speaker was an American—said crisply, "It's not locked. Come on in."

COMMUNICATIONS

VANDENBERG, EUGENE R.
#4076
OVMI SCORES: 109, 126, 117, 136, 120.
TIME: 1:05 P.M.—3:45 P.M.

COMMENTS: *Subject possesses above-average though by no means unusual intelligence. Superficially, he shows some indication of cooperation, though making little effort to conceal deep-rooted distrust and resentment.*

—*C. Eugenev, Medical Div.*

HE OPENED the door and went in. A thin young man at an oak table rose to greet him.

Below average height, he wore a short-sleeved print sports shirt, slacks, and loafers. He came out from behind the table, extending a hand. "Hello. My name is Walters. Andy Walters. Glad to meet you. Here, have a chair."

He listened to Walters' introduction, glanced at the proffered hand, finally shook it, and then sat down in a chair on his side of the table.

The room, he saw, was almost bare. There was the chair he sat in, the oak table, Walters' chair, an ashtray, a typewriter on a steel stand, and beside it a dictaphone. There was no phone. Stacked manila folders were piled at one end of the table. The walls were cheap plywood painted green; he could see the configurations of the grain beneath the paint.

Walters went back to his own chair and sat down, pulling it closer to the table. The window behind him was open. Vandenberg heard a jay chattering somewhere outside.

"Let's move along, shall we?" Walters said, glanced at him. "We have about an hour. The first session is supposed to be in the nature of a briefing. I'll do my best to give you an idea of the setup here and to answer your questions."

"I have a few," Vandenberg said drily.

"I'm sure you have."

"You're an interviewer?"

"I'm one of them. There are eight of us," Walters said. "You've been assigned to my case load. That means we'll be seeing a lot of each other. In fact, in a couple of months, the notion of coming into this room may make you want to puke."

Suddenly he grinned across the table at Vandenberg. "That's the name of the game, you know. We keep at you—wear you down. Invidious. The trainees say we're merciless, and I understand they think I'm one of the worst."

He paused, waiting for a response, but Vandenberg did not reply.

"Officially then, I'm your interviewer. That does not mean interrogator, third-degree specialist, father-confessor, couch-therapist, or anything else. I'm an interviewer, period. Very simply, the idea is that we establish a line of communication—a relationship. Not necessarily a friendship. Actually, you could hate my guts, and we could still achieve success. Conversely, we could be pals, and not get a damned thing done. As I said, it's the establishing of a relationship that permits communication.

"You will, I'm sure, admit that it's not a simple task. A new man is intimidated, suspicious—it's understandable. The Colonel —Brushnevesko—is all for running the camp as though it was an annex of Devil's Island. The technical staff—those of us in medical and education—we do what we can to keep him calm, but it's still a tight camp, as you've seen. It's not an easy job. We all work a full six-day week, and it's a twelve-hour day. The goal is your rehabilitation and release. I've already laid out your schedule. We'll go over it at the end of this period. Aside from work details, weekly inspections, and the like, it's divided into group lectures and instruction, small group discussions, and individual interview periods. You'll see me at least six times weekly. You can if you like call me Comrade Walters, but most of the bunch call me Andy."

"You say rehabilitation is the goal," he interrupted. "Suppose it doesn't happen?"

"But that's pointless," Walters replied. "Everybody rehabilitates. The time varies from man to man. You'll see. Nobody's interested in keeping you here."

Walters spoke engagingly, but Vandenberg was only slightly impressed. He sat there listening, watching the man behind the table, deciding that Walters (or Andy, as he obviously wanted to be called) was older than he'd first thought, closer to forty-five. He displayed a kind of nervous energy and enthusiasm that at first made him seem younger. There were crow's feet around his eyes, and the hair over his temples was gray.

He was also astonishingly untidy. Vandenberg had noticed, when Walters rose to greet him, that the tail of the garish sports shirt had come untucked from his trousers, and a shirt button was missing. Walters' hair, dirty blond and of indeterminate length— it looked like a grown-out crew cut—was unkempt, as though he combed it once at the start of each day by running his fingers through it. His teeth were crooked and stained with nicotine— the index and middle fingers of his right hand were also a saffron brown—and the bony cheeks were pocked and riveted with ancient acne scars. Except when he grinned, the forehead was furrowed into a frown. The eyes were watery blue, the nose a prominent thin blade, the flesh drawn tightly across it. His entire frame was bony and wiry with hunched, drawn-up shoulders, and the arms, revealed by the short sleeves, were thin and covered with a pale-brown shag. Vandenberg was reminded of a coyote with its long, skinny legs, scraggly tail, and washboard ribs.

Walters offered him a cigarette, took one himself, struck a match, exhaled a cloud of smoke, and went on speaking in his distracted, rapid-fire style. "If there's one thing I want to make clear at the start, it's that here in this room you don't have to be afraid to say what you think."

"Oh, come off it," Vandenberg said. "Your people throw me in jail, cart me up here, shave my hair, don't let me call a lawyer, and now you tell me I don't have to be afraid to speak up."

Walters grinned. "Every trainee gets the same treatment. They survive. A big, burly bastard like you, you're no more delicate than anybody else."

"Mister, you're not getting through to me," Vandenberg said. "I can't see any reason to talk to you or anybody else until I find out what charges are held against me, why I'm here, and when I get representation."

"You afraid of self-incriminating statements?"

"I haven't done anything incriminating."

"Afraid you might let something slip that'd be held against you?"

"It's your ball game," he replied. "And until I know the rules, I'm not playing."

"Then nothing happens."

"What do you mean?"

"You stay."

Vandenberg stared at him.

"Rehabilitation isn't possible without communication. And that means talking," Walters said. "No rehabilitation, no discharge from our happy little mountain resort hideaway. You're worried to death you may say something that could be construed as derogatory evidence. For Christ's sake, Vandenberg, use your skull. If we wanted to rig a charge against you, would we have to Mickey-Mouse around like this? You think M.G. couldn't stash you away for twenty years if it wanted to? D'you see me as a shill—you really think I'm trying to set you up so we can hang a tough sentence on you? D'you think maybe there's a mike in one of these plywood walls that's connected to a recorder over in Administration, and that the recorder is going right now? Hell, yes, the room is bugged. Sure, the talk is being taped, partly to get down your initial reactions, and partly to score my own performance.

"You worry about incriminatory statements. Balls. None of that's important. You could confess right now that you headed up an active counterrevolutionary group dedicated to creating anarchistic mayhem among M.G., and it wouldn't shorten or lengthen your stay here at Cowles by fifteen minutes.

"This whole goddamned camp is bugged, from one end to the other. You so much as fart during calisthenics, we can tape it. Listen, there's a couple of private rooms in Administration with porcelain embalming tables with gutters to catch your urine and feces, where, if they want, they can make you say anything. We've got a polygraph here, and one of the psychiatrists—old Orlov—has a thing for hypnotism. They've got something brand-new up here that's part psychedelic and twice as powerful as LSD, with none of the organic brain-damage syndromes your classic hallucinogens inflict. Man, the medical staff mainlines you with *that,* they can damned near take you back into gestation. You'll go the whole route. Everyone does.

"Listen, don't get the idea that this is a two-bit operation, just because the buildings are jerry-built and you have that dumb-assed electrified fence. It's more than a maximum security stockade. It's costing S.M.G. on the average eight thousand dollars for someone like you to spend time here. For that money they could shelve you in the state pen until your teeth fell out.

"Do yourself a favor and stop worrying about being framed. What you want to keep in mind is that with a Cowles discharge you can appear before a People's Court anywhere in the country, plead guilty, and pick up a suspended sentence. Does that get through to you? You'll be on probation, but so what?" He paused. "Friend, we're all on probation."

"Plead guilty to what?" Vandenberg asked.

"Seditious tendencies." Walters motioned with his thumb toward the topmost manila folder. "There's your dossier. It's not complete yet. Garbage is still coming in from the Vet's Administration, the Army, from Chicago, where you grew up. School transcripts. Even the CIA, that horse's-ass polo club, and the FBI had disposition sheets on you."

"FBI? I don't believe that."

"Why not?" Walters demanded. "They've had a file on you since '50, when you applied for a job as an illustrator with Los Alamos' scientific lab. You were a poor risk, even then. You probably never knew why you didn't get the job. The report indicated that you were shiftless, irresponsible, too radical in your thinking, immature, a chronic complainer. Your employment history was scattered, spotty. You were on the juice. They even mention drug addiction—were you ever on anything?"

"No," he said. "I'd try marijuana once in a while. A friend of mine used to bring in peyote—it made me throw up."

"No difference—they needed you on the Hill like they needed

cancer. What the hell ever made you apply for such a dumb job?"

"My wife was pregnant with my son," he said. "She had a bad time of it, and we had medical bills. I needed steady money—a salary. Later that year I sold some paintings and that helped." He thought for a moment and then said, "I didn't think they'd hold on to a routine personnel investigation that long."

"They had reason to," Walter said. "In 1966 you threatened to throw a Molotov cocktail at Ladybird Johnson when she visited Santa Fe plugging that Keep America Beautiful program Lyndon scratched up to keep her busy."

At first he hadn't the slightest idea of what Walters was talking about, and then he smiled. "Do they really have that in my file? It was a joke."

"Some joke."

"No, I mean it. Sure, I was drinking that night—down at the Montana—"

"That Montana Bar has gotten you into more trouble than you think."

"Maybe so. Anyway, some friends and I were hitting it pretty good, I guess. I remember it now. It was the night before she was due to fly in. There was this young, fat longhair who'd got in with our table. Said he painted. From Denver. Somehow, the conversation got on Ladybird, and he came on in a big way about what a pain in the ass she was—everybody at the table went along with it. Hell, you couldn't go wrong, picking on her.

"Anyhow, this kid's up at the bar, buying us another round—which seemed strange in itself—and one of the guys at our table, Phil, said something like, 'I dig him for one of J. Edgar's bird dogs. Ten-to-one says they moved him in ahead of her plane to scout the scene.' Another friend of mine said, 'Look at the ass on that kid—they don't make pear-shaped agents.' But this Phil said, 'Don't let that fool you—watch the way he moves—he's had karate training.' And he did in fact move in an agile way— light on his feet. Another thing we noticed was that he was pretty sober—he'd been boozing with us for hours, and we were all feeling it. So when he started back to our table with another tray of drinks, Phil said to me, 'Okay, let's hassle him.'

"When he sat down, we began coming on about organizing a reception party for Ladybird the following morning, out at the airport. That's when I mentioned the Molotov cocktail. We were all kind of watching this fatty to see how he'd take it. I said something like, 'We don't actually want to *hit* her with it—just lob it out on the apron, where the camera can get a good shot of it. We'll show 'em what Santa Fe thinks of the Keep America Beautiful campaign.' Well, this guy went along with it. Said it sounded great. We were all laughing and making wisecracks, but now that I think of it, I suppose you couldn't really tell how serious we were. Of course we were putting him on. Next morning when her plane landed, I'd forgotten it—I was out at the ranch, drinking coffee, hung over.

"We didn't figure him for an agent—even Phil didn't, really. And he was one all the time—that's really very funny."

"You wouldn't have thought so if you and your pals had gone out to the airport that morning," Walters said. "Among the crowd waiting to cheer their patriotic hearts out when the First Lady deplaned were probably a dozen or so plainclothesmen and agents who'd studied your mug shots. If out of mere curiosity you'd driven out there to rubberneck with the rest of the citizens, you'd probably have been hauled off on the spot."

"I still can't believe it," he said. "I suppose I ought to resent it, but really it's laughable. It's the kind of thing a Yippie would've labeled police state tactics—"

"The kind practiced now?" Walters said, looking at him.

"Sure. I can't see them going to that much trouble. Sending in an agent. Getting all fired up by a couple of drunk painters mouthing off in a bar."

"Listen," said Walters, "it was routine to spot a man in a town a few days ahead of a VIP's arrival. It doesn't take long to pick up the mood of a town, and it takes only a little longer to bird-dog the troublemakers. They knew the cocktail lounges and bars where the action was. The Montana was at one time a very in place. And there you were, jacking off at the jaws. It might have been a joke to you, talking about Molotov cocktails, but something like that is enough to really prime an agent.

"That wasn't the only time you mouthed off," Walters went on. "Did you really think you could get away with telling people, Fuck the Russians this and fuck the Russians that? Talking about Gandhi and passive resistance and all that crap? Really, Gene."

"Are you saying I was arrested for talking when I had one too many?"

"Not exactly. Let me put it this way. When you first attracted the attention of our counterintelligence, they ran a check on you, both locally and in Washington. The evaluation was not particularly good, although it's not nearly as bad as some we have with us. You're Category III. That means you were potentially dangerous and that periodic surveillance was advisable. It doesn't mean that you're subversive—all it means, really, is that we were aware of you. Sooner or later, CIC would have issued a warrant on you. If not now, then next year or the year after."

"For sedition?"

"It's as handy a charge as any," Walters said. "It's the kind of charge where almost everything depends on you. It means, literally, nothing . . . or it can mean everything. Like a confession, such an accusation is open to interpretation."

"If it means so little, I wish to hell they'd have let it go for a couple of years. Why did they pick me up now?"

Walters said, "Simple. We happened to have room for you here. We decided we might as well get it over with as quickly as possible."

"Get *what* over with?"

"Why, your rehabilitation," Walters said, looking at him.

"LISTEN, WHAT'S all this rehabilitation business actually mean?" He motioned to Walters' pack of cigarettes on the table, and Walters shoved it across. He shook one loose and lit it.

"Call it an in-depth profile," Walters replied. "We're interested in why you're discontented—why you can't function adequately under Communism."

Vandenberg stared at him, listening.

"It's no Dale Carnegie course we run here, but it's not a concentration camp either," Walters went on. "We're interested in working with you toward achieving a sounder adjustment to life outside."

"Sounds like a joint cooperative effort," Vandenberg said drily. "Doesn't a trainee sometimes give you trouble?"

"Trouble? No. What kind of trouble?"

Vandenberg shrugged. "I don't know. Breakouts, that sort of thing."

"Don't be ridiculous."

"They all cooperate?"

"Certainly. But, listen, Gene, you're not here to be a yes-man. You can't coast through Cowles by parroting what you imagine are right responses—we can spot that a mile off."

Vandenberg puffed at his cigarette. "Have you heard anything about my son?"

"No. Your file says he's retarded. How badly?"

"Bad enough. He's never been away from me."

"Security has probably picked him up," Walters said. "Let me make a few phone calls—I'll let you know what I find out." Walters looked across the table at him. "Incidentally, about this charge of seditious activity, at the present time do you plead innocent?"

"Certainly," he said. "Hell, I'm not a joiner. Politics never interested me."

"Ever demonstrate? Anti-Vietnam—that sort of thing?" Vandenberg shook his head, and Walters said, "But you're basically against Military Government?"

"Who isn't?"

"I'm not interested in others—I'm asking you."

"Okay, I'm against it—but that doesn't mean I'm seditious."

"I didn't say it did."

"You can't lock up everybody because they don't love your high-powered little Occupation." He added, "You can't rehabilitate a couple of hundred million people the way you're rehabilitating two hundred here at Cowles."

Walters smiled. "That's true, isn't it?"

And from the way he said it Vandenberg understood that this was exactly what S.M.G. was aiming for: the country, its borders sealed, would become a three-thousand-mile-wide camp. Walters stood up, glancing at him. "Well, don't worry about it—the problem right now is yourself and getting you out of here as expeditiously as possible, right? I've enjoyed the chat. Let's call it a day."

"All right."

"Here's your schedule. You'll see from it that I've scheduled you at eight in the morning. Are you a coffee drinker?"

"Yes."

"I usually stop at the cafeteria and get a potful to start the day. I'll bring you an extra cup." He handed Vandenberg a typed sheet with a schedule on it, and then a second sheet. "Check the bulletin board in the study hall for special details—you should pull kitchen police about once a month, and fatigue duty in the dorms. You're free now. Walk around the camp, get acquainted. Don't go near the fences, and don't go into any classrooms where groups are working—the lecturers don't like interruptions."

"All right."

"On the second sheet I've typed four questions. I'd like you to study them for tomorrow morning and be prepared to talk with me about them."

Vandenberg got up and turned to go, then stopped. "Can I ask you something?"

"Certainly."

"You're American, aren't you?"

"Yes. I'm from Philadelphia."

"But you're with them—of your own choice?"

"Certainly."

"That seems unusual."

"Why? Lots of Americans have. If you're really curious, sometime I'll tell you about myself."

Vandenberg looked at him. "Sort of an Inside Andy Walters?"

"Why talk to a perfect stranger? I certainly wouldn't, in your place."

"Everything is slanted toward encouraging the line of communication?"

"Gene, that's it, exactly."

HE PAUSED on the wooden steps outside, blinking in the sunlight, feeling its heat on his shaven skull, scanning the schedule Walters had given him. At the bottom of the page was a notation: *The only authorized preemptions are 1. Sick Call 2. Special Examinations 3. Psychiatric Counseling 4. Work Details.*

The second sheet listed the following questions:

a. Who is to blame for the recent conflict? The U.S.? Russia? Both?

b. Could the conflict have been avoided? How?

c. Are you optimistic or pessimistic about the future and what it holds for you and the U.S.? Are you more optimistic—or pessimistic—than you were in the late '60s?

d. There are differences between Communism and capitalism as methods of government. How have these differences affected you and the lives of those close to you?

He read them a second time and then folded both sheets and put them away in the breast pocket of his coveralls. Then he went for a walk around the compound, as Walters had suggested. Less than five days had passed since his arrest.

He was still confused over what had happened, but he believed that were it not for his son he could take Cowles in stride without being bothered or affected by it. He knew that he was enormously stubborn, and that now, at his age, they would have a time trying to implant pro-Soviet ideas in him.

In other times the rehabilitation they spoke of here would have been called brainwashing or political reindoctrination. Reorientation of political and social values. Call it whatever you want (in the Catholic hierarchy, Cowles would have been a mountain retreat, a sanctuary, a place of meditation and rediscovery for troubled Church intellectuals).

He thought, they've got almost two hundred intelligent people up here. How in hell do they sell it to them without trouble? What happens when they go back home discharged? Finney says plenty have gone out—but there's never been a whisper in Santa Fe about the high-voltage fences or the watchtowers. What do they do, swear us to secrecy with a Boy Scout oath?

These men—it was obvious—weren't frightened. Nor did any that he had met so far display the symptoms of the genuine penal inmate—fear, hatred, distrust, qualified defiance.

HE TOURED the compound in ten minutes. There were the four Quonset-like dormitories, the cafeteria, the study hall, and the three small classroom buildings. In back of the cafeteria was a broad grassless plot; he assumed this was the calisthenics area. Thumbs hooked into his coverall belt, he strolled up to the front gate, checking the buildings outside, and noticed again the joint Russian-American flags flying over the main building, the neatly parked vehicles in the motor pool, and the recoilless rifle. He inspected the fences but did not approach closely. Stapled to the outer mesh at eye level were red-and-white metal signs warning of high voltage. He noticed a guard in the closest tower watching him. Vandenberg looked up at the man for a moment, and then turned and walked back to the dorm.

At five, when the day's classes were over, the dorm filled again with men. Emil Harris, the physicist, came over. "How'd it go?"

"Not bad," he said. He closed a book he'd taken out of his footlocker, a condensed outline of Soviet economics.

"Who'd you get for an interviewer?"

"Someone named Walters."

"Andy? He's good."

"Do you have him, too?"

"No, I'm with Pornagian—Armenian."

Mel Finney joined them, and Harris said, "He got Andy Walters."

"Andy's a good man to work with," Finney said.

"Do you know anything about him?"

"The talk is that he was a big wheel in shaping pre-Invasion policy," Finney replied. "He's American, you know—was in the Air Force. Supposed to have defected in the sixties."

"He doesn't look like a wheel to me," Vandenberg said.

"He may have been," Finney said. "He'll tell you he asked for the assignment up here—being an interviewer—but I always wondered if he didn't play his cards wrong somewhere, and they shanghaied him."

"Can you believe anything of what he tells you?"

"Andy'll level with you, from what I hear."

"He mentioned polygraphs and scopolamine—does everyone go through that?"

"Everyone," Finney said. "They haul us up to Administration periodically, and put us under to see how we're shaping up."

"You don't mind?"

"Are you kidding? Hell, yes, I mind—we all do. You take those sessions on an empty stomach, y'know, and even then you're throwing up parts of what you ate four days earlier. They have to carry you out. We call them talk sessions. That's one thing around here nobody gets used to. Some of the tapes they record they play back to you, later. It's not very pleasant. It's like a verbal enema, the stuff they flush out of a guy. You feel about an inch high."

"Yet you—everybody—takes it?"

Harris interrupted. "A guy named Banks died last month. He

had cancer of the stomach. We all knew about it. He got out. But he's been the only one to make it through that main gate without a discharge slip, see?"

Conversations With Andy

The next morning after calisthenics, he met with Walters in the same room. Walters, good as his word, had brought a pot of coffee. He had on a fresh sports shirt, but today he had not bothered to tuck it in at all. "How'd you sleep last night?"

"Pretty soundly. I only woke up once," he said.

"Good."

"It's odd, because usually I have trouble sleeping in a strange place."

"It's the altitude. Everything else all right?"

"Is there any way I can get cigarettes?"

"You'll be issued a carton every Saturday. I can lend you a pack till then."

"Have you heard anything about my son?"

"No," Walters said. "I had a special session last night until nine. But I'll have some free time this afternoon. I'll make some calls. Did you have a chance to do any reading?"

"I looked through a book on economics."

Walters poured two cups of coffee and tossed an open pack of cigarettes on the table. He opened a drawer, took out a legal-sized pad of yellow paper and a pen, lit up, and said, "What did you think of the questions I gave you yesterday?"

"Not much," he said.

Walters grinned. "I know how you feel. They were pretty corny. Still, we have to start somewhere."

"It would seem so," he said.

"How about the first question—who would you blame for the war?"

"Both countries."

"Would you blame one more than the other?"

"With respect to what?"

Walters shrugged. "Oh, say, U.S. foreign policy. Soviet pighead-edness over mutual disarmament?"

"I'd like to think it wasn't our fault," he said. "Or that it was less our fault than Russia's, but I can't. How can you be objective when you know your country's been fed as much pap as another?"

"Exactly. There you have the advantage—and the weakness— of insularity. Other countries besides the United States and the Soviet Union indulged themselves in the luxury of soft-pedaling their roles in history. The advantage lies in that you can train a large group of people to think and feel a certain way about themselves. The trouble is that other countries may, and probably do, think otherwise. This country was spoonfed a line of crap for so many years that to this day most Americans cannot accept the fact that the rest of the world regarded the U.S. as an essentially war-like nation. The same goes for the notion of Uncle Sam lending a helping hand to impoverished countries—Christ, when was the last time this country ever *really* gave something away for the hell of it? But, to return—you'd say, then, that both countries, and per-haps their allies, were equally to blame?"

"I suppose so."

"Do you believe the official Communist Party interpretation of the events leading up to the war—that there was a formal plot in Washington to attack us first?"

"No."

"What if I proved to you that you were wrong?"

"I'd still doubt it."

"Why such skepticism?"

"I suppose because it's hard to think of one's country as being fundamentally treacherous," he said. "It's possible, but the idea sticks in my craw."

"Do you believe that we attacked without provocation?"

"I think provocation, of one sort or another, must have existed, to a degree."

"What in your opinion constitutes sufficient cause or provoca-tion for war?"

"Nothing. No cause is sufficient. To me the risks were too great. Also, Russia like the U.S. had too much of a good thing—a war-time economy for thirty years. War, or a climate of war, makes for progress, you know. An all-out thermonuclear exchange would have put an end to that."

"Do you think that the temperament of the Russian people and its leaders is essentially more warlike than that of Americans?"

"I wouldn't think so," Vandenberg said. "But people can usually be stirred up, if you work at it."

"Do you know how many casualties there were in Russia during World War II?"

He shook his head.

"Nineteen million. Frightening, no? Imagine that many inside the U.S. After a loss like that, wouldn't you think it would take a lot of 'work' to create an aggressively warlike community?"

"Yes," he admitted. "But your leaders have had years to accomplish it."

"Do you believe people, any people, are basically aggressive or basically peaceful?"

"Aggressive," Vandenberg said. "I'd like to think otherwise, but there's nothing in history to indicate a . . . natural urge toward peacefulness."

"The Bible?"

"Oh, come on."

"You're not religious, then?"

"No."

"Do you think people can be educated—sophisticated—into being peaceful?"

"That'll be the day."

"Do you think the U.S. has become more peaceful, in spirit, in mood, since the Occupation?"

"No." Then Vandenberg corrected himself. "Yes."

"How do you react to the official Party reference to the Occupation as the 'noblest of social experiments in human history'?"

"It's a crock of shit."

Walters smiled, and lit a cigarette. "Here, have more coffee." He refilled their cups. "How about the next question—could the war have been avoided?"

"I think it could have been."

"How?"

"Both sides should have withdrawn from the arms race," he said. "Less powerful allies would have followed. Censorship should have been completely removed."

"What would that have accomplished?"

"For one thing, it would have made for a more humane climate than we have here in this country right now under Soviet rule."

"It's only temporary."

"I'll bet."

"No, I mean it. How about disarmament? Do you think there was any integrity on either side during the talks?"

"Yes, I do."

"Why was so little accomplished?"

"Censorship again. Fear. Mutual distrust."

"On both sides?"

"Yes."

"It wasn't all black or white then?"

"When is it ever? Mutual stupidity."

"Why stupidity?"

"They couldn't break away from . . . what? Not from a compulsion for national security—which is only another term for being territorially stronger than anyone else. That term as it was used in this country during the last years had so many ramifications that, to me, it became meaningless, until finally everything was involved with national security. No one ever spoke of national *in*security, which would have been much more accurate. Take Vietnam. Sure, along with Laos and Cambodia, it was a fulcrum for the big Asian power play. But you can look at a school kid's globe and pick out a hundred similar fulcrums, from Antarctica to Uganda—none of them, of course, penetrating the borders of either the U.S. or Russia —the idea being to fight 'em on foreign soil, rather than on ours or yours. And, if you'll admit that there were a hundred possible fulcrums, then both countries could not help but look forward to continuous war. It would have gone on, until somewhere, someday, someone would have gotten too jittery, too worn-out, and then one of the big monster computers would have gotten that special programmed tape that would have started it."

"You didn't approve of Vietnam then?"

"I don't approve of war anywhere," Vandenberg said. "You don't really accomplish anything. You change things around. Somebody wins, somebody loses. In a few years, there's another flareup, and a few years later, still another. You end up with a lot of corpses, that's all. The cadavers themselves aren't so tragic as the knowledge that it was all so pointless—nothing served, nothing accomplished. All this bullshit about national security, or insecurity, sovereignty and autonomy, is for the birds."

"Then you refute individual nations?" Walters asked.

"Not necessarily. But individual nationalism certainly contributed to the appalling state to which the world has progressed."

"Do you see World Government on the way?"

"Hard for someone like me to envision."

"Perhaps. But consider the alternatives. What others are there, really?"

"You may be able to do it, if you get China under control."

"China is only one leg of a long journey."

"She occupies a sizable portion of this planet's land surface," he said.

Walters glanced at him. "And we occupy the remainder."

"True."

"All the old farcical business about power plays between the 'free' and the 'Communist' worlds—that's done with," Walters went on, using a ball-point as a baton. "Mark my words. The war marked the date of bona fide U.S.-Soviet joint efforts. We'll do more in the next ten years than you can imagine, and it won't be under the false cloak of national defense or progress."

"Somebody'll have to pay," Vandenberg said. "Landing manned rockets on Mars cost money. Tax money—here, in Russia, or anywhere else. Listen—let me ask you—how much of a threat is China? Really?"

"She's a real threat, all right."

"It isn't all propaganda—what we hear on television?"

"Some is. Not all of it though," Walters said.

"ICBM's?"

"Hell, yes. More every month."

"I thought all that talk about her missile sophistication had been exaggerated—blown up—to provide Americans with a fresh emotional target."

"Of course we play it up big—but she's the real thing, friend. We're *all* scared of China."

"Sooner or later something'll happen."

"Why? Everything pointed to a U.S.-Soviet nuclear war, but it didn't happen."

"Instead of a bomb, you—they—used something else. The effect was the same."

124

Walters dropped the subject.

"How do you feel about the third question," Walters said. "What about the future? Pessimistic or optimistic?"

"Pessimistic."

"For yourself?"

Vandenberg nodded.

"For the United States?"

He nodded again, and said, "It's bad now in this country, but I believe it's going to get worse. Not just for the next decade or so, but from here on out. The world I grew up in and knew is gone—like Zhivago's world."

"Was it such a good place?"

"It was the only world I had. I complained about it, but it wasn't that bad—I preferred it to what we have now."

"What do you see for yourself?"

"Nothing good—I'm fifty now. I don't have many years left."

"You could be useful."

"I don't want to be."

"You think life under Communism is that bad?"

"Maybe not. All I know is that in the old days I lived my life by no means as fully as I would have liked to, but I got by. As long as I made even a token show of following society's rules, I was more or less left alone. When I blatantly ignored the rules, there were practical consequences, like being picked up for being drunk. I don't imagine anybody thought of me as being a useful citizen, but neither was I a deficit. The American middle-class mentality can tolerate a great deal in a man as long as he's not a tax burden—a welfare recipient. I probably alienated some people, but not to the point where they felt they had to do something about me. The real difference between then and now is that now I find myself up here at Cowles. And that's bad, friend."

"What do you think will happen to the United States?"

"Who the hell cares?" he said. "I'm interested in me. I think, very shortly, that somebody like me will be so out of tune, so out of place and out of grace, that death will be welcome. Another year or so and I won't recognize the country—hell, it had gotten pretty chickenshit for me by the Kennedy Administration. Listen— maybe a great new people *will* rise out of the Soviet Administration of this country, as M.G. insists it will. All I'm saying is that I tend to approach such matters very personally. And I know that Gene Vandenberg's time is running out."

"You find that much difference in life now?"

"Yes. Ten years ago I'd bring my kid up here, and we'd fish the Pecos and collect mushrooms. Today I'm locked up in this fucking zoo you've built."

"Does our system of electoral representation strike you as being different?"

"Yes," he said. "But it doesn't trouble me. I don't vote. Never have."

"What did you think of Johnson?"

"He bored me."

"Kennedy?"

"He'd have made a great Republican president."

"Goldwater?"

"Likably direct. A born loser, considering the mentality of the people he was appealing to."

"Nixon?"

"Oh, come on."

"You felt so strongly, but never voted?"

"Why bother? Leadership by majority's rule is better than a dictatorship . . . but only slightly better."

"What other differences have you found under Occupational rule?"

"A lot that isn't too important," he said. "Gas and food rationing, censorship. We're getting a taste of what Germany experienced in 1945, a feeling that it's not even your country anymore, that it's owned and operated by an absentee landlord. That'll pass, I imagine. People can't survive with that sort of demoralization."

"True," Walters said. "People have a psychological resiliency. Survival at any cost is more attractive than extinction."

He paused. "Well, this gives me an idea of your thinking. You have some very mixed-up ideas, do you know that?"

"I'm not defending them," Vandenberg said. "You're the one who's hung on establishing a relationship between us."

"At least you were trying to be honest. Some of your responses were so ass-backward, they *had* to mirror real feelings—no one

126

trying to channel me the proper answers on a pretuned wave length would have talked that way."

"Am I scored on these interviews?"

"No," Walters said, lighting a cigarette. "Later, I'll dictate my opinion on the machine, but there's no score."

"What's your opinion then?"

Walters shrugged. "You really want it?"

"Why not?"

"Okay. It'll take more than this first interview to convince me, but my initial reaction is that you probably never should have been sent up here."

"I'll drink to that."

"You've got a couple of decades' frustration built up inside," Walters continued, puffing at the cigarette. "You're a malcontent, all right—a real one. But you're basically harmless. You're a talker, Gene, a windbag—no offense meant—but you're not dangerous. You're full of shit, that's all. If you'd stayed out of the Montana Bar on Saturday nights, you'd never have had a warrant put on you. I think you were busted because they were worried that a couple of *real* hotheads might overhear you and take it from there, get the picture?"

"Yes."

"The problem is now that you've been admitted, you have to take the course."

"There's no way out of it?"

"No. With luck though, you could be a short-timer."

"How short?"

"Three months."

"That's minimum?"

"Yes. And after discharge, a probationary period."

"How long is that?"

"Life."

Vandenberg gave him a look.

"It's not that bad, really," Walters said. "The coffee's cold—you want any more?"

"I don't mind it cold." He held out his cup. "We might as well get on with it."

"Fine," Walters said. "I'd like to get some personal background."

Vandenberg gestured toward the dossier lying on the table. "Isn't it all there?"

"There are a lot of facts," Walters said. "The name of the doctor who gave you a diphtheria shot doesn't really interest me."

"What do you want to know?"

"Tell me about painting."

He disliked talking about painting. "What is there to say?"

"You made your living at it?"

"That's not saying much."

"Did you paint in oils?"

He explained about egg tempera. "I'd developed a palette all my own. Muted shades, perfect for this Southwest light. No one else in this part of the country could come near my palette."

"How well known were you?"

"Limited. It took me four or five months sometimes to do a panel. Tempera is slow work—it doesn't like being rushed. You can't splash it on, like acrylics. So I had to charge a stiff price. Not many could afford it. I sold quite a bit in southern California in the fifties and sixties. But I was never big-time, like Wyeth or Hurd —they also worked in tempera."

"This satisfied you?"

"Yes. I was making enough to support myself and my family. Representational stuff. For a few years I did portraits, but I didn't care for the people who could afford me. They all wanted to be entertained, you know, and some even wanted to come out to my ranch to pose. Curious, you see—dying to observe the artist in his natural habitat. I didn't need that sort of thing."

"But you think you were really good?"

"Yes, and that's not a put-on. Of course, the later stuff got to be cut and dried, I suppose. Like a pianist doing Chopin exercises over and over, when he should have been going on to tougher scores. That's when I lowered my prices. Two, three hundred, whatever I thought a panel would fetch. One year, though, I worked hard. Cora, my first wife, was alive then. Made eleven thousand, some of it through a Los Angeles gallery, some through private local sales. That was the year I bought the ranch. Kevin, my boy, had just been born. I spent two years rebuilding the old ranch house. I worked mornings on construction; afternoons, I'd paint. I was twenty-nine then. I could work hard and drink at night, and it never bothered me. Twenty-nine is a hell of a good age for a man to make a thousand dollars a month, part-time, doing something that wasn't really work at all but fun. I felt good. And Cora was still in her middle twenties.

"We used to laugh at Santa Fe together. The phony art colony, the would-be writers. Everybody making the scene as hard as he knew how. With the ranch, we turned our backs on all that. People thought we were crazy for buying ninety acres of unimproved grazing land, a wrecked house, no water, no well, no electricity.

"That was, I suppose, the first time I got really pissed off at the government. We went to Albuquerque, to the VA, to see if we could swing a GI loan so we could fix the place up. Not as a working ranch—we didn't know a thing about cows. I knew I could get something a lot better than beef out of the place: my paintings. They took a lot of time explaining to us why Uncle Sam wasn't about to loan five cents on a busted-down ranch. Uncle wanted his vets to have decent housing. No tar-paper shacks, no kerosene lamps. 'Nothing's too good for our boys.' They were asshole deep in greenbacks to loan on FHA-approved homes. Beehives. Housing developments. Levittowns. But not a cent for a sixty-year-old abandoned ranch that didn't even have a clear abstract or title examination.

"I tried to tell them we weren't interested in a neat little development box-house. A waste of breath. They were polite, but it was no go. I was ready to tear up my army discharge in front of them, but Cora stopped me. We walked out and never went back. And we bought the ranch anyway. I damn near flooded the market with Vandenberg temperas that year, but we paid off the place. Never did get electricity or a phone. I put in a butane kitchen, butane fridge, the works. Fireplaces and panel rays in each room. Cora got to love that place. Nine miles from Santa Fe, far enough for privacy, close enough for shopping. The next winter we put a camper on my pickup truck and went to Mexico. That was the only vacation we ever had together. Hit Guaymas, and then drove down the coast to Mazatlán, but it wasn't any good—Cora was already worried about the boy.

"So we came back, and we began the tests, and it was one specialist after another. We'd sweated it all along, you see. He was a seven-months baby, and we understood about oxygen starvation and damage, and then, one afternoon—Cora—she was on her way back to the ranch, and she misjudged a curve on the Taos bypass. They found where the right front wheel hit soft gravel. The pickup only rolled once. She was unconscious for two and a half days in the hospital, and then one morning she went, just before noon. A nurse had looked in on her and then gone out for a few minutes, and when she came back Cora was halfway out of the bed, dead. I buried her at the ranch.

"Later, I started drinking hard. Usually, I'd take the kid with me. It was having him with me that finally straightened me out. I couldn't booze and take care of him too. So I eased off. It took over a year. That's when the temperas became cut and dried. Not as good as they could have been, see? Except once, say, in every dozen paintings there'd be a hint—maybe in the way a head was turned, or the expression of a mouth, or the reflection in a pane of window glass— never an entire painting, only a part of it, and you had to look carefully to find even that much, but when you did find it you knew that for a while, maybe no longer than a day or so, I'd been getting it down the way I wanted, not just going through the motions."

"You married again?"

"Yes, about two years later," he said. "That was Helen. Her name is Perkins now—she's remarried. Lives in Connecticut."

"What sort was she?"

"A fine girl. Bright. Very female. She had money—and she'd just gotten divorced. She was out here for a change, which was another way of saying she'd headed west to find love and happiness. She'd no sooner hit town and rented a house before word got out that a new mark was on the scene. Every deadbeat, chiseler, and dying survival-artist in Santa Fe was out to try his luck, but she took it with a laugh. She told me later that she'd had four serious proposals within a month."

"Yours included?"

"Yes."

"She didn't dig you as a bum?"

"I was making money. When I took her out, I didn't have to sponge egg off my only tie with kerosene, the way some did. Also, I suppose I was a lot younger and better-looking than I am now. We were all right together. She was a hell of a woman. She'd walk into a bar and stop the place cold. She knew about Kevin, and she knew about the drinking. By then, though, I'd slacked off. She liked the ranch and the way I lived, at least she did for a while—almost five years. By then, we'd had two girls."

"What happened?"

"Different things," he said. "She wanted a place in town—and, of course, she could have afforded it—for the convenience, she said, and she wanted a more active social life than I could stomach. Basically, I guess I liked being off by myself too much. The ranch suited me, and I wasn't about to move into town. It took her six months to get up nerve enough to make the break. And when she did, the first thing she did was buy a house, like she said. We tried a reconciliation—I moved in with her. It only lasted a few months. I found fault with everything. Finally I took Kevin and went back to the ranch."

"You didn't think about marrying again?"

"No," Vandenberg said. "I was thirty-eight by then. We'd inflicted a lot of damage on each other—some pretty bad fights. I wasn't interested in taking a chance again."

"How about the two daughters?"

"She took them with her when she headed east."

"And your son—how bad is he really?"

"It varies. Sometimes, he's not much more than a baby—next minute, he acts like a teenager."

"Is he ever difficult to handle?"

"Kevin? Lord, no."

"No violence?"

"Never."

"If you were released tomorrow, what would you do?"

"Get my kid—presuming he's in custody somewhere by now—and go home."

"You really couldn't see yourself doing anything else?"

"Such as?"

"A more meaningful existence?"

"Such as?"

"I don't know," Walters said. "I'm just throwing out feelers to you."

"Listen, I can find faults aplenty with the way I live," he said. "Don't think I don't wish some of it could be different."

"Have you sold any paintings lately?"

"No," he said. "Money's tight. I traded some small panels a few months ago for stuff like liquor and cigarettes."

"That'll pass. Various cultural programs are already in the planning stage."

Vandenberg did not comment.

"Would you be at all interested in doing any sketching while you're here in the compound?"

"No."

"Why not?"

"I work alone," he said. "Anyway, you've got me on a pretty tight schedule."

"That's true," Walters said, "but if you change your mind, let me know." He glanced at the clock on the wall. "Let's take a break. We've been at it for an hour."

"Suit yourself."

"How about some hot coffee?"

"Can we get some?"

"Take the pot around to the back of the cafeteria and give it to the cook," Walters said. "He'll know who it's for."

"Okay."

"While you're gone, I'll organize some of the notes I've made so far. Take a cigarette with you and have a smoke."

It was obvious that Walters wanted to be alone. Vandenberg took the pot and said, "I'll be back in ten minutes, okay?"

"Fine." When he had left, closing the door after him, Walters turned to the dictaphone and slipped a fresh plastic belt into place.

COMMUNICATIONS

VANDENBERG, EUGENE R.
#4076

(Extract, narrative entry)

INTERVIEW #1—INTERIM OBSERVATIONS

During the course of this initial interview, a number of standard topics outlined in TP-1219 were discussed, including a superficial exploration of the subject's political and sociological rationales.

My primary feeling is that we have here a subject possessing immature, ambivalent, and shallow orientations, especially politically.

Distrust, suspicion, and conflict are apparent in his responses. Continuity is significantly lacking in any attempt by him to present political theories. He gives good indication, however, of superficial cooperation. This last is based partially on curiosity over his present situation and the hope that spurious cooperation will provide insights into his predicament. Also he appears to have grudgingly accepted the fact that cooperation is mandatory.

Responses toward interviewer are ambivalent. Reservation and distrust are apparent and only thinly veiled.

Concerning political immaturity, it should be noted that his reactions, though ineptly thought out, are deeply ingrained and, as such, will be immensely more difficult to cope with than prejudices stemming from conventional democratic indoctrination.

Though he cannot verbalize it, he is profoundly apprehensive over his present situation. He appears unaware of prescribed medications already begun and reports that he has been resting well at night.

The interview was permitted to veer from political themes for the purpose of sounding out his feelings about his past life. A pattern of marital discord became evident; he also idealizes his first marriage. The relationship with his current inamorata (see case record) was not raised. Aware that the subject had been an artist and that he had in the past been able to earn a living from his vocation, I asked about his feelings toward painting. Initial responses were disinterest, bitterness, disgust, and resentment over not having achieved success. I believe this may constitute the most important aspect of successful rehabilitation and that with proper indoctrination and encouragement a useful role for this subject may be found in some department of the Ministry of Culture, possibly as an instructor or teacher.

—A. Walters, Dictaphoned

WHEN HE RETURNED with fresh coffee, Walters was at the table waiting for him. They refilled their cups, lit cigarettes, and Vandenberg said, "Shall we go on?"

"All right."

"What of yourself?" Vandenberg asked. "I heard you were pretty important."

"Did you? Where did you hear that?"

"Scuttlebutt."

Walters smiled. "Don't place too much value on gossip."

"I'm wondering how much value I can place on anything I hear."

"Gene, whatever I tell you about myself will be the truth," Walters said. "If you ask me about anything that's classified, I'll simply refuse to discuss it, but I won't lie to you. Fair enough?"

"I guess so," Vandenberg said. "Is your name really Walters?"

"Yes. I was born in Philadelphia, in 1922, but my family moved west when I was a kid. My father was in insurance. I majored in government at UCLA and did a hitch in the Air Force, mostly in England. After I was discharged, I got married and did graduate work at Columbia's Russian Language Institute."

"Is your wife here with you?"

"No. We were divorced years ago."

"Were you always interested in the Soviet Union?"

"No. At that time, I wasn't sure where my interests lay, but I suppose I was growing more dissatisfied with what I saw here. Government service repelled me, although I was aware by then that the Soviet bureaucratic system was if anything even more screwed up. It would have been easy enough to settle into some twelve-thousand-dollar-a-year job in Washington, but I was hostile. Not that I wasn't highly critical of the Soviet Union at that time— I was—but I was sickened more by what I'd seen here.

"So, there I was, still in Air Force Reserve. I signed for another tour of duty. They sidetracked me to Wiesbaden for almost a year, and then, as I'd hoped, the Russian studies paid off and I was transferred to Berlin, in intelligence. To make a long story short, one evening I simply took the train to the Russian sector and at East Berlin military headquarters asked for asylum."

"You'd thought it all out, ahead of time?"

"Oh, yes."

"You weren't frightened?"

"Not so much frightened as—lost, for a while," Walters said. "Later they showed me some of the stateside papers that carried the story on me. Not that I was ever big news. In this country, I was just one more mixed-up guy who'd gone over. Not that I cared about what they thought. By then I was convinced I'd done the right thing. I've never regretted it. Of course, I had a hell of a time convincing my Soviet hosts I was on the level. They put me through the mill. You'll get the treatment, too, Gene, before you walk out of here. There's no cleverness left anymore, no subterfuge. This has become the age of honesty. Nowadays, nobody fools anybody. We can literally pick your brain to pieces. No more secrets, even from yourself. They found out aspects of Andy Walters I'd kept hidden from myself all my life. Very depressing. Ultimately, however, I was cleared for classified work. That's why I wanted the tests. Without them, I'd have ended up in some trivial post as a kind of oddball consultant, and that wasn't what I was after. Despite the weaknesses my tests revealed, they also showed that I was categorically convinced that the Soviet Union possessed the key to peace."

"What do you mean by that?"

"Perhaps the climate was—healthier," Walters said.

"Stronger?"

"If you insist, yes," Walters said. "Not that I buy the line of reason based on newer countries having more vitality than old ones. Let me put it this way—despite America's sophistication, the country seemed lost—adrift. U.S. foreign policy alone, from '58 on, certainly mirrored this. There was also an almost unbelievable aura of adolescent petulance about this country's not getting its own way. I ended up finally in the Division of Foreign Statistics—FORSTAT was the English code name. Still under surveillance, of course. It was a curious place to work. At any rate, six other Americans and I spent nearly seven years with FORSTAT, and in certain respects I'd say some of the research we were involved with contributed directly to the success of the Invasion."

"And this is how they showed their appreciation?" Vandenberg asked.

Walters looked at him. "You think my being here is some sort of punishment, Gene? I requested the assignment. I could have accepted an advisory post in Military Government—gotten myself a fancy apartment, a chauffeur-driven sedan. But remember, I'd been in Russia over eight years. I'd fallen out of touch with the very subject I was supposedly an expert on. Sure, we had books, articles, reports, TV shows, films. But I missed working with people. Also, I still had that aversion to being swallowed up in the machine."

"Weren't you swallowed up in this FORSTAT?"

"No. It was a pretty unique division," Walters said. "It was also high enough to be directly supervised by a member of the Central Committee. I can't think of any close parallel over here, except perhaps the old Rand Corporation. FORSTAT's role was to explore in depth various courses of action relating to the United States and other western powers."

"This isn't classified?"

"It's not important," Walters said. "We expect to publish a definitive account of the events leading up to the war. In a year or so. I can sketch it out roughly for you. The group I was with evolved a theory. In itself, the theory had no great sweep of imagination—but it took imagination to grasp that it was workable. Anyway, once we got the idea across, the rest of it—the Invasion and the Occupation—became simple. The military, fiscal policy, economics, administration, government—all that could be worked out, much of it with the help of computers. There were still problems, of course, that couldn't be run on a computer tape, and one of these is what we came to refer to as the nonconforming group, which is what we have here at Cowles. I don't mean radical splinter groups, far left or far right. In the first place, all these existed via the tolerance of this country's last few administrations. With the Occupation, naturally, all that was done with. We simply told them what they were going to do. Not surprisingly, we did have problems with hard-core elements in certain security groups, such as the FBI. Men who'd been exposed to a lifetime of unilateral indoctrination. There was nothing to be done with them. No hope of rehabilitation."

"Were they executed?"

"No. You know that the death penalty has been abolished."

"I suppose they simply disappeared," he said drily.

"Let's just say they're out of circulation. But these people, statistically, were only a drop in the bucket. We were concerned with the broader spectrum of citizens. It wasn't simply a matter of intelligence, by the way. Some of the brightest—and stupidest—minds presented no difficulty. It was more a question of temperament. The sort that, by nature, goes against the grain—it's an old, all too familiar personality type that exists in the Soviet Union as well as here. And, too, there are many more—yourself, for one—who are not especially troublesome, but who, we know, possess that unpredictable factor that might trigger an incident. You will,

I think, agree when I say you can't have a sprinkling of hot-heads running around in a country you're bent on remaking. You either execute them—which is expedient, though apt to blur the image you're trying to convey to the rest of the country—or you isolate them; hence, Cowles."

"Are you saying that you had something to do with the planning of camps like Cowles?"

"We did, indeed. Isolation camps—think camps—aren't new in Europe, or here, either. We've carried it a step further, that's all. Treatment on an individual basis. Very expensive."

"But there must be tens of millions of candidates for such camps."

Walters gave him a patient look. "My friend, don't overestimate the mettle of your fellow Americans."

"Unless you have fifty thousand camps like this—"

"Don't be ridiculous. Five thousand rehab centers like Cowles would be a needless extravagance," Walters said. "As I said, it's an expensive program. But well worth it. We're salvaging some of the best people in the country—certainly the only exciting ones. You can probably guess that there are officials in M.G. right now who feel otherwise, those who can still condone the *kulak* persecutions. They speak in terms of the cost of a rifle cartridge as opposed to the cost of rehabilitating one of you, forgetting that this is not the Soviet Union of the twenties and thirties. They forget, too, that they couldn't do that today in Russia. Some attitudes die hard."

"The velvet hammer," Vandenberg said.

"Precisely," Walters said, smiling. "Americans are used to pla-cation and circumspect handling. It would be stupid to indulge in harsh treatment now."

"And all you can do with a corpse is bury it."

"It makes excellent fertilizer. Anyway, all this was a challenge. I wanted to see the theory in practice. Unfortunately, these camps are becoming a catchall for anyone with a borderline evaluation. M.G. is getting lazy."

"And you like working up here?"

"Yes," Walters said. "You see, if I can still communicate with people like you—the maverick breed—then I'm worth my pay. If we can return III's, IV's and V's to society, think of the implication. We will have solved a problem that in earlier eras was relegated to the dungeon, the penitentiary, the *auto-da-fé*. Really, isn't it infinitely more civilized to sit here over coffee and cigarettes, chatting, than to face one of Torquemada's inquisitors, or a jackbooted storm trooper . . . or for that matter a jackbooted Los Angeles cop with a rubber truncheon in some precinct basement? Isn't this preferable to the firing squad, the fascist concentration camp? Indeed, my friend, the insane asylum, traditionally, has absorbed many of society's more precocious nonconformists."

"You'd call Cowles successful?"

"Indeed, yes," Walters said. "Out of camps like Cowles is coming a new breed: nonpartisan, nonchauvinistic, nonethnocentric. The first genuine social creature."

"A conforming social creature."

"Some conformity is necessary."

"Not at the expense of individuality."

"Gene, that's a dangerous thought."

"You talk of ethnocentricity, yet obviously if there was a choice between Russia and the United States, you'd choose Russia, wouldn't you?" he asked.

"The choice no longer exists, Gene," Walters said. "Man, can't you get it into your head, the Soviet Union and the United States are one country?"

COMMUNICATIONS

VANDENBERG, EUGENE R.

(Extract, narrative entry)

INTERVIEW #1, *10:30 A.M.–11:30 A.M. A standard RPI-12 Memory Erase will be indicated for the above noted period. Positive reinforcing interviewer-trainee elements may remain vestigial, if they do not readily extinguish.*

—*A. Walters, Dictaphoned*

AFTER LUNCH, VANDENBERG, in accordance with his schedule, reported to one of the small classrooms in Building Six. There he met the rest of his study group—five others, including Jerome Fein, the broker who had been admitted with him. The instructor had not yet come in, and he and Fein had a moment to speak. Fein introduced him to the others. "This is Don Haskell. Harry Deutsch. Duane Perrin. . . ."

He shook hands with them. None was familiar.

"Listen," Fein said, "has Walters told you yet about the tests they give us? I could do without that."

"Maybe you won't remember it," Vandenberg said. "They may have a drug that automatically cancels out the experience. Like with electroshock. I had a friend who had EST. No pain, nothing— he never knew anything about it. They anesthetize you before they wheel you in, so there's less chance of broken bones during the spasms. He wouldn't have even known he'd taken treatments if his psychiatrist hadn't told him."

"Yes, but did it help him?" Deutsch asked.

"As a matter of fact, it did," Vandenberg said. "He was suicidal before."

"And afterward?"

He shrugged. "He wasn't the same person. At least, I didn't think so. But he wasn't suicidal."

"You wouldn't want to go through that, would you?"

"No, I wouldn't."

"You don't seem very concerned, Vandenberg," Deutsch said.

"Neither do you." It occurred to him that none of them did. They might have been discussing a forthcoming visit to a dentist.

Their instructor walked into the room and shut the door. He was a young Russian whose name, he told them, was Alyosha, and he began immediately:

"Gentlemen, this afternoon's discussion period will cover introductory aspects of world peace. . . ."

Conversations With Andy

They were in private interview one afternoon three weeks later when Walters suddenly asked, "Gene, who's Marjorie Heller?"

"Terry?"

"The name's listed several times in your dossier."

He was by now reasonably sure that knowing him would not make her subject to harassment, yet he had never mentioned her to Walters. He said, "If you've got her name, what more do you need to know about her?"

"She's a blank—as far as your history is concerned. Known her long?"

"Seven or eight years."

"She teaches school?"

"Yes. Fifth grade."

"Not married?"

"No."

"Is she your mistress?"

"At times, yes," he said.

Andy smiled. "She somebody else's mistress the rest of the time?"

"I didn't mean that. We're friends. Sometimes—not very often —we're lovers."

"She appears content with this arrangement?"

"I don't know," he said. "We don't talk much about it."

"Ever thought of marrying her?"

"Yes."

"What's stopped you?"

"She's over twenty years younger."

"Is that important?"

"At my age? Hell, yes."

"Yet you must get along fairly well together—else the relationship would have died."

"We get along," he said. "Largely, I think, because of the distance we've maintained. She's free. I've always told her that. So am I."

"You're satisfied with this sort of setup?"

"No. But I'm damned glad to have that much," he said. "I'm not the only middle-aged guy, I imagine, who's been drawn to a young girl. It's very nice. But I'm not about to push my luck. Ten years from now, if I'm alive, she'll still be a young women, but I'll be an old man."

"Is she pretty?"

"Yes—I think so."

"Do you think you're a father image to her?"

"Some."

"This doesn't trouble her? No hang-ups with the sex angle?"

"None."

"How does she feel about this limited relationship?"

"She understands that it's either that or nothing."

"Is she a submissive type?"

"No."

"Do you think she loves you?"

"Yes. Otherwise she'd have dropped me."

"You love her?"

He nodded.

"Does she know about your son?"

"Oh, yes." Walters had finally learned that Kevin had been placed in a foster home, and this information had eased the worry that had gnawed at Vandenberg since his arrest. Walters went on: "She's been to your ranch then?"

"Many times. Also, I'd go out to her house, in San Sebastian."

"You told me you never permitted visitors at the ranch."

"I didn't say that—I said I didn't like anybody dropping in on me. What I have out there is mine, and I was always careful about who I shared it with. With her, I didn't mind."

"What do you imagine this Heller girl sees in someone like you?"

"I've never asked her."

"Not security?"

Vandenberg shook his head.

"Nor loquaciousness, either."

Vandenberg said nothing, and Walters went on. "You can really clam up when you want to."

"Look, what do you expect?"

"Progress."

"There are analysts who spend years trying to break barriers— we've been talking for only a couple of weeks," he said.

"By now, most trainees would have accepted the situation for what it is."

"I've accepted it."

"With qualifications."

Vandenberg shrugged. "Sure. I'm here against my will."

"You insist on rejecting rehabilitation."

"I don't want to be rehabilitated. If it's all the same to you people I'd a hell of a lot rather not be rehabilitated at all."

"You enjoyed that limited, sterile existence out there in the hills?"

"Immensely."

"That shitty life?" Walters was in a sour mood this morning.

"Shitty by some standards, not by mine. You ought to spend a few days at the ranch with me. Sit around. Relax."

"Ask your fellow trainees about your existential existence— see what they think."

"Damn it, I've told you a dozen times, I don't care what other people think."

"I don't believe that."

"Suit yourself. I don't give a damn what you think, either."

"Yes you do," Walters said. "You have to."

Vandenberg said nothing.

Walters continued. "You wouldn't want to be discharged as the same mixed-up, cranky old bastard you were when you came in, would you?"

"Frankly, yes."

The glance Walters gave him was serious. "You realize what you've said?"

"I think so."

"The length of your sentence depends largely on your attitude." Walters stubbed out his cigarette. "To return again to this Heller woman—"

"Must we?"

Walters paused, and then continued stabbing the butt into the ashtray. "No, if you'd prefer not to. . . ."

"Has she been interrogated or arrested?"

"Of course not."

"Then let's talk about something else," Vandenberg said. "I wasn't lying when I said we were casual friends. I'm not really that interested in talking about her."

"Okay, we can drop it."

"Suits me."

142

VANDENBERG, EUGENE R.
#4076

(Extract, narrative record)
INTERVIEW #24, 8:00 A.M.–11:30 A.M. *A rating of Unsatisfactory is indicated for this interview. As noted in the last four interviews, the subject's obstinate retention of immature political values remains the same.*

And, stenographer, would you be good enough to send off a messagegram to District Headquarters, advising that we strongly recommend that HELLER, MARJORIE P., be designated Category III until further notice? Our subject doth protest too strongly about the insignificance of their friendship.

—A. Walters, Dictaphoned

THERE WAS SOMETHING wrong, but he had never been able to find the answer, and now, on this night, stretched on his bunk, he thought about it again.

Except for the sounds of a few snorers and one or two others who moved restlessly in their sleep, the dorm was quiet. From a bed farther up the narrow aisle, a man broke wind softly, moaned, then became silent again. Another, lost in some deep dream, talked unintelligibly, but most of those in the long Quonset hut were silent except for their measured breathing. They slept like animals. In a cage. Fed regularly. Exercised, both physically and mentally.

Except for a dim night light, it was dark. Vandenberg glanced at Sorensen, the big psychiatrist, who slept in the next bunk. Sorensen's forearm was thrown across his face as though shielding his eyes from a bright light.

Vandenberg himself was nearly asleep. The others attributed their sound sleeping to the clear mountain air. He'd been a poor sleeper for years, because of nocturia. At the ranch he would have gotten up three or four times during the night, but here he slept heavily, so that when the bitch box roused them at 5:30, his bladder was painfully distended. Now, he felt a mild urge to urinate. He decided to wait. The gentle urge, along with the vague feeling that something was wrong, kept him awake awhile longer.

143

"You ask me how much we've done?" Walters asked irritably. "Come on, Gene—I expect more of you than that. Man, admit the faint possibility—we might be capable of accomplishing *something*."

"I'm not saying Communism won't do a lot," he replied. "Any time you have a strong approach, you cover ground fast. Look at what Ataturk did for Turkey."

"He was interested in doing the most good for the most people."

"I told you before, I'm not interested in the largest number of people, or what's good for them. I'm interested in me."

"All right, you as an individual, then. But you're still a member of a group. You're a white Anglo-Saxon Protestant—a classic example."

"I'm a white Anglo-Saxon drunk."

"A drunk then. You're still an artist. You're engaged in creative work. Ostensibly imaginative. Ostensibly intelligent. There are tens of thousands of men and women like you across the country. Painters, writers, composers, poets, musicians. Aren't you interested in the roles they'll play in this new society?"

"Jesus Christ, no."

"Why not?"

"Because there won't be any difference from the roles they played under democracy," he said. "Among the group a few will be good. The rest will be jerks. One King Kong to a million Callicebus monkeys, the way it's always been. I don't see why I ought to feel differently now."

"Quit using withdrawal as a device to explain your own mediocrity."

"Nonsense. They were never interested in me, nor I in them, that's all."

"Suppose you were a Negro, would you feel the same?"

"I'm not a Negro."

"Supposing you were though."

"The concept is beyond me."

"Are Negroes so different then?"

"A shade different."

"Do you think they're as good as you?"

"Quit rooting around, like a boar-hog after a truffle—I'm not a racist, if that's what you want to know. I wasn't trying to put down blacks when I said I couldn't put myself in their place," he said. "And there isn't a Negro alive who could put himself in my place. They're different people, that's all. They've earned the right to be."

"There's a faint stink of whitey in that kind of come-to-me-go-from-me approach."

"Depends on the situation," Vandenberg said. "I've been called worse than that. Seven, eight years ago, there was this big black writer—a fucking *poète manqué*, who knows?—who was making the scene around Santa Fe. I kept running into him in bars. A seven-foot-high Nat Turner with granny glasses and a Lion-of-Judah goatee. I despised this character. We had some mutual drinking acquaintances, and a few times we all ended up at the same table. He sensed I didn't buy him, and so he didn't think much of me either. He'd been on the marches, and Jesse Jackson was a hero of his. He'd pushed pot in Haight-Ashbury, and Cleveland, and Mexico City, and he'd been in and out of stir in a dozen states. I never read any of his stuff, but some of it had been published in little quarterlies, and I heard it was all right. He had the Peace-Allah syndrome. Two hundred and fifty pounds, and not an ounce of fat on him, and shot through with gentleness. He'd paid his dues, you see.

"He had a kid traveling with him at the time, a St. John's College girl. Long, pale, waist-length blond hair, steam-ironed. Maybe nineteen, with drooping, dreamy, acid-stoned green eyes . . . one of those brassiereless handmaidens of destiny. Sulky-mouthed. Tall, and rangy-bodied, and blown clean out of her Terre Haute skull by that great big chocolate cock.

"Well, with the goatee and the shades and a Hebraic peace greeting, he came on like a blue-skinned Jehovah. But I dug him for a crybaby who was so hung up on that pelt of his that he couldn't think of anything else. That plastic black bastard not only expected the world to love him, he wanted it to support him.

"He nailed me one night for being a fascist and for being hostile, and he was dead right, mainly because I wanted a little of that ultragorgeous pampered pussy he'd commandeered. I was prejudiced, all right, but not against blacks—I didn't like *him*."

"Would it interest you to know that over four million blacks have joined the Party since last year?" Walters asked.

"Red Uncle Toms?"

"Perhaps. But they joined."

"Why shouldn't they? Christ, they died by the thousands to make a dent in this country! Did you think they'd all give it up? Military Government would have had real trouble if it'd tried to put them all the way back down again. So Negroes are joining—so what?"

"It could be because the Communist Party thinks all men are equal."

"That's the most moronic assumption in mankind's history, and it's been the cause of untold trouble. The Party doesn't believe that crap—neither do you."

"It's a goal worth working toward," Walters said.

"In any social group, you have a hierarchy," Vandenberg said. "Reward incentive demands it."

"Nonetheless, we've encountered little resistance with militant black power."

"You promising them a slice of the action?"

"What, and invite further white backlash?"

"Listen, if there's one thing I'm not arguing, it's the fact that M.G.'s keeping the lid on—I bow to Mother Russia, and I'm not being sarcastic."

"Gene," Walters said, "we're at least attempting honesty. Take religion. We regard it for what it is, an idiosyncrasy, in which many people have a token interest. A way to lubricate the day. Isn't that less hypocritical than the In-God-We-Trust drivel wherein the family and nation that prays together stays together? Religion doesn't make a people stronger, when the chips are down. There's no one easier to corrupt than a man whose gods have failed him."

"I wonder what the Roman Church would say to that?"

"The Roman Church exists today because its leaders are shrewd enough not to venture outside their own turf. Russian orthodoxy has survived—so has Jewry."

"But in a relatively proscribed fashion."

"Russian Jews have weaned themselves of relying entirely on religious mysticism."

"I find it difficult to imagine a Jew—Russian, American, or Eskimo—weaning himself completely of the Talmudic tradition."

"It's possible. That's the point, Gene," Walters said. "I keep telling you, the barriers are coming down." He shifted ground. "Do you think it's all one-sided, that the Soviet Union will remain unchanged by the American Occupation? Why, just the other day I read in a paper that a Soviet enlisted man in Spokane applied for permission to marry his American girl. Such marriages are prohibited at present, but regulations will relax; in the next few years there'll be tens of thousands. Elementary Russian has already been introduced in public schools, to the lasting horror of American school kids who heretofore have been able to complete high school without learning even English. In fifty or a hundred years, the U.S. will be very different than it is now. But so will the Soviet Union. Cities will be decentralized—after all, the megalopolis isn't the ultimate logical end of industrial specialization."

Vandenberg smiled. "Are you advocating a return to cottage industry?"

"No, but there's a place for it—there's a place for everyone."

"For me?"

"Yes, if you want it."

"Suppose I don't?"

"Then face the consequences. Frustration, bitterness, isolation, being left out of the greatest movement in history. Is this what you want?"

"Yes."

"Some men march to the beat of a distant drummer—is that really you, Gene?"

"Don't be ridiculous. But I liked my ranch. It was a good place for me." He paused and stared at Walters. "How do you think I behaved out there? Sullen, irritable—the way you accuse me of being here?"

Walters did not reply.

"My boy and I would work around the place. I'd paint and sketch. My house is on a hill, and at night I could look for miles in any direction and not see a neighbor's light. We could see the beacon at the Santa Fe airport, and a red light on one of the radio towers, and the lights on the crest of Sandia Peak, seventy miles away, but that was all. The kid liked birds, and I built feeder stations out of dowel and scrap plywood all around the house, and in the morning we could look out the window and see hundreds of birds, all kinds, flickers, jays, robins, starlings, hummingbirds, and if you walked outside they'd all fly up—it was pretty noisy.

"So few people knew about my ranch that when a car drove

up my road—in summer, this would be, because the road was mostly blocked in winter—it was an occasion. It might be a quail hunter out lost, or some Spanish teenager and his girl looking for a place to park, or it might be a friend, but no matter who it was, it was an occasion. It wasn't any great place, understand. The house itself had once been a line shack, when the place was part of a larger spread—you know, just a couple of small rooms, with a stable and corral attached. A place a ranchhand could hole up in if he was out riding fence in bad weather. Then somebody added a couple of extra rooms. I built on a few more. I found lintels in the walls of one room that must have been the original stable—it'd been walled up.

"It was the sort of place you couldn't stand for five minutes—or else you never got enough of it. Once a friend of mine who was teaching school at Santa Barbara came out to visit. He'd gotten used to that California scene, and the ranch blew his mind in two days. He couldn't stand the quiet. The sky was too big and empty and bright blue for him. He kept asking me what I did out there. Wouldn't believe me when I told him I was always busy. Sure it got lonely. That's why I liked going into town once in a while, to raise a little hell. Then I'd be ready to go back out. It's a good place. If you could ask my son, he'd tell you I was happy there. Nothing fancy, only the privacy.

"To tell the truth, I never thought I'd have it this long. I figured the town would grow in that direction and that eventually I'd have another suburbia. But it's stayed empty. The nearest neighbor, the nearest phone and electricity, is a couple of miles off. I'd take you out there sometime and let you see for yourself, but I don't think you'd like it."

"You've managed to avoid the population explosion," Walters said.

"For me, it doesn't exist," he said. "It does for all of you."

"We're working on it."

"You better work on that one fast."

"You'll see," Walters said. "Within five years, there'll be mandatory birth control. Until we increase food production to the point where every citizen on earth is getting his two thousand calories a day, there'll be no more babies except on an authorized basis. Mass registration. A married couple will have their choice of an IUD, hysterectomy, or, for the man, a vasectomy."

"For everyone?"

"You're damned tooting," Walters said. "There'll be no more of this bullshit about wooing poor whites and blacks to practice birth control, because they can't feed their progeny. A growing child occupies just as much space on this planet and needs just as many carbohydrates and proteins whether his name is Snopes or Rockefeller. In the sixties the U.S. helped lead over six million couples in India down the vasectomy-IUD route, and now about twenty million young American Doris Day moms will join ranks with their Indian sisters. The fact that the U.S. is exploding less explosively than, say, Brazil, is incidental.

"The only way the American girl next door—or her Russian sister—will be able to indulge in the ancient custom of getting knocked up will be when someone, someplace in the world, *dies.* A one-to-one replacement system. Until the world population everywhere is existing on an adequate diet—maybe then, the one-to-one ratio'll be relaxed. And that, my friend, should cause a couple of second thoughts. The American male's tender jewels will no longer be objects of sacred regard—neither will Mom's Fallopian tubes. Mark my words, Gene, the venerated senior citizen may soon be viewed by his child-starved granddaughter as a miserable old prick who's too mean to die."

"How would M.G. enforce this kind of thing?"

"Legal. Medical."

"It sounds too complicated, somehow," Vandenberg said.

"It's so simple, it's breathtaking," Walters said, smiling. "A lottery."

"A sterilization lottery?"

"Of course!"

"It sounds wild."

"Gene, for God's sake, it's not a bit wilder or more insane than the notion that the United States and Russia had stockpiled over one hundred thousand atomic devices apiece—the equivalent of thirty tons of TNT for every man, woman, and child on the planet—and then programmed fail-safe systems, activated—on both sides, and this is really insane—by computers, machines!"

"The ultimate weapon became the ultimate absurdity."

Walters looked at him: "It still strikes me as incongruous— you're a sensitive man, and you feel strongly—yet you did nothing?"

"What could I have done? Joined a pacifist movement? Voted?"

"You didn't consider yourself some kind of cranky hippie?"

"Certainly not."

"Other people did."

"Why? Because I didn't buy the whole ridiculous middle-class routine—the decent house in a decent neighborhood with a decent car and job and wife? Hell, I grew up with all that."

"You come out here in the forties?"

"In 1948," he said. "We'd only been married a short time. Santa Fe was much smaller then. The art colony has always been a farce— a cul-de-sac for washouts—but I loved the climate."

COMMUNICATIONS

VANDENBERG, EUGENE R.
#4076

SEPTEMBER STATUS REPORT-39271

An overall rating of Unsatisfactory is indicated. Subject still gives indications of fear, hostility, aggressiveness, and spurious cooperation. There are, however, signs of a more positive trainee-interviewer rapport developing.

Medications are to continue, as prescribed.

Also, I am postponing an initial full-scale neuropsychiatric interrogation and will be rescheduling it for the twelfth instead of the ninth week, due to this man's continuing poor responses.

—A. Walters, Dictaphoned

"CHLORPROMAZINE—THORAZINE—is bitter. So is Thioridazine, which is Mellaril."

Sorensen, the psychiatrist, was speaking. He and Vandenberg had grown friendly, and now, lunch finished, they were sitting in the sun outside the dorm, Vandenberg with his eyes shut, head tilted back against the wall. He said, "Is that why most of the stuff is put up in coated pills?"

"Yes." Sorensen, near sixty, beaknosed, bald, with the massive build of a worn-out pro football player, glanced at him. "Why don't you, and I"—he smiled lazily, wickedly—"complain to the Food and Drug Administration, eh!"

150

Vandenberg liked Sorensen's dry detachment, the cynicism, the sly, snotty humor. He said, "Doc, you think it's possible?"

"*Amigo,* who knows?" Sorensen said. "For thirty years, I've made a close study of my own behavior. Up here, it's different. Perhaps, as they claim, it's the brisk mountain air and the altitude."

"You seem to be taking it in good stride."

"I'm a philosopher," Sorensen said, lighting a filter cigarette. "A cynic, a Stoic, with a blend of Epicureanism. Read Apollonius. Transactionally speaking, it's a child's game they're playing up here."

"But you're going along with it?"

"My ratings, Gene—and I venture yours, too—have been unsatisfactory."

"There's no way to beat the system?" Vandenberg asked.

He borrowed a smoke from Sorensen, who said, "In Albuquerque, I have a pleasant home and a family and a wife I'm inordinately fond of—a beautiful, lovely broad." He leaned closer to Vandenberg, grinning slyly again, as though he were about to share a tremendous secret: "Man, with assets like that, d'you think I'm about to fuck around with this operation?"

"You're going to get out?"

"By playing their game," Sorensen said. "They've got all the equipment, and we play by their rules, but short of a lobotomy, they can't touch you."

"Brain surgery?"

"Brain *cutting,*" he chuckled. "They used to go in from the top of the skull, sawing little holes so they could probe the prefrontal area. Later on they simplified it—they'd insert an ice-pick probe into the skull opening at the corner of the eye socket, alongside the nose, and yammer it back and forth. Prefrontal chopmeat, see? The unconscious effectively separated from the conscious, and only a black eye to show for it, a gorgeous mouse. The patient no longer presented problems—no restraint, no more chemotherapy—*nada.*"

"But they wouldn't do that here?"

"No. Too obvious. Besides, it'd be illegal." Sorensen laughed. "But I'll venture a guess that their pharmacologists and chemists have come up with something not covered in our contemporary medical literature."

"Why haven't you told the others?"

Sorensen blew a cloud of smoke. "I'm no gadfly. That's a sucker's game."

Inside the dorm, they heard the bitch box telling everybody to fall out.

Conversations With Andy

"The real idea—the first intuitive insights—came out of FOR-STAT's conclusions about how masses of people react during severe emotional stress," Walters was saying. "For our study, we chose the most traumatic event in recent U.S. history. I mean, of course, the assassination in Dallas."

Another week had gone by. Halfway through a morning's interview and bored with talking about himself, he had recalled Walters' account of his defection and on impulse asked to hear more. To his surprise, the interviewer had not objected.

"Why choose so morbid an event?" Vandenberg asked now.

"My group's assignment was emotional reactions, should war be declared—for our purposes, the assassination contained interesting parallel factors. It held a clue."

"A clue?"

"Kennedy's death showed us it could be done. This became, for FORSTAT, not merely the gunning down of an enormously powerful and appealing figure by a warped ex-Marine. Nor were we interested in all the sentimental garbage that rose up within days around the legend of the man, although I will admit that the plethora of tripe—the photo essays, the statuettes, the endless commemorative programs—served to underline the fact that Americans were after all, emotionally speaking, children. We knew this already, of course, but we had to have indisputable proof to show the top men."

"His death sparked more than mere sentimentalism though," Vandenberg said.

"All right—grief, if you will. Please understand that for our purposes this was one of the three great disasters to hit the American mind in the twentieth century. The first was the crash of '29; the second, naturally, December 7th, 1941. Earlier calamities—the death of Lincoln, even World War I—were small-time."

"Are you talking about impact?"

"You're close. Communication!" Walters replied. "It was right there in front of us. The United States had evolved the most advanced system of communication in history. Press, radio, TV, movies, periodicals—everything—and it was *big*. Gene, just thinking about it takes your breath away. This all-encompassing ability to reach people—the facilities available—imagine, if you will, the entire communications industry as a single instrument, a device, or as admen would say, a package—juxtaposed with a nation fundamentally unstable. What an explosive setup.

"Naturally, at FORSTAT we had regarded this package, this system, with admiration and envy long before the Dallas incident. The argument, however, against attempting a coup was that there was no way, really, to take over all aspects of it simultaneously. It was too huge, too amorphous. We would have had to place thousands of key personnel. A few hundred we could have managed, but not thousands, not with your internal security groups. There would have been a leak.

"But in the months following Kennedy's death, when as a matter of procedure our researchers gathered every scrap of information on the assassination and what subsequently transpired, something got through to our group. An idea that was almost too fantastic to contemplate. That was the most attractive thing about our theory, you know—it was incredible. But then Dallas itself was incredible, wouldn't you agree?"

"It was that."

"Anyway, it took a long time, but in December, 1968—I remember that there was snow on the ground—a breakthrough was reached. I don't know how to describe it, really, except to tell you that at a conference one afternoon, with about thirty of us present, something happened. I remember we were discussing the risks involved in detonating a device over Washington. Then, for the first time, we abandoned argument. There was a kind of . . . epiphany, I suppose, on a group scale. At that moment we all knew, without the slightest doubt, that it could be done. The theory had become fact. We had not been in conflict over whether the theory would work, but over our own doubts. It was, I think, one of the behavioral scientists who stopped us all by going back to the original propositions and remarking something like, 'Ladies and gentlemen, in all this have we not pushed so far ahead that we have lost sight of the two demonstrable clues provided by the Dallas incident?' "

"What was he referring to?" Vandenberg asked.

"He meant the nationwide paralysis caused by those first hysterical announcements over radio and television."

"I remember," he said. "I had the transistor turned on that morning—I was out in the yard working—"

Walters gave him a wolfish grin, and pointed a finger at him. *"Touché!* How very interesting. You, Gene—a misanthrope, a recluse—even you happened to have a transistor with you that morning. But, to continue . . . the announcements that Kennedy had been gunned down. Et cetera. Then, the first confirmation. The rush to the hospital. The waiting. The rumor that Johnson, with a heart history of his own, had had a coronary. That whole, terrible, incredible first thirty or forty minutes, including the plea, actually given over national networks, for people everywhere to stop and pray, culminating, as everyone sensed it would, in the solemn pronouncement: 'The President is dead.'

"No one knows exactly, of course, but it was FORSTAT's opinion that within an hour and fifteen minutes after Oswald acted, over one-hundred-and-seventy-million people knew they had lost their leader. Before the day was out, better than ninety-six per cent had been informed. Think of it! That was the first clue—this vast, omnipresent, beautiful communications system that could transfix a nation."

"And the second clue—the effect the news had?" Vandenberg asked.

"Right," Walters said. "Not merely the events of that weekend—the pomp and circumstance of the Washington funeral, the grandly controlled grief of the Kennedy family, the child saluting on the steps—all this was secondary to what occurred during the first six or seven hours. We had the picture, and it was there for anyone to see, of an entire nation incapacitated, fragmented, waiting simply to hear what would happen next. Sure, there were inferences, rumors, military alerts. But there wasn't a general officer anywhere in the world, not in SAC or Europe or the Far East, who was primed to commit himself or his men to doing any more than the rest of the citizenry—namely, sitting tight. We checked on that, friend. It didn't last long. The condition was too perilous to be permitted

154

to continue. Johnson, whatever you may think of him, Gene, was simply marvelous, the way he stepped in, shouldering the Irish Mafia aside. Brilliant—all the more so because of the man's lackluster personality, the lack of size, as the English would say."

"Was germ warfare used on Washington?" Vandenberg asked.

"That's classified. Anyway, *how* it was done never particularly interested me. It worked—that's what counts. The President might have enjoyed knowing that he and four million other Washington area residents achieved the same heights of martyrdom as Kennedy. It was a cheap price to pay."

"Four million of anything isn't cheap," he said.

"Be practical, man. What the hell's four million compared to, say, a round billion?"

"It could have gotten that bad?"

"Yes! Instead, it turned out to be one major city. It worked—thank God it did. The military were committed by the end of summer to back us all the way, in case of a misfire. No telling what might have happened. Our military pundits always swore we could take the U.S. without retaliation—but I never believed that, and down deep I don't think anyone else did either."

"And then? All that crazy business on TV and radio? Was any of it true?"

"That was premise two," Walters said. "By then, we had a few key people in the wire services and at the networks, and they released different versions. That Washington was a smoking ruin, which was not true. That Chicago, New Orleans, Los Angeles, and New York—shit, right there you've got close to thirty million—had been reduced to rubble. That an armistice had already been signed. The networks went crazy. And everywhere, the magical placebo, repeated over and over: keep calm—watch for further reports. There were other aspects, which I can't discuss with you, but surprisingly it didn't take that many people to accomplish it. The ethological concept of *noyau,* as a label for a society of inward antagonism, was valid—the collapse of the French will to resist in 1940 is another example.

"Here, less than twelve hours after the first reports were sent over the wires, almost forty thousand troops had been airlifted via the polar route. The theory worked. The shock of actual Soviet infantry troops in full battle dress, carrying live grenades and ammunition, appearing on the streets of American cities—and within a week, towns—was too much. It was a gamble, and it produced a quick checkmate. Why else would West Germany, Italy, France, Scandinavia, the Benelux countries, and all the rest of them have agreed so quickly to the invitations Moscow extended? Complete and unconditional capitulation."

Walters' next remark was a Parthian shot. "It was really very easy."

COMMUNICATIONS

VANDENBERG, EUGENE R.

#4076

(Extract, narrative entry)
INTERVIEW #32, 10:30 A.M.—12:00. *A Standard RPI-12 Memory Erase will be indicated for the above noted period. Positive reinforcing interviewer-trainee elements may remain vestigial, if they do not readily extinguish.*

—A. Walters, Dictaphoned

AT LUNCHTIME that Friday, Sorensen's bunk was bare, stripped of blankets, the footlocker empty, too. None of the other trainees knew anything about it. Vandenberg questioned the men in Sorensen's study group, but they could tell him nothing.

That afternoon he asked Alyosha, his political instructor.

"Doctor Sorensen?" Alyosha said. "Yes, of course I know him. A wonderful gentlemen—such a brilliant mind. He became ill this morning, with his interviewer."

"Ill?"

"His heart—a mild coronary," Alyosha said. "I was in Administration when they brought him in. Doctor Orlov examined him. He's been sent down to Santa Fe to the hospital."

Vandenberg frowned. "He seemed perfectly all right yesterday evening—we played chess in the dorm until lights out, and then talked for a while afterward."

"Oh, he wasn't a well man. He didn't like to talk about it."

Vandenberg did not answer, and Alyosha looked at him and

said, "A shame, really—our staff will miss him. He had a little difficulty adjusting to the pace here at first, but later we came to think of him as being the perfect example of what an intensive course like this can do for a man."

HE BEGAN the experiment the following Wednesday by deliberately restricting his food intake, convinced that the food and beverages served in the cafeteria provided the only means by which drugs could be administered.

Fein, the broker, had already begun his talk sessions, and he admonished Vandenberg for his lack of cooperation, pointing out that he was only making it tougher on himself.

"They can release me whenever they get tired of having me around," Vandenberg had said.

"You're crazy—by this time next month, I'll be home. And I'll bet you'll still be in basic indoctrination."

He knew Fein was right, yet he could not tolerate in himself the attitude they all expected of him. And the possibility of his and the others' food being doctored made him furious. If true, it would explain the atmosphere of relaxation, their amenability. Vandenberg knew himself well enough to realize he should have been bellicose— not with the veneer of disagreeability he was revealing to Walters, but with an overt, nasty, sullen intractability.

At lunch that Wednesday he stood in line with the others, holding the steel food tray, and passed along the counter, accepting regular servings of hamburger, mashed potatoes, bread, butter, coffee, cookies.

The men ladling out the food were trainees. During his K.P. assignments, he'd tried to verify Colonel Brushnevesko's statement that everyone—Soviet and American—ate the same food. Perhaps the menu for the Russians was the same, but it was cooked and served somewhere outside the fences. None of the interviewers had ever been seen eating in the trainees' cafeteria. The chief cook did not have the habit of sampling his cooking—he did drink coffee, but served himself and those trainees on K.P. that day from a five-gallon coffee maker kept on the stove, not from the big fifty-gallon job. Vandenberg noticed that the morning coffee he by now customarily fetched for Walters came from the same five-gallon pot.

He took his tray and found a vacant spot at a bench. Buttering a slice of bread, he ate it slowly, and then said to the man next to him, "You want any of this? I think I've got an abscessed tooth starting."

The man, a newcomer named Schwartz, looked like a heavy eater.

"Take the milk too—as cold as it is, if it hits my tooth . . ." Schwartz ladled most of Vandenberg's food onto his own tray. Presently, Vandenberg got up and placed his empty tray in the wash rack and left the cafeteria.

By four that afternoon, he was hungry. Alyosha had led the study group through the intricacies of the new international trade laws, and Vandenberg found it difficult to concentrate.

At five they returned to the dorm to wash up. Vandenberg was waiting for the bitch box to announce chow when Schwartz's group came in. The men with Schwartz were kidding him, and one said, "Lord, what a winner."

Schwartz grinned goodnaturedly and shook his head, and his companion said to the man in the next bunk, "You should have seen him—fell asleep three times."

Vandenberg walked over to them. "Hello, Schwartz—how's it going?"

"Okay." Schwartz stared at him, smiling. "How's the tooth?"

"Still hurts." Then he said, "Some of these classes get boring."

"I was pretty sleepy this afternoon."

"The instructor didn't chew you out for it, did he?"

"No—he didn't seem to mind."

"That's good," he said. "You want to stay on the right side of your instructor."

Conversations With Andy

"Gene, how'd you like to be dorm captain?" Walters asked. This was on Friday, two days after Vandenberg had stopped eating.

"I wouldn't," he said.

"Finney is due for discharge next week. Somebody has to take over his job."

"Why me?"

"I thought you'd be good at it," Walters said. "A transcript of

158

your military record finally came in—you never told me that you won a battlefield commission or that you'd gotten a DSC."

"You never asked. Besides, what the hell does a DSC have to do with this place?"

"I showed your service record to Brushnevesko. He agreed with me that you might make a good dorm captain. It could shorten your stay here."

"Tell you what," he said, "you get me a weekend pass, and I'll take the job."

"Be serious."

"I am. You ask me to be a hatchet man? Why? 'Shorten my stay.' I'm tired of that crap. Get me a weekend pass, and lend me a car and some clothes so I can go to town and get drunk and get laid, and I'll make that bunch in the dorm look like West Point cadets."

"Brushnevesko will probably call you up to the front office after inspection tomorrow morning—you can tell him yourself."

"Great. I haven't been outside the fences in over three months." Walters stared at him. "Say—what's eating you?"

"Nothing. I'm in a rotten mood."

"Why?"

"I've got a tooth that's bothering me."

"Report on sick call."

"I will, if it doesn't get better."

"Is there anything else?"

"I'm fed up with this place, and we don't seem to be getting anywhere."

"That's true," Walters said. "Maybe we can do something about it."

"Such as?"

"One of the psychiatrists and I were going over your interviews the other day," Walters said. "He agreed about your progress being —well, it isn't what it should be. We're scheduling you for a special session next week."

"A talk session?"

"Something like that."

"I wish you hadn't," he said.

"Don't let it worry you," Walters replied. "These specials aren't that bad. We'll have to get to the bottom of what's holding you up.

To be honest, when I first met you in July I figured you for a short-timer."

"Will they use a polygraph?"

"Don't worry about it."

"Scopolamine?"

"Something like it."

Vandenberg did not speak.

"Gene, don't get in a sweat—it's not as though you were going to come out a different man."

COMMUNICATIONS

VANDENBERG, EUGENE R.
#4076

(Extract, narrative entry)

Status Report-20271

RATING: *Unsatisfactory, with indications of major deterioration.*

I am scheduling a Level II neuropsychiatric interrogation for Tuesday, 10/5.

And, steno, please notify Dr. Orlov of the above, and advise him that the subject may not cooperate.

We'll want a blood morphology and urinalysis on this man after he's on the table, along with medication–level responses for the first twenty-four hours after he comes out of shock.

—A. Walters, Dictaphoned

IT HAD BEEN clouding up all that afternoon, with gray thunderheads moving in from the west, and around four o'clock it rained, so that the corrugated steel skins of the dorms shone wetly when the sun finally came out, and the neatly mown plots of grass between the buildings were a fresh, bright green. At five the men fell out for chow and then had a free hour before assembling again. The instructors had been showing an evening movie in the main study hall that week, and tonight it was Three's turn.

At supper he got away with it again, scarcely eating anything. Since Schwartz had almost passed out in class, he had not dared give his food away and had taken a chance on not being seen when he scraped his still-full tray into the garbage cans. A few men had asked him why he was not eating, and he told them about the tooth. Except for bread and butter and long drafts of cold water at the drinking fountain in the dorm, he had not eaten since Wednesday morning, and he could tell he was losing weight. The worst part was mealtime itself, having to sit there for fifteen or twenty minutes with the food-heavy tray before him, seeing the potatoes, the gravy, the thick slices of meat. He was in a murderous mood, which he blamed more on hunger than on the possibility that the drugs were clearing out of his system. His size and weight demanded bulk intake. He felt irritable and dizzy. His eyes were sensitive to light, and at night his legs cramped up on him.

After supper, back at the dorm, he went to the water fountain, drank, and then smoked several cigarettes. It began raining again. He knew his experiment was pointless. If they had scheduled him for a session, they'd learn—strapped on one of those porcelain tables in Administration, he would reveal everything. He wondered if they could make him forget it later.

The bitch box over the door came on with an announcement that slickers would be necessary when the time came to fall out for the film. There was a general stir as men went to their clothes racks and took down raingear.

At six they assembled in the rain, and by now there was thunder and lightning, and in the twilight he could see pools of water forming on the lawns. It was late in the season for rainstorms. Under the fatigue cap he wore, his glasses were spotted with drops of water. His mood, which had been bad enough in the cafeteria, grew worse.

Finney had them wait until Alyosha, accompanied by three guards, appeared. Then they moved out under the glare of the floodlights, the political instructor leading, the guards following at the rear, the men dogtrotting in a double column down the shining boardwalks in the pouring rain.

At the study hall they filed in and took seats, folding their wet slickers and placing them in their laps or on the floor at their feet, talking, lighting cigarettes, growing quiet when the lights were switched off and the film began, the sound of the music and narration coming thin and tinny from the box speakers on either side of the portable screen. The story was about the destruction of Great

161

Britain's missile sites, caused for the most part by Soviet subs that had massed off Dogger Bank for the attack of November 28, and Vandenberg, distracted by hunger, hot, perspiring in the stuffy room that smelled of wet and rubbery raingear, wished it were over. Halfway through the second reel, there was a sizzling clap of thunder, and the projector stopped; the power was out.

The men of Dorm Three sat there for seven or eight minutes, relighting cigarette stubs, the spurt of matches unnaturally bright in the darkness. One of the guards rolled up the shade on a window and opened it to let in fresh air. From where Vandenberg sat, he could see that the entire compound was dark. There was supposed to be an auxiliary power plant in the motor pool, and he wondered if they were having trouble starting it. Then, sitting there with the minutes slipping by, he began to understand that this was it, and the longer they waited there in the dark the surer he grew, thinking, if the power stays off, I can do it. It could be done in about ninety seconds.

He found that his hands were trembling; he felt nauseous. Sitting there, he told himself in a kind of endless, silent monologue that if the lights came on he would forget it but if they didn't, he might try it. If it looked all right, that is. It would have to look really good before he would try it.

A guard went out and came back with a flashlight. The white beam shone back and forth across the rows of faces. More time passed. Alyosha left, and then returned to announce that the film would be exhibited again tomorrow night: "You can go back to the dorm, and when the power comes back on begin cleaning for inspection tomorrow."

They went back out into the rain, forming a column again. Mel Finney gave them a right face, and they took off at a trot toward the dormitories, flanked by Alyosha and two guards, the beam of the one flashlight jogging and bouncing in the rain. As they turned a corner, Vandenberg—weak with fear, scarcely thinking now— muttered to the man beside him, "Damn—I'm losing my shoe," dropping out, gambling that no one would look around to see if he was still on the boardwalk, moving quickly now, getting into the doorway of one of the small interview buildings as the last of the formation, followed by the third guard, trotted past, the rain coming down, it seemed, even harder. He stood there a moment, listening to the pounding of feet on the boards grow fainter, wondering how long he had.

He thought, if it wasn't for those fools, I'd have until morning census. Alyosha won't take a roll call in this rain, but the minute the lights go back on some idiot is going to ask where the hell I am. That's as long as I'm going to get. The minute they realize I'm not with them, someone—Finney, probably—will use the bitch box.

With that he broke from the doorway into the rain, heading toward the north side of the camp, running blind in the darkness past the back of the cafeteria—a dim flash of lightning lit the sky just then, and he saw the neatly lined-up jerry cans on the back platform. He saw he was headed in the right direction—he'd get to the fence midway between two watchtowers, and he was thinking, if the lights go on I'll have to stop, and stop fast, because they'll spot me right away from the towers and they'll shoot.

Swearing, knowing that the odds of getting over both fences were bad, still running, his feet slapping into pools of water, he hit the inner fence hard and bounced back, stunned, his cap gone, eyeglasses knocked off. Seconds passed while he knelt, searching, fearing more than anything else that the power would go back on, scrabbling in the mud and water with both hands for the glasses, and then he found them, fingering the lenses quickly to see if the glass was intact—it was—and slipped them into the breast pocket of his coveralls, buttoning the flap, not even bothering to wipe them clean, because it was too dark to see anything, and now he thought, I can stop right now and walk back to the dorm—tell them I fell in a puddle. . . . They may suspect but they won't know for sure, or they'll find out when they put me through the session, but if I start over the fences, there's no coming back, I won't have the nerve to.

He chose the fences—clumsily hoisting himself up the twelve feet of inner chain link; going up was not too bad—that was easy compared to the barbed wire at the top, four strands, stapled to angle irons. The wire was bad; careless now and moving too fast, he fought it. His hands tore, the barbs cutting but not hurting at all, he was that tight, dangling from the three lowermost strands like a huge spider, finally hooking a leg over the fourth wire, hauling himself up and over and then falling into the no-man's-land walkway, leaving most of his ripped slicker and pieces of skin up in the wires. He crouched in the walkway, and then with two long steps he was across it and going up the outer fence, grunting with exhaustion as he scrambled up the chain link, moving quickly; but this time he almost did not make it over the outer fence's four strands, leaving more clothing and flesh in the wire, over now, and down the other side, his fingers clawing ineffectually at the mesh—the strength gone from them—and he could not brake his fall and landed heavily, the wind knocked from him, on the outside.

He rested a moment and then managed to rise, staggering, thinking that they, the security men, would have something to look at in the morning—the clothing and rubberized fabric caught in the barbs—they would know it had not been easy, and they'd know, too, that he'd hurt himself badly on the wire and would not be able to travel far.

He tried to run but couldn't, everything in him so used up that even walking was agonizing, trying to see a little in the rain and darkness, beyond caring now if the lights came on or stayed off, or if they saw him and opened fire, limping slowly up the cleared slopes north of the compound to where the first stands of spruce began, and then he was among the trees, concealed now from the blacked-out camp below him, still panting but a little stronger now, and taking comfort in the knowledge that the rain was washing out his tracks, so that by dawn the best bloodhound in New Mexico wouldn't be able to track him twenty yards.

Later, high on one of the slopes, he paused on a deer trail, took the filthy glasses out of his breast pocket, wiped them against his sleeve, and slipped them on. The rain was still coming down and it was dark and cold, but the glasses made him feel complete, and he thought, now let them find me.

3
Free

THE FIRST DAYS were the worst.

That morning at daybreak he stopped at a stream and carefully soaked and washed his cuts, clenching his teeth as he scrubbed the proud flesh, spreading open the long, jagged tears in his skin so that they were exposed to the icy water, knowing that if the wounds festered the accompanying fever would leave him helpless. The water he drank eased his hunger pangs, but he was so sore he could hardly walk. He judged he was only about a mile from the compound.

At noon, when the sky finally cleared, he was farther up in the mountains but too exhausted to go on. He stopped at an outcropping of rock. At its base a natural alcove took in the sun, and he curled up in this and slept, resting against the warm stone, scarcely stirring until late in the afternoon when the alcove grew shadowy. The sleep helped. He got up, stretched, still feeling pain, and then moved on again. A short time later, he found a fruiting of *A. campestris,* or meadow mushroom, and ate several dozen. At dusk he struck a trail that looked familiar, and followed it, circling to the east and south of the compound, heading for lower elevations.

TWO DAYS PASSED. He found more mushrooms, and some wild garlic and asparagus. By now his stomach had shrunk, and he was having dizzy spells.

He walked through the mountains slowly and with apprehension, knowing they would be searching for him, always heading in a southerly direction. On the third day he reached the Pecos River, a few miles above Terrero.

He stayed on the high slopes of the valley, sticking to deer trails that meandered among the heavy scrub oak. The river was far below him, and the road, too, a serpentine dirt lane. Summer cabins, closed since the Occupation, were what he was looking for. There had been four in the last half mile.

At sunset he descended to the river and broke open the back door of one cabin, but the owners had taken everything. There was not a can of food on the shelves in the musty-smelling kitchen, and the refrigerator had been turned off and the door propped open. In a closet he found a woolen work jacket—there was a large rip in one sleeve, but the garment fit, and he took it, along with two worn-out blankets covered with dog hair. He left, not bothering to close the cabin's door. It was dark now—the days were growing shorter—but he kept well back from the road that paralleled the river, moving among the willows and thick rushes that grew along the banks. Years ago he would have worried about watchdogs, but now the whole stretch of river-front lots was silent and deserted.

The next cabin was also empty, but the third try was better. He broke out a window with a rock, not caring how much noise he made, climbed inside and went from room to room, groping in the dark with outstretched hands. He found a small padlocked store-room off the kitchen, and managed to kick the door loose. Inside, he found canned goods, pots, pans, matches, candles—he lit one immediately—half a carton of stale Chesterfields, an eiderdown sleeping bag, work clothing, two fly rods, and, in the corner, wrapped in a scrap of cloth, a remodeled Springfield sporter with a telescopic sight.

Standing in the middle of the small pantry, inspecting the rifle, he wondered why the owner had never returned for the weapon. He set it down, opened a can of Spam, and scooped out the contents with his fingers, relishing the rich, fatty meat. When the can was empty, he lit a cigarette and examined the bore of the rifle. The Springfield was an oddity—a man might close up a summer cabin and leave a little food behind, but not an expensive weapon. On a storage shelf, he found a cardboard box that contained five cartons of surplus military ammunition.

He wasn't sure he wanted the rifle. He hated the compound, but if it came to a confrontation he did not know if he could shoot a man, Russian or otherwise, no matter what the circumstances. The war had been different. I don't want any trouble, he thought. If they'll just leave me alone, I swear I won't bother anyone. But he knew better, and thought again, it won't work that

168

way. You say you won't bother them—the way the longhairs used to preach peace, but you will, friend, exactly the way the long-haired kids bugged the establishment. They won't let it work out that way. You went over the fences, and they're not going to forget it. If you turn yourself in, they'll ship you right back to Cowles. They may turn you loose, but it won't make any difference. You'll be left behind, stored on reels of tape. Everything's on their side. They'll be waiting for you with open arms.

He felt bitterness over the way his life had gone—the marriages, the loneliness, all of it—he felt baffled, outwitted. And now? He had meant it when he'd told Andy Walters that all he wanted was to be left alone, but somehow, the way he wanted it, on his terms, it seemed like wanting the world. It was too much to ask, and they weren't going to let him have it, and what he feared most now was the image of himself as he'd seen others, nearly thirty years earlier, in the war, the human debris of Heurtgen Forest, headless, limbless, torsos burst asunder, the green-and-gray flesh putrefying slowly with the thawing snows.

Taking matches, he went into the kitchen, checking the butane range, wishing he dared turn on the light. The stove worked, and he lit all four burners, went back to the storeroom and selected a large can of pork and beans and a skillet. He opened the can and emptied it into the skillet on the stove; when the beans were hot, he sat down at the table and ate them directly from the pan in the faint blue light of the burners. When he finished, he lit another cigarette, feeling sleepy.

He checked the rest of the cabin without haste, finding more things he could use: a razor, a flashlight, first-aid ointment. He stacked it all on the kitchen table, packing the canned food into a cardboard box, planning to carry everything a quarter of a mile up the ridge above the river, where he could make a cache. It was slow work. By midnight he had buried most of the canned goods at the base of a tall spruce, going to some trouble doubling back and forth on his tracks; he still feared dogs, and knew he'd have trouble if they brought in bloodhounds.

He left the sleeping bag and several days' supply of food for the last trip. When he got back to the cabin, he went through it once more. He rolled the clothing and a ration of food into the eider bag, tied the ends of the roll with scrap wire, and then made a carry-ing loop so that he could sling it across his back. He stood there a moment longer and then went into the storeroom and got the rifle, filling the pockets of the woolen jacket with boxes of cartridges. Then he turned off the stove burners, blew out the candle, and left. At the river, he stepped into the shallows and waded upstream for several hundred yards.

COMMUNICATIONS

The *Santa Fe Journal-News,* Santa Fe, N.M.

PECOS BREAK-INS BLAMED ON ESCAPEE

Oct. 5th. A rash of housebreakings in the Pecos-Terrero area are believed to have been committed by Eugene R. Vandenberg, 50, the Santa Fe Sheriff's Department said Tuesday.

Vandenberg, who escaped last week from Cowles Rehabilitation and Training Center, north of Pecos, is known to be a political extremist. His behavior at the training center was described as excellent, and he was to have appeared before a review board for possible release next month.

Burglarized were three summer cabins owned by H. A. Harris, Houston, Tex.; E. L. Graves, Austin, Tex.; and R. P. Tomlinson, Santa Fe, N.M. A full report is being delayed until the owners can be contacted. The burglaries were discovered late Monday by District Game Warden Eduardo Salazar, 29, an employee of the Game and Fish Department.

THEY BROUGHT in dogs two days later, and he watched them for the better part of an afternoon from a crest of rimrock, half a mile off. He had stayed in the vicinity, resting and letting his cuts heal. They had not become infected, but they were still tender, and the thick scabs broke easily. He had begun to think it might be best to stay along the river—there were scores of summer cabins to choose from—when he heard the dogs.

Earlier that afternoon he had watched two sedans and an Occupation truck drive up and park at one of the cabins he'd ransacked. Later a pickup truck arrived with the hounds, and the sound of their baying carried faintly to where he watched. The men, he knew, would be finding heel marks that showed the special V-cleft.

Within half an hour, they'd examined the vandalized cabins. He heard the hounds working his trail, and a few minutes later spotted them, a pair of big black-and-tans on long leashes, moving slowly up the far slope, followed by the men. They ranged back and forth through the scrub for over an hour, tracing out different trails he'd walked over. He did not know hounds, but it had not rained since the night of his escape, and the dogs sounded to him as though they were working a strong scent. He stayed where he was and waited.

The dogs and men disappeared among the trees, and then he caught sight of them again, higher up, near the big spruce he'd chosen for the cache. Vandenberg was not concerned now about whether they would find the buried food. He was gambling on having the hounds strike the main trail he'd made on this three-day trek that had started north of Cowles. If the dogs hit that, the men with them would have a long walk, all of it in the wrong direction. It would end at the rocky alcove he'd slept in the first afternoon, or they might be able to follow it a mile or two farther, to where he'd washed in the stream that morning.

He watched the tiny figures on the bluff across the valley. The late afternoon sun was behind him, and they were easy to pick out. The hounds were still baying, and he knew that the men with them were working along the top of the bluff, heading north. He saw them among the trees two or three more times. The baying grew fainter, but he heard them, from time to time, for another quarter of an hour, the sound always from the north, on the trail back toward Cowles.

COMMUNICATIONS

The *Santa Fe Journal-News,* Santa Fe, N.M.

ESCAPEE BELIEVED ARMED

UPI—Oct. 8th. Eugene R. Vandenberg, 50, an inmate who walked away from the Cowles Rehabilitation and Training Center, north of Pecos, is believed armed, State Police Chief E. W. Freeman said Friday.

Vandenberg, arrested last July and charged with seditious activities, had been given a psychiatric examination, which confirmed severe psychological deviations in his personality. He escaped from the minimum security training center on Oct. 1, during a severe storm that knocked out electrical power in the Pecos Valley.

Last Tuesday, a series of thefts in summer cottages along the Pecos River were investigated by members of the Santa Fe Sheriff's Department and USSRAOOUSA CIC.

The owner of one cottage, Mrs. H. A. Harris, of Houston, Tex., told authorities her late husband, Henry A. Harris, a retired building contractor, may have neglected to turn in one or more firearms he had owned and which may have been left at the cottage. Harris died last year after a protracted illness. A check is being conducted at the Houston offices of the Ministry for Public Safety to see if Harris's name is listed on rosters of confiscated weapons. Harris's widow stated that they had left a supply of canned food and clothing in the cottage.

Bloodhounds from the State Penitentiary in Santa Fe were enlisted in the search of the surrounding area. A detachment of USSRAOOUSA mounted cavalry may be called in to assist in the manhunt.

Fingerprints were obtained from all three cottages and have been forwarded to the Bureau for National Security in Washington.

Vandenberg is believed to be still in the Pecos area, and is described as husky, about 6'4", ruddy complexioned, wearing spectacles. State Police Chief Freeman emphasized that Vandenberg, an artist, had not been considered dangerous despite emotional disturbances.

MIDWAY BETWEEN PECOS and Terrero there was a general store called Pando's that in years past had done a fair business supplying sportsmen with liquor and various sundries. Outside, a large machine dispensed ice at fifty cents a block, which, packed in polystyrene carriers, would last a party of hunters a weekend. One night less than two weeks after he had escaped, Vandenberg pried open a rear window of the store. During that time he had broken into four more cabins along the river but had found almost nothing. On this night, he had left the rifle and sleeping bag a half mile up the road in a clump of bushes. A gibbous moon shone through scattered black clouds.

Inside, he worked quickly, moving up and down the narrow aisles, striking matches from time to time. He located an empty box and filled it with food. In a corner he found what he needed most, boxed pairs of rubberized shoe-pacs, with heavy climbing cleats. Still striking matches, he found a pair of size twelves and changed into them, leaving the work shoes that had been issued to him at Cowles. At the far end of the aisle was a clip-on rack of *carne seca,* and this was valuable because of its light weight and high food value; he helped himself to a dozen large packages. He found cigarettes, took a carton; on impulse, he tossed a pair of cheap Japanese-made binoculars into the box, and up by the cash register, where the wine and liquor was displayed, he took down a fifth of Bellows, twisted off the cap, drank several times, and then slipped the bottle into the box. There were a dozen other things he could have used—most of all he wanted a packrack. Last, he chose a sheath knife and a belt axe.

Suddenly the lights came on, and he saw a heavyset man wearing trousers and an undershirt, standing in a doorway. The man was barefooted and had obviously been asleep in the quarters adjoining the store. Squinting at Vandenberg, he spoke in Spanish and moved toward him. Then he stopped and said in English, "What the hell you want?"

"Go back inside," he said.

The man swore and came toward him, moving quickly. Without altering his stride, he reached under a counter and brought up a butcher knife. Vandenberg grabbed the belt axe and swung as the man rushed at him.

From the adjoining quarters a woman's voice called, "Armando —qué pasa?"

COMMUNICATIONS

The *Santa Fe Journal-News,* Santa Fe, N.M.

STORE OWNER ASSAULTED

UPI—Oct. 21st. Armando Ulibarri, 46, owner of Pando's General Store, north of Pecos, N.M., was admitted to St. Vincent's Hospital in Santa Fe early Thursday morning, suffering from severe lacera-

tions of the face and scalp, received when he grappled with a thief who had broken into the store.

More than sixty stitches were required to close head wounds received by Ulibarri, whose condition was described as fair. Santa Fe Sheriff's Department officials said that Ulibarri was not as yet able to give a formal statement on what had occurred. They added that a tentative identification of the assailant had been made by the store owner from city police photographs.

The *Santa Fe Journal-News*, Santa Fe, N.M.

ESCAPEE NAMED ASSAILANT

UPI— Oct. 22nd. Eugene R. Vandenberg, 50, an emotionally disturbed political deviationist who escaped three weeks ago from Cowles Rehabilitation Center of Pecos, N.M., was identified today by Armando Ulibarri, 46, owner of Pando's General Store, as the man who assaulted him.

Early yesterday afternoon, Ulibarri picked out a mug shot of Vandenberg without hesitation. Vandenberg, a local portrait artist, is known to be at large in the Pecos area.

"There is no doubt that this is the man," Ulibarri stated. He said he surprised a thief about 2 A.M. Oct. 21 in his store. "I heard noises," Ulibarri told police. "I went in and turned on the lights. At first I thought it was kids."

Pando's General Store has been burglarized five times in the past four years. Ulibarri and his wife Macedonia live in an adjoining apartment.

"It was a big guy," Ulibarri said. "For a second, we just stared at each other. I had a knife I keep under the counter. But then he began hitting me with a small axe."

State Trooper E. B. Miller emphasized the brutality of the act. "Whoever did this is dangerous," he pointed out.

A hunt has been on since Oct. 2 for Vandenberg, who escaped from the training camp during an electrical storm. He was considered a model trainee, authorities said. Vandenberg was due to appear before a review board within a month, Col. A. R. Brushnevesko, commandant of the training center, said.

A mounted platoon of the 17th Reconnaissance Squadron (USSRAOOUSA), stationed at Glorieta Assembly, and about eleven members of the Santa Fe Mounted Sheriff's Posse, under the direction of Deputy Sam Becker, are combing trails and logging roads between Pecos and Terrero for signs of the escapee. Vandenberg was arrested on July 23 for sedition.

IN A NARROW RAVINE, a quarter of a mile off the road below Holy Ghost Canyon, Vandenberg sat at a U.S. Forest Service picnic table, drinking bourbon. The table and its benches had been bolted together out of heavy spruce logs split lengthwise and stained dark brown. A sign nailed to a nearby tree warned picnickers against littering, and a green-painted fifty-five-gallon drum had been placed beside the tree for garbage. He was on one of the hiking trails that wandered through the woods in this part of the forest. There were no hikers anymore, but the campsites and their tables and crude native-rock fireplaces would last for years, longer than the trails themselves, which were already becoming blocked in places by underbrush.

He had built a small fire, drunkenly fumbling in the dark for pieces of deadwood. Part of the nonperishable supplies he'd stolen, including canned goods, had been cached in a pile of rocks not far from the general store. It had taken several hours of walking to return this far north, and the sky that showed through the dark trees above him was already turning light. It was cold and damp, and his breath condensed in streams of milky vapor.

He had eaten two packages of *carne seca,* and now he drank again from the bottle and opened a fresh pack of cigarettes, reminding himself that when the bourbon was gone he would have to save the bottle for a canteen.

The fire was warm, and his feet felt comfortable in the new shoe-pacs. He'd been lucky with those; shoe sizes in this part of the country seldom ran above a nine or a ten because the Spanish had small feet.

He was drunk by now and did not care. Later he would have a thumping hangover, and he didn't care about that either. Nor was he especially worried over what he had done to the store owner, whom he had left on his hands and knees in a welter of blood. With an air of indulgence, he unscrewed the cap from the bourbon and drank again.

Shortly before he passed out—it was light, by then—he heard the sounds of a vehicle driving along the road below. He listened, waiting to hear if it would stop, but the sound of the motor continued, growing fainter. It was headed south, perhaps the morning courier from the compound. Or perhaps it was a patrol, searching for him. They'd be after him in earnest after what had happened in the store. Still listening, he raised his head in the direction of the vehicle's sound and said aloud, "Piss on all of you."

COMMUNICATIONS

The *Santa Fe Journal-News*, Santa Fe, N.M.

OCCUPATION JEFE DENIES LAXNESS

Santa Fe, Oct. 25th. Lt. Gen. S. M. Mischenkovitch, Assistant Commandant, 32nd District, USSRAOOUSA, categorically denied laxness on the part of Occupation personnel in the Oct. 1 escape of Eugene R. Vandenberg, 50, wanted on charges ranging from sedition to felonious assault. Vandenberg is believed armed, and is considered dangerous by the authorities.

"Until he escaped, we had no reason to believe Vandenberg could not be rehabilitated," Gen. Mischenkovitch said in a prepared statement. "He was well-liked by both his fellow trainees and staff personnel."

Vandenberg, a painter, is still at large, and is believed hiding in the Pecos Wilderness. He is the focus of a manhunt encompassing several thousand square miles. Vandenberg is known to be an expert woodsman and outdoorsman.

"As a trainee, Vandenberg was not subject to maximum security," Gen. Mischenkovitch said. "None of the Cowles trainees is. The camp is operated on an honor system basis."

Vandenberg was identified earlier this week as the person who assaulted a store owner, Armando Ulibarri, 46, of Pecos. Ulibarri's condition was described by St. Vincent's Hospital as satisfactory.

A CLEAR TRAIL suitable for both horses and men strikes north from Cowles for three miles, following Panchuela Creek, and then angles west at the junction of Panchuela and Cave Creeks, following the latter for several more miles to crest finally at a ridge, on the other side of which lies Horsethief Meadows. East of the meadows is Horsethief Canyon, a six-mile-long trough impossible for a horse and barely passable for a man on foot; two other trails head west and north for several more miles, to Beatty's Cabin and Pecos Baldy respectively. Horses can be used on these trails but are useless off them because of the dense tangle of underbrush and fallen, rotting trees; it is here, at altitudes of nine thousand feet or more, that the wilderness begins.

He returned to it on foot the day after he'd broken into the store, hung over and bearing his supplies on a crudely constructed packboard he had fashioned of aspen saplings lashed together with wire. In the bedroll he had a dozen packages of dried apricots and other fruit, chocolate, coffee, powdered milk, oatmeal, and the rest of the *carne seca*. During the day, when it was warm, he tied the woolen jacket to the bedroll. He was still sick from the bourbon he had drunk, but the three-months-long stay at Cowles had built him up. Except for his wind, which was poor from smoking, he was in good condition, and, more important, he knew how to pace himself. It was Vandenberg's opinion that unless he grew careless, he could in the next few weeks outwalk them all.

COMMUNICATIONS

SPECIAL: TO KOAT-TV, KGGM-TV, KOB-TV—EVENING REPORT

MANHUNT WIDENS.

ADDITIONAL MOUNTED PATROLS OF THE 17TH RECONNAISSANCE SQUADRON FANNED OUT NORTH AND EAST OF TERRERO, N.M., THURSDAY IN THE WIDENING MANHUNT FOR EUGENE R. VANDENBERG, 50, A MENTALLY DISTURBED PATIENT WHO ESCAPED FROM A TRAINING CENTER ON OCT. 1.

VANDENBERG IS BELIEVED ARMED AND IS CONSIDERED DANGEROUS. ABOUT EIGHTY-FIVE MEN, INCLUDING MEMBERS OF THE SANTA FE MOUNTED SHERIFF'S POSSE, ARE INVOLVED IN THE SEARCH, AND A NUMBER OF FOUR-WHEEL-DRIVE VEHICLES FROM THE NEW MEXICO SEARCH AND RESCUE ASSOCIATION HAVE ALSO BEEN ASSIGNED

TO THE AREA. VANDENBERG IS KNOWN TO BE AN EXPERT OUTDOORS-
MAN. AUTHORITIES BELIEVE THEY HAVE HIM CONTAINED IN AN AREA
ROUGHLY TEN BY FIFTEEN MILES. TWO HELICOPTERS FROM KIRT-
LAND AIR FORCE BASE ARE SCHEDULED TO JOIN THE SEARCH FRIDAY.

HE MADE CAMP in Horsethief Meadows and rested for two days, but on the third he was spotted by five riders who came over the trail from Cave Creek. He heard the sounds of their horses while they were still some distance up the slope. By the time the men on horseback rode out of the trees and into a grassy park, Vandenberg had the pack on his back and was trotting for the opening of Horsethief Canyon. One of the mounted men shouted at him, and then someone fired, the sound of the rifle shot echoing back and forth from the rocky ridges above, but the range was too far— seven, maybe eight hundred yards. They fired several more rounds before he disappeared into the tree-filled canyon. There the horses would be useless, and he doubted that they would follow him very far on foot.

An hour later he stopped, climbed part way up the side of the canyon, and waited to see if they were behind him. He had the Springfield loaded, but he was still not sure if he would use it. He waited. No one was following him. Then, because he assumed the riders would have walkie-talkies and would probably try to get more men at the mouth of the canyon, five miles below him, he climbed to the top of the ridge. As he neared the rimrock he heard the helicopter, its engines making a raw, chugging sound as it cruised slowly above the canyon, and then a minute later the sound of the jets. He saw them, two swept-wing MIG-21A's, with pods beneath their wings.

Moments later, they circled at the mouth of the canyon and then dove into it, making three passes, the sounds of their guns crashing thunderously. For a moment Vandenberg thought the jets were after the five riders who'd fired at him, and then, astonished, he realized they were after him.

COMMUNICATIONS

The *Santa Fe Journal-News,* Santa Fe, N.M.

DRAGNET TIGHTENS

UPI—Oct. 29. Radio reports received Friday at 17th Reconnaissance Squadron Headquarters at Glorieta Assembly, N.M., said that Eugene R. Vandenberg, 50, wanted for sedition, escape from confinement, and felonious assault, was cornered in a narrow canyon about thirty miles north of Pecos.

Vandenberg, who escaped on Oct. 1 from a training camp near Cowles, N.M., has eluded authorities for over three weeks by doubling back and forth on his own trail in the nearly impenetrable Pecos Wilderness area. Most of the search has been restricted to a 250-square-mile area of the mountainous country.

Vandenberg, who is described as being armed and dangerous, was sighted by a detachment of Soviet mounted cavalry around 11 A.M. Friday. Shots were exchanged, but it is not clear yet whether the wanted man was wounded. He was seen heading into a narrow box canyon, which was later strafed by two jets from Kirtland Air Force Base. The jets were directed by radio from the ground and from a nearby helicopter. The planes were armed with napalm, but it was not used because of the unusual dryness of the forest at this time of year.

The *Santa Fe Journal-News,* Santa Fe, N.M.

PAGOSA SPRINGS, Colo., Nov. 5th. (AP) A hitchhiker fitting the description of Eugene R. Vandenberg, 50, wanted for sedition and felonious assault, was arrested and released here Tuesday.

The man, who carried papers identifying him as Vernon W. Lemoine, 52, of Baton Rouge, La., was picked up by Pagosa Springs city police who spotted him standing beside a road sign on U.S. 84. Lemoine objected to accompanying the officers, and a brief scuffle ensued. He was later treated at Pagosa Springs General Hospital for minor bruises and lacerations. Lemoine described himself as a migratory worker, and said he was on his way back to Louisiana after completing seasonal agricultural jobs in California and Arizona.

NORTH OF LOWER COLONIAS, miles past the sawmill, on a dirt road that eventually peters out in the high hills, an old man was walking, not far from a defunct fishing resort called Honeyboy Haven. The fishing spot was mainly a series of large, spring-fed ponds, which at one time had been planted with rainbows. Less than a mile past Honeyboy lay the national forest, and an hour earlier three riders had come down out of the woods. They wore faun-colored Stetsons and gabardine shirts and trousers, tailored so that there was a suggestion of both military and Western styling. Tied to their saddles were rifles in engraved leather scabbards. Lashed to the back of one of the saddles was a small transceiver.

They had stopped for a break, dismounting beside a wooden drift fence, lighting cigarettes and talking. One of the men said, "Howard, I think that pilot's got us off on a wild goose chase."

"Sure looks like it."

Earlier a Piper Cub belonging to the local civil defense unit had radioed that it had spotted a man north of Honeyboy's ponds, and the three riders had been dispatched from the main posse to check out the report.

Suddenly the third man stood up straighter, peering across the grassy flats of the fishing resort. He flipped his cigarette over the topmost rail of the drift fence and said softly, "By Christ! Howard, look there."

The others looked and saw the man. He was about two hundred and fifty yards off, coming out of the trees and onto the flats, diagonally, to the east. All three went quickly to their horses and slid the rifles from their scabbards. The weapons were expensive sporting models, with engraved and carved receivers—bolt-actions, with low-mounted telescopic sights. The one named Howard told the others, "All right, now, let's just take it easy."

"Somebody had to find him," the first man said. He eased a round into the chamber of his rifle. "I never thought it'd be us though."

"Ben, you just take it easy," Howard said. "What d'you think the range is?"

"I'd say three hundred," the third man said. "Why, hell, that's three hundred, easy. That's a long shot."

Howard went over to the drift fence, got down on one knee, and slid his rifle forward between the bars. The other two did the same, and he said, "Ben, with that .264, you got the best chance."

"She'll shoot flat to four hundred," Ben replied.

"Well now, let's not go getting all bent out of shape," Howard said. "I want you to listen. We want to get him, and get him fast. What I'm goin' to do is yell at him to halt. If he doesn't stop, I want you to place a shot near him, to let him know we mean business. Don't hit him though—Ben, you understand?"

"Sure."

"If he doesn't stand for us, we all three open fire," Howard said. He spoke in a leisurely, matter-of-fact tone. The man they were watching was halfway across the flats by now, with the nearest cover more than a hundred yards off, and they knew they had him.

Howard looked at his companions. "Set?"

They nodded, and he called loudly, "Hey, there! Stand where you are."

The man in the field kept walking.

Howard shouted again. When there was no response, he said, "All right, Ben."

Ben moved his cheek a shade farther forward on the comb of the stock, setting himself, and said, "I'm going to lay this one right at his feet. About a yard in front of him. Y'all watch."

Several seconds passed, and then the Magnum rifle crashed; the 130-grain, ogive-spired, copper-jacketed pellet left the muzzle at close to four thousand feet a second, and when it struck the ground in front of the walking man, almost exactly where Ben had predicted it would hit, it was still going fast enough to disintegrate, exploding a geyser of dirt and pebbles into the air. The man leaped as though he himself had been hit, and then began running. Howard looked up from his telescopic sight and shouted once more for the man to halt, and then said, "Okay, boys."

COMMUNICATIONS

SPECIAL: TO KOAT-TV, KGGM-TV, KOB-TV—NIGHTCAP NEWS

NOV. 6TH. A TRAGIC ACCIDENT OCCURRED TODAY WITH THE DEATH OF A PECOS RANCH HAND, SEVERINO VIGIL, 63, WHO WAS MISTAKEN FOR ESCAPED PSYCHOTIC EUGENE R. VANDENBERG, BY MOUNTED PATROLS HIGH IN THE PECOS WILDERNESS.

VIGIL, WHO WAS ON FOOT, WAS APPARENTLY SEARCHING FOR STRAYED CATTLE ON THE T. P. WILLIAMS RANCH, WHERE HE WAS EMPLOYED. HE WAS SPOTTED BY MEMBERS OF THE SANTA FE MOUNTED SHERIFF'S POSSE, WHO WERE IN THE AREA UNDER DIRECTION OF A CIVIL AIR PATROL OBSERVATION PLANE THAT HAD EARLIER REPORTED SEEING A MAN.

VANDENBERG, WHO ESCAPED FROM CONFINEMENT ON OCT. 1, IS KNOWN TO BE ARMED AND IS CONSIDERED EXTREMELY DANGEROUS. AN INTENSIVE MANHUNT HAS BEEN IN PROGRESS FOR THE PAST TWO WEEKS, BUT VANDENBERG, WHO IS SAID TO BE AN EXPERT OUTDOORSMAN, HAS SO FAR ELUDED CAPTURE.

THE ACCIDENT OCCURRED ABOUT 11 A.M. THIS MORNING. ACCORDING TO DEPUTY HOWARD V. MILLER OF THE SHERIFF'S POSSE, VIGIL IGNORED REPEATED ORDERS TO HALT, AND THEN BEGAN RUNNING AFTER A SERIES OF WARNING SHOTS HAD BEEN FIRED. VIGIL WAS STRUCK THREE TIMES. THE TRAGIC PART OF THE ACCIDENT, CONFIRMED LATER BY THE RANCHHAND'S WIFE EDUVIGEN, WAS THAT VIGIL WAS HARD OF HEARING AND CUSTOMARILY WORE A HEARING AID. SHE SAID THAT WHEN HE WORKED, HOWEVER, HE OFTEN DID NOT WEAR THE DEVICE. AN INVESTIGATION IS PENDING.

HE WONDERED HOW much longer the good weather was going to hold. By now there should have been snow at the higher elevations.

He knew that a storm would stop the search. In deep snow, horses would be useless, and ski- and snow-vehicles would be restricted to the main trails. He could recall only one man in Santa Fe, an engineer, who really knew anything about living outdoors during the winter at elevations above ten thousand, where conditions were arctic. The man had been good at it, and had taken groups of youngsters out above the timberline for weekends in December and January, without tents, carrying only food, clothing, and sheets of polyethylene in which to wrap their sleeping bags.

Winter would be hard on him, too. He'd been on winter deer hunts, and had once been stranded for three days in a December blizzard in the Jemez, near Regina, but that had been three days, not three months. He still remembered how good a hot shower had felt when he and the people he was with had finally got out of the mountains.

He thought again of Terry. He could hide at her house for a few days, and rest and make plans—provided, that is, she let him in.

THAT SATURDAY NIGHT they spoke about him in the Montana Bar, Hugh and Phil and some of the others who knew him. The temperature was down to freezing, and later Abilene Tixier came in, his cheeks ruddy with cold.

The bar talk had to do with how long he could avoid capture. Nikos drew a beer for Tixier, and asked, "What do you think, Abilene? You and him were friends."

"Any day, now," Tixier said, drinking. "He can't last much longer."

"He may be in Mexico by now," Phil Gibbs said.

"How's he going to get there?" Tixier demanded. "Fly now, pay later?"

"He might make it up there—he knows the country," Hugh Rogers said.

"He's a dude," Tixier said. "Hell, I've seen Gene Vandenberg lose himself half a mile from camp. He's got the worst sense of direction I ever seen in a man."

Nikos thought about this. "He'll probably turn himself in."

"He will if he's smart," Tixier said. "Else he'll get himself killed. I'd say this—we got about another week of warm weather. Then the goddamned bottom'll fall out of the thermometer. I've seen Indian summer hold on like this—hardly any frost at night, and warm in the daytime. You get to thinking there ain't going to be any winter at all. And then"—Tixier snapped his fingers—"first deep snow, Gene'll freeze his nuts off and come running down—if he can find his way, that is."

The Greek liked gambling. He said now, "Let's make a pool." Between serving other customers, he drew on a sheet of cardboard a calendar for November and December, ruling the days off in small boxes. "This is November 8th. Take your pick, any time after the 9th. Two bits a throw. Write your names in the boxes you pick." Nikos himself took the last four days in November. Tixier chose the 18th, 19th, and 20th of November. Hugh Rogers, on impulse, chose Christmas Day. Gibbs, who was broke, went on the cuff for December 7th and 8th.

Nikos went up and down the length of the bar with the sheet. Seventeen or eighteen more chances were sold to customers, some of whom knew Vandenberg, some of whom had only heard of him. By midnight, almost all the boxes were filled. Nikos propped the calendar on top of the cash register. Across the top he had printed the legend:

E.R.V.—HOW LONG?

AT DUSK he would stop and make camp in as concealed a spot as possible, so that the light of the small fire he built would only be seen a short distance. The *carne seca* was gone by now, but there were still several boxes of dried fruit and the tin of cocoa. He was filthy and unshaven, his hands and fingernails caked with dirt, a half-inch of stubble matting his cheeks.

Vandenberg squatted beside the fire, tending it with twigs, a blanket draped like a cowl over his head and shoulders. Two days ago they'd found his trail and had stayed with it. After eating, he planned to move on in the dark.

Yesterday they had been so close he had heard the sounds of their horses, the thudding of hooves against rocks carrying through the woods to where he lay hidden. He had walked last night, trying to put distance between himself and them.

At dawn this morning, he'd seen their campfire in the valley he had crossed in the night, a gray tendril of smoke rising undisturbed for a thousand feet above the forest, until it met a cold layer of air that trapped it and spread the smoke in a fine, delicate band of haze that hung unmoving over the valley.

Now, after drinking several cups of cocoa, he moved on. He was exhausted; the last three weeks in the forest had hardened him, but this pace was too much. Moving slowly he followed a deer trail until late that night, when he stopped again. He had covered perhaps three more miles.

He made camp at the base of a high ledge of rock. Below the ledge it was boggy, and Vandenberg discovered a shallow, spring-fed pond of clear water. He built another small fire and heated a can of water for coffee. He drank this and had a cigarette. Then he spread out the sleeping bag, lay down on it fully dressed, and drew it around himself.

He slept for almost seven hours, waking shortly before six, with the sky in the east already blue. He sat up quickly, yawning and shivering in the cold, his shoulders hunched, angry at having slept so late. After urinating against a nearby tree, he lit another cigarette and rolled up his sleeping gear. When he finished the cigarette he went down to the pool and drank, rinsing his mouth, the water so cold it made his teeth ache, finally removing his spectacles and splashing water on his face. He stood up, wiped his face on the sleeve of his jacket, and put the glasses back on; he was still tired. As he went back to where he'd left his gear he wondered if the smoke from their fire would again be visible.

On the north side of the high ledge there was easy footing, and taking the rifle he climbed to the top until he was perhaps twenty feet above his sleeping bag. He crouched there a minute, waiting for his breathing to slow, and this probably saved his life, for the figure of a small man appeared below him, and Vandenberg stayed perfectly still, too frightened to move.

He watched as the man came closer, and then he began to understand. It was an Indian, he was almost sure. The face and head were hidden by a broad-brimmed hat, but the man's hands, holding a Winchester high and ready, were coppery brown, a color you rarely found among the Spanish, no matter how much time they spent outdoors. That, he understood, was how they'd stuck so close the past two days. It had not been the posse but an Indian the Occupation had hired to track him. He was still frightened as the little man moved closer, and then he saw what the Indian intended doing.

The man was coming around the base of the ledge, one slow step at a time, catlike, placing his feet with enormous stealth and care, the Winchester still held chest-high, hammer at full cock, right forefinger on the trigger. The Indian meant to kill him, and with that, Vandenberg moved the Springfield around, easing the safety off—it gave a faint click, and the Indian stopped, his Winchester held straight out now, hearing it or perhaps merely sensing something, but unable for a few seconds to pinpoint the direction the sound came from. He started to make a half turn to look behind him, and at that moment Vandenberg shot him once through the back of the head, and before the echoes had died he had scrambled off the ledge and was running for his gear, ignoring the wildly convulsing body less than five yards from his packboard.

He grabbed the pack and began trotting up the trail, glancing once at the man, who lay face down, the loaded Winchester beneath him. He saw that it was, in fact, an Indian. In striking, the shot had knocked the broad-brimmed hat flying, and had created an enormous wound, and blood was still pouring from the mouth, nose, and ears. The head, with its matted wet hair, lay in a bright pool; Vandenberg had forgotten that it was possible for so much blood to come out of a man.

COMMUNICATIONS

The *Santa Fe Journal-News,* Santa Fe, N.M.

GUIDE KILLED

UPI—Nov. 10th. The body of Juan Reyes Sandoval, 57, was found Wednesday morning high in the Pecos Wilderness by mounted troopers of the 17th Reconnaissance Squadron (USSRAOOUSA).

Sandoval, a Picuris Pueblo Indian, was a well-known guide and tracker for many years in the area. He was hired earlier this week by Occupation forces to assist in the search for Eugene R. Vandenberg, a mentally disturbed inmate who escaped five weeks ago from a rehabilitation center near Cowles.

Sandoval had been shot once through the back of the head. A manhunt has been underway for several weeks in the mountainous country for the fugitive, who is known to be armed.

FOR TWO DAYS, banks of low, dark cumulus had been moving in from the northwest, shrouding the upper peaks in chill fog. On the third day, the temperature did not rise beyond the thirties, and by early afternoon the first snow began falling. Several hours later it stopped.

He had walked almost twenty miles into the wilderness, stopping when the snow came to make a camp, near Jicarita Peak. At daybreak the next day, a herd of mule deer passed within eighty yards of him on their way to lower elevations, and he used the Springfield to bring down a young doe. That afternoon he gorged himself on venison. The carcass of the doe dressed out around a hundred pounds, and he could not move far with that much meat. He stayed there for several more days, eating heavily. It snowed again, and then the temperature dropped sharply, and he had to keep a fire going most of the day.

He found the shack less than half a mile from his camp. A *jacal*, really, made of split logs plastered with mud, hidden in a ravine. Whoever had built it had known the country, for they had situated the hut under the lee side of a cliff where a minimum of snow and rain could reach it. It was a crudely built single room, perhaps eight by ten, with no windows, and a dirt floor. The roof was of dirt, too, supported by a decking made of lengths of aspen. There was a small fireplace in one corner. The door had been made of rough planks. It sagged, and moisture had worked through the roof near one wall, but this could be repaired. Outside, he found a midden, and he poked around in the rubbish, unearthing fire-blackened and rusting tin cans, bits of broken bottles, and the like, but was unable to guess how long it had been since anyone had used the place. Two, maybe three years at the least, he decided, maybe longer. Farther up the ravine was a spring.

He'd found places like this before. Sometimes a sheepherder might build one, if he knew he would be in the area for a time. Once in a while you came across an old ruin, all that remained of a shack put up by a miner years ago. He had found several such places not far from his ranch. One had been built of natural field-stone, no telling how many years ago—the roof had completely disappeared, and only the walls stood. He'd found another curiosity near his place, a small adobe cabin no bigger than a closet, no more than three by five feet, so small that a couple of ordinary fence posts had been used for ceiling beams. He'd asked Spanish people about these isolated places, and a *viejo* had once told him that they were built to provide a hideaway, a retreat for men who were fed up with wives and family and town living, and who wanted to get away for a few days, out in the country by themselves, with a gallon of wine.

Pack rats and field mice had made a filthy mess inside, and he spent several hours cleaning the place out. By the following afternoon he had moved all his gear, including his supply of venison, to the *jacal*. That night the temperature went lower, and it began snowing again; it snowed for forty-eight hours.

COMMUNICATIONS

The *Santa Fe Journal-News*, Santa Fe, N.M.

CHARGES FILED

UPI—Nov. 14. Charges of first degree murder were filed Sunday against Eugene R. Vandenberg, 50, of Santa Fe, by the District Attorney's office.

The charges rose out of an investigation into the shooting death of Juan Reyes Sandoval, 57, of Picuris, N.M., a professional guide. The shooting occurred on Nov. 9. Sandoval was assisting Occupation forces, who were searching for Vandenberg.

Simultaneously, the Judge Advocate-General's Office of Soviet Military Government released a statement that a reward of $1,000 had been posted for the capture of the fugitive.

HE HAD CUT a bundle of green willow rushes and carefully bent two of the thickest pieces into teardrop-shaped frames which he then latticed, securing the pieces with the last of his scrap wire and lengths of cord cut from the sleeping bag. He used the leather sling from the rifle to make crude footstraps. It was slow work, and he would have given anything for a drill, a box of screws, nails, rivets, but he finally managed to get the snowshoes strong enough to support his weight. He did all this by the light of the fireplace. Outside, it was snowing again.

COMMUNICATIONS

The *Santa Fe Journal-News*, Santa Fe, N.M.
Editorial, Nov. 20.

NO ROBIN HOODS, PLEASE

The publicity recently accorded to alleged murderer Eugene Vandenberg strikes us as being out of proportion. Some of the more liberal intellects of this community have invested him with the glamor and charisma of that legendary righter-of-wrongs, Robin Hood.

A moment's objectivity, if you will.

1. Vandenberg is a criminal, wanted on a number of charges that include: murder, grand larceny, felonious assault, escape from confinement, and sedition.

2. As far as we know (and we did a little checking) Vandenberg, even in his heyday, was something less than an asset to this community. He was not a registered voter. He belonged to no civic group or organization. Though professing to be an artist, he never exhibited at any show or museum here, nor did he ever, that we know of, win a prize or award for his art efforts. A check with the county assessor's office revealed that he is four years delinquent in property taxes. As a matter of fact, the only place we did find his name turning up was on the city police blotter: to wit, drunk and disorderly, DWI (Driving While Intoxicated), abusive language to a police officer, creating a public disturbance, indecent exposure (attending to a private function in public), and so on.

The champion of Sherwood Forest possessed a discernible amount of nobility and graciousness, but we must confess that we find none in Eugene Vandenberg. Not only that, we doubt if he knows which end of an arrow goes first.

The *Santa Fe Journal-News*, Santa Fe, N.M.
Letters to the Editor: Nov. 21.

Sirs:

I agree utterly with your column. And those you were talking about who think he's doing anyone any good ought to be shut away with him.

> *Very truly yours,*
> *R. Cutler.*

Letters to the Editor: Nov. 22.

I knew Gene Vandenberg he was a good old boy, no criminal, sure liked a drink and maybe was a little rough in his talk, but who of us isn't? Now everybody is down on him and says he's no good, why? I'm speaking as one who knows from personal experience, I'm seventy-four, no kid anymore, out on a pension and crippled with the rheumatism, no family, and more than once he staked me to a meal, bought me a beer, would sit and talk with me, and now he's a killer and Lord knows what else! All I'm telling you is that he was a pretty good old boy and many's the time I seen him be kind when he didn't have to.

Name withheld by request.

Letters to the Editor: Nov. 22.

Sir:

The snide attitude in your Vandenberg editorial was unwarranted and served only to demean your customarily excellent reportage.

The man is obviously mentally ill. As such, he is not legally responsible for his acts. If blame must be placed, place it on those who permitted a criminally insane man to practically walk away from confinement.

True, there is nothing of Robin Hood in Vandenberg—but it is not necessary to be amused over what he actually is: a sick, pathetic creature.

Sincerely,
Howard and Denise Roberts
La Bajada, N.M.

Letters to the Editor: Nov. 23.

Gentlemen:

In the interests of accuracy I would like to comment on the Vandenberg editorial. I knew Gene Vandenberg for a number of years, and while it is true he did not exhibit at any of the museum shows here, he did have many one-man shows from 1949 to 1958. He usually exhibited at the now-defunct Hoovan, Del Monte Sol, and Potpourri galleries, on Canyon Road, and in several shows all of his temperas sold out. I also know that he exhibited in California, Scottsdale, Ariz., Dallas, Houston, and Fort Worth. In 1948, he was elected a Fellow of the Chicago Institute of Painting and Sculpture. The number of private collections, my own included, which carry his work are too numerous to mention.

Thank you,
(Miss) Dawn Riley
Secretary, Santa Fe Ass'n of Fine Arts.

IT WAS Nikos' habit to serve free Tom-and-Jerrys on New Year's Eve, one to each of his steady customers, perhaps two or three— no more—to the best spenders. He would also have a small keg of fresh oysters flown in, which were more of a novelty than a delicacy in this landlocked state. A mariachi band would be hired, and the back of the bar festooned with strings of varicolored crepe paper. At eleven forty-five, Nikos would circulate among the tables and booths, distributing noisemakers and party hats, many of which he managed to salvage the next morning and put away for the following year's celebration.

By midnight on this New Year's Eve, several fights had started and had been squelched. The city cops had been in a number of times. Abilene Tixier was loudly declaiming undying love for two *pachucos,* total strangers, who sat beside him at the bar with stony, hostile faces. Hugh Rogers, the painter, had been hired by Nikos for the night as an extra barman. Phil Gibbs was sitting at a table with four bucks from Cochiti Pueblo, and he was telling them how much better life for the American Indian would be under Soviet rule. The bucks had been on beer and Jim Beam all evening. They listened politely to what was being said, and then the one nearest Gibbs fell forward, out. Behind the bar, Hugh remembered the pool they'd made on Vandenberg, and he said to Nikos, "Looks like nobody wins."

"Unless they caught him already and never announced it," Nikos said.

At the far end of the bar, the one they called El Cabrito, The Goat, luxuriously sideburned, Stetsoned, weight 108, leaned forward on his bar stool, opened his legs, and vomited between them. Wearily, Nikos picked up the bucket of sawdust and started toward him. "I got sixteen highballs to mix, and he does that. Not only that, he's been down at El Cid's all night, drinking on the cuff, and now he comes in here and orders a twenty-five-cent beer and does something like that. Who needs it?"

The air was hot and stuffy. The noise was worse. The mariachis had set sail for Venus with a third rendition of "Auld Lang Syne," the two trumpets vying for tenor lead. Outside, the main plaza of the town was icy and deserted, the street lights illuminating the snow- and ice-laden elms.

TEN MILES EAST of Santa Fe is San Sebastian, a settlement of a dozen or so homes, scattered across a broad slope a quarter of a mile off U.S. 85. For most of the houses there is privacy—they are set back as far as possible from the main lane, and the piñon and shagbark cedar that grows everywhere has not been cut except where necessary.

He appeared at one of the smallest places late in February. He'd watched the house for over an hour, and before that had circled the driveway to see if any cars were parked in the area. Finally, he walked up to the portal and knocked. After a moment she opened the door, and he said, "Terry?"

She couldn't make him out in the shadows of the portal, but she recognized his voice immediately. "So—it's you."

"Can I come in?"

"You're back. Yes, for God's sake, come in."

He stepped into the kitchen, blinking in the light, and she shut the door, turning. "I was wondering when you'd come."

"I didn't want to take a chance on making trouble for you."

"What kind?"

"I thought they might be watching the house."

"Why would they do that?"

"They had your name in my dossier."

"There's nobody watching the house," she said, staring at him. "Gene—what's wrong with you?"

"I don't know. Bronchitis, maybe, or pneumonia—both."

"You look terrible."

"Thanks."

"You must have lost thirty pounds. Where did you get those clothes?"

"Found 'em."

"Where've you been?"

"In the woods."

"All this time?"

"I found a shack," he said. "It must be thirty-five miles from here—I walked for three days. Got lost, twice." He sat down at the kitchen table.

"Do you want a drink?"

He nodded. She got a bottle of port wine that had already been opened and two glasses and set them on the table, but she did not sit down with him.

He poured a glassful, drank it off, refilled the glass, and then filled hers.

"Got a cigarette?" She brought a pack from the counter, and he lit one. "What's the date?"

"February 27th."

"I wondered how long I'd been out."

"You escaped the first week in October."

He looked at her. "How do you know?"

"It was in the paper. And on radio—and television."

"Really? I'd have thought they'd have hushed it up."

"I saved some of the clippings," she said. "I knew you'd come, sooner or later. I thought you might be interested in what they had to say about you."

"None of it's true."

"Sandoval, too?"

"Sandoval? Who's that?"

"An Indian. He was helping them. Did you really shoot him?"

He stared at her. "Yes."

Her brow furrowed. "I was hoping it was a lie, that maybe someone else had done it."

"I had to."

"Gene, you have to give yourself up."

"Jesus, Terry," he said. "I've been running like a rabbit since October, I've lost Kevin, and the first thing you tell me is to give myself up."

"What else can you do?"

"I don't know," he said. "But I do know that if I turn myself in, it's going to be the last you hear from me."

"But, Gene, they'll find you anyway."

"Why say that?" he asked. "They had God knows how many men up there and they couldn't get me. I'm still loose."

"Look at you—you're a wreck."

He looked at her. "You don't seem especially pleased to see me."

"That's not true—you know that."

"You're shook up about the Indian."

"Of course I am," she said. "Why shouldn't I be?"

"It was self-defense."

"Tell that to the authorities, Gene."

"I'm telling you."

She shook her head. He said, "Do you want me to leave?"

"Oh, for God's sake, stop it," she cried out. "Look at you—you can't walk ten feet."

He'd started to shake in the heat of the kitchen, but he kept on: "If you want to be a good citizen, you can get on the phone."

She grew angry over that. "Oh—you're still just as stupid . . ."

"I've had enough of good citizens. That compound up there is filled with them." He finished his wine and poured a third glassful. "Listen, I'm sick, Terry. If you want me to go, say so. But don't start being righteous until you have some idea of what you're talking about."

"You can stay—you know that."

He looked up at her and tried to grin. "Terry, you're an absolute doll."

"And you're still a first-class son of a bitch."

He raised his glass. "I'll drink to that."

"You think you can do all these dreadful things, and then walk in here and pick up where we left off. It doesn't work that way."

"I didn't have anyplace else to go."

"If I have anything to say about it, you're going to turn your-self in."

"Get on the phone then."

"I want *you* to phone," she said. "I'm not going to see you wreck your life."

"Honey, it is wrecked."

"I thought about you, you know. The papers said you might try to get to Mexico, but I was sure you'd stay around here."

"Did you really think about me?"

"Oh, the hell with you," she said, moving away from the table. "I'll cook supper. You look starved."

"I need a bath," he said, getting up.

"Come on." He took the bottle and his glass, and followed her. There was a shakiness in his legs that did not come from the liquor.

The bathroom was small and cheerful, and it was obvious that its only user was a woman. She bent over the tub, ran hot water into it, and rinsed the sides. Vandenberg dropped the lid of the toilet, sat down, and stared at her back. He set the bottle of port on the floor. "Do you have any medicine here?"

"Aspirin," she said. "Some cold tablets. And there are a few penicillin capsules left—I had a strep throat last month."

"Is there more wine?"

"There's another quart."

"Do you still have any of my clothes?"

"Yes. There's a shirt and a pair of pants, in the closet. Socks, too."

"Later, you take the underwear I have on and burn it in the incinerator. Get me a paper bag, and I'll put them in it."

"I'll wash them."

"No, you won't. And I'll want scissors and your razor."

"The razor's in the medicine chest—let me put a new blade in it."

She went out, and brought him what he wanted, and then closed the door. He undressed and clipped his beard, letting the hair fall into the sink below the mirror, and then climbed into the tub, gradually raising the temperature of the water with the hot tap. He soaked for half an hour, shampooed his hair, shaved. When he was done he dried himself, dressed—his old clothing hung loosely on him—took four aspirin and three penicillin capsules, washing them down with port, and then used her comb on his hair. He cleaned the mess he'd made as best he could, and then took the wine and went out to the kitchen, where she was cooking.

"Tomorrow night you can give me a haircut if you want."

She looked at him. "You look worse. Without the whiskers, you're gaunt."

"Clean, though." He sat at the table, lit another cigarette, heavy-eyed now after the bath and wine, already half asleep, head nodding. She saw this and said, "Gene—I've got a steak here—stay awake until you eat."

"I will."

"It'll be ready in a minute."

"Smells marvelous, Terry."

"What did you live on up there?"

"Venison. Rabbit. I didn't have any salt, though. I've been dying for salt."

"You found a cabin?"

"A hut. Can't keep it warm, though. This is the first time I've been warm all winter."

She served him. He ate most of the steak, but she could see he'd never finish, and finally she got up and took him by the arm. "I'm going to put you on the couch in the living room tonight. It's warmer there than my bedroom, and I think you'll be more comfortable."

He did not argue, but followed her without speaking, drunk now in addition to being exhausted. She quickly made up a bed on the couch, and after he'd stretched out she covered him. He was almost asleep now. "Terry?"

"Yes."

"I heard Kev was put up for adoption." She frowned, and then said, "They told me he'd been sent to La Madera."

"You talked to them then?"

"Yes."

"They arrest you?"

"No—why would they do that? I went to them and said I was a friend of the family."

He said, not opening his eyes, "You're a winner."

"Nobody knew where you were. This was before you escaped. Nikos told me you'd been arrested. They were really very nice."

"They told you he'd been sent to La Madera?"

"Yes. A woman at Military Government found out for me."

"They have no business putting him in a place like that."

"She said he was doing quite well there."

"What about my ranch?"

"They said it had been confiscated."

He shook his head. "Why did they have to put him in La Madera?"

"He'd been made a ward of the court."

"Even so."

"I know. Don't worry about it for now, please?"

He was silent; then, "Terry? What day is tomorrow?"

"Thursday."

"You'll have classes?"

"I'll call in sick—don't worry."

"If it's all right, I'd like to stay here a day or two."

"Stay as long as you want."

"I'm beat."

"I know."

"I feel all shot down."

She said nothing.

"I won't stay too long—don't worry about that."

"It's all right."

He was almost asleep. "You know why I broke out of there?"

"It's not important."

"You know what they do to you there?" he said. "They take your mind apart, and put it back together again. You wouldn't believe it, Terry, but those crazy bastards have built a regular brain factory up there at Cowles."

"Tell me about it tomorrow."

HE HAD KNOWN her how long? Seven—eight years? A sometime lover, he'd told Andy Walters. There was more to it than that. What else could he have added? That they were good in bed, whenever they did sleep together, which happened more frequently than he'd led Walters to believe? Or that he cared for her as much as any woman he'd known, including Cora? He'd been telling Walters the truth when he said he would have married her in a minute if he'd been ten years younger.

She was very pretty without being beautiful, with features that in the old days used to be described as classic, meaning, usually, Anglo-Saxon: finely arched, thick brows, and brown eyes that were direct and unflinching. High cheekbones. Small, square teeth and a sensitive, mobile mouth. She customarily wore her hair in a chignon; loose, it reached to her buttocks. She had an extraordinarily small waist, and was a shade heavy in the legs, soft-breasted, and he liked all this. Her parents were dead. Two aunts in Pennsylvania had raised her. Soon after completing the courses that earned her a teacher's certificate, she'd contracted tuberculosis. Like Vandenberg, she'd come West for the dry climate. He had met her one night at a party, and had been so open and direct in his admiration that she responded. After they became lovers she continued to go out occasionally with other men, and he believed her when she said she didn't sleep with them. They saw each other at least once a week and during the summer almost every day.

One year she spent part of her vacation back East, and he discovered that he missed her more than he cared to admit. He told her about this when she returned, and she seemed pleased. On several occasions they spoke of marriage, but nothing came of it. The summer before the Invasion, a former fiancé, to whom she'd been engaged while still in college, came out to visit her. Vandenberg had done nothing to discourage the situation, but was sick with jealousy. After several weeks the fiancé had gone back East, and Vandenberg felt relieved. They settled back into their old routine, and very likely this would have continued indefinitely had it not been for the Occupation and his subsequent arrest.

HE STAYED the weekend, sleeping ten and twelve hours at a stretch. On Friday, at his insistence, she went to classes.

That night she cooked supper, and at the table he told her what he needed. "Do you have any money?"

"Yes. How much do you need?"

"I want you to buy some things for me."

He gave her a list he'd made out while she was at school, and she read it. "Fishing line, hooks? Where can I buy them?"

"Tiano's. If anyone asks, say you're buying them so you can take some of your culturally deprived slum kids fishing this spring."

"Socks—two pair, size twelve."

"Heavy work socks. Buy four pair, if you can find them. And work gloves. The leather-palmed kind, with cotton backs."

"Salt."

"Yes, don't forget that. And dried fruit—apricots, prunes. Instant coffee. Cigarettes. Soap. A razor—I'd gotten hold of one, but I hid it with some canned goods and never went back. A comb, small mirror. Small can of three-in-one oil, for the rifle—it's starting to rust. A file. Ball of heavy string."

"I'll have to go to several places."

"Rationing?"

She nodded.

"Listen, are you still able to find those cheap little transistors? I sure could use a radio."

"I've one here you can have."

"Can it be traced?"

"I don't see how."

She glanced at the list again. "This'll take time. I've got some other shopping to do though."

"I'd appreciate it."

She looked at him. "Was it quiet here today?"

"Yes. I slept till past noon. Why?"

"Nothing." She paused. "It's only that—well—you seem nervous."

"I'll be leaving Monday."

"All right, if you like." She smiled. "You can stay longer though. I'll worry about you even more now, you know." When he did not answer, she went on, "How will you carry all this?"

"I left a packboard in your carport," he said. "Wire. I forgot to put that down. There must have been a hundred times I could have used wire."

"Do you want liquor?"

"Life's blood—only I'll be carrying plenty, as it is. Some cold pills would be good. Something you don't need a prescription for. Can you buy vitamins?"

"Yes—I'll get you some."

"The multi-purpose kind."

She poured a glass of wine for herself. "When will I see you again?"

"A month? Two months?"

"That long?"

"I can't make a habit of hanging around here."

"What will you do up there?"

"Sweat it out until spring."

"And then?"

"I don't know."

She looked at him across the table.

"I really don't, honey."

"What you're doing—it's so pointless."

"You're probably right."

"If you turned yourself in—what would they do to you?"

He shrugged. "A stiff sentence—at the least."

"But there'd be parole."

"Not really," he said. "If I was convicted of the charges they have, and if the sentences ran concurrently, how long would it take before I could apply for parole? Ten years? Fifteen? Longer? I'd never make it."

"But, Gene, as a fugitive you can't live."

He shrugged. "Somebody has to stand up to them."

"You?"

"Who else?"

"It won't work."

"I can try."

"But—why? Why you?"

"Because there's nothing else for me to do," he said irritably. "I found out something while I was in there. And I've thought about it all winter. I'd lie in that sleeping bag all day during those blizzards—didn't even dare go out for firewood—and I'd think about what has happened. It got so I was like a goddamned bear hibernating in that shack. I'd bring a chunk of half-cooked venison inside the bag with me, wrapped in a rag, and keep it warm with the heat of my body. There were plenty of times when I'd spend less than an hour a day outside that bag. The rest of the time I'd curl up inside it, trying to keep warm. Honey, I not only spent time thinking about them and this country, but about myself—my whole life. I got so I talked out loud—I'd spend days inside that bag, with the wind howling up a storm outside, holding conversations. It's not only Cowles—or the other compounds they have. It's the whole thing, Terry. Nobody has done a damned thing. Sure, there have been TV seminars, and open discussion panels, and debates on the major issues, but there's only one real voice."

"What do you want to do—defy them?"

"Yes."

"My God, Gene, at your age you're developing a savior syndrome?"

"I'm not a savior, nor a revolutionary either," he argued. "But it has to start someplace, don't you see? There has to be dissension. Maybe nothing big, but there has to be a start—something to make people compare!"

"Maybe Americans are tired of comparing," she said. "Maybe, for a change, they enjoy a straight Party line—did you ever think of that?"

"Yes," he said, "your whole life tied up in one neat package. Well, why not? A housewife in a supermarket used to have to mull for half an hour over a score of soap powder brands, all of which were pretty much the same—now, she's damned well tickled to get her hands on a box a month, any brand. Very intriguing, having variety removed from your life. So now it's all black and white— America is going to become the greatest peaceful nation in history."

"I'm for peace," she said.

"So am I. Listen, that was the line they handed us in the compound. The great brotherhood of man. The reason it sounded so good was because the alternative sounded so final—peace, at any cost, or the alternative."

"I'm still for peace."

"But part of the cost of their way of peace is Cowles." He'd told her about Cowles, but she had difficulty accepting his story.

Now she said, "I think some of the other inmates would have complained, if it was that bad."

"They must have a way of blanking out most of it," he insisted.

"Some of them were very important people, you said."

"Sure."

"But you're the only one who knows what it's like?"

"Me. You. And the ones who run the shop."

"Still, you *could* have made it," she said bitterly.

"Yes. Eventually, they'd have discharged me. But I'd have been a shade different—like all the others. That's what I couldn't stand."

"Sure—your old way of life had such integrity, it was so valuable."

"It was the only life I had. You seemed to enjoy it."

"What little of it I had," she said, and looked down at the table in front of her.

"What's that supposed to mean?"

She shrugged. "Nothing."

"Let's not argue about it. You know, when I first broke out—those first few days when the drugs were wearing off and I was starting to think straight again—I wondered if the real reason they'd arrested me was to put me through Cowles as a kind of test case. No—I'm not being paranoid. I mean, Terry, I was a nobody, really, as far as they were concerned. I had no affiliations in Santa Fe, or anywhere else. Christ, my paintings are the least controversial stuff imaginable. I had no influence, and didn't want any. I hated M.G., but so do a lot of people. And I never believed any of that hoke they gave me about talking too much in bars. If that were true, they'd have to lock up ten million drunks. Why the hell didn't they simply ignore me?"

"You were too charmingly irresistible."

"In a way, you may be right," he said. "Because long before the Occupation, I'd divorced myself from most of the middle-class goals. Money. Success. Approval. Recognition. There were years, after Cora died, when Kev and I got by on fifteen, sixteen hundred a year, and, you know, we lived pretty well? The point is that the Soviets themselves can't wait to become a middle-class country. They still talk about the great working class, but, Jesus, who the hell wants any part of it? The whole basic reward-incentive operating in the Soviet Union is that with luck, if things go right, Ivan Ivanovich may someday become a nice, fat, comfortable bourgeois citizen. He's not the least interested in having himself and his children working their asses off in some factory or farm commune. If he has a bike he wants a motorcycle, if he has a motorcycle he wants a car, if he went to gymnasium his kid has to go to university. He wants his neighbors to envy him. He wants to be mildly successful—but not too successful. For the time being he'll probably still accept a work-quota achievement medal for his lapel, but he'd probably rather have a new TV or an extra bedroom in his flat.

"Andy Walters was right—can you imagine the impact this country will have on the hundreds of thousands of troops they have here? All those Russian kids in their thick blanket-wool uniforms and clodhopper boots? You've seen them rubbernecking around town. Too shy or unsure to talk to anybody, but they're taking it all in. Every one of them with an English phrase book in his jacket pocket—that's the first thing comes out when they're in a store shopping, and with that Military Occupation currency they're buying everything that isn't nailed down, crating it up and shipping it back to the Urals or wherever. I don't know what the Occupation is going to do to us, but it may help in producing a middle-class mentality in Russia."

"But where do you fit in?"

"I'm telling you. The Russians are working with middle-class values, both with us and themselves. That was the reward-incentive —the big banana dangled on a string—at Cowles, the promise that if we behaved and cooperated and played their fancy little game we would get back to our happy little existences. But I'd left all that. Andy wanted to help me get into the Ministry of Culture after I'd been discharged. He was right in thinking that the kind of academic representationalism I painted would appeal to the Ministry. He couldn't understand why I laughed at him. I don't think he ever believed me when I said I'd withdrawn from society not to prove a point but because I wanted as little as possible to do with it. I think they picked up enough information on me to know I was eccentric by our standards *and* theirs, and maybe they wanted to see what would happen to me if I lived under conditions where they were the button pushers. Would I react to the proper stimuli?

Conform? What would happen to my thinking if the insignificant inventory of items I valued were removed? The ranch. Kevin. My books. My God, how could they have made such an error? Who better than they should know that the man who'll give you static is the one with nothing to lose? Andy, I think, had an idea that in me he was going to *prove* something, the jerk."

"But what can you hope to accomplish?"

"I want people to know about Cowles," he said.

"And you're going to tell them?"

"Who'd believe me—hell, you don't really."

"Then—who?"

"I don't know."

"You have a plan?"

"Not really."

"You want to expose the place?"

"That'd be part of it."

"And then?"

He looked at his glass.

She said, "Suppose you try. Suppose no one listens to you, and they go on believing what's in the papers, about its being minimum security . . . a center for the politically disoriented instead of the chamber of horrors you insist it is. Where will that leave you?"

"Up the creek, I suppose."

"What you're objecting to is that life has gotten tougher—that Military Government is leaning on the general public a lot more than any of the old administrations would have dared."

"Of course."

"And, too, isn't Gene Vandenberg objecting because *his* life has gotten rougher—because for the first time in years, he hasn't been able to go merrily about his own affairs?"

"Granted."

"You still won't consider turning yourself in?"

"No."

"And where do I fit in?" she asked. "Am I supposed to go on being some kind of ideal, plucky, Hemingwayesque handmaiden to destiny? God damn it, Gene, you know me better than that. I was never a mirror to your ego—I've got too many of my own needs to wait around until you snap your fingers. Is there any sort of future for me in all this?"

"Was there ever?"

She paused at that. "At least we had something."

"But no future really. That's what you're really talking about, isn't it?"

"I suppose you expect me to go on helping you."

"I don't expect you to go on doing anything, honey. But if you want to help me, I won't refuse."

She gave him a steady look. "You say you got away from that place before they did anything to you, but that's not true. You've changed."

"I suppose I have."

"I'm not sure I like you nearly as much now."

"I can't say I blame you."

"You were never easy to get along with."

"And now I'm worse?"

She shrugged. "You've changed."

THAT NIGHT, HE WENT to her bed. He could tell she was awake from her breathing, but when he slipped in beside her she did not move. They both lay quietly for several minutes, and then he turned on his side and placed one hand over her breast. He could feel her breathing through the nightgown, and finally he whispered, "Terry?"

She gave an angry moan and turned quickly to him and as they met she parted herself with her fingers to make his entry easier, her right leg over and around his waist, crying once in anguish as he thrust into her. She could not remain silent or motionless but urged him on, almost weeping, and then very quickly she came, her breathing coarsening as though she'd run some distance, and he went, too, almost with her. Later, she said simply, "Thank you."

"I wanted that very much—thank *you*." It was an old affectionate exchange.

She moved until she was up against him. "At least this is still the same."

THE NEXT MORNING she drove in to do her shopping, getting everything on the list and bringing something extra, a fifth of gin, setting it on the kitchen table with the other stuff she'd brought. "Heavy or not, you can use it."

204

"We'll drink it tonight," he said. "Martinis."

"There's another bottle in the sack," she said. "This is to take with you. And don't park under the nearest tree and drink it all at once."

He helped her put the food away. "Have you had any trouble with roadblocks?"

"Not since a raving maniac named Vandenberg escaped last October," she said. "They stopped me three times then."

"Just you?"

"No—they were stopping everything on the highway."

"Monday morning when you go in to work, I'll leave with you —you can drop me outside town."

"What the hell do you want to go near town for?"

"There're a few things I have to do. It'll be all right, if you're sure we won't be stopped."

THAT MONDAY THEY LEFT while it was still half dark, and she drove him far out on West Alameda, past the radio towers. By then she knew where he wanted to go, but she stopped the Plymouth when he asked her to, and they sat for a minute in the warm interior. She said, "It's the ranch, isn't it?"

"Yes."

"Why?"

"I want to see it again."

"Let me drive you out there," she said.

"Too risky. Someone might spot the car. Besides, the road is probably blocked. You've done enough. I can walk it from here in a few hours."

They spoke awhile longer and shared a cigarette. West Alameda was deserted. She said, "When will I see you again?"

"Five or six weeks, maybe."

"I don't see how you can go back up there in this awful weather."

"I don't want to."

"You could stay at the house—at least until it's warmer."

"The two of us living on your ration card?"

Finally he said good-bye, kissed her, and got out. It was cold. He slipped into the packboard, waved, and moved off, heading north beyond the last houses, where the first foothills began.

AT HIS FENCE LINE he saw the small metal signs that read: STATE PROPERTY—TRESPASSING FORBIDDEN, but there were no tire tracks along the road that climbed the hill, and when he got to the house he saw that it was deserted.

The windows were gone, including the one in the studio. On the weather side blowing snow had drifted into the living room and kitchen. He walked around to the front and saw that the heavy planked door had been ripped from its hinges. Whoever did it had used a crowbar.

It was worse inside. They had taken the gas range and the butane refrigerator. A litter of broken glassware, plates, and crockery lay on the floor. The door of the broom closet hung by one hinge, the butane wall lamps had been ripped loose. The other rooms were the same. Someone had set fire to the big bed, and the ceiling *vigas* over it were scorched. Cora's old treadle sewing machine had been broken to pieces. The bureaus, chests, mirrors, the paintings of his that he'd hung on the walls, the photo albums, his books—all gone. The doors of the closets had been torn off, the contents scattered about with the rest of the garbage—clothing, canvasses, brushes, painting supplies. In one corner of the bedroom, half buried under a scattering of what had been blankets and quilts, he recognized the brown and buff fur of one of his Siamese cats, the carcass shredded by rats. Through all the rooms there was the steady sigh of the raw February wind. From time to time it rustled the pages of a torn and rotting book or flapped what was left of a curtain hanging askew in a glassless window. The house was otherwise silent.

He spent the day there. He went from room to room, carefully inspecting everything, as though he intended to begin tomorrow with a shovel to clear away the rubbish. In the bedroom he sat down on the raised fireplace ledge and ate a handful of dried fruit. He lit a cigarette, puffed at it, and then let his head drop forward until his forehead rested against his knees, sitting that way with his eyes closed until the cigarette had been reduced to a stub and was beginning to burn his fingers.

The second shock came later that night, when he went to Tixier to ask the old man for help.

"YOU WANT ME to ride with it then?" Vandenberg had asked.

Tixier nodded. "That's my advice exactly. Beg for clemency.

206

That's what they want to hear." The old rancher went on for several minutes more, his thick white hair highlighted by the overhead kitchen light. "What'll you get—twenty-to-life? You'll be up for parole in six or seven years. You're still young enough. Here, let me pour you another drink."

He refilled Vandenberg's glass. "When you get out, you can start working angles. You're not going to accomplish anything up there in the mountains. Do it the smart way. You think you got something to say to the world? Why, Christ, I can get you a goddamn printing press."

Vandenberg had looked at him. "A press? You could promote something like that?"

"Could be," the old man said. "Get legal first, Gene. And the day you get out of the pen I just might make you a present of a twelve-hundred-dollar Multilith to play with."

"Abilene, you're putting me on."

Tixier shook his head. "I could get it."

"Where?"

"That's my business."

"Damn it, Abilene, where?"

"It's in one of the Capitol warehouses. Crated, brand-new—never used. Fellow who can get it, he owes me a favor."

"One of your boys?"

Tixier was unruffled. Vandenberg did not push it; he said, "A machine like that could be useful."

"Useful! Why, man, with a rig like that you can run off two, three thousand copies an hour."

"How about paper? Ink?"

"It could be gotten. Anything can be gotten."

Vandenberg looked at him. "All right, let's get it then."

"You just slow down a bit."

"I've got a place up there where it'll be safe."

"How much you think you're going to get done, with a murder charge on you? You think they won't start looking for you again, soon as spring comes?"

"Why the hell are you so anxious for me to give myself up?"

Tixier was silent a moment; then he said, "Gene, I've always admired you. Why use up what years you've got left on the run? That kind of life ain't worth a shit. I know."

There was a great deal, he realized, that he didn't know about the old rancher. Olga herself had told him that Abilene had come out of World War II with enough to buy the eleven-thousand-acre ranch they'd owned east of San Ysidro—Abilene, who'd never been more than a technician fifth-grade in an army medical unit. And he also knew that the old man, in all the years they'd been friendly, had never worked, had always had money. And now this, the vague offer of printing equipment. It wasn't altogether a come-on, he knew that. Somewhere, probably, Abilene had heard of a crated duplicator, one perhaps not carried on inventory. Perhaps the old man had stored this item of information away with the idea that someone, someday, might be willing to pay for such a piece of equipment.

Despite the country-boy style, he knew Tixier was shrewd. He guessed now that the old rancher was edgy over his friend's lawless status. Perhaps, for Tixier, the real pleasure in breaking the law lay in maintaining a veneer of respectability. To operate an underground press with Vandenberg, who was wanted on half a dozen charges, was merely dangerous; to operate one with an ostensibly rehabilitated felon might be something the old man would relish.

Tixier leaned closer. "Why'd you blow off that Indian's head last fall?"

"I had to."

"I don't doubt it." Tixier finished the whiskey in his glass. "You never would listen to reason. And now you've pushed your luck too far." He stared down at his glass. "I know one thing for sure— you keep on this way, you'll turn mean."

When he did not answer, the old man went on. "There's ways to get around everything. The law hasn't been made you can't get around, if you want to. I don't give a goddamn who's running the country. Why, shit, if the Ivans had any brains at all they'd of shipped me off to Cowles long before they ever got around to thinking about you. But they can't prove anything, and that's the way I like it. Having you here in my house is the closest I've come to sticking my neck out in years. I know, you think I'm turning my back on you. And I am. I ain't out to prove anything. Fuck 'em. I take care of Olga, and I'm always ready to help a friend, but old Abilene is number-one stud around here. I've always operated that way. You tell me you want to bust open that compound and turn everybody loose, you're out of your skull."

"It's got to be done."

"Not by me. And you know why? Because I'm smart. That's the difference between you and me, Gene. I'm no more legal than you are. Never was. But I'll tell you something. I own this house and three others like it that bring in steady income—at least I did till those low-life motherfuckers passed that law—and I got an old woman to take care of me, and when I want a bourbon high, why, she mixes it and serves it to me, and I can go to the john and sit down with a magazine and take a crap, instead of squatting behind some piñon in a foot of snow without even a piece of lousy toilet paper. If I need a cigarette I say, 'Olga, baby, fetch me a smoke.' I don't have to walk no three days to get it.

"Nobody's going to take a potshot at me, but they will at you, and they'll get you, too, one of these days. I ain't the least bit interested in dying with my boots on. If I can help it, I'm going to die in a nice warm bed with a fifth of bourbon inside me, and a hard-on that won't quit, and not a worry in the world. Gene, you go serve your time, and when you get out, I'll help you. That's a promise. I'll work with you, and it won't cost you a cent. I'll do it out of friendship, because I love you, you ornery bastard. But all this other phony shit, count me out. I ain't no goddamned Boy Scout, Gene. It'll take more than old Abilene to set this world straight. You ought to know me better."

SPRING AND SUMMER came, and in the high grassy parks alpine flowers bloomed. He worked most of the summer building his own cabin in a ravine midway between Elk Mountain and Hollinger Canyon, in a virtually inaccessible part of the forest. It was more of a cave, really. Using a pick and shovel he'd stolen from a road gang, he had tunneled into the side of the ravine so that the floor, roof, and three sides of the room were part of the cliff itself. He built up the outer wall of narrow aspen logs, and after mudplastering the inside, shoveled several tons of dirt against the wall, leaving only a small entrance door and a vent for a crude fireplace. If no fire was burning, the place was undetectable from a distance of thirty yards, and later that summer, when grass and weeds took seed in the raw earth, it was better still.

That July, almost a year after his arrest, he stole three horses while returning from San Sebastian. By then he'd worked out a walking route that passed near the compound, then headed south, skirting the valley until he could strike west through Apache Canyon.

The compound by now had a greater fascination for him than ever, and he spent hours watching it through the binoculars. In one of the notebooks Terry had bought for him, he'd drawn maps of the camp complex. Several times he approached close enough to hear the shouted commands of evening census, but none of the faces of those he watched was familiar, nor did he ever see Andy Walters. So great was his absorption with the camp that several times during the long, warm summer he sat from dawn to dusk under a huge fir on a nearby slope, unmoving, watching. In the same fashion, he learned a great deal about the cavalry detachment billeted at Terrero, seven miles below.

The horses he had chanced upon one afternoon in a rough corral atop Glorieta Mesa, near the overnight camp of three Soviet cavalrymen. He'd watched the troopers for a while through the glasses. One gathered scraps of deadwood, while another made tea. He guessed that this was a routine patrol, one of those run regularly out of Glorieta Assembly. He lingered on, seeing how easy it would be to take their horses. At first he dismissed the notion, not because it would alert them to the fact that he was still in the Pecos area— he was sure they knew that—but because the mounts would restrict him to easier trails that could be traversed by other mounted men. On the other hand, he'd been on foot for nine months now, and he knew that if he was ever forced to make a break the horses would enable him to cover ground.

When it was dark, he moved in among the horses quietly, whispering to them, not touching them, giving them time to grow accustomed to him. Fifty yards off, the light of the patrol's fire was visible through the trees.

There was a big, short-coupled gray that looked easy to ride, and two chestnut geldings. In the faint starlight he could see that they were well cared for. Their blankets and gear had been hung on poles nearby. Moving quietly, he got two saddles, hung them over a corral rail, and then went back for the blankets and bridles and a coiled stake rope. The gray was docile, and he saddled him without trouble, but the other two were nervous. He spent another five minutes getting them bridled, and then opened the corral gate, and after tying the chestnuts' bridles to the stake rope, led all three out.

For a quarter of an hour he walked them along a trail, and then mounted the gray. The moon would be rising soon. He found a cowpath that cut back and forth across a long, steep slope, and gave the gray a slack rein, letting the animal pick its own way.

IT WAS TERRY who located Kevin. During the summer, Vandenberg had settled into a routine of visiting her every few weeks, staying for several days at a time. He still made these trips on foot, leaving the horses hobbled near his cabin, because there was no place near her house to graze them. She'd worked through part of the summer doing remedial reading with a class of sixth graders, and one weekend night he had no sooner got inside the door and kissed her than she said, "Gene, I've found Kevin. He's right here in Santa Fe."

For a moment he was too astonished to speak.

"He's with a foster family in Agua Fria Village."

"How did you find out?"

"Through a student of mine—or through his father."

"How is he?"

"All right. They apparently discharged him from La Madera this spring."

"He never belonged there in the first place."

Later, he would be able to piece together from Kevin himself how badly he had done at the state institution for the mentally retarded. It was there that his son had for the first time in his life shown intractability, refusing to do what he was told, losing weight, and becoming dispirited and sullen. By the time a foster boarding home was finally found for him via the welfare department, his hair had grown to his shoulders and he had needed a delousing.

They had done something else to him, too, that Vandenberg could never positively identify, perhaps electroshock, or it could have been merely an orderly who'd mistreated him, although at first, seeing the terror in Kevin's face as he tried to describe life at the institution, Vandenberg thought they had castrated him. He'd known for years that, sexually, he would become more of a problem, and for this reason had never been punitive when he came upon Kevin masturbating, condoning the boy's self-abuse rather than have the worry of what might be triggered if he got near a woman.

"Well, he doesn't belong in this foster home either," Terry said. "I wanted to walk right into that welfare office and tell them off."

"Don't do anything like that. You start raising hell about him, and they'll be on your back. Don't think they're not looking for me."

"Even so—"

"What happened?"

"The boy in my class—Leonard Suazo—lives two houses down from the family who has him. Lennie's father stopped by after class the other day to talk with me. Suazo senior is active in the PTA."

"Skip the family history."

"Well, anyway, we were talking about children, mostly Mr. Suazo's brood, and the problems they were having, and he mentioned a family named Gutierrez up the street who'd taken in a retarded boy, a young Anglo they called Kevin. I practically fell out of my chair."

Suazo senior had not understood her sudden interest, but he was a man who liked to talk. He was not partial to morons, as he called them, living on the street where he'd been born and raised, but it turned out that this was an excuse to complain about the Gutierrez family, with whom Suazo had apparently feuded for years.

"Why should you be interested in them, Miss Heller?" he'd asked. "To tell the truth, I don't care for them—they're not friendly people, if you understand what I mean. A cousin did a stretch for first degree murder. Half the boys are in Springer Reformatory, and only last winter the grandfather was arrested for maltreatment of his wife with a chair. They're hard people, don't like anybody. Money, that's all Gutierrez is interested in. Both the older boys are out of school already, one in a gas station, the other doing Lord knows what, maybe black market, and now they've got that big simplehead from the insane asylum. I thought to myself when they took him in, why have a mental cripple like that around the house, with two girls—one eleven, the other fourteen—I wouldn't feel right in my mind. Not that I have anything personal against idiots. Those types are to be pitied. Actually, he's a sight better than the Gutierrezes, knows some manners, how to say good morning. Not that you see that much of him. They keep him in back, working.

212

So the old man gets a strong back and sixty dollars a month from Welfare, but Gutierrez, he isn't that dumb, getting hold of a big fellow like that, because he's working him to death making 'dobes. Keeps him locked in a toolshed at night out back, and that's not right either, treating someone like that like he's an animal. I'd complain to Welfare myself, but it would just be something for Gutierrez to hold against me."

She'd questioned Suazo more, wanting to know exactly what sort of work the Gutierrezes had Kevin doing, and he told her what he'd seen from his back fence. Adobe-making by hand, mixing and molding the heavy kaliche soil into thirty-pound bricks. Hard, back-breaking work, done now by fewer Spanish families, a moribund trade because of the grueling labor and the fact that cinderblock is cheaper to build with.

"What's so tough about that?" Vandenberg asked. "Kev and I have made any number of adobes together at the ranch."

"Gutierrez is in business. Suazo claims he's got Kevin turning out something like a thousand a week."

If that were true, something had gone wrong with the social workers responsible for Kevin. Working together, he and the boy had made as many as five hundred a week. He said now, "You really think it's Kevin—not somebody else?"

"How many tall, mentally retarded young men are there around here named Kevin? That's the name he gave the neighborhood kids when they asked him. After school, I drove out. The Gutierrezes' house is set back from the road. I thought I might be able to catch a glimpse of him, but there's a high wall around their property. I didn't want to park."

His first reaction was wariness. Conceivably, they might be using Kevin as bait, intentionally placing him in a home near one of her students. The father of the student might have been primed to relay the information to her. She was watching him. "You think it's a trick?"

"Possible."

"That's one thing they've taught us," she said sourly. "Distrust."

He nodded. "Yet, you drove out there?"

"I had to see! Gene, what are we going to do?"

He frowned. "I might be able to get to him, Terry—but what am I going to do with him afterward? It's not safe in the mountains."

"I know."

"I've had the best run of luck you'd want," he said. "With the new cabin, I'll be all right this winter. The point is, though, I might be able to make it up there for ten years, or then again maybe next week sombody will spot me—understand?"

"Gene, let me keep him here."

"It wouldn't work," he said.

"I could try."

"He wouldn't stay put longer than a week or a month, not with you away all day. He needs somebody with him. He'd be wandering all over San Sebastian."

"Are you going to leave him there?"

"No," he said. "I'll see for myself how he's being treated."

"When?"

"Tonight."

But he knew he'd take the boy with him. If in fact it did turn out to be Kevin, he wouldn't be able to leave him behind.

That evening he did not unpack his packboard. Out in her garage he found pliers and a screwdriver, and he took these, along with her flashlight.

They drove into town after midnight. Sitting beside her, he glanced at her face, illuminated by the green dash lights; she was tense, but she did not seem frightened. "Are any of these Gutierrez kids in your class?"

"No. Why?"

"Just wondering."

"Don't worry about me."

"No, listen. If it turns out to be him—assuming I can get close enough—I'll probably take him with me."

"I know."

"If I do, one of two things can happen—as far as you're concerned. If it's Kev, and he's been planted there, they'll trace all this to you. If that happens, it won't be pleasant."

"Suppose I simply confess?"

"It's prison then. And I'll lose my only contact with civilization."

"I never thought of myself as a link with the civilized world," she said drily.

"The other possibility," he said, "is that Suazo's mentioning Kev was in fact a coincidence. In that case, I doubt if they'd be

214

able to involve you. They'd check the Gutierrezes and the other people in the neighborhood, but I doubt if they'd check out a neighbor's children's teacher."

"Oh, is that why you asked if I had the Gutierrez kids in my class?"

They were far out on Agua Fria now, outside city limits. Agua Fria Village was actually a suburban extension of Santa Fe. Most of its residents were working-class Spanish-Americans. He said now, "Dogs. I'll lay odds there are dogs around."

Years ago he'd gone with a Spanish girl in Agua Fria, and he could remember nights when one dog would begin barking, to be followed by another, and still another, until the area sounded like a kennel gone wild.

"Drop me near the house," he said. "After I get out, drive on for a couple of miles along Agua Fria—then turn around and drive back. When you approach the house, slow down. If you see me step out into the road, stop. Otherwise keep on. If the house is lit up when you drive back, get the hell out of here, fast. If it's dark, and I'm not out front, do the same thing again—drive a few miles, turn around, come back, and slow down. But not if you see another car. If the lights are on, that'll mean trouble—don't stop. Don't worry about me, I can get away on foot. I know a lot of the side streets."

She found the Gutierrez residence with its high cinderblock wall and stopped the Plymouth. He got out. Far down Agua Fria a single street light burned. He stood a moment, waiting for his eyes to adjust to the dark. Then, moving to the corner of the lot where there were no bushes, he hoisted himself over the wall, running his hands gingerly along the top first, to see if they'd imbedded fragments of broken glass in the concrete cap.

In the yard he dropped into a flower bed. There were no lights on in the house, and apparently no dog either. Stepping carefully, he walked to the rear of the property, and in the faint light he saw that he was in the right place. Adobes, perhaps five thousand of them, were stacked in a small field that lay behind the house, neat, straight, waist-high rows of them, the topmost layers covered with strips of scrap tar paper. He frowned. This was crew work —for this many bricks you used a gang, two men to puddle and hoe, two more to feed the forms, a fifth, maybe, to trim and stack.

You didn't use a single man. The Spanish themselves would not do it single-handed.

He found the shed, hoping that Terry's Mr. Suazo was right and they were not keeping the boy in the house. It was a small storage shack built of rough lumber. He went up to it, walked around it, found the door, delicately feeling with the tips of his fingers for the lock and hasp, then put his lips to the jamb and whispered, "Kevin? You in there?"

There was no reply from inside. He called the boy's name six or seven more times, and then he heard a movement, someone stirring, and Kevin's voice, sleepy. "Who's there?"

"Kev. It's Daddy. Wake up."

And this was his worst moment, because there was the chance that they might have told the boy the wrong things, so that he would blame him for everything, for his being left alone, for being picked up and shuffled from one frightening place to another. He whispered again, "Kevin—it's Daddy. You hear?"

From inside there was a movement, and then the sound the boy made when he wept. Something was knocked over or fell to the floor, and then Kevin was at the other side of the door. He felt the wooden door sag as the boy strained against it; one of the hinges broke part way. "Daddy? You out there?"

"Hush, darling," he whispered. "Jesus, keep quiet, will you?"

"Daddy? Is that you?"

He was alarmed at the sound of Kevin's voice, cracking and rising in near hysteria. "Kev, keep quiet, for Christ's sake, will you? You hush, hear? I've come to get you. Just keep quiet a minute."

"I knew you'd come," Kevin was saying from the darkness inside. "I knew if I waited, and was good, you'd come for me."

By then he was working with the screwdriver, trying to find purchase on the rusted and paint-coated screws holding the hasp and padlock, and he could not see, and finally, losing his temper completely, he slipped the blade of the screwdriver between the hasp and the wood and wrenched, bending the steel shank of the screwdriver, making a lot of noise but ignoring it now in his anger. Something in the shed went over with a crash. He wrenched again at the hasp, and the door came loose, swung open, and he stepped

216

inside. His son grabbed hold of him. "Daddy, you won't leave me here now, will you? I hate it here. You're going to take me with you?"

"It's all right, honey. Keep quiet," he whispered. "Yes, you're going with us." He took out the flashlight and snapped it on. "You got a coat? Shoes? Get them on."

The circle of light moved around the interior of the shed. There was an army cot against one wall and a pair of heavy work shoes set neatly under it, the way he'd taught the boy. "Hurry, will you?"

Then, as Kevin sat down on the cot and began pulling on the shoes, not bothering with socks, still talking, a light came on at the rear of the main house. Vandenberg switched the flashlight off, hushing the boy.

A man opened the back door and came down the steps. In the light of the doorway, Vandenberg could see that he was dressed in trousers and slippers and an undershirt. He walked slowly toward the shed, peering in the darkness.

"Kevin? *Qué pasa?* What in hell you think you're doin', making all that noise for?"

Feeling in a trouser pocket now for a key, not seeing the already open door. Coming almost up to the shed before he realized, still squinting in the dark, that something was wrong—on guard now, fist clenched, the arm drawing back, but too late: Vandenberg, standing in the darkness inside the door, reached out swiftly, wordless, stepping forward, one hand looping up to grab a handful of thick hair; he yanked, dragged the man off balance and into the doorway, the flashlight whipping against the man's temple, forcing a gasp of pain, and twice more, across the face and skull. The head of the shattered flashlight burst off, both batteries in the case going too, to bounce off a wall somewhere in the shed; a spray of blood spackled the back of the hand that still clenched the man's hair, as Gutierrez went down. Heavy fist cocked, Vandenberg stood over him, panting, then wiped his bloodied hand on his jeans. "Kev—let's get the hell out of here."

Outside he ran, crouching low, Kevin behind him with the laces of his shoes untied, the shoes flopping. They trotted past the stacks of adobes to the front yard and were over the wall.

He was still panting. He stood on the sidewalk, looking down

Agua Fria. There were no headlights. He cursed and, too jittery to stand still, did a little hopping dance of impatience. "Goddamn her, where the hell is she? Come on, Terry."

A minute passed, two. There was still no sign of headlights. The house behind the high wall was still dark. Kevin, too, was so keyed up that he could not stand still. Then, far up the road, lights appeared, coming fast. He said, "Hide—it may not be her."

They trotted over to a thick clump of bushes near the wall and crouched down.

Kevin said, "Is that Terry, Daddy? Is that her in that car?"

"I sure hope so," he said. "If it isn't, we got some walking."

Near the house the car slowed; he touched his son on the arm and they ran out into the road. The car came abreast, then braked, and even before it had stopped he had a rear door open, shoving Kevin inside and scrambling in himself. "Get moving, Terry— we've got to get out of here fast."

She shifted, hitting the gas hard, and the Plymouth moved off. "Trouble?"

"Yes."

"Bad?"

He heard the fear in her voice. "I smacked a guy—Gutierrez, I think."

"Did you have to?"

He did not answer; after a minute, he said, "Slow down—keep it under fifty, will you?" He wished he'd hit the adobe manufacturer harder—if Gutierrez recovered and got to a phone, the police would be alerted in minutes.

They made it back, though, without trouble, reaching San Sebastian about two. As they pulled into the garage he said, "I'll get my pack and rifle, and we'll go. Get right to bed. Let's hope they don't check you in the next hour, before the motor's had a chance to cool."

"Gene—they won't check."

"Probably," he said. "Kevin and I will stay up at the cabin for a couple of weeks. I'll be listening on the transistor, but I don't think they'd play up something like this. When we come back down, if you think the house is being watched, park the Plymouth outside the garage the way I told you, okay?"

He and the boy got out and he shut the door. She rolled down the window on her side, and he leaned in and kissed her. "We better go now."

"Be careful."

"We will," he said. "Listen—thanks."

"That's all right."

"I couldn't have done it without you."

"Just be careful."

"Yes." She smiled at Kevin. "You take good care of your father."

"I will, Terry."

"I'm glad we finally found you."

"Me too."

THAT WAS THE BEGINNING of their retreat into the Sangres. He felt no regret over the beating he'd given Gutierrez. The boy's fingers and nails, split and crushed from handling the heavy mud bricks without gloves, took weeks to heal. Later he was able to tell his father a little of what had happened in the past year.

"That time when you didn't come home, I waited for you at the ranch, and there was nothing to do. I looked at all the magazines we had, cooked something to eat, and that night I was scared, and all the next day, too. Couple of times I walked up to the top of the hill to watch for our truck, but you never came. Then some soldiers drove up, and they took me to town."

"Did they do anything to the house?"

"They looked all around, that's all." He knew then that it had been vandals—probably town kids—who'd wrecked the place. "One soldier, he found your old .22 in the closet. They put a sign on the door. They put your papers in a box and took them. They brought me to town. Then I went to a big place, where you couldn't go outside. Then they sent me in a car to another place, a long way from here. I was scared there, too. I didn't think I was ever going to see you again."

By the end of the summer Kevin had regained the weight he'd lost. Together they rode the high trails, and fished upcountry streams and lakes that had not been visited since the start of the Occupation. They traveled to San Sebastian three times before first snow. Terry had heard nothing about the abduction. That fall, she surprised Vandenberg by giving him and Kevin mackinaws and new boots, which she'd obtained somehow on the black market.

It was then, too, that she gave him something he wanted as badly as clothing: looseleaf notebooks and several drawing pads, and an assortment of ball-point pens and conté crayons. That winter he began the first journal, using Terry's collection of books as a reference library, often writing all day beside a small window he'd made from a piece of scrap glass he had found. He began drawing again and made sketches of Kevin and the cabin, dozens of them, as though he had a need to record this life in a medium other than the journals.

They were passably comfortable. The horses, however, fared poorly, and had such a bad time of it that they were not fit to ride until the following April.

By and large, their life was not greatly different from the way they'd lived at the ranch. There was wood to be cut, water to be fetched. In the evenings after supper, they listened to the transistor. In mid-December he killed a cow elk with the Springfield, and its meat lasted the rest of the winter. As long as the snow blocked the trails there was no need to worry about patrols. His greatest worry was that he or the boy would become sick or be hurt—pneumonia, influenza, a broken leg: something as minor as an abscessed tooth could end it for them. Alone, he might have gambled on his ability to pull through an illness, but if anything happened to Kevin he knew he would give up and come down. In time this caution became almost morbid—he'd always been careful with tools, but was more so now, and an axe or a knife or a gun was treated with extreme respect.

4

The Raid
at Terrero

AT DAWN the following morning Tixier's high spirits of the night before had vanished.

Kevin was first out of his sleeping bag. By the time Vandenberg was up, he had a fire going and coffee on. Next came Tixier, limping over to the fire in long underwear. He squatted in front of it. "Is there any beer left?"

"We drank it last night," Vandenberg said.

Tixier picked up a bottle of bourbon and poured a spoonful into a metal cup, rinsed his mouth, spat, then poured an inch and slowly drank it.

"Abilene," Vandenberg remarked drily, "you are a man of iron."

"Merely a drop, to break open the tubes," Tixier said.

"You've got a lot to do today."

"Thousand times rather have a cold brew." Tixier turned to Kevin: "Son, would you mind very much fetching me my boots and pants?"

There were times when Tixier still looked good—Vandenberg had seen him fresh from the barber's chair, cheeks pink and shining after a hot towel and massage, shaved, talced. Today, however, in the raw light of dawn, he looked seventy. His eyes were darkly circled, and the craggy face looked doughy. The mane of white hair stood up in matted spikes. He seemed physically ill.

Willie Deaguero and Reuben were up by then. Abilene got into the boots and jeans Kevin brought and then limped down to the stream, removed his dentures, scrubbed them briefly in the icy water, and slipped them back into his mouth.

Vandenberg had Kevin put half a dozen leftover baked potatoes in the fire to heat. Abilene sat down beside him and poured more bourbon into his cup.

"Feeling better?" Vandenberg asked.

"I can't tell yet."

"After breakfast, you and Willie and Reuben better move along."

"You know, it's a shame anybody who enjoys drinking as much as me has to suffer this badly," Tixier said. "What's for chow, Gene?"

"Steaks again." He knew Tixier was forcing himself to appear cheerful. Deaguero and Reuben came over and sat down, and he said, "How're you boys feeling?"

Deaguero smiled ruefully. "*Poco bien,* Gene."

Archuleta said, "How much did we drink last night?"

"Two fifths, two six-packs."

Deaguero shook his head. Vandenberg said, "You'll feel better after breakfast."

COMMUNICATIONS

You will encounter among the Spanish-Americans in our part of the Southwest a higher percentage of the type potentially dangerous to the Occupation than anywhere else. Broadly speaking they are immature, suspicious, sullen, and exhibit all the weaknesses of an insulated ethnic group. They are, moreover, a dispossessed ruling class (having conquered this territory and opened it to trade centuries ago), which has since been reduced to ignominious servitude through laziness. The Iberian mentality is ill-equipped to cope with the Anglo's practicality. The Spanish, emotionally, are inveterate romantics. And they have a fatalistic attitude toward life —which is too often evidenced by an awesome disregard for it.

I would have men of Spanish-American ancestry with me not because they are braver, and certainly not because they're more dependable, but because they will kill. They will rally to a call that would leave the Anglo prudent and cautious. Truly, like the Arabs, they can be swung on an idea as on a cord. Let me point out that not a single trainee at Cowles was of Spanish-American descent. Either the Soviets are unaware of the combustibility of the Chicano, or else he has been able, to date, to avoid attracting attention— running, so to speak, submerged.

—The Journals

AFTER CHOW HE REVIEWED with them the tasks he had assigned. By then the sun was warmer, and they sat in a circle around the campfire.

Tixier said, "Gene, what're you going to do while we're down in town and Willie's getting the dynamite?"

"Go back to my cabin. The extra ammunition for my rifle is there. And I want to check the compound again."

"Going to make sure it's still there?"

"Sort of. I've got maps at the cabin, too, of the compound and Terrero."

"Maps? A regular military operation," the old rancher said.

"With them I can show everyone in five minutes what'll be going on."

"In the Army I was never much good at maps," Reuben said.

"You'll be able to read these."

"Gene, can I be your second-in-command?" Tixier said.

Vandenberg glanced at him. "You already know you are, Abilene."

"How far's this cabin of yours?"

"Half a day's ride."

"You going to bring us up there when this is over?"

"I may."

"Whyn't we ride up today?" Abilene asked. "I'd like to see how a dude like you lives so stylish up here."

"Let's get things squared away first," he said.

"I still wish we had more men."

"Just don't go starting a recruiting drive."

"Would you object if I bring more whiskey back?" Abilene asked.

"I wouldn't mind that a bit."

"Sometimes, Gene, you act so coldblooded you amaze me," Tixier said. "You act like raiding this camp was nothing. How do you do it?"

Vandenberg did not answer.

THEY LEFT by midmorning, with the promise that they would return by sunset the following day. He and his son watched them ride back down the trail. Kevin was disappointed over Abilene's leaving. Vandenberg glanced at the boy a moment and then said, "You like Abilene, don't you?"

"He's great. You think they'll really come back?"

"They may."

"I sure hope they do," Kevin said. "Daddy?" He looked at his father. "All that last night—about the compound—was that just talk?"

"If they don't come back, it was just talk, Kev."

"You really going to do it?"

"If Willie gets the dynamite, we may go ahead and try it. If nothing goes wrong."

"And that other—about having to hide—did you mean all that?"

"Yes."

"Abilene didn't like that part," Kevin said. "I could tell."

"I can't say I blame him."

"I think he meant it about all of us going fishing. I'd like that."

"We may do it," he said.

"Then it wasn't true about us having to hide *all* the time?"

"I wanted Abilene to understand that it won't be easy. But afterward, he and I are going to sit down and have a long talk— we'll figure out what to do."

The two knelt on the ground and began packing their gear. Finally Kevin said, "You think we'll ever go back to our ranch?"

"Hard to say."

"Not now—I mean, someday?"

"Someday, maybe," he lied.

"I'd like that best," Kevin said. "I miss the ranch. That was the best."

Vandenberg looked at him affectionately. "Maybe we'll get back there. I liked it best out there, too."

"You remember how I used to feed the birds?"

"I sure do."

"I thought about my birds a lot when I was in that place. They must be starving with no one to take care of them."

"They're wild, Kev. They find their own food."

"You mean they won't be there when we go back?"

"They'll come back—we'll put out the stale bread in the feeders, the way we used to, and in a week or so they'll all be back."

"I'd like that fine."

"Well then, we just might do it one of these days."

They continued putting away the cooking utensils and sleeping gear. Kevin said, "We going to see Terry?"

"No. Like I told them, we're going up to the cabin. Why?"

Kevin shrugged. "I thought you might want to ride down to see her, but didn't want to tell Abilene."

"There's no time. You're right, though, about Abilene—I'd rather he didn't know about her. You didn't mention her?"

"No. But I think he knows we visit her. He's awful smart."

"He probably does. But let's not say anything about it anyway."

"I wouldn't tell," Kevin said. "Wasn't I good, all yesterday? I hardly said anything."

"You were just fine."

"I did what you told me, that's all. I didn't say anything or do anything at all I shouldn't have."

"You're a good boy," he said, and then asked, "Do you like Willie Deaguero?"

"He's all right."

"How about Reuben?"

Kevin thought. "I don't think he likes me."

"And Abilene's the best?"

"He's the best." His son smiled. "That's for sure."

IN THE COMPOUND trainees were visible outside the dorms. It was lunch hour, and they would be enjoying the fresh air before reporting to afternoon classes.

They had tethered the horses in an aspen grove a quarter of a mile off and had walked south along a foot trail to the camp.

With Kevin beside him, he scanned the camp through the glasses for half an hour. The boy had wrapped a leftover steak in a rag, and they divided this and ate. "You looking for something special?" his son said finally.

"No. I only wanted to make sure things were the same."

"Are they?"

"Seems to be," he said, chewing at a piece of the cold steak.

"You want it that way—the same?"

"Yes."

They watched awhile longer and then made their way back to the horses.

BY MIDAFTERNOON TIXIER and his friends reached their concealed truck and horse trailer. They had parked the rig at the end of a logging lane near Holy Ghost. Tixier dismounted, groaning. "That Vandenberg—making us ride our asses off . . ."

"He was sure in a hurry," Deaguero said.

"He's waited this long, he can wait a little longer." Tixier massaged his buttocks and the insides of his thighs. "I sure wish there was some way to ride a horse for the first time in a year without feeling permanently crippled." He limped over to the pickup truck, unlocked the doors, and took out a fresh fifth from under the seat. He opened it, drank, then passed it to Willie. "That Gene's a *loco* bastard."

"He wasn't chicken, though," Deaguero said.

"No, but he was suspicious—and he'll stay that way until we all come back."

"You know what I think?" Reuben said.

Tixier looked at him. "What you thinking about, sugar?"

Archuleta said, "I think this whole deal's screwy, that's what."

"You do?"

Archuleta nodded.

"Why you think it's screwy?"

" 'Cause he's *serious*," Archuleta said. "He's goin' to keep fucking around till he gets us all killed."

"And you ain't serious, Reub?"

"I ain't ready to die."

Tixier stared at him. "You think I was kidding when we talked about this?"

"Matter of fact I did," Reuben replied.

Tixier glanced at Willie. "Hear that? He thought it was a put-on. With a five-year stretch attached to those .30-30's." He turned back to Reuben. "You want to ease out?"

Archuleta's mouth tightened, but he said nothing.

"Would you like me to fix it, if we raid that camp, for you to stay with the horses?"

Archuleta looked at the older man as though he were a stranger. "You mean you're really going to do it?"

"We might. Then again we mightn't," Tixier said. "Gene himself isn't sure what he wants."

"But that'll be asking for real trouble."

Tixier gave him a calm look. "You been in trouble before."

228

Archuleta shook his head. "Not like this."

Tixier turned to Deaguero. "Here's one little fucker you never want to sell short. He went and burned a guy in Albuquerque, six years ago. Had to tell old Abilene about it. How old were you then, Reub? Twenty-two? Got pissed off at this boy. Boy sitting in a car. Parked at the curb on North Fourth. Something to do with a girl. That was when you were still trying to play it straight, right, baby?"

Archuleta was silent.

"Went up to the car—stuck a .38 through the open window. Popped that kid right behind the ear," Abilene went on. "How about that? And got away with it. Just walked away. Threw that motherless .38 in a culvert. That's Reuben's brag, Willie. You ever kill anybody?"

Deaguero shook his head.

"That's just a story," Archuleta said angrily.

"You might lie to others—but not to old Daddy Tixier," Abilene said. "Right?" Archuleta said nothing. "Of course, now that he's got away with it, he wants to stay square."

Archuleta said, "I just don't want to see anybody get hurt."

"The way you hurt that boy in the car?"

"Abilene, lay off."

"Okay," Tixier said. "I'll lay off. And I'll fix it so's you watch the horses, same as you're going to do tonight, while Willie and me are in town."

"I want to come in with you," Archuleta argued. "I ain't going to stay up here with these dumb-assed horses. Why can't we load them into the rig and all go down?"

"Because we can't go driving an outfit like this all over the state without being checked," Tixier explained. "Gene's not dumb. He figures we have the mounts up here already, let them stay. That permit I got for us expired four days ago."

"Let's stake out the horses and go in together," Reuben insisted.

"That might work—providing Gene isn't sitting up on one of those ridges right now, watching us through his field glasses."

"You think he'd follow us?" Deaguero said.

"He's cagey enough to. And if he found out things weren't proceeding exactly according to schedule, he just might not be around when we come back."

"I ain't staying," Reuben said.

"It would please old Gene to know you were up here."

"*Por qué?*"

Tixier shrugged. *"Por qué no?* I had a hunch he might've been worrying about you—like maybe wondering if, while we were in Santa Fe, you might use a telephone to get a slice of that reward on him."

Archuleta protested, "You know I wouldn't do anything like that."

"I believe it," Abilene said, taking the bottle away from Willie. "But whyn't you do me a favor and stay?"

"I don't *want* to."

"I sure wish you would," Tixier said. His voice was gentle. "If you stayed, baby, I think that'd be the smart thing to do."

Young Archuleta looked rebellious; then he frowned and turned away.

"That's a good boy," Tixier said. Archuleta said nothing. "That's one thing I always loved about this kid," Abilene said to Deaguero. He drank from the bottle. "He's not muleheaded—always ready to listen to reason."

Once again Reuben said nothing, and then Tixier came on with it cold and flat: "You stay, baby, not because Gene wants you to—*I* want it, *sabe?* You fuck me up, and you won't be hiding from him —you'll have to hide from *me*. And I'll find you. We're gonna do this my way!"

"Okay," Archuleta said. "Suit yourself—but how come Gene thinks he's doing it his way?"

"Don't worry about that," Tixier said. "Let the silly son of a bitch think whatever he wants."

"What'll you tell him when he finds out you're bullshitting him?"

"Let me worry about that," Tixier said. He smiled. "Listen, all I'm asking is for you to mind the horses."

"Will you leave me the bottle?"

"No." Tixier's tone was definite. "But I'll bring you some more." Archuleta did not respond. "And, if you want, I'll put you with the horses when we hit the compound."

"I don't care about that," Reuben said. "But from what Gene said, we need about forty guys—" He objected several more times, but it was settled. They passed the bottle back and forth, had a smoke, and then Tixier and Deaguero unhitched the trailer and rolled it out of the way. Their gear—the saddles, bedrolls, camping equipment, rifles—was left behind. Tixier climbed in behind the wheel, and Deaguero got in beside him, slamming the door. Reuben came up. "When d'you think you'll be back?"

"Tomorrow afternoon, if we're not stopped," Abilene said. He started the engine. "If we ain't back by sunset, you'll know something went wrong."

"I'll wait here."

"You do just that. I'll bring you a cold beer." Tixier backed the truck. Archuleta walked beside it. "Reubenito, you tend those horses."

"I will."

"I don't aim to run all over these fucking hills looking for them."

"I'll watch 'em."

"That's my boy."

He shifted into first, and Archuleta called out, "You're coming back, aren't you—you ain't going to leave me here?"

Tixier grinned at him through the open window. "Leave you? Why, you mean little bugger. Old Abilene, he might do a lot of things, but he isn't about to go and do something foolish like that. Just don't you worry."

COMMUNICATIONS

MESSAGEGRAM

TO: L. A. INGRAM, CHIEF
    SANTA FE CITY POLICE
FROM: 1237 CIC, USSRAOOUSA
DISTRICT-32

SUBJECT: TIXIER, HOWARD A. (AKA "ABILENE"): DEAGUERO,
         WILLIAM R.: ARCHULETA, REUBEN A. (REFER TWX THIS
         HQS DTD 10/7)

WHEREABOUTS ABOVENAMED STILL UNCLEAR. REPEAT: TIXIER, H. A.
IS CATEGORY IV. REQUEST HOUSECHECK, 3956 CERROGORDO, SANTA
FE, AND NOTIFY THIS OFFICE OF FINDINGS.

THE DRIVE DOWN Holy Ghost was rocky, and Tixier took it slow, the bourbon propped between his thighs; after they had driven awhile he said, "Willie, there's aspirin in the glove compartment—get me three or four." Deaguero found the tin; Tixier chewed up four of the tablets, washing them down with a sip of liquor.

Deaguero said, "Damned if I understand how you can drink this early."

"It ain't easy," Tixier said. He lit a cigarette.

They were silent, and finally Deaguero said, "You laid it on Reuben hard."

"Won't hurt him."

A mile farther on Deaguero glanced over at him. "You were right, though—Reuben had something on his mind."

"He's not a bad kid," Tixier replied. "You need to keep an eye on him, that's all." Deaguero did not speak. "Kid like that needs a little extra attention." Deaguero slid his rump forward on the seat until his knees were propped on the edge of the dash. He tilted his Stetson forward over his eyes. Tixier glanced at him and smiled. "You don't cotton to Reuben?"

"I don't reckon I do," Willie said. He folded his hands across his paunch. "He's as useless as tits on a goose."

"My hunch is that he doesn't care all that much for you either."

"That's his problem," Willie said agreeably.

"He probably figures there was once something between us," Tixier said.

Beneath the Stetson's brim, Deaguero's eyes were shut. "Now, where'd he get an idea like that?"

"Probably from me," Tixier said. "But he's got no reason to be jealous."

"It was a long time ago," Deaguero said. "Ain't he a mite old for you, Abilene?"

"He's a good boy," Tixier said again. He uncapped the bourbon and took a drink. "And so were you—only I don't know how you ever got so fat—why, I recollect when I could put both my hands around your waist."

They were silent. Finally Deaguero said, "You feeling any better?"

"Some. What I need is about ten hours' sleep and a cold six-pack."

232

"What you going to do after you drop me at Rowe?"

"Drive over to Pecos and see Cip. Then I'll go talk to your dad. I got a lot of moving around to do—got to stop by the Military Government office again."

"What?"

"Going in and talk to Ivan."

Deaguero lifted the brim of his Stetson and looked at him incredulously. "You're *loco!*"

Tixier grinned. "Our pass expired four days ago. We never reported in."

"You mean, you're going to walk right in there? Now?"

"We don't want to break the law."

Deaguero thought about this. "I don't think I could do it. Not now." He shook his head.

"All you need is an honest face. Like Gene used to be—he had the look of a real honest dude. Innocent. Not much left of that now. It always surprised him when people never turned out to be what they told him they were. A real jerk. Now it's too late. He's done for and he knows it. Ain't nobody going to wipe his nose for him except maybe that little cunt he used to run with—and I'll bet he's still sneaking down to her place every once in a while to get his ashes hauled."

"I never knew her," Deaguero said.

"Smart little bitch," Tixier said. "Only sign Gene ever gave that he had a speck of brains is that he never married her. Why buy a cow, when buttermilk's cheap?"

"You knew her?"

" 'Course." Tixier drank again from the bottle. "She knew I was wise to her. We used to sit in the Montana, and she'd tell me how brilliant she thought he was." The old rancher's expression was cynical. "Sh-i-i-t. She just couldn't get enough of that Vandenberg cock, that was all. Why, I'll bet he's hung like a bull."

"You're putting him down," Deaguero said, reaching for the bourbon. "And yet you still want to make him a hero?"

Tixier smiled. "Hell, why not?"

"Can't make something big out of somebody doesn't want to be big."

"Oh, he'd like being big, don't fool yourself. He'd give both eyes for a chance."

"Then why didn't you tell him everything?"

"He's too spooky," Tixier explained. "Why, just having the three of us find him got him so jumpy he didn't know whether to shit or go blind. With a dude like Gene, all you can do is let him think he's running the show."

"When're you going to tell him?"

"Tomorrow night maybe."

"I thought this morning you were going to."

"I never like to rush things," Tixier said.

Deaguero glanced at him. "He knew we weren't being straight with him—suppose he doesn't show?"

"He'll show."

"You're sure?"

"He's suspicious—but he's just like an old stand-up whore about to step inside church for the first time in twenty years—'fraid to move, more 'fraid not to. He and his kid'll be at the mica mine, you'll see."

"Listen, you really think we can do it?"

"He thinks so."

"With that many sentries?"

"He's got a plan," Tixier said. "Only I got one, too. He just doesn't know how big it could get. His feelings about Cowles are all personal—he's plumb pissed off at what they did to him up there and what they did to his place. As crazy as he is it's a wonder he hasn't gone and shot up that camp single-handed. Why, if we work it right, the way folks exaggerate, it'll sound like a handful of us wiped out half the Russian Army, how about that?"

Deaguero looked at Tixier again. "Who wants to be a hero now?"

"Not this boy," Tixier said. "Fact is, though, you and I were the only ones in the organization who could have tracked down Gene, and by God we did. Willie, you want to use your head more. Gene wouldn't have any part of the organization—and they wouldn't want any part of him, *que no?*" Deaguero nodded. "On the other hand, they ain't got guts enough to do anything more than sit around talking. Someone like me, I ain't about to be a hero. All I am is a . . . liaison man. The group won't move—but Gene will. He's crazy, but he'll go after that camp. If nothing goes wrong, we can get us some pictures that'll be worth a mint. Why, it could get to be like one of those chain reactions even."

"Or a misfire," Deaguero argued. "Personally, I got nothing against old Gene. But he ain't no chain reaction. He's nothing but an old drunk who broke jail and killed a guy, maybe by accident, but he ain't no hero."

Tixier glanced at Willie. *"Mira,* don't you see, that's the funniest part of it? I know it. You know it, and so does Reuben. Gene's a zero. But nobody else has to know it. It's what people think of you that counts. If everything goes right, you may hear his name all around the country. We're liable to end up being the only ones who know what a horse's ass he really is."

DEAGUERO HAD LEFT his pickup behind a Mobil station on the outskirts of Rowe four days earlier, when he and Tixier had rendezvoused.

Like other towns in the northern part of the state, Rowe existed partially on welfare subsidies and partially on intermittent incomes earned by its male citizens who traveled to larger towns to find employment. It was less a village than a scattering of forty or fifty run-down adobe and frame buildings. The big four-lane highway on which Deaguero was employed as a heavy-equipment operator bypassed the settlement, half a mile to the south.

The pickup was where he'd left it. As Deaguero got out of Tixier's truck, Abilene said, "When will you see Nat?"

"Right now."

"Not going to report in for work?"

"Hell, no."

"Listen, if you're stopped by M.G., tell them you were with me, the way we planned," Tixier said. "Tell 'em we got lost and that I've gone in to town to get our pass extended, so's we can find our horses."

"You really going to try and get that pass?"

"Sure. Can you get the other stuff?"

"I'll get it."

"I'll see you at Holy Ghost tomorrow then."

"Stay sober, Abilene. When you see my dad, tell him I'll be waiting for him."

"I'll do that." Tixier raised a hand in farewell and drove off. Deaguero stood by the gas station, watching the cloud of dust the truck made, until it drove up on the shoulder of the four-lane and turned west toward Santa Fe.

THAT AFTERNOON THEY REACHED the cabin. The sky was perfectly clear, and the sun shone, but it was growing late enough in the year so that its heat did not really warm, and they wore woolen shirts. The distance from their camp near the mica mine was not great, but the trail they had taken was bad, with difficult grades, and the animals were tired.

They spent an hour unpacking their gear and rubbing the horses down before turning them out to graze, and then some more time at the mouth of the ravine working with willow branches, sweeping dirt over their tracks. "When we leave tomorrow, we'll do the same thing again," he said.

"You don't think they'd follow us?"

"They might. The cabin's our ace in the hole. If anything happens we can turn the horses loose and walk in. If we don't light a fire, we can stick it out for weeks."

They walked back up to the cabin. The sun had already disappeared behind a high bluff to the west. It was the best time of day, quiet and turning cool, and he placed an arm across his son's shoulders.

Kevin looked at him. "Will we really come back here?"

"I imagine so. Why?"

"Oh—all that talk last night—with Abilene." Vandenberg did not reply, and his son went on. "You sounded like maybe all this was done with."

"It might be different," he said. "It's hard to say. He might not come back."

"I don't want you to get hurt," Kevin said.

"Don't worry about it."

"You're always telling me that."

They reached the clump of willows that hid the cabin and crossed the stream. His son filled a pot with water and built a fire.

He poured himself a little whiskey from one of Tixier's fifths and sat down in the doorway and began cleaning the Springfield, using a straightened coat hanger for a rod, stroking out the barrel with scraps of oiled rag. When he was satisfied with the bore he worked on the bolt, leisurely wiping it clean and free of dust. In the fading light he went over the stock and exposed metal with the last piece of oiled rag. He'd pampered the scope-sighted gun in the time he'd had it, and despite the bad weather and knocks it had taken, very little of the deep bluing had worn from the metal, except along one side of the barrel, where it rubbed against the scabbard he had made. He had grown fond of the Springfield. It shot well, far tighter than you had any right to expect from a lightweight sporter, and he was sure it would group under two inches at a hundred yards. He had never been a good marksman—he tended to let off a round too quickly—but in a prone or sitting position he could shoot very well with this gun. In the time he'd had it, he had used twenty-six rounds, taking eleven deer, two elk, and now the calf he had killed yesterday.

When he was done he stood the gun in a corner and got the cloth sack that held the ammunition. He emptied it, counting: three of the boxes were unbroken, and the fourth had fourteen rounds in it. Seventy-four rounds.

While Kevin was frying meat for dinner, he unrolled their sleeping bags on the raised earthen pallets he had built along the inner wall.

They ate at the table while there was still daylight, and afterward Kevin made coffee. Vandenberg struck a match to a cigarette and went over and sat down in the open doorway. After the boy had rinsed their dishes he joined his father, moving a stool close to the doorway. Neither spoke, and finally Vandenberg flipped away the stub of his smoke.

"Why're you so quiet tonight?"

Kevin did not reply.

"Cat got your tongue?"

"I don't feel good," Kevin said. "All that talk."

"It bothered you, eh?"

"A little," his son said. "And quit telling me I shouldn't worry."

He tilted his head back against the jamb of the door, regarding the boy. "Do you still remember what I told you to do, in case I get hurt?"

"Why do you have to talk about that?"

"Do you remember?"

The stubbornness persisted. "If you ain't going to get hurt, why do I have to remember?" The boy's face was sullen. "I have to go to Terry's house."

"That's right. What else?"

"I have to go at night. And look all around, 'cause somebody might be watching."

"Why, you remember every word."

"And I have to take the notebooks to her—all of them," Kevin recited. "And I mustn't get them wet. If it's raining, I have to wrap them in the plastic sheet."

"That's perfect."

"And I have to do what she wants," his son concluded. "Right?"

"Right," he said. "Most likely I won't get hurt. But if I ever did, you'd have to know how to get along."

"I don't see why I couldn't stay up here."

"You could, Kev, but not forever."

"Or I could bring Terry up. We could take care of you, till you got better."

"That'd be fine, except we don't want to make any trouble for her."

"She'd come," the boy said. "I bet old Terry wouldn't mind at all." He was still angry at being forced to speak about possibilities. "I don't understand why you want to mess around that compound for anyway."

Vandenberg said nothing.

"Because they put you in there and did bad things to you?"

"Not only that—it's really a bad place. The hospital you were in at La Madera was bad, but this is worse."

"If I didn't like a place that much, I wouldn't hang around it, the way we are. I'd go someplace else."

"If I could think of a place to go, I'd forget about the camp and Abilene and the others in a minute," he said. "We'd pack our stuff and go get Terry and say the hell with all this."

"That'd be great."

"Let me work on it. One of these days, I may think of just such a place."

Kevin glanced at him. "Ah, that's just talk."

"No, it isn't really."

"It is too. If you wanted to find a place like that as bad as you want to think about that camp, you'd have found it long ago."

He smiled. "Why do you say that?"

"Because you can do anything you want."

"I wish that were true."

"It's true," the boy said. "Terry told me once. She said there wasn't a thing in the world you couldn't do if you once made up your mind about it."

"What else did she tell you about me?"

"Lots of things, only I can't remember. She said you were crazy."

"Maybe she's right."

"I just don't want you getting hurt," his son said again.

He let it drop, and lit another cigarette. Later he got out several of the maps he'd drawn and the latest notebook, and, sitting by the fire, writing slowly, made an entry.

WHILE DEAGUERO was seeing Natividad Gabaldon, Tixier visited the District Office of Soviet Military Government. He had already stopped at Pecos to talk with Cip Griego, and on the way in had detoured at Cañada de los Alamos to visit Ben Deaguero.

The Travel Permit Division was located near the Bureau of Motor Vehicle Registration in one of the older buildings that made up the state capitol complex. The high-ceilinged corridors were cool and quiet and almost deserted, and Tixier's spike-heeled boots sounded against the parquet floors; he passed large offices, with opened doors, that were filled with white-collar workers at their desks.

He found the room he was searching for. A few clerks glanced at him with curiosity. Tixier was either unaware of or did not mind his appearance. Beneath the banks of blue fluorescent lights, the filthy jeans and work jacket, the stubbled chin, the cocked Stetson, were all emphasized.

He went up to a counter, took the expired permit out of his wallet, and presented it to an official. "Howdy. You made this out for me last week."

The man behind the counter looked up. "Hello. I remember you." He took the pass. "This expired, three—no, four—days ago."

"We had some trouble."

The official frowned. "You had a burial permit, didn't you? Were you able to take care of that?"

"We took care of it. Two friends came along to help." The official nodded. "We had some horses with us. They got away."

"You know, you should have gotten in touch with this office."

"No phones up there."

"I guess it's all right," the man said. "The pass is void, but since you're back—"

"I've got to go back up tomorrow," Tixier said. The man stared at him. "One of the fellows with me broke a shock on his pickup. Hung it in a ditch. Other kid is up on Rowe Mesa with the horses. I've got to buy a shock, get some tools, and go back and give 'em a hand."

"I don't see how that'd be possible."

"Why not?"

"Your permit is void," the official said. "We'd have to make out an entirely new one—I couldn't extend this. You'd need gas and oil vouchers."

Tixier propped an elbow on the counter. "Sure 'nuff."

"I'd have to get an okay from the Transportation Officer."

"I'll wait."

"He won't approve it. He countersigned the original permit because it was for a special purpose—to bury your wife, as you explained. He won't okay a new permit just to bring in a couple of horses and a disabled vehicle."

Tixier looked down at his boots, and nodded. *"Amigo,* I understand. You guys have more damned forms to fill out. . . . But listen, these guys took off from work to help me in a bad time. I can't just leave them up there."

"I'm sorry."

"Isn't there something you could do?"

"Afraid not."

"Those fellows up there don't have any pass," Tixier insisted. "If they get picked up, they'll be in real trouble. You wouldn't want to hang six months on them for traveling without authorization." Tixier paused. "One of them is my late wife's godchild."

The man behind the counter looked irritated. "All right—I'll talk to the major. But he'll probably tell us both to go to hell."

"I appreciate it," Tixier replied. "Take your time—like I said, I got all afternoon."

The man left with the permit and Tixier waited. He lit a cigar-

240

ette, slouched against the counter, removed the Stetson, ran a hand through his matted hair, put the hat on again.

It took about five minutes. The official returned, smiling. "This is your lucky day." Tixier looked suitably grateful. "The major okayed a new permit. I swear, I don't understand that man—one minute he'll give permission, the next he won't."

"Friend, I want you to know I appreciate this."

The man took a pad from under the counter, slid carbons into the multicolored copies, and wrote a fresh permit. "I can only make this forty-eight hours."

"That's all right," Tixier said. He tilted his head to watch the man's writing. "Have it start first thing in the morning."

The man recopied the necessary information from the old permit, tore loose the perforated sheaf, and handed the original to Tixier. "The major wanted to know if it's an American custom—burying someone on private land."

"It used to be, around here."

"Me, I'm a vet," the man behind the counter said. "When I go they can put me up in the National Cemetery."

"Me too," Tixier said. "That way it doesn't cost a cent." He folded the permit and tucked it into his wallet. "Thanks a lot."

"Glad I could help."

Tixier left. He was still feeling bad, but his mood had improved, and he began whistling to himself, the shrill sound echoing in the quiet corridors. In the office the man behind the counter turned and said to a girl seated nearby, "Could you smell him, Imelda?"

The girl smiled. "He's been celebrating."

"Smelled like a distillery. His wife just died."

"Do you know him?"

"Never saw him before last week."

"What'd he want?"

"New permit. Poor old devil."

Ten minutes later Tixier was having his first cold beer at the Montana Bar.

NATIVIDAD GABALDON, forty-two, graying now at the temples and with six front teeth missing, was courting a fifteen-year-old high-school dropout, name of Darlene Fresquez, when Deaguero showed up. Gabaldon's style involved large and continuous servings of homemade red wine, which he got from an uncle near Mora. The girl had been in his ramshackle three-room home for two days and her parents in Santa Fe had an all-state alarm out on her, but Gabaldon did not know this: both had been drunk since day before yesterday when he'd picked her up at a Tastee-Freeze on Cerrillos Road.

When Deaguero, who was his best friend, knocked at his door, Natividad greeted him delightedly and immediately suggested that Willie open another half gallon of Mora red and have a go at the girl. Deaguero, who had seen some of Gabaldon's girl friends, insisted on having a look first. Natividad tiptoed with him to the door of the bedroom, where the girl was either asleep or passed out atop a torn quilt, nude. Deaguero regarded her for a moment and then said, "I ain't got nothing to do until midnight."

" 'stá bueno," Gabaldon said. "All you got to do is give her a shove. She's always ready. She goes right off, just like a pistol."

"You ever get your clap cured?" Willie asked.

"It's pretty good now."

They went back to the kitchen. Deaguero said, "We got something big we're planning."

"Fun?" Deaguero nodded. "Count me in. Trouble?" Deaguero nodded again. "If you say it's good, I'm in," Natividad said.

"You'll have to get rid of her though."

"Send her home? Now?"

Deaguero drank from his half gallon. "In a couple hours."

COMMUNICATIONS

We need not stir about among buried recollections to recall that in the autumn of 1962 an irreproachably innocent Kremlin directed the secret mounting of nuclear missiles in certain shy Cuban preserves. Since the missiles were directed at various American capitals, they constituted a territorial intrusion of magnitude. The Americans, however, were believed to be fat, they were rich, they were preoccupied with the material things of life, they were politically divided at home and diplomatically irresolute abroad. That they were all of these things is indisputable, yet such indulgences did not add up to a noyau, *for American society was not held together by*

inner antagonisms and we remained a biological nation. The threat was revealed. And while a helpless, watching world suffered a succession of cold sweats and heart attacks, the American put his Cadillac in the garage, returned his two-inch steak to the frigidaire, turned off the television set and the air-conditioning, kissed his wife and the children and the stock market goodbye and marched as one man to the confrontation. The Soviets withdrew. And the world in a dead faint was carried out of the ball park.
              —R. Ardrey, The Territorial Imperative

But this time around, it didn't work that way—what happened?
              —The Journals

HE WAS MORE FRIGHTENED than he would have imagined. Earlier, with Gabaldon, he had felt no nervousness at all. Drinking with Nat there had been an air of intrigue and excitement. They had wakened the Fresquez girl, gotten her clothes on, and taken her to a neighbor, who promised to drive her back to Santa Fe. Later Deaguero had borrowed a broad-head axe and a pry bar. It was dark when he said good-bye to Gabaldon, promising to meet him the following afternoon at Holy Ghost. Gabaldon planned to ride his horse from Rowe. By then both were drunk.

Deaguero was fine until he drove out of Rowe and onto the four-lane. Then he sobered up and began getting rocky. He lit a cigarette but this did not help. He remembered that he had not brought blankets as Vandenberg had directed, so that he could pad the explosive.

He knew that if he were stopped by a prowl car he would never be able to fool them. He drove carefully, staying within the legal limit. Several cars passed him, heading toward Santa Fe. By the time he came to the section of highway under construction his broad, round face was shining with perspiration.

It had been almost a week since he'd left the job site, but nothing was changed. He passed the monstrous metal-and-concrete culvert cylinders that had been dropped by the supply gangs, and a mile farther on he made his turn off the highway, where the supply and engineering shacks were located. The broad beams of the pickup's lights swept across ranks of parked equipment, the big, bright-yellow Cats and Euclids.

He parked near the superintendent's shack, turned off the lights and engine, and waited. A car passed on the highway, going fast. Finally he got out of the truck. His hands and fingers felt numb.

Standing beside the pickup, he peered around in the dark, began whistling softly, and then, finally, felt around on the bed in the rear, searching for the axe and pry bar. He found them, and like a mongrel dog began scouting around the shacks and parked equipment, reassuring himself that he was alone. There was a ghostliness about the area. He had been used to it during the day, used to the clattering roar of the big earthmovers. He felt strange without his hardhat.

Satisfied that he was alone, he walked quickly to the superintendent's shack. The nervousness in him had built up now. He set down the pry bar, placed one foot on the lowermost wooden step of the shack, and swung the axe fiercely. It struck the plywood door just above the deadbolt lock so hard that the door burst open, and, as though he were facing a physical enemy, Deaguero charged inside, axe held ready. He fell over a wastebasket, skidded headlong, skinning the knuckles of one hand, scrambled quickly to his knees.

He struck a match, seeing familiar objects—desks, metal file cabinets, drawing tables—and got to his feet. The desk was locked. Deaguero found the axe he'd dropped, felt in the dark, and smashed the center drawer, releasing the lock fasteners on the side drawers.

In the bottom left-hand drawer, along with cartons of .22 explosive cartridges for the Ramsets, he found the blasting caps, coils of wire, and two small hand detonators in heavy canvas bags. In the shallow center drawer there was a handful of keys, each with a circular cardboard disk tied to it, for the other shacks and the equipment. One of them was for the corrugated steel shed behind the parked equipment, near the edge of the woods.

Breaking in had only taken a few minutes. Deaguero paused now, and went to the open door to listen. He was still alone. Taking the detonating gear and his tools, he went back to the truck, opened the door on the driver's side, and placed everything on the seat. It would be almost an hour before he would remember that Vandenberg had told him to put the caps in the back.

He got behind the wheel and drove down the line, not putting the lights on. At the steel shed he got out and inserted the key he'd taken into the padlock on the door. At first it would not turn, and then it did, and the lock snapped open. He stepped inside, striking another match. Stacked against the walls were half a dozen new spades, a bundle of surveying stakes, two transits in rosewood boxes, tripods, raincoats hung on nails, an open carton of scaffolding nails, and the blasting dynamite, six cases of it. Almost in a leisurely way now, Deaguero carried out two unopened boxes, one at a time, placing them in the back of the truck.

He got back behind the wheel, started the motor and turned around, and was almost ready to switch on the lights when far down the highway headlights appeared, quickly growing brighter, and all his terror returned. He swore, turned the motor off, opened the door part way, ready to abandon the truck and dash for the woods if the car on the highway slowed, but it did not. Sitting there, he watched it speed past, and when it was gone he sighed, slammed the door weakly, and started the motor again, easing the truck up the dirt lane away from the rows of silent machines until he felt the wheels hit the smooth concrete of the road, and then he switched the lights on and floored the gas pedal, wanting more than anything else to put distance between himself and the site.

He lit a cigarette, forgetting the dangerous caps on the seat beside him, and puffed hard, his hands tight on the wheel. He was almost back to Rowe before he thought to glance at the speedometer, the nausea returning again: the indicator quivered between ninety and ninety-two. He eased off the gas, so that when he finally got the Dodge back down to sixty-five, it felt as though the truck was crawling along in first.

BENEATH THE PALE MOON the compound was silent, its perimeter marked by bluish mercury-arc floodlights. In the towers the sentries sat beside small electric heaters. Within the fences the dorms were silent and dark except for night lights in the latrines. In the old trout pond bordering the road outside the compound a thin sheet of ice had begun to form along the shoreline.

AT TEN THAT EVENING, the sergeant on duty at City Police Headquarters received a radio message and gave the patrolman who'd sent it a stand-by. He dialed the number of USSRAOOUSA Counterintelligence at St. John's. "This is Officer Ramirez, City Police. I have a confirmation on a Category IV suspect."

The Russian officer at the other end asked him to hold on until he got pencil and paper. In a moment, he was back on the line. "Go ahead."

"This is in reference to a TWX from your office, numbered"—Officer Ramirez flicked through a sheaf of teletype messages clipped to a board—"hold on, please. Here it is—number two-four-one-three-B. The name is Tixier—Howard, initial R—AKA Abilene. Do you have your copy there?"

"No," the Russian officer said. "Will you please read back the contents."

Ramirez scanned the message. "This man overstayed a special permit, which expired last week. No arrest is indicated, only that your office be notified."

"Where is he?"

"In a bar downtown, drunk," Ramirez said. "I just had a radio call on him."

"Here in Santa Fe?"

"Yes."

"Where, Comrade?"

"The Montana Bar on the plaza."

"But no pickup was indicated in the TWX?"

"No."

There was a pause. "All right—I'll make a note of it for the duty officer in the morning. What was that number again?"

"Two-four-one-three-B, as in baker."

"Thank you."

"No trouble," Ramirez said. There was a click at the other end of the line and he hung up the receiver. He went to the radio room and took the mike from the night operator. "Five-oh-one—come in."

From the grilled loudspeaker above the transceiver a distorted voice replied: "Five-oh-one—go ahead."

"Sanchez—on that Category IV—no pickup is indicated. Repeat, no pickup."

"Roger."

"What's Abilene doing?" Ramirez asked. He had known Tixier many years ago.

"Intoxicated," the loudspeaker replied.

"Disorderly?"

"No more than usual."

"When will you check the Montana again?"

"About twelve thirty."

"If he's still there, tell Nikos to call a cab and run him home."

"Roger." There was a pause. "I could give him a lift."

"You some kind of taxi-driver?"

"Negative."

"All right then."

"Roger. Ten-four."

Ramirez put the mike down and went back to his desk and the *National Geographic* he had been reading.

IN THE MONTANA Nikos was ordering Tixier to finish his drink and go home, but there were only a few customers and Abilene knew the Greek was only going through the motions. Nikos always threatened to cut off his noisier customers.

"What do I want to go home for?" Tixier demanded.

"Get yourself some sleep. You been here all night."

"I just might never set foot inside that house again," Tixier said. "No heat turned on. Empty. All locked up."

Nikos knew about Olga's death and he said nothing. He disapproved of Tixier, and considered him a bad drunk and very risky in the morals department, but the old rancher had been one of his steadiest, and he paid cash. Still, Tixier was often unmanageable when stoned, and tonight was no different. His mood at present was convivial and sentimental, but could easily turn nasty. Nikos knew that while Tixier would not ordinarily start a fight, he would not back down from one. On top of it, Sanchez, the local cop, had been in twice. Now Tixier, as though he were offering a bribe, leaned across the bar. "Mix me *one* more—and I'll go home."

"You don't need another."

"Just one—"

"All right. But this is the last."

Nikos made a bourbon-and-water and sorted through Tixier's change on the bar.

"Things're going to be different after tonight," Tixier announced, looking around at the other drinkers. "Going to change."

"You going on the wagon?"

"New leaf."

"That'll be the day."

Tixier did not reply. Nikos asked, "Everything go all right up at the ranch?"

"Just the way she would have wanted it," Abilene said. "Two-by-eights, solid cedar, copper screws. Set me back forty-six bucks. We put her on the high slope behind the main house." He sipped, looked around again. "Anybody want to buy a house? Authentic 'dobe, herringbone aspen ceilings, two-hundred-year-old *vigas*. Sell it cheap."

"How much do you want?" Nikos asked.

Tixier shrugged. "Pointless. Property transfers all frozen. Merchantable title's a meaningless phrase—hell of a way to run things."

"Write your congressman," Nikos advised.

"We were married thirty-one years," Tixier said. "It ain't easy to turn around and make an adjustment like that after thirty-one years. You take that house—I don't feel like going into it. Don't feel like cooking up a meal or turning on the TV, don't feel like watering her goddamn flowers."

The Greek nodded. "Why not go down to El Fidel and rent a room?"

Tixier shook his head. "The hell with El Fidel. I'll show them."

Nikos smiled. "Show who?"

"You just watch the papers in the next few days."

"What page? You going to make the front page?"

"Listen, Nikos, you're putting me down," Tixier warned. "I know what you're thinking. All of you, always putting me down. Vandenberg and that whole bunch. You can't fool me."

The door of the Montana opened, and a man in a dark overcoat and an Astrakhan hat entered. Claude Remington was a middle-sized, handsome man in his late forties, with patrician features and dark, wavy hair. He saw Tixier, glanced around at the other drinkers, and went over and joined the rancher. "Tixier, my friend, where've you been keeping yourself?"

"Hello, Claude," Tixier said, looking up.

"Nikos?" The Greek nodded a greeting. "Slow night," Remington observed, looking around the bar.

"Been a bad month."

"To cheer you up then, draw me a fifteen-cent beer," Remington said.

"Take it out of this," Tixier said, gesturing toward his loose change.

"Dutch treat," Remington insisted, feeling in his pocket. "I'm not about to return the gesture by buying you a double Heaven Hill. Haven't seen you around."

"Been away. We buried Olga."

"It take a week?"

"There was something I had to take care of."

Remington's beer came, and he tasted it. "Ah . . ." He took out a cigarette and fitted it into a black plastic holder.

"What's new with you, Claude?" Nikos asked.

"Money's tight," Remington said sourly. "Lately, there hasn't been enough action to cover the rent. Gladys is looking at me like a barracuda again."

"She coming in later?"

"How the hell am I supposed to know what that dame's going to do? All I know is that she gave me the barracuda look tonight, so I thought I'd take a walk."

"Gladys is a good gal," Tixier remarked.

"She's a twenty-one-carat, blue-white diamond," Remington agreed. "Only sometimes I can't stand her vibrations."

"You ought to appreciate your wife," Tixier remarked sententiously.

"She bites the hand that feeds her."

"A wonderful, patient woman . . ." Tixier was insisting.

Remington considered this carefully and then said, "Bullshit."

"Ah, Claude—"

"Listen, you imitation Wyatt Earp," Remington said, "I appreciate that broad. What do you want from me, a black band on my sleeve because you're having a rough time? I like you. But because I come in for a lousy fifteen-cent beer, it doesn't mean I'm going to use up a box of Kleenex sympathizing with you. You want to cry, Abilene, do me a favor, go off and cry for both of us."

All this was said without rancor, and Tixier took it easily, smiling and nodding. "You never appreciate someone till she's gone."

"Listen, if Olga'd had sense, she'd of run your ass off twenty years ago. The only thing you're sorry for now is that there isn't anybody to post bail for you the next time you get busted."

"She had a hard life," Tixier admitted.

"She loved it," Remington said. "A classic masochist pattern."

"She never had to worry about money. I gave her everything."

"You gave her old age."

"We all grow old."

"Nikos, would you mind reaching me the slop bucket—I think I'm going to throw up."

Remington had been around Santa Fe for years. Depending on his mood when asked, he described himself variously as a publicist, free-lance promotional manager, or simply an entrepreneur. None of these vague professions were really viable in a city the size of Santa Fe, yet the fact remained that Remington had managed to survive, always involved in some get-rich-quick scheme he'd created, never making it big but never going completely under, expending more energy, it seemed, in the business of avoiding legitimate work than any conventional job could have ever exacted.

In past years he had sold insurance, cars, and mutual funds, had enrolled most of the town's health cranks in a food supplement plan, had at the height of the folk music boom imported countless long-tressed girl harpsichordists, lutists, and twelve-string guitarists for one-week stands in the various cocktail lounges that featured entertainment.

If there was one thing Remington confessed to being hooked on it was culture, just as he admitted that he regarded himself as a kind of *guru* of sophistication, dedicated to upgrading Santa Fe—a town, as Vandenberg had once pointed out to him, so absorbed with its own clouded image as an art world focal point that it could barely tolerate the most mundane outside talent, to which Remington had cheerfully remarked: "Culture's here to stay! I'll ram it down their fucking throats if I have to!" In this mood he went on bringing in minor poets and third-rate novelists and writers of travelogue books, along with flamenco groups, singers of *Lieder*, a French *mime*, and, once, a Nisei *origami* expert from Marin County, who spent the better part of a month showing the lady members of some of the town's garden clubs how to make boats, vases, and flowers out of folded paper.

He had lately involved himself with the organization in which Abilene Tixier was a member, thinking, perhaps like Tixier, that this might provide a medium leading to hard cash. The inherent dangers of being associated with a group revolutionary in nature

250

and seditious in intent made him nervous, but ultimately his feelings were perhaps again similar to the old rancher's in that he found a certain attraction in the sheer illegality of such a venture, and too, he believed that if you're going to make a little money you have to gamble a little. The group, made up of about thirty men, did indeed have a high-speed duplicating machine loaned them by Tixier, as well as quantities of paper and ink, and Remington had agreed to act as an advisory member in the fields of publicity, distribution, and editorial know-how, with the strict stipulation that his involvement be disclosed to as few others as possible. In this Remington had not been as successful as he had hoped.

Now Tixier, elevated to heights of wild creativity by the alcohol content of his blood, leaned conspiratorially closer on his bar stool, almost falling off. "Claude? How'd you like to make a scoop?"

"A scoop?" Remington said. "Chocolate? Vanilla? What're you talking about?"

"You know . . . a *scoop*," Tixier insisted.

Remington stared at him. "You filthy old man, I do not know what you're talking about."

"You've done newspaper work."

"Indeed I have," Remington said agreeably. "But I happen to have left my big story newspaper reporting hat at home tonight, the old porkpie with the brim turned up all round and a press card stuck in the band. Nikos, *un otro, por favor.*"

"Large or small?"

"Small," Remington said, and while the Greek drew a fresh beer he turned to Tixier. "Why would I be interested in a scoop, as you insist on calling it?"

Tixier shrugged. "Money. This'll be big."

Remington smiled. "You're out of your skull. There are no more big scoops. Everything comes through the State Information Bureau."

"Including everything you write?"

"Certainly—I'm first in line at the censor's desk with my handouts."

"Everything?"

"Abilene, are you implying that I might be guilty of illegality? Of underhandedness? Chicanery? Are you implying maybe that I'm the type who'd fuck around with the fourth estate?"

"I ain't implying you of anything."

"Good," Remington said. "Because if it's one thing I don't need, it's a loudmouthed old horseshit artist like you leaning on me, see? I play it strictly straight, understand?"

He looked at Tixier with arrogant distain. "Don't you understand, that's how I've made it in this whistle-stop dump for so long? Claude Remington plays it straight and true. If I have Gregory Lipshitz from the Berkeley Poet's Corner, that's who I tell you you'll hear, not Graves or Creeley or anybody else. I've built my reputation on being level, no fancy stuff, everything aboveboard. Listen, I've got a small yoga association I'm trying to get off the ground, so why do I need you or your crummy scoops? Man, I've got a fakir from Roswell who sits naked in a basin of water and sucks nearly a gallon of water up into himself. It has something to do with stomach muscle control. I've already got almost a dozen garden-club old girls enrolled, and when they see my fakir do *that,* they're going to go out of their fucking minds!"

"It sounds disgusting," Tixier said.

"No sound at all, except maybe a little gurgling noise."

"Ugh," went Tixier and looked away. Then he said, "You remember Vandenberg?"

"Who?"

"Gene Vandenberg."

"Who could forget a knothead like him?"

"I just spent a couple of days with him," Tixier said.

Nikos, returning with Claude's beer, had overheard. The Greek was astonished, and then alarmed. "Abilene, hold it down."

"Goddamn it, I am," Tixier said.

Nikos looked around quickly, checking to see whether any of the other drinkers had overheard. He glanced at Remington, then back to Tixier. "Just hold it down, will you?"

"Son of a bitch's gonna do something big," Tixier continued. "You'll see." A hand was placed on his shoulder, and the old rancher looked up to see Remington regarding him. "Dear old dirty-minded dad, whyn't you and I go sit in a booth?"

"Go on, Abilene," the Greek advised. "I'll bring your drinks over."

"Remember that hoary expression—'even the walls have ears'?"

Remington said, with vague amusement. He helped Tixier off his stool and steered him toward the rear of the bar and an unoccupied booth. "You silly, stupid, loudmouthed old bastard."

"Whyn't you help us?" Tixier asked.

"Only last night I checked in here for a quick one," Remington said, seating Tixier. "And a CIC cat was *platzed* right up there at the bar, with a beer, looking as naive as Lucifer. Muscleskull, you keep warbling about scoops, and you'll find yourself totally and irrevocably busted by Ivan, understand?"

"He's alive and well—Gene. Ain't that something?"

"It surely is."

"The minute you walked in, I knew you'd be perfect—should'a thought of you before." Claude stared at him. Tixier rambled on. "You can write. And you can use a camera."

"Abilene, do you see this impressively elegant nose of mine?" Remington said. "It's never been broken. It's never even been struck in anger. The reason for that is, I'm careful never to stick it into places where it doesn't belong. You think I'm some kind of nut?"

"That's a lot of crap."

"C. Remington never lies."

"You're already mixed in with a certain bunch in this town," Tixier said.

"Now where did you ever hear something like that?"

"I got ways of knowing," Tixier said mysteriously. "Anyway, you don't fool me. You're always covering yourself. And if the Soviets pulled out of this country tomorrow, you'd want to be able to say you'd been in with those who were against them. Always on the winning side."

"I'm on Remington's side."

"And if you ain't sure which side'll win, you'll play both," Tixier said. "This'll be big. There's money in it."

"Like how much?"

"Whatever you could make out of it."

"As I thought," Remington said. "I ought to know better than to listen to a fruity old lush like you."

"You know Cowles?"

"Where they have the training camp?"

"We're going to dynamite it," Tixier said softly.

Remington shut his eyes, as though by doing this he could obliterate what he had just heard. "Good luck."

"Vandenberg and me and some others. You know how to handle a camera."

Remington sighed. "Old Gene is wanted, my friend, for murder. He's—how can I put it—bad luck."

"You're scared."

"You're wrong. I'm not scared—I'm terrified," Remington said. "Listen, Tixier, I wouldn't take a Kodak Brownie up to a place like that. I don't even know where it *is*. In World War II, I was in Special Services, a movie projectionist. I brought the best of Betty Grable, Danny Kaye, and Abbot and Costello to our intrepid lads in Europe, and when hostilities were over I was commended by a lieutenant general for bringing my portable silver screen through the war without a single bullet hole—mainly, you freak, because I made it my business never to get within thirty miles of the front lines. I came through with four battle stars, and I never got my goddamned fingernails dirty, what d'you think of that?"

"If we get pictures of what's going to happen, they'll be worth a fortune."

"Who'll buy? *American Heritage?*"

"Goddamn, don't you see, it could be a historical event!"

"Chum, if you had a suitcase full of Occupation scrip for me when I got back, I'd tell you to shove it," Remington replied. "The idea is not only pie-in-the-sky, but, personally, I want nothing to do with Gene Vandenberg. We were never exactly friends."

"I still say we'd have something on film that had never been done."

"Abilene, are you looking to get your picture taken? Which side of your face photographs best?"

"We got it all lined up. And you'd have something nobody else anywhere would have."

"My very own bullet hole."

"Then will you *lend* me a camera?" Tixier asked.

Remington shook his head.

"Come on, Claude."

Remington glanced at him. "I never lend my equipment. It's expensive and, nowadays, irreplaceable." But he was interested. He

254

ordered another beer, and when the Greek brought it he said, "Nikos, you've forgotten any incoherent remarks our beamish boy here might have mumbled, haven't you?" Nikos nodded glumly, and Remington added, "Matter of fact, he was merely drunk, and I am sitting here trying to sober him up, right?" Nikos grunted as though he wished all this had happened in somebody else's bar, and walked off.

"How long will this debacle take?" Remington asked, turning back to Tixier.

"A day. Less."

"Do you have all the necessities. Like men?" Tixier nodded. "Any of them know me?"

"Gene does. That's all."

"Ah—Gene." Remington paused. "You're sure you've seen him? This isn't some whiskey-soaked, depraved fantasy of your brain? You're not lapsing into Korsakoff's?"

"Hell, I just spent two days with Gene."

"I thought maybe he'd died, or had made it to old Mexico."

"He's been within forty miles of Santa Fe for the last couple of years."

"That creep," Remington said, and smiled. "Supercilious bastard. I always liked his paintings. Did you know that one time I wanted to represent him?"

"What'd he say?"

Remington shrugged. "He laughed. I could have made a few bucks for us both. That was his failure—never could see beyond the end of his nose. I even used to mail him brochures and fliers on the better stuff I was bringing into town."

"He didn't buy?"

"He told me once that he never read junk mail, threw it away unopened. After that I dropped him from my lists, the antisocial prick. Junk mail!"

Tixier changed the subject. "Claude, if you *were* coming in, how would you do it?"

Remington shook his head. "You're a smoothy. Who was going to take your pictures before I walked in tonight?"

"No one. Olga has an old 35-millimeter at home. That's what I was going to use."

"You know anything about photography?"

Tixier nodded.

"I'll *bet*. Listen, you don't need one camera, you need at least two. Three would be better, two 35's—one with black and white, the other with daylight color—and a reflex. And if it was me, I'd take the 16-millimeter Bolex."

"Movies?"

"Christ, yes. People have a thing about watching home movies in which the extras get all shot up with real bullets."

"But how'd you develop them?"

"For you, that would be a problem. Me—I have my own darkroom."

Tixier had managed to sober up a little. He knew that he almost had Remington, but not quite, and he said now, "How do you think I ought to write it up?"

For the first time, Remington admitted his complicity. "Man, they've got that little Multilith, and they don't know what to do with it."

"Could it print photographs?"

"Sure. But, so what? Suppose you run off five thousand copies of a little four-pager, illustrated. You going to sell them on the plaza, at two bits a throw?"

"One thing at a time."

"Listen—does Gene know about this?" Abilene shook his head. "I thought so. What's he going to say when he finds out? He may not buy it."

"He'll have to," Tixier said. "He's waited too long."

"You wouldn't be setting your pal up for Ivan, would you?"

Tixier said earnestly, "Listen, Claude, come on in with us. Until we started talking, I didn't realize how big it could get. We were just going to blow the place, take a couple of snapshots, and come back."

Remington said under his breath, "Crass amateurism. You'd have to beef it up. Human interest. Overwhelming odds. Heroic gesture by a few determined men—all that shit. Your problem though is Gene—he'd get lofty."

"That's his problem."

"You're wrong, my friend—you want folks to react favorably, you got to have a likable leading man, someone they can admire. No fathead's going to buy Gene for a minute. He's about as likable as a grizzly. Not only that, he's"—Remington searched for an appropriate word—"he's eccentric."

"I didn't say it would be easy to write," Tixier told him. "Gene's no prize, but that doesn't mean you have to tell it that way."

"Okay, we make him a hero," Remington smiled. "But if he gets it into his head to write his version, or if he ever gets near a microphone, a nosepicker like him will ruin it for sure."

"We'll worry about that later."

"You think it would only take a day? How much danger is there? Really."

"Some. But the camp's a sitting duck," Tixier lied. "How about it, Claude?"

Remington paused. "I have exclusive rights to the pictures and story?"

Tixier nodded.

"I'm strictly noncombatant—I'm not carrying any gun."

"Nobody's asking you to."

Remington paused, frowned, then shrugged. "I'll think about it."

"Okay," Tixier agreed. "Only let me know by ten tomorrow morning, because I'll be leaving then. The new travel permit goes into effect at six."

"That quick?"

"That's right."

"Where can I reach you?"

Tixier glanced at the clock. "One thirty. I'm going to have me one more nightcap and then go on home. You call me at the house tomorrow morning."

"I'll think about it."

Tixier nodded. "You do that."

COMMUNICATIONS

Such an abundance has been written on the inherent goodness in man that even a cynic must think twice to remember that all these euphoric arguments have their roots in the awareness that man, as a creature intrinsically evil, is an apparition too terrifying to behold. Out of them have come an abundance of rubbish: gods, religions, love, guilt, conscience, morality—all dedicated to proving that man is indeed the highest order of animal, on a quest for immaculate perfection; all of which is refuted by a philosophical trick as nettlingly simple as the gratuitous gesture, wherein it is impossible to show that in all our short history not one man has ever been spontaneously impelled to do his neighbor good.

—The Journals.

BY MIDMORNING the next day, Vandenberg and Kevin were ready to leave. While the saddled horses waited in a grove, they again used willow branches to brush away most of their tracks. Then they mounted and set off at a walk, heading south. Vandenberg rode in the lead. Kevin, leading the pack gelding, said, "I still don't see why they couldn't have all come up here to meet us."

"They don't have to know where this cabin is," he replied.

"We going to ride to Holy Ghost to meet them? Supposing they don't come?"

Vandenberg did not reply.

"I sure hope nothing goes wrong," his son said.

"Nothing'll go wrong."

"But how do you know?"

"I don't. I'm like you—I hope nothing'll go wrong, that's all."

At the mouth of the ravine they came out of the dark shadows cast by its high walls and into the bright morning sunlight. They felt the heat of the sun immediately, and the horses lifted their heads and stepped out. A few alpine flowers were still visible among the stretches of high grass.

On the north slope of the ravine a man squatted motionlessly near the base of a corkbark spruce, watching. He stayed there like that for almost an hour after they had disappeared, and when he was sure it was safe he clambered down the slope, and, carrying his rifle in the crook of his arm, slowly began searching the ravine.

NORTH OF HOLY GHOST, Reuben Archuleta was having trouble saddling the four horses left in his care. A city dweller, he was out of place here and had been unable to sleep during the night. He finally got the job done and sat down and waited, growing increasingly restless as the sun rose higher. The horses, with bedrolls and

258

weapons lashed to their saddles, grazed quietly nearby, their teeth from time to time sounding against the heavy steel bits.

When alone, Reuben had a habit of talking aloud, and he was doing this now as he sat against a rock, smoking, shoulders hunched. "He ain't going to come back."

"That damn' Abilene."

"They catch you up here—"

"*Muy estúpido.*"

"*También loco—*"

"Ah . . . man."

He sighed, chewed at his lower lip, shook his head irritably, stood up, paced back and forth, sat again, cursed, his hands balled into fists and jammed into the pockets of his work jacket. "If he comes back, and you ain't here—"

"Should have left Willie, not me."

"Should have took me with him—"

"If he comes back and—" He wept a little, got up again, wandered around the grassy park aimlessly, urinated against a bush, carefully examined his penis in the bright sunlight for signs of syphilis or gonorrhea, two diseases he greatly feared, found nothing, zipped his jeans, and went back and sat down by the rock. He felt a weariness as the sun warmed him. Finally he stretched out on his back, tilted his Stetson over his eyes, and fell asleep. The horses, which were not staked but loose, with only dropped reins to hold them, continued grazing, working their way slowly up the slopes, until they finally disappeared among the trees.

NATIVIDAD GABALDON, MOUNTED on a deep-chested black, was high in the upper reaches of what had been the old Running W Ranch, north of Rowe. He had with him his last half gallon of Mora red, and he rode with it held atop the pommel, keeping his horse at a fast walk. Gabaldon was somewhere between being badly hung over and drunk again, but he was familiar with this part of the country. Holy Ghost Canyon lay eleven miles to the north, and he knew he would make it by midafternoon. He had left his place at Rowe while it was still dark, leaving Willie Deaguero passed out on a couch in his living room. The pickup, loaded with enough explosive to flatten half the village, was parked in Natividad's front yard, among the irises.

At a distance Gabaldon might have passed for any Spanish ranchhand riding the high meadows in search of stock, but his appearance up close was more impressive. Before leaving he had dressed in a style favored by the local *charros,* in a black shirt with a bright crimson kerchief knotted at the neck, black jeans, heavy engineer's boots, and a wide-brimmed black felt Stetson, tilted low over his eyes, its crown shaped in what was known as a Cheyenne crush. Strapped to his waist was a 9-millimeter Luger automatic, and he wore two extra cartridge belts, filled with rounds, slung crosswise from his shoulders and across his chest. Across his back was an extra rifle, a .30-caliber carbine he had stolen while in the army. In a fancy hand-embossed scabbard forward of his knee was his heavy deer rifle. As he rode he worked steadily at the wine, between sips humming a song popular around the holidays: *"Mamacita . . . dónde está Santa Claus?"* He was in a fine mood, pleased by the formidable impression he imagined he would have made on any stranger who met him on the trail.

SPRAWLED FULLY DRESSED on the double bed in his Cerro Gordo house, Tixier snored loudly, his angular, bony chin pointed ceilingward. His shirttails were out, and the big silver-and-turquoise belt buckle had been loosened. He had managed to get one high-heeled boot off.

The bedroom drapes had been drawn so that the interior was cool and dark, but a bright bar of sunlight, laden with dust motes, shone through a narrow gap where one pair of drapes did not quite meet. The bar of light fell diagonally across the big bed and Tixier's chest.

On a small night table beside the bed, a Princess phone was ringing. It had been ringing for some time, the sound of its muted bell cutting through Tixier's sonorous rumbling. After a while the old rancher stirred, frowned in his sleep, worked his toothless gums, swallowed, groaned, then began moving his lips as though speaking silently to the still ringing phone.

What is lacking in this country is a climate of unrest. A certain air of mewling discontent does exist, but it is too similar to the affectionate bickering young lovers indulge in as they jockey for the role identities that will endure between them for the rest of their married lives. Except for your criminal elements, who through circumstance or choice are the pariahs of any society, I defy you to find nowadays any of the implacable ferocity that must have been extant in the Jacobin, Cromwellian, pre-Revolutionary American, and Czarist-ruled societies.

—The Journals.

REUBEN ARCHULETA SPENT the rest of the morning locating the horses he'd lost, clambering over the steep slopes. Their tracks were easy to follow, but the climbing exhausted him, and by the end of an hour his face and hands were scratched and bleeding in a dozen places from falls he had taken.

He found one quickly, its reins tangled in a thicket of scrub oak, and rode it back to the rendezvous point, this time staking the animal. He finally located the others, several miles up the canyon, grouped near a small spring of fresh water. Riding one and leading the other two, he got back to the first horse in time to be badly frightened by Natividad Gabaldon, who had followed Deaguero's instructions for reaching the mouth of the canyon.

THEY RODE UP to the abandoned mica mine shortly before sunset, eight riders and two packhorses, halting in front of the old shack: Natividad drunk again, Willie, his father, Ben Deaguero, Cipriano Griego, who had brought his sixteen-year-old grandson, Luis Vialpando, Reuben, Abilene, and, lastly, Claude Remington.

Lashed to the packhorses were the explosives and a fresh supply of beer and whiskey, promoted by Tixier before leaving Santa Fe. He had shaved and showered that morning, and was dressed in expensive, custom-tailored gray whipcord. His cheeks were smooth-shaven, and except for the bloodshot eyes there was no sign he had been drunk for a week.

Remington brought up the rear. He was a poor rider and did

261

not try to hide it, but he was using a 35-millimeter Nikon to take pictures even now, as the group reined to a halt before the little cabin. Tied to the back of his saddle was a large cowhide camera case. Remington himself wore an Austrian loden coat with buttons of pine dowel, a felt Tyrolean guide's hat, wraparound sunglasses, slacks, and suede desert boots. He smoked steadily, the black plastic cigarette holder clamped between his teeth. Stuffed in the pockets of the loden coat were cartridges of fresh film.

Like his friend Natividad, Deaguero was a long way from sober. He had not washed or shaved for several days.

From a stand of trees on the slope behind the cabin, Vandenberg watched them approach. He put the binoculars on them, counted the riders, tried to identify them, but the light was fading. "There's too many," he said angrily.

"Can you see who they are?" Kevin asked.

"No. One's dressed like an Anglo though." He watched through the glasses. "He had no business bringing in extra people."

"Should we go back to our cabin?"

He hesitated, and then shook his head. "No. We'll go down." He paused again. "If Abilene's got this many together, he's serious."

He and the boy stood up, and Kevin said, "It wasn't just talk, after all."

"With Abilene, there's always talk. For once though, he meant it."

He and his son mounted their horses and began riding down the slope at a walk, leading the packhorse.

At the cabin the riders had dismounted and were standing around, lighting cigarettes and opening cans of beer that Tixier was handing out. Willie Deaguero's father said, "Where's that old son of a gun, Gene? I thought you said he'd be waiting for us, Abilene."

"Give him time. He'll show up," Tixier said.

Then Luis Vialpando, Griego's young grandson, pointed. "Look."

The others turned and saw the two men riding toward them in the dusk, the one in the lead tall and heavier, followed by the boy and the pack animal, the legs of the horses hidden by the thick growth of scrub oak through which they stepped, so that in the

262

fading light they appeared to be almost swimming, belly-deep, through a sea of thick, brown foliage.

SOMETHING OCCURRED during the first few minutes—no particular word or gesture but nonetheless discernible—that removed Vandenberg, who had always been aloof and apart, still further. Perhaps it was the physical confrontation with a man they all knew had committed murder and who was wanted for the crime. He himself sensed it in the barely perceptible formality in their greetings, the shaking of hands, the dip of a head, the salutations almost stiff—except in the case of Ben Deaguero, who came on with an ornate, courtly greeting in formal Spanish, first placing both hands on his own chest, then embracing Vandenberg: "My old and dear friend, I am honored and filled with pleasure to see you again. . . ." All this, though old man Deaguero had never been more than a casual acquaintance, often not seen from one hunting season to the next.

Abilene, hearing Ben's effusiveness, wisecracked to Gabaldon, "My God, he's a bigger bullshitter than me at my worst."

Almost as artificial was Claude Remington's greeting: "Gene— Jesus—it's great to see you again."

They shook hands. There was no sign in Vandenberg's face that he was surprised to see the entrepreneur. "Hello, Claude."

"Baby, I've got to tell you—you look just great!"

Vandenberg frowned, not understanding.

"You've got it all, man—the suntan. You've lost weight. And that hat. That hat's a classic—strictly William S. Hart."

He frowned, and Remington went on, "Abilene was gracious enough to invite me along on this *petite espièglerie* he's dreamed up."

"He did?"

"Yes."

Vandenberg stared at Remington, who said, "Decided it all should be recorded, for posterity's sake. Rightfully so."

"You?"

Remington snapped to mock attention. "Who else? The eye of the shutter clicks, and having clicked, moves on. Abilene convinced me last evening that we have something brewing that is out

263

of the ordinary, do you agree? Good. *Ergo,* dauntless Claude Audubon, everyman's own ornithologist, is Johnny-on-the-spot to obtain priceless negatives of a wildassed *rara avis* in its own native habitat, namely you, how about that, you big, distinguished-looking ugly old sourpuss?" Remington glanced around, then made a sweeping gesture toward the towering mountains. "This . . . is what it's all *about!*" He paused. "Surprised to see me, Gene?"

Vandenberg did not reply.

"What's the matter? You look all bent out of shape."

"We'll talk about it later," he said, turning to Gabaldon. "Nat, *com' está?*"

"*Bien,* Gene—long time no see."

"I'm glad you're with us," he said seriously. "We need you."

"I told Willie I'd be glad to do what I could," Gabaldon said modestly.

"We can use a good man."

Gabaldon did not accept the flattery completely, but it got to him; he adjusted his Stetson, weaving slightly. "Willie, he told me all about it—I told him I'd help."

Vandenberg moved on to Cip Griego, in his late seventies, a stern, fierce-eyed old man with shaggy brows. Griego said, "You remember me?"

"I remember."

"One time I run you off the old Rolling-R," Griego said, not smiling. "That was years ago. Before I knew you."

"It was during deer season."

"Your son was with you."

"I remember."

"This is my grandson," the old man said, gesturing toward the boy with him. "Luis Vialpando."

Vandenberg shook hands with the boy, then turned to Griego. "You have a fine grandson."

"*Si*—he's a good boy."

"Does his mother know he's up here?"

"The mother is gone," the old man said. "I'm all he has."

To Deaguero: "Willie, were you able to do any good?"

Deaguero nodded. "I got it, Gene—and the caps, wire, and detonators."

To Tixier: "Is this everybody?"

264

"You want more?" Tixier asked, and then he pushed it too far: "Hell, we already got a couple of extra people."

"I noticed."

"You ain't sore, are you, Gene?"

Vandenberg stared at him. "For two cents I'd call it off."

"Ah, you don't mean that."

"Don't tell me what I mean and what I don't mean."

He turned away and walked off, leaving them all. In the fading light, standing back a dozen yards and using a telephoto, Remington had got three pictures of him in conversation with Tixier. He called out, "Did anyone ever tell you, Gene, that when you lose your cool you look Olympian?" Vandenberg glared at him.

Natividad glanced at Ben Deaguero. "How come he's pissed off?"

Willie's father shrugged. *"Quién sabe?"*

"Don't pay him no mind," Tixier advised. "Leave him alone till he cools off. Let's get these horses unsaddled before it gets dark."

SEATED ON A DEADFALL away from the campfire, Tixier listened patiently as Vandenberg cursed him. "Drunks. Old men. Kids. And that idiot, Remington. Some sideshow!"

"Gene, I did the best I could."

"I don't remember Remington being mentioned."

"He was spur-of-the-moment. We need everyone we can get."

"And Griego's grandson."

"Gene, I swear I didn't know Cip was going to drag him along."

"Natividad'll be okay when he sobers up," he said. "Willie's good. So are Ben and Cipriano and Reuben. But Remington—Christ!"

"He wants to take pictures, Gene." Vandenberg stared at the ground. "He's even brought a movie camera—he's goin' to take movies of it, Gene."

"Of the compound?"

"Sure."

"He knows about the camp?"

"Not much. I figured you could brief him."

Vandenberg peered at his old friend. "Abilene, what's this all about?"

Tixier lit a cigarette, the spurt of the match flaring in the twilight. He said finally, "If we wreck that camp, the only ones who'll know about it are the Russians and the guys in there—you want that?"

"Word'll get around."

"How? By carrier pigeon? Come on! M.G. will play it down for sure. Now maybe you don't care what people think, but you ain't going into this alone, Gene. You can't ask a man to do what you're asking, and then let the Russians tell it their way. I want it told our way. I'll argue with you on that."

"Who're you going to tell it to?"

"Everybody."

Vandenberg did not reply, and the old man went on. "I got a little more to tell you, and you better listen. You remember one time I told you I could get you the use of a printing press?"

Vandenberg nodded.

"Well, we got it. She's ready to go, paper and all. We're going to print this up big, with photographs and everything. Claude says it'll print pictures. If we have to we can put those black bars across the faces, like when they don't want somebody identified."

"Who's going to do all this?"

"We got a little organization down in Santa Fe. About thirty of us. They don't care much for the Occupation."

Vandenberg was silent. Then he said, "And they want to demonstrate against the Occupation. Only, they don't know where to begin. And we're supposed to show them?"

Tixier looked at his companion in the dark and grinned. "Old buddy, you hit the everlovin' nail smack on the head."

The anger in Vandenberg came up again. "And you're just telling me all this *now?*"

"Now's as good a time as any. Gene, I know you too well. You'd have put me down if I tried to tell you at the start."

"You were damned right I would have. Listen, if you've got your own bunch of friends, why come looking for me?"

"We need you," Abilene said simply. "Otherwise, I can guarantee you, I wouldn't have ridden all over these mountains looking for you till my ass was crippled."

"Deaguero—Archuleta? Were they in on this joke, too?"

"Willie belongs to the organization. That half-breed ain't nowheres near as dumb as he looks. Reubenito knew a little. I told them to keep their mouths shut."

"And Olga? Is she really dead, or was that a come-on, too?"

"No, Gene. She died last week."

"You in it for money? Do you have an angle working for you?"

"Nothing like that," Tixier said, and his voice was bitter. "I was thinking about it when Claude and I were driving back up here this afternoon. All you smart bastards. Remington, he thinks I'm an alcoholic with the start of a wet brain. To you, I'm an old closet queen. That's all right, Gene—I don't mind. But I'm telling you, you're making a mistake when you say I'm *just* this or that."

"You still didn't need me," he insisted. "You could have found out what you needed to know in a week, by hanging around the camp."

"Had a little problem there," Tixier explained.

Vandenberg waited.

"That bunch with the printing press, they mean well, but they kind of don't know how to go about doing anything. I been to a couple of their meetings, but all they do is bullshit. Hell, it was *me* got them the press, and now they don't know what to do with it. Sure I could have brought some of them up here, and Willie could have gotten the explosive, and we could have figured out that camp, but I'll be honest with you, Gene, I think we might have gotten everything lined up, and then none of them would have fired a shot."

"So you picked me for a setup?"

"I knew you wouldn't back out."

"Matter of fact, Abilene, I thought you'd be the one to chicken out," he said. "It sounds to me like you're asking me to pull a chestnut out of the fire for you, so you can go back and be a big shot."

"There's no chestnut," Tixier argued. "Gene, I can't do it without you. But you can't do it without us. Admit it. Two days ago, you were just a bum on the run. And I was somebody with an idea."

"Who gave it to you?"

"All right. You did. I ain't looking for the credit. It's a good idea. I didn't understand how good it really was until last night when I talked with Claude."

Vandenberg looked at him. "Were you at the Montana?"

Tixier nodded.

"And you and Claude talked about it—in the Montana?"

"Nobody heard—except Nikos—and he's okay."

"You were drunk!"

Tixier was silent.

"In the Montana. . . . You silly son of a bitch—"

"Olga had a good camera up at the house," Tixier interrupted. "I was going to bring that and take pictures. Then I saw Remington—he's in the organization, too."

"Him?"

"Doesn't attend meetings, but he's involved," Tixier said. "What a splash we could make. He'll develop the prints. We'll do up a couple of thousand copies. The compound—don't you see—they'll believe pictures of that! With Route 66 running smack through Albuquerque we can get copies to New York, Chicago, in a couple of days. There's other groups, don't kid yourself."

Vandenberg did not reply, but he was swayed.

"And Claude can do it—after he phoned me this morning, I went over and picked him up. God, he must have fifty pounds of cameras and film. I know you don't like him, Gene—but he ain't all that bad."

"I just don't think he belongs here."

"He doesn't think so either," Tixier said. "But he came."

"Can he handle a rifle?"

"He doesn't want to."

"He gets one anyway. Nat brought an extra one."

"Why not let him fool with his cameras?"

"He gets a rifle."

Tixier shrugged.

"What about the Vialpando boy?"

"You don't get any argument from me on that count. Cip shouldn't have brought him. What do you want to do?"

"Put him with Kevin and the horses, I guess. Where's his mother?"

"Cip's raised him. His momma's a whore down in Albuquerque or Belen somewhere."

"She a Pecos girl?"

"Born and raised there—I remember seeing her when she was fifteen, sixteen," Tixier said. "She was giving it away then. Luis was a woods colt. I don't know why she hung the Vialpando name on him. From what I heard, she had him till he was seven or eight, and then Welfare nailed her with child neglect and Cip got custody. He's old-fashioned, old-time Spanish. Just an ordinary working ranchhand, no education, no fanciness, but he's his own man—he's tough. He ain't very big, but when he was younger, he was nobody to fool with. Never talks much."

"Does he have a family?"

"Cip? He's got six or seven kids besides Luis' momma. All grown and moved off. About forty-three grandkids—but he lives alone with the boy. I guess Luis is his family now. He's country Spanish. Put him in a big town, he'd die. He's ridden and walked over every inch of these mountains. Years ago he used to drive herds cross-country from Tres Ritos to Mora, right through the mountains. Never lose a cow or a calf, and at Mora they'd weigh in the same as when they were in summer pasture at Tres Ritos. Fifty—sixty head, and he'd do it alone. You couldn't want anybody better. You see the way that boy rode exactly two paces to the rear of him? That kid dotes on Cip."

"Go bring him over," Vandenberg said.

Tixier got up and went over to the camp, and came back with Cipriano and three fresh beers. The moon had risen above the trees by now, casting a white, cold light. Cipriano did not look in his seventies. His bearing was military, and he would have looked even younger if it had not been for the paunch that bulged out over his jeans. His torso was broad and powerful, set on very short, bowed legs, and he had that broad, square face of the Southwestern Spanish-American, the brows in a permanent scowl, the eyes reptilian in their steadiness, the nose a shapeless lump of flesh, broken and badly reset. The mouth was drawn down at each corner, a hating mouth, the kind you used to see in those old wet plates taken of Indian chiefs back in the 1880's, who even now stared out at you from foxed and faded brown prints with murder in their glittering eyes.

Years ago, when they'd hunted the area, Tixier had once taken Vandenberg to a cabin that Cipriano used until the first snows, located at around eleven thousand feet, and he had seen the old man's Spartan preferences: a round-bellied sheepherder's woodstove, a bag of flour for tortillas, beans, a side of bacon, coffee, canned milk, tobacco, a gallon of wine, and an army cot. That was all. There was no doubt in his mind that the old man would be good up here, but he said, "Cip, why is the boy here?"

"Por qué no?" Cipriano asked.

"Did Abilene tell you it was all right?"

"I don't ask him."

"It's no place for a kid."

The old man shrugged. "You don't want us, okay. We can go back."

"I wouldn't want him to get hurt, that's all."

"Everybody has to take his chance," Cipriano said. "Next year, the Russians, they will put him in the army. They say his work at school is bad. Two years from now, he could be in some foreign countries fighting. So? Now? Two years from now?"

"I wish you hadn't brought him, Cip."

In the moonlight, Cipriano's face was serious. *"Compadre,* you ever hear of the Silva gang?"

Vandenberg said he had.

"When I was Luis' age, Silva still had his gang in the mountains west of Mora, where I lived, and it was said that the youngest outlaw was only twelve."

Vandenberg had heard vaguely of the Mexican bandit, no revolutionary like Zapata, but an out-and-out stick-up artist who had pulled a series of jobs in pre-World War I days in this part of the country, from Mora and Vegas and Watrous as far west as San Juan Pueblo, north of Espanola, where the gang held up Kramer's Mercantile. Silva had become a folk hero to many of the old, ranching Spanish. Was that what Cipriano had in mind, Vandenberg thought, Robin Hood? It wasn't important—what counted was that he wanted Cip, and Cip wanted his grandson with him. He said, "Luis can stay with my son, who will take care of the horses when we make the raid. I don't want either of them around the shooting."

Cip nodded. *"Bueno."*

Vandenberg said, "I saw that he has a rifle."

"It's an old Winchester of mine. I told him to bring it."

Vandenberg thought, if the boy was older, I'd use him—even a year older. That's what's wrong with Remington. He'll come up here and refuse to touch a weapon, but he'd sit and let a sixteen-year-old mix into it. So that makes seven, not counting the boys and Remington. We could use half a dozen more. Abilene knows it, too. He said to Cipriano now, "Why did you and Luis decide to come up?"

270

The old man thought about this. "I don't like what is happening."

He could not articulate abstract impressions, but Vandenberg thought he understood. It was the old problem again—what to do with obsolete classes of citizens who would not, or could not, adapt to newer social concepts. It was himself—Tixier—Gabaldon, with his dossier of felonious violence. They were the least visionary, a full dimension removed from both communism and the original precepts chartered by the founding fathers. Anachronisms, gathered here not to participate in a gesture that might improve man's lot, but to turn the clock back to a time in which they had been not worthier men but more patiently tolerated.

To Vandenberg the raid was still a personal gesture, but Tixier, Remington—they would not permit so private an experience. True he would use them, but they would use him more. At that moment, all things considered, he'd have as soon packed, ridden down to the nearest Occupation post, surrendered and gone on trial and served his time, however long; and then, finally released, he would have donated the ranch to the state, moved into town, joined all the quasi-patriotic movements, applied for membership in the Party, and in all ways possible fitted into this "noblest of human experiments."

He wondered if he would have been more complete if as a young man he'd lost himself in something other than art. Law had always fascinated him, as had sociology. Certainly, at twenty, the huge energies he knew he had at his disposal should have suggested something more than this, nearly three decades of creative mediocrity. Did that explain his years of growing hostility? The self-lubricated withdrawal that became hostile isolation? The increasing inability to discover anything gratifying in contemporary life? Did it explain the years of heavy drinking? The self-destructiveness? The fits of depression that became almost suicidal? Was it the loss of one wife by incompatibility and another by death? Was it the special hunch he'd had about himself when younger, that he was good enough to win at anything he tried? Tixier and the others bored him now. He cared nothing for Cip Griego, or his grandson Luis, or why they had chosen to come here. He was weary of Cowles itself, and the immolative nature of their raid on it. What he wanted now was to live and die in peace.

Cipriano was looking at him in the moonlight. "We stay, then?"

"Yes. Stay," Vandenberg said. He stood up. "Let's get back to the fire."

The three of them returned. Kevin and Willie were setting out pots and pans. Young Luis and Natividad had unsaddled the horses and stacked the gear in a neat row. He saw that the cases of explosive had been placed to one side.

Claude Remington was sitting near the campfire. He looked up as Vandenberg approached. "Gene, this life is fantastic—all this sky. Stars. The thundering silence. You must love it. Why, it's just like being in the country."

Vandenberg sat down with him. "It's a pain in the ass."

"I got some tremendous shots of you in the last light."

"Fine."

Remington waggled his head. "Crazy."

"What?"

"This whole production."

Vandenberg nodded.

"You're really going to do it?"

"Yes."

"Driving up, Abilene told me about the compound. It doesn't sound easy."

"It won't be," he said. "Claude, can you handle a rifle?"

"I can hand it to someone else. No guns. I told that to Tixier."

"Natividad has an extra gun. It would help if you made noise with it."

"And attract attention to myself? Gene, I'm your official historian."

"You see how few men we have."

"You, General Vandenberg-Fingeroo, are appealing to my better nature. You're playing on my sympathies. You are giving me, Remington, a fucking *pep* talk." The entrepreneur paused. "Okay, if it makes you happy. But I guarantee you, nobody's going to be hurt with it."

"Just make noise with it."

"I couldn't just whisper bang-bang?" Remington asked. "Listen, I want to get together with you later—I need info on that lobotomy club they have in that camp. They really produce zombies in there, like Abilene said?"

Vandenberg nodded. "They reorient political and social thinking, using drugs, hypnosis, and instruction. I think they have some method for removing or erasing most of what we experienced."

Remington dipped his head toward Natividad, on the far side of the fire, lowering his voice. "I'd hate to meet Pancho Villa, there, in a dark alley."

"He'll fight—that's all that's important."

"How good are our chances?"

"Fifty-fifty," Vandenberg said. "But keep your mouth shut about that."

"And if we manage it?"

"Scatter."

"And then?"

Vandenberg shrugged. "After that, it's yours, Claude. Write it up. Use your pictures. See what you can do with it."

"After this is over, you think you may organize another raid?"

"That's too far ahead. Some of us may be dead by tomorrow."

Remington thought about this. He glanced at Vandenberg. "Somehow, friend, I hear a voice whispering in my ear. And you know something? It tells me you feel several ways about all this."

"After the raid I'll write it all out for you."

"You do that, Gene."

"And listen—about tomorrow. I'll spot you where you won't be hurt."

"Say that again, would you—slowly and earnestly," Remington said. "You know how I feel after hearing that encouraging little remark? Now I *know* I should have stood in bed."

COMMUNICATIONS

There are places like Cowles everywhere, and some of their borders are thousands of miles apart.
—The Journals.

AFTER DINNER Willie made coffee, and Vandenberg built up the fire and then took from his pack roll a small plastic bag containing sheets of paper. He placed them on the ground near the campfire, weighting their corners with pebbles. "These are maps I drew last year," he told them.

"This is the camp. The double fences form a box roughly one hundred and fifty yards on each side. Sentry tower in each corner, a fifth one beside the gate. In front, the recoilless rifle. Did Abilene and Willie tell you about Terrero? They've got a half-track weapons carrier down there. If we get that, we have the whole camp.

"There are local people living in the houses—they won't bother you. The cavalry squad is in this building. Willie and Abilene will be here." He turned to them. "Like I told you, it's a frame house. You'll have cover if you come down from the north side—brush, plenty of scrub oak. At night there's a sentry. My guess is that he's also a nighttime charge-of-quarters, to answer a phone or whatever. There are twelve men and a noncom in the squad. You want to be set by four in the morning. He makes a tour around that chain link fence once an hour."

"No dog?" Deaguero asked.

"No. Wait till he finishes walking his rounds, then you'll have to get the explosive positioned. It's not that dangerous—you can stay in the underbrush almost all the way to the house—maybe fifteen or twenty yards in the open. At that time of night, the guard will go back inside and catch a little shuteye. Make up two bundles of sticks. I'll be keeping a few for the power poles at Cowles. Keep the caps wrapped in a handkerchief, in your shirt pocket, with the flap buttoned. Willie, you know about wiring the cap?"

Deaguero nodded.

"Good. You want to be at least seventy-five yards off. Strip the ends of the wires and attach them to the cap, and then insert the cap in the stick, not before. On the way back, be sure you don't trip over your wires."

"Suppose we do it, and it doesn't go off?" Tixier asked.

"We'll test everything before you go. But if nothing happens at six o'clock, when you twist that detonator handle, I don't know. I'd say leave it, Abilene. Leave the whole damned setup and walk away from it on foot."

"We ain't going to have our horses?"

"If it works you won't need them—you'll have the half-track. I'm sending Luis, here, with you. We'll be all set at Cowles. If we

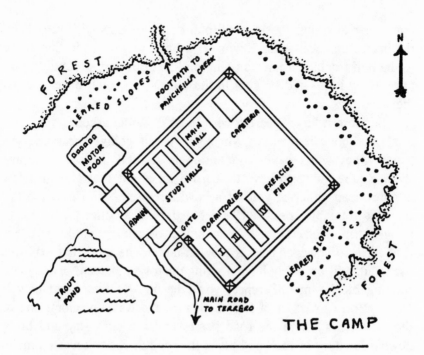

FOREST

CLEARED SLOPES

FOOTPATH TO PANCHEILLA CREEK

MOTOR POOL

STUDY HALLS

MAIN HALL

CAFETERIA

ADMIN

GATE

DORMITORIBS

I II III IV

EXERCISE FIELD

CLEARED SLOPES

FOREST

TROUT POND

MAIN ROAD TO TERRERO

N

THE CAMP

TERRERO

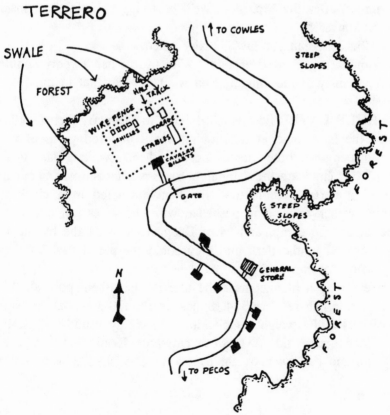

TO COWLES

STEEP SLOPES

SWALE

FOREST

HALF TRACK

WIRE FENCE

VEHICLES

STORAGE

STABLES

CAVALRY BILLETS

GATE

STEEP SLOPES

FOREST

GENERAL STORE

FOREST

N

TO PECOS

don't hear anything by six, we'll pull out, too. Luis will bring back the horses and wait with Kevin. You have to get inside that fence to the half-track. It'll have an ignition lock, but they probably won't have a key in it—it'd be kept in the billets—so you'll have to cross the wires."

"Suppose it has a steering wheel lock?" Willie asked.

"Let's hope it doesn't. When you get it going, check the gas gauge. They won't have ammunition in it—it'll be in the storage shed. You're going to have to learn a lot about that gun in a few minutes. Can either of you set a howitzer fuse? No? Up at the tip, there's a rotatable cone. It'll be safetied, with a cotter pin or something—strip it off. There'll be numbers on the rotatable part. Set it at zero, so you won't get a time-on-target, the kind that explodes overhead. It'll probably have a swing-open type breech, or maybe a rotating block—no difference, you'll be able to figure out how it works. You can let off a few rounds on the way up, along one of those stretches where the road passes under a cliff—try and bring down a few tons of rock and block the road. But don't waste time— remember, after the explosion, we'll be trying to hold them inside the buildings."

"How long can you last?" Tixier asked.

Vandenberg glanced around. "With five of us? Twenty minutes maybe. Thirty at the longest. You want to keep that in mind."

AN HOUR LATER he was still talking to them. By then they had tested the hand detonators, running out a hundred yards of wire from a reel, wiring the ends to a cap, and then walking back to the campfire to hook up the detonator. Each mechanism was about the size of a portable radio, and the handle rotated in a clockwise fashion rather than being pushed down. The wires ran out into a field below the camp, and when Deaguero twisted the handle the cap went off in the dark and they could see a red flash of light. The sound of it was like a .22.

He spread a blanket near the fire and had them pool all their ammunition. There were 314 rounds for the .30-30's, hunting stuff, in various bullet weights. Gabaldon had eighty rounds of .30-06, and Vandenberg said, "I've got seventy-four. Keep what you have."

Cipriano had twenty-eight rounds for his old .32 lever-action, and there were four full banana clips for the army carbine Remington would carry. Vandenberg and Tixier began dividing the .30-30 cartridges into equal piles, and Reuben Archuleta said, "Luis, here, he had only four shells to start with. He and your kid, they'll be with the horses. What's he need so many shells for?"

"He might not need them at all," Vandenberg said. "But if any of those sentries get out of that camp, I wouldn't want him to have just four cartridges."

"Why the hell did he come up here with only four rounds? Archuleta insisted.

"He came. And he gets his share."

"Reuben, there's plenty enough," Tixier said.

"There isn't plenty," Vandenberg said. "This isn't like hunting, where your first shot counts the most. You have to keep firing all the time to keep them inside the buildings and watchtowers."

Gabaldon picked up the maps and tilted them so that they were illuminated by the firelight, and Vandenberg said to him, "When we get to the camp, I'll go around with each of you and show you the best places. Ben, I'll be giving you the roughest spot, on the north side—you'll have two guard towers to take care of."

Deaguero's father, a huge, amiable-looking man with a mournful basset hound's face, said, "Two, Gene? How I'm going to do that?"

"Get the sentry in one right away," he said. "Then get back into the woods and move down to the next tower. Reuben, you'll be on the east side. Natividad, you take the west. Cipriano and I will be down by the trout pond. Its banks slope down about four or five feet—that's the only cover anywhere on the south side. Natividad, Reuben—when you take care of the guards in your towers, get down to where we are fast, because there'll only be the two of us to hold down the big Administration Building and the officers' billets."

"You really want to try it tomorrow morning?" Tixier asked.

Vandenberg nodded. "We'll leave here after midnight."

Tixier's expression was pained. "Man, I only had about four hours' sleep last night."

Vandenberg thought about this. "Stretch out, if you want. But I'll bet you won't sleep. Nobody'll be sleeping tonight. How much whiskey did you bring back?"

"Six fifths."

"Open a couple. Let's have a drink. I'll make up some more coffee."

Claude Remington spoke. "Gene, why so early—there won't be any goddamned light. How about making it at seven?"

"At seven, the whole compound's up and going," he said. "I'd make it earlier, but at five thirty, you can't see the front sight of of a rifle."

"Friend, I've got sixteen rolls of Kodachrome Daylight. You're not with me."

"Use black and white. You were taking pictures this evening in the twilight—there was less light then than you'll have tomorrow."

Tixier came over with a bottle and handed it to Vandenberg, who poured an inch into his cup before passing it on.

CIPRIANO GRIEGO and young Vialpando were by their saddles, packing away the ammunition that had been given to Luis. He was a slender, compactly built boy, not very tall, dressed in jeans, a chocolate-brown Stetson, and a heavy woolen sweater. He said now in Spanish, "I want to stay with you tomorrow."

"He wants you with the horses."

"His son is with the horses, too. I'm going to tell him I want to stay with you."

Cipriano shrugged. "I don't think he'll change his mind."

"Abilene told us he would be in charge." He glanced toward Vandenberg, who was by the fire, speaking with Remington. "Is he any good?"

"He's not so bad," Cipriano said. "Abilene and Ben Deaguero would bring him up during the hunting season. He was a very bad hunter then."

"That son—what's wrong with him?"

"Something in the head. He's simple."

"And tomorrow I have to be with him."

"You can't always do what you want," Cipriano said. "That's the sign of a man, someone who can do something he doesn't care for."

Luis was silent.

278

"Also, tomorrow, it would please me if you watched out for his son. Like a brother, understand?"

"I will, *viejo*."

The old man nodded.

Luis said, "But I still wish I was with you."

NATIVIDAD BROUGHT his carbine and the clips over to Claude Remington and sat down crosslegged opposite the photographer. "You as good with a gun as you are with the cameras, mister?"

"No." Remington saw that Gabaldon was still somewhat drunk. He took the carbine. "Is it loaded?"

"No. But you are supposed to look for yourself." Gabaldon showed him. "Clip goes in here. Give him a smack with your hand, so. Snap the bolt, she's loaded. See this button, by the trigger? Slide him forward, he shoots one shot at a time. Slide him back, it's automatic—keeps shooting until the shells are all gone." He placed the tip of his tongue against the roof of his mouth and made a machine-gun noise, pointing a forefinger at Remington. "You take good care of this gun for me."

"Keep it if you'd rather not lend it to me."

"I don't want it back with scratches in the stock. Don't drop it." Gabaldon leaned forward. "And listen, do me a favor, mister."

"All right."

"I don't like somebody taking my picture. You know, I don't look like no movie star, do I?"

"I'll make sure your face won't be seen." Gabaldon frowned, and Remington explained what he meant.

"That's a good idea," Natividad said. "Even so, you take pictures of Ben or Willie or Abilene—they like it—not me. Okay?" Remington nodded. "And take care of my carbine. A guy offered me eighty bucks for it once. That's a valuable gun."

SOMETIME AFTER MIDNIGHT a man suddenly appeared at the edge of the circle of light cast by the fire.

One moment there was no one, the next he was there, standing by the row of saddles, a small, thin man, his old man's face sharp-featured and as dark and wrinkled as a piece of sun-dried leather, Spanish and maybe some Indian, too, wearing boots and jeans, a

279

sheepskin jacket that was blackened and split with age, and an old fedora.

He stood there a moment, leaning forward a little, peering at them, then stepped over a saddle and came closer, not shyly but with hesitation, unarmed, at last recognizing someone he knew— Cipriano Griego—to whom he bobbed his head. Vandenberg had risen from the group of men, glancing at Tixier, who was watching the old man with astonishment.

Now the man spoke to Cipriano in a soft voice, almost a murmur but very rapidly, in Spanish, so fast that Vandenberg could not catch a word, the phrases emphasized by brief hand gestures. When he stopped Vandenberg said, "Cipriano, what's he want?"

Cipriano had risen, too. "He say he hungry and that he saw our camp. He has not had food for three days."

Cip went to the fire and got a pan of leftover beans and brought them over to the old man, who nodded several times and then squatted, eating with his fingers, scooping the beans swiftly into his mouth, ignoring the men who were watching him.

After a minute he looked at Cipriano and spoke again. Vandenberg said, "Does he speak English?"

"No."

"What does he say?"

"That he was watching us from the trees, up there, all evening. He was afraid to come down. He said he could smell the food, all the way up there."

The little man continued eating, and Vandenberg said, "Who is he?"

"This is Olguin," Cipriano said, giving it the northern pronunciation: Ol-*geen*.

"You know him?"

Cipriano nodded. "He's a *viejo*—old-timer." Vandenberg said nothing. "He been around for years—used to live by Mora, then I saw him by Tres Piedras."

"A rancher?"

"Rancher? No. Olguin's *nada*," Griego said. "They used to call him *El Solitario*—The Lone One. A little crazy, you know, from living alone so long."

"He's a long way from home."

"No home. He goes all over," Griego said. "Sometimes, I see

him in Pecos—he buy a little flour, tobacco. He was old-time sheepherder."

"No family?"

"*Nada*, Gene. *Viejos* like Olguin, he don't know where he come from, where he was born, who was his people. Never baptized. No school. *Nada*. Too old now to take care of the sheep. Doesn't even know how old. Seventy-five. Eighty. Eighty-five. Maybe more, no telling. His kind, they don't like towns, don't like people. Been up here in the mountains too long to come down, live inside a house."

"What's he do up here, all alone?" Vandenberg asked.

"*Quién sabe?* Just walk around. Couple of times, I run into him. Mostly, I think he hides if anybody around. One of these years, he'll get caught in blizzard, freeze to death—couple of more years, somebody finds a few bones. He's crazy, that's all."

"Do you think he can be trusted?"

Cipriano shrugged.

"How harmless is he? I mean, is there a chance he'd go to the Russians?"

Cipriano shook his head again. "No. Old-timer like this, I don't think he knows who is Russian, who is American. Maybe never seen a television—probably scare hell out of him."

"If Mora and Tres Piedras was his territory, what's he doing this far south?"

Cipriano shrugged. "Old man like Olguin, he might turn around and walk up to Canada or down to old Mexico without ever coming out of mountains. Likes to be by himself, go where he pleases, maybe half the time doesn't even know where he is, other half doesn't care. Looks up in the sky, sees big airplane, don't even know what it is, says, '*Mira*, look at that.' In old days, man like Olguin would watch the sheep for a year, two years, make a few hundred dollars. That last him a long time, you know?"

The little man set down the pan of beans and spoke again. Cipriano said, "He wants to know if we have a few shells to give him. Any kind."

Vandenberg looked at the old man and said, "Cip, ask him why he wants cartridges, if he has no rifle. Ask him, too, if he's alone, or if he has friends with him."

The translation went on, and Cipriano said, "He is alone. And he has a rifle. He says if we give him some shells, he can get a deer or an elk for the winter, but that he'll starve if we don't. He told me he was in a town this summer, but that none of the stores have ammunition."

Vandenberg looked at the old man again, trying to guess his age. Certainly at least in the seventies. The narrow-shouldered build was skinny, wiry, but he was probably stronger than he looked, and it occurred to him that Olguin might indeed be able to undertake a trek such as Cipriano had mentioned, to Canada, although it was difficult to imagine anyone doing such a thing in these times. He acted retarded and perhaps senile, too. He felt an uneasy stir of realization that such a man could easily have spied on him and Kevin, stalking them from camp to camp. And now he was here. What other thoughts were in the old man's mind besides a few cartridges and a free meal?

As if in reply Olguin began speaking again to Cip Griego. Vandenberg let them talk, but he noticed the sharp look Natividad gave Willie Deaguero, and finally Cipriano turned to him, his face sterner than ever. "He wants to know if we are going to attack the camp?"

"What?"

"Cowles. He calls it the little prison. He says he will help us."

"Why would he think that?"

Cip shrugged, staring at the ground.

"Ask him."

There was another exchange and Cip said, "He saw the horses, the guns. He says either we are running from the Soviets, or we are getting ready to fight them. He calls them the foreigners."

"And he wants to help?"

When Cipriano had translated this the old man replied again, but this time directed himself to Vandenberg, grinning slyly and dipping his head obsequiously. Cipriano said, "He's telling you he is good with a rifle and that he is not afraid. Also he knows of a valley north of here where no soldier has been, where we can hide, and where there is deer and elk and bear."

"Is that all he said?"

"Mostly that he was not afraid."

Vandenberg asked, "Would you trust him?"

Old Cip frowned. *Quién sabe?*

282

Tixier leaned forward. "Cip doesn't know how to describe it, Gene. Best thing with an old fucker like this would be not to have to trust him. Then you wouldn't have to worry about him. But if you had to trust him, then okay, and if it turned out okay, then that's fine, *pero* if it turned out otherwise, then don't be surprised either, *sabe?* A *viejo* like this, one day he's one thing, the next day he's another." Abilene turned to Cip, "Is that how it is?" Cip nodded. Tixier grinned at Vandenberg. "You thinking of taking him with us?"

"I don't know."

Olguin was standing by Cip, listening to the talk, his expression impassive, and Vandenberg thought, he's not stupid. He may be senile and ignorant, but he's not stupid—we could watch him for a month, even Cipriano, who's a *viejo* himself, and not know what he's thinking. And he's not afraid. It took real nerve to walk into the middle of this the way he did. He knows we're illegal, yet he came in. And if we run him off he might head straight for Cowles, or Terrero, or Pecos. Or he might take a shot at us—or he mightn't do anything. To Cipriano, he said, "Ask him why he left his rifle up in the woods."

They talked, and Cip said, "He did not want to frighten us."

"Tell him to fetch his rifle."

When Cip had finished, Olguin stared at Vandenberg for a moment and then grinned, showing a ruin of yellowed and black-edged stumps. He turned and trotted off into the darkness. Vandenberg asked Tixier, "What do you think of him?"

"Old fart like him is better off dead," Abilene said.

"Olguin—what kind of name is that?"

"Old name," Cipriano said. "Mexican—up in Rio Arriba. Real old. Maybe Indian, too."

Olguin returned quickly. Under one arm he carried a lumpy blanket roll, tied with a piece of rope. Slung from his shoulder was his rifle, and Vandenberg thought, my God, it's an antique. It was a .45-70 Springfield single shot with a trapdoor breech, the metal parts worn shiny and smooth with age, the stock almost black in the light of the fire. Probably a shade over a century old. A black-powder rifle—a charcoal burner—an anachronism in this age, the equivalent of a ballista matched against a jet fighter. It would spurt out a heavy slug as thick as a man's index finger, at a trajectory resembling that of a thrown snowball, but the shocking power of the bullet was such that in its time it had taken the biggest game in North America.

Olguin set down the gun and untied his blanket roll. He spread it out and spoke to Cip, who said, "He wants to show you that he was not lying when he told us he had no food."

There was no food and very little of anything else inside the filthy blanket: an old metal candy box for odds and ends, a small frying pan, a pot, the remnants of a blue cotton shirt.

Vandenberg said to Natividad, "Give him a shot of that bourbon—thin it a little, we don't want it to hit him too hard. Cip, ask him if that's the gun he wants to go to war with."

Cipriano translated; Olguin again revealed the ruined mouthful of teeth in a grin. "He says he bought it before the First World War, before New Mexico was a state, for six dollars, and that it has killed more deer than he can remember."

Vandenberg and Tixier exchanged glances. Natividad fixed a watered-down bourbon for the old man and gave it to him.

Olguin sniffed the cup, his face splitting into that chimpanzee grin again, nodding—he let off another burst of soft Spanish, then drank, and Nat said, *"Por nada, compadre. . . .* He says it's the first drink he's had in over a year. He says that if he'd known you had real whiskey, he wouldn't have waited up in the woods for such a long time."

"What's he think he's going to do for ammunition?" Vandenberg asked.

Cipriano translated. "He say if you have ten cartridges, .30-30's or anything, he can produce twenty rounds for his gun."

"He's using smokeless powder in that coffee grinder?" Abilene said with surprise. "He'll blow his goddamned head clean off."

Olguin knelt on his outspread blanket and opened the metal candy box, taking out the contents, which were wrapped in a cloth. He lined up a number of big, conical, hand-cast slugs, a bullet mold, a small, flat box of primers, and a handful of brass cartridge cases. He spoke and Cipriano said, "He say he has forty-six primers left, but only twenty bullets. The primers he bought two years ago. He makes the bullets, he say, out of the lead from inside old car batteries."

Vandenberg said, "Natividad, mix him another drink, will you?"

He went over to his belongings and broke open a box of military .30-06's, took out ten rounds, and came back, laying them on Olguin's blanket. "Here, old man."

"*Sí,*" Olguin said, looking up. "*Muchas gracias.*"

With another drink beside him and a cigarette, he set about manufacturing his ammunition. He inspected each of the brass cartridge hulls by the light of the fire, looking for dents, and then used the point of a pocketknife to pry out the old primers. Vandenberg noted with some surprise the care the old man gave each hull, reaming out the primer pocket, blowing through it, checking the lip for roundness and reaming that, too, so that it would accept the leaden slug. After that he turned to the .30-06's, using the handle of his knife as a hammer now, resting the neck of each cartridge against a rock and tapping it until the neck gradually expanded and released the copper-jacketed slug. Carefully, he emptied the smokeless powder into a borrowed coffee cup.

"I guess he doesn't even bother to resize the necks," Vandenberg said to Tixier. The others watched the old man with interest because they had never seen cartridges handloaded under such primitive conditions.

Claude Remington said, "Why don't you let him have that carbine of mine?"

Cipriano shook his head. "Old man like Olguin, he like his own gun."

Olguin gently reprimed the .45-70 cases, pressing each tiny copper cup of fulminate into the primer pocket with the tip of his knife, and Vandenberg wondered how the old man had managed to avoid blowing open a finger in the years he had been doing this. Then he measured the powder into each case, using a teaspoon, scooping about a quarter of a spoonful out of the cup, gauging by eye alone the proper amount.

Vandenberg said, "Cip, does he know what can happen, loading them with smokeless that way?"

Cipriano asked the old man and then translated. "He say he always loads them this way. The powder in one .30-30 makes two cartridges for his gun. With black powder he fills the case all the way, but he say he like this smokeless better because it don't make the bore dirty. Also, it gives the bullet power."

"I'll bet," Vandenberg said drily.

Olguin was nearly finished now. He had worked with surprising speed. After measuring his charges, he fitted the conical hand-cast slugs into the necks of the cases, tapping the point of each slug until it was seated. He then inspected each finished cartridge—holding it to his ear and shaking it to hear the powder, finally wiping the finished product briskly with the old shirt. He was on his third bourbon and had smoked cigarettes throughout the operation, the ash-laden, glowing tip sometimes inches from the cup of powder. He spoke now to Cip, who said, "He wants one more thing—butter." Cip got him a foil-wrapped stick of margarine, and Olguin cut off a small lump, which he rubbed between his fingers; then he massaged the cartridges. "He say butter makes them fit in the rifle easier. Also the bullet goes faster."

Olguin spoke again and Cip said, "He wants you to know that these shells will shoot very well, though they don't look like the ones you buy in the store. Sometimes, he says, one misfires, but not often. He say to tell you that with these twenty rounds he could live through the winter and all through next year, maybe longer, but that if we want him he will stay. He knows we are going to do something at the camp. Don't ask me how. If we don't want him, he will go in the morning, and he say thanks for giving him the shells and the whiskey and the cigarettes. He also wants to tell you that he will not say anything about what he has seen here."

Vandenberg looked at Tixier, who said, "It's one more man, Gene."

"I'm wondering if he's really any good with that old blunder-buss."

"He might surprise you," Tixier said.

Vandenberg did not reply.

"Would you use him at the compound, Gene?"

"Yes. Another man wouldn't make any difference to you and Willie, at Terrero."

He would have liked to have more time to consider Olguin, but there was none. They would be leaving in a few hours. Finally, as with other choices he had been forced to make, he felt that it did not make that much difference—either way—and he said to Cipriano, "Tell him we can use him. Sit down with him and explain the whole thing so that he understands it. If he wants to stay, we'll put him at the camp. But if, after you tell him, he wants to back out, tell me. We'll figure out what to do with him."

SHORTLY AFTER ONE they were ready. The weapons were checked, and Vandenberg insisted that no one carry a rifle with a chambered round. The explosives had been uncrated and tied in bundles, with Vandenberg keeping four sticks, several caps, and one of the detonators. The fire was extinguished. They grouped together near the cabin, illuminated by the moonlight. He and Willie Deaguero timed their wristwatches. At one thirty he said to Abilene, "Better move along."

There were no farewells. Tixier, Deaguero, and young Luis, who would return with the horses to the rendezvous point north of the camp, mounted and rode off at a walk. The blanket-wrapped bundles of explosives were lashed to the back of Deaguero's saddle. Tixier rode lead. He claimed to know a trail that led straight to Terrero.

"We should be at Cowles around four thirty or five. Let's stick together. Go ahead and smoke, if you want. It's an easy ride. Like I said, when we get there I'll go around with everyone, so you'll all know what to do."

There were no questions, and he said, "All right, then."

They went to their horses. In the moonlight, a tendril of smoke rose from the buried campfire. They mounted and rode slowly away from the ruined cabin beneath the mine tailings.

THEY REACHED THE PARK he had chosen by four, a sloping meadow, seventy or eighty yards across, surrounded by steep, forested slopes. The camp lay fifteen minutes' walk to the south. A hundred feet below the park Panchuela Creek flowed. They dismounted and gathered around Vandenberg, lighting final cigarettes. The moon would be setting soon.

He lit a cigarette himself and nodded toward an old equestrian trail that still had a hand-carved Forest Service trail sign. "The camp is that way. There's a rise, about three hundred yards down the trail, and then you can see the floodlights shining through the trees. Kevin'll wait here with the horses." He turned to his son. "Not out here in the open—I want them up in the trees. Don't unsaddle them."

"I'll watch them," Kevin said.

Vandenberg waved. "We'll see you in a while."

Kevin smiled.

"Don't go wandering off," he said. "Luis should be up here in another hour or so. Have him bring his and Abilene and Willie's horses up in the trees, too, Keep them all together and keep them calm. No matter how much noise you hear at the camp, stay with them. When it's over, we'll want to get out of here fast." He noticed Claude Remington standing off from the others. "Claude, you all right?"

"If I'd known riding made you feel like this, I'd have walked— I mean it."

Vandenberg did not reply. While they smoked, he went to his pack saddle, and took out a fresh fifth, opened it, and handed it around. "Everybody take a couple of stiff shots—I've got another bottle, for a last one, when we get there."

He unpacked the hand detonator, wire, and the sticks. Reuben Archuleta and Ben Deaguero had canteens of water, but none of them carried food. He had told them that the raid would not last beyond seven o'clock—he knew they could never contain the security guards for longer than that.

BELOW THEM was the compound, lit by the last of the setting moon and the mercury arcs atop the watchtowers, a broad rectangle of glaring blue light.

They were crouched at the foot of a scattered pile of rocks, listening as he talked to them in a low voice. He had wanted to bring them to this high spot so they could see and understand as much as possible about the place. "There are the dorms. Over there's the cafeteria. The big building outside the fence is administration and enlisted men's living quarters. That small building alongside it is for the officers—Colonel Brushnevesko is there. Over there on the right is the road that goes to Terrero and Pecos. Five watchtowers and the little sentry box at the gate—six men on duty all the time. If you're going to get the tower men, you'll have to do it in the first five or ten seconds after it starts. They won't know what the hell is coming off for the first few seconds, but after that they'll be a bastard to handle. They have submachine guns."

"The most important, then, is how it goes at the start?" Ben Deaguero whispered.

"Yes. If each of us has a man picked out and is ready to shoot, we can get the sentries right away. If you miss, you'll be in trouble."

"You'll fire first?"

"At six," Vandenberg said. "As soon as I hear the dynamite go at Terrero."

"How close must we be?" Cipriano asked.

"Stay out around seventy-five yards. That's a good range for the Winchesters, but it's just far enough for those submachine guns to start shooting wide."

He did not tell them that he had already reconnoitered the perimeter of the camp long ago, checking firing positions, and that he had found plenty, the only fault with all of them being that once a man opened fire he would inevitably be pinned down. That was the weakness of their number. They could not lay down the kind of smothering counterfire that would guarantee a successful withdrawal if something went wrong. Once it started they would find out for themselves. They would have to kill the entire security detachment or be killed in turn. He said, "There are plenty of things in our favor. At six, the light will still be poor—unless you stand up, they'll have a hell of a time spotting you."

"Muzzle flash?" Natividad asked.

"It won't show—not like it would at night, anyway."

"Gene, they have any hand grenades in those towers?" Ben asked.

"I don't know," he said. "They probably have vomiting or tear gas, in case the trainees riot. I wouldn't worry about it. The thing is, they'll have trouble seeing you, but you'll be able to see them in the towers, outlined against the sky, and that's good. Also, those towers are built of planking, maybe two-by-twelves, with hinged glass windows to keep the weather out. I'll bet a .30-30 will shoot clear through—so if you can figure out where a guard is crouching inside, you can let off a shot at the side of the tower and maybe hit him that way."

He thought for a moment, and then said, "That's it, then. If the dynamite at Terrero doesn't go off, we do nothing. If the weapons carrier doesn't make it up here, we get out. Don't panic when you hear a lot of submachine guns firing. Cipriano and I will try and keep them from crewing that recoilless, but if we can't, don't get scared. And we'll take care of the auxiliary power plant in the motor pool, too. After I fire the first shot, we'll explode the power poles. All of you be ready to fire, with a target picked out—the guards in the towers have a chair or bench they sit on, and they're visible from the chest up. The whole thing is to get as many as possible in the first seconds. They have field telephones in all the towers, maybe battery-powered, and the first thing they'll do is start ringing each other to see what's up, and if there's no answer they're going to be scared. If you're sure you've gotten the men in the towers along your side, get back into the woods and move down to the trout pond. We'll need as much help as we can get. There's maybe forty men in that big building."

"Gene, why don't all of us stay with you and Natividad and Cipriano?" Ben asked.

"Because those men in the towers may have orders to fire on the dorms—we don't know. They don't want anyone to escape, I know that. Cip, you explain to Olguin all I've said. Make sure he understands."

Cipriano spoke for several minutes with the old man. Olguin nodded from time to time, asked several questions, and then pointed to the floodlit camp. "Does he understand?" Vandenberg asked. "Does he still want to be with us?"

They spoke again, and Cipriano said, "Yes. He thinks maybe we could make an army with all the men inside, but I tell him they are useless, like you said, that they would not fight, and Olguin say it is too bad that they are *chingasa*."

"Yes. Too bad," he said. They left the high point and went into the woods. He passed the word back to walk softly now. Among the big pines it was dark and silent, and they moved slowly. He stopped finally. "Reuben, I'm putting you here." Archuleta came up and stood beside him. "There's good cover here. Stay down, don't take any chances, and be ready."

"I'll be all right," Reuben said. For a moment Vandenberg stared at the young man, not liking him even now any more than he ever had, dismissing him too easily, perhaps, for the way he followed Tixier. Then he motioned for the others to go on.

Keeping in the woods and heavy underbrush, they reached the

290

north flank of the compound, and here, beyond the cleared areas, there was a steep slope, thickly forested and high enough so that they were actually above the guards in the towers. The nearest corner tower was only about fifty yards away. They crouched, watching; there was a yellow spurt of light from the tower as the guard in it lit a smoke.

Vandenberg whispered, "Ben, pick your spot in here someplace —I'll leave it to you. You know pretty much how it's going to go." He uncapped the last bottle of liquor. Ben drank, then handed it back and moved down the slope a few yards by himself.

Along the west flank of the compound, almost at the start of the old Windsor Creek Trail, he found Olguin a good position among a pile of boulders. He waited silently while Cipriano whispered to the old man, Olguin nodding, then replying, shaking his finger in negation. Cipriano said, "He wants to tell you not to worry about him."

"I won't," Vandenberg said.

"He says he will wait for your shot. When he hears it, he will shoot, too."

"Does he understand about the submachine guns?" Cipriano nodded. "And that he must not shoot only to wound?"

"He knows that—he say at this range he can make a good head shot every time."

"Tell him not the head," Vandenberg whispered angrily. "Tell him to aim for the chest, not the head."

Cipriano spoke to Olguin again, and the old man grinned and nodded. Cip said, "He say all right, he will not do a head shot. In the chest. He say he will shoot the foreigners exactly through the center of the chest."

"Let's hope so."

Olguin spoke again, and Cipriano said, "He wants you to know that between now and dawn he will make a prayer."

They moved off again, wading Windsor Creek, and Vandenberg positioned Remington on another steep bluff, behind and above Olguin. From it, the photographer would have a panoramic view of the entire compound.

They left him to set up his equipment and worked their way around to the south flank, near the Administration Building and officers' billets, which were brightly illuminated by the arc lights.

They were very close at this point, maybe sixty or seventy yards off. This was the weak spot. If the men inside guessed there were only him and Cipriano and Natividad, they would rush. Besides the guards in the sentry box and the tower beside the gate, they had the power poles and the generating plant to take care of. He was more worried about this part of the raid than anything else, and he thought, in the war if I'd ordered three men into something like this, they'd have laughed at me. And I couldn't have blamed them.

The most valuable weapon was the Springfield. No one in the buildings would have a rifle that good, and no one would be expecting it. With the three-power scope and careful shooting, he knew that at seventy-five yards he could place five shots in a group a twenty-five-cent piece would cover. Also, most of his ammunition was armor-piercing military surplus, the copper tips painted black. The AP slugs would shoot completely through the frame buildings, and he knew that even if he did not hit anyone they would keep low inside when the slugs tore through the thin partition walls.

Cipriano would be good with the old Winchester, too; at this range, even with iron sights, the old man would not miss if he got a chance for a clear shot. Vandenberg thought, myself, and Nat, and Cipriano here. The security men will be too surprised for a while to do anything. They've had it easy. All routine. They won't be soft, but they'll be surprised, and if we can get a few right at the start, then we'll be all right. And if nobody answers the field phones in the towers, they'll be worried. But not too worried. They'll know damned well all they really have to do is sit tight. But if Abilene and Willie get that half-track up here, they'll be in for the surprise of their lives.

He and Cipriano and Natividad were hidden behind a thick growth of bushes that bordered the old trout pond. No one fished here now except some of the men in the security detachment. As an inmate, he had watched them from the other side of the fence, standing on the pond's steep banks with open-faced spinning rods.

The road leading out of the compound passed directly in front of where they were hidden. He said, "Cip, how does it look to you?"

"It will be worse for us here than for the others, *que no?* How many are inside?"

"Thirty. Forty. Something like that."

"All with guns?"

292

Vandenberg nodded.

"Very bad," Cip said.

"We only have to hold them until Tixier and Deaguero come."

Cipriano shook his head. "You count on Abilene too much, Gene." He looked at the Springfield. "How good is it?"

"Very good."

"You can use it?"

"Yes."

"You will have to do some good shooting with that telescope."

"I know."

"If you kill some right away with the telescope they'll be afraid to come out," Cipriano said. "Until they understand there are only three of us. We should move a little, from one place to another."

"Yes," he said. "It's dangerous, moving like that, but it may fool them." He hoped Cipriano's talking would give the old man confidence, and he let him go on.

"I'm glad Luis is with the horses," Cipriano said gloomily. "Before, I thought to myself, we stay together, else we go home. But now I'm glad he's not here. It's no place for a boy." He paused, and then said, "No place for old man either."

"Do you want to quit?" Vandenberg said.

"No. But I think we could be killed here, very quick."

"That's possible."

"Gene, you were in the war, *sí?*"

Vandenberg nodded.

"You were in the fighting though?"

"Yes."

"Then you know. I was never a soldier," Cipriano said. "And I have never shot a man, not in my entire life, so I don't know. But to me this looks bad, *que no?*"

"It's bad," he admitted. "When Abilene and I talked about it, I thought we could do it. But now that we are here, I wish we had fifty men—a hundred."

"But it can be done?" Cipriano insisted.

Vandenberg thought about this for a minute, and then said, "Yes, with a little luck. No, not a little—a lot."

The old man nodded without speaking. Then he said, "But then, nothing is certain."

Vandenberg could tell that the old man was starting to feel

better, and he said, "Cip, we still have some work—the power poles."

"*Si.* There isn't much time."

"It won't take long."

"Let's do it then."

They left their rifles with Gabaldon and moved down to where the main road curved sharply at a corner of the trout pond. The poles that carried the power and phone lines ran along the road. He unstrapped the hand detonator, set it on the ground, and tied two sticks of dynamite to each of two poles, down low. He wanted to be absolutely sure that at least two poles would go. A substation somewhere would register the breakdown, and it would be a warning that something had gone wrong with the lines to Cowles. But it would take time to figure out what was wrong, and during that time the camp would be without power.

He knew that if they managed to radio a message to Santa Fe or Glorieta Assembly it would make no difference whether the half-track got there or not, because they would call in an air strike. At that moment, thinking of what a flight of jets could do, Vandenberg accidentally nudged the detonator in its bag, and the small heavy device rolled down the slope of the trout pond and splashed into the water. He and Cipriano did not move. They both glanced toward the compound. A minute passed and Cipriano whispered, "They didn't hear. They would think it was a fish jumping." He nodded, and Cipriano went on. "Maybe we can find it."

"No. The banks are steep—it was built that way, no shallows. It may be six or eight feet down. It's gone. Christ."

"Can we explode the poles another way?" the old man asked.

"Yes," Vandenberg said, furious with himself. "But the detonator would have been best. Listen—pile up a lot of dead leaves around the dynamite. Like this." He worked quickly, arranging a mound of dry leaves. Then with care he took a cap from his pocket and primed one of the sticks of explosive. When he had finished, he took off his Stetson and placed it over the mound. "At six, come down here and strike a book of matches to the leaves and then run. There's no telling when the burning leaves will explode the cap. Once they're burning, you want to get away. The hat will keep the dew off—but when you light the fire, bring it back. This hat was at my woman's house. I've had it a long time, and I don't want to lose it."

Cipriano nodded, and they moved down to the second pole and rigged the charge in the same fashion, using his Stetson this time. They rested a moment and Vandenberg said, "Remember, you'll have to be very careful."

"I will," Cipriano said. "Something always goes wrong, *sí?*"

"Always."

"A bad sign?"

"No. You have to expect such things. But I could kick myself in the ass for losing that detonator." Together they moved back to where Natividad waited. Across the flat, open stretch on the other side of the road, the buildings of the camp personnel were silent. Vandenberg looked at his watch and saw that it was after five.

THEY FOLLOWED a narrow deer trail to Terrero, Tixier in the lead, sitting slouched in the saddle. None of them spoke much except for a few whispered comments or questions, and a number of times they had to bend low in their saddles to get through tangled stands of young aspen and oak. Tixier finally halted; they were high on the rocky slope north of the settlement Vandenberg had drawn on the map, and he said softly, "Willie, now I want to ask you, am I or am I not the best goddamned trailfinder in New Mexico? By God, we hit within fifty yards of where I wanted to take us."

Below them in the moonlight, perhaps five hundred yards off, the small frame building that housed the cavalry squad was visible. The fence, too, showed clearly, closing in a field a hundred yards on each side. Inside the field they could see the dark shapes of the vehicles and the stables and storage shed. Willie said, "I sure wish we could figure a way to take their animals. Seems a shame to leave 'em."

"Horse is more damned trouble than it's worth," Tixier said. He dismounted, groaning softly. Willie got down and they began untying the ropes that held the explosives and equipment. Abilene loosened the buckles on one of his saddlebags and took out a full fifth. He opened it, drank, and handed it to Willie. The boy, Luis, watched them.

They placed what they were going to take with them in a pile on the ground. Abilene was nervous now. There was a strange, detached expression on his face as he regarded the moonlit building below them. Finally he turned and said to Luis, "Son, you better go along now, like a good boy."

"You can get down there all right from here?" the boy asked.

"We can make it fine," Abilene said. "Can you find your way back to where Kevin has the other horses?"

"Yes. I think so."

"Just stay on the trail we came down until you hit the Willow Creek cutoff, then follow the road. It'll take you right to Cowles. Make sure you stay away from the camp itself. Kevin will be north of the camp, a quarter of a mile or so."

He helped the boy rig a lead rope to their horses. "You ought to be back up there before daybreak, if you don't waste time. Do like Gene said—stay with Kevin. And don't you worry or get nervous. Everything'll be all right."

"Will there be a lot of shooting?" the boy asked.

"I'd say so," Abilene replied. "And it may go on for quite a spell. But don't you worry. You and Kevin sit tight."

"All right," the boy said. In the moonlight, he looked as though he wanted to shake hands but was too shy. Finally he did nothing, only nodded, then mounted his horse, taking the lead rope. "Be seeing you."

"Take care, little buddy," Abilene said. They watched as he turned his horse and expertly led the riderless animals back up the trail. For a minute they heard the faint sounds of the horses' hooves, then it was silent.

Abilene said, "Come on."

They began descending the slope, moving with caution through the scrub oak, their Winchesters slung on their shoulders. The farther down the slope they got the slower Abilene moved, ducking and crouching now in open places. He stopped behind a heavy growth of juniper and waited for Willie to join him. The building, some eighty yards off, was dark except for a light that burned in a window beside the front door. Tixier said, "This is close enough."

"Plenty close," Willie whispered. For a minute they watched the building and then he said, "When you figure that goddamned guard's going to come out?"

"No telling." They set their bundles on the ground beside them. Abilene got farther behind the juniper, and said in a low voice, "Shit, I'm going to have a smoke."

296

"Better not."

"The hell with it," Tixier said. He got out a cigarette and a match and took off his Stetson, sticking his face and one hand into the crown and fumbling until the match ignited. He puffed at the cigarette, blew out the match quickly, and then put the hat back on, cupping both hands over the glowing cigarette. He passed it to Deaguero, who took a couple of drags and then handed it back. Tixier got the whiskey out again, and they had a few drinks, Deaguero taking too big a swallow once and going into a near-silent fit of coughing. When he regained control of his breathing, Abilene looked at the house, regarding it soberly. "Well, what do you think?"

Willie said, "You think we ought to?"

Abilene had another drink. "Hell, we might as well. Why not?"

"You want to then?"

"Damn it all, yes." They did not want to, but they knew they would try it. Abilene glanced toward the darkened house again. "All right, Mister Guard, shag your ass out here and let's have a look at you."

They waited another twenty minutes, and then the night man came out, a brief rectangle of light showing as the front door opened and then closed. They heard him come down the steps and then the sound of his boots on gravel. They sat very quietly as he walked off, and stayed that way for the ten minutes he took to patrol the fence perimeter, until, faintly, they heard the measured tread, and then saw the dim figure approaching in the moonlight, the man in uniform, the round steel helmet visible, taking his time. He went back inside. They saw his silhouette briefly in the lighted window, and then Tixier said, "I guess we can get started."

"You ready?"

"No," Tixier said. "As a matter of fact, I ain't the least little bit ready, now that you ask." He was feeling the whiskey.

"You want to wait awhile longer?"

"We wait till I'm in the mood, we're liable to be sitting behind this motherless bush for two weeks."

Willie grinned. "What do you think is the best way?"

"Same way you swiped the dynamite," Tixier said. "Walk up like you owned the place. Just don't make any noise. That guard'll probably be having himself a nap. Just go do what you have to do without making a racket—I'm going to sit here and cover that door with the rifle. If he comes hopping out I'll let off a shot at him, while you run for it."

Willie set down his rifle, leaning the muzzle against the juniper, and unwrapped the blanket protecting the two bundles, got one under each arm and waited while Abilene fumbled with the reel of plastic-covered wire. "What's the matter?" he asked finally.

"It's tangled," Tixier whispered. Willie stood there waiting while Tixier fooled with the wire, stripping turns off the reel, trying to find the snarl, until fifteen or twenty yards of wire lay in loose coils at their feet. Abilene was swearing softly. "Jesus, did you ever in your life see such a goddamned mess? You'd think they'd make a reel of wire—Why don't they— Ah, *shit!*"

Finally he got more wire off the reel, took out his pocketknife, and cut the tangle at his feet, giving the fresh ends to Willie. "Here—wrap it round your waist. I'll hold the reel, but if I get another snarl don't yank on it, you'll only make it worse. Stop and give me time to get it clear."

Willie looked at the house again. It was still dark except for the one window. Then he moved out, walking fast, bent low, a bundle under each arm, the wire around his waist. From behind he could hear the faint creak of the revolving reel held by Abilene. The open flats that had to be crossed seemed much longer. Then the side of the house loomed up, the north side Vandenberg had chosen, with the hedges. He got in between them and the wall without making any noise and crouched there until his breathing slowed, and now he felt fear, a real horror. Tixier was out there behind the juniper, safe. He could run for it. But Deaguero could not, and for a minute his stomach was so tight he could not move.

He finally set to work, overly cautious now, so that stripping the wire and tying it round the bundles and then wiring the caps took longer, and, too, it was dark on this side of the building, so that most of what he did had to be done by touch. Once he dropped a loose cap on the ground, his whole body knotting in an almost spastic convulsion as he felt it slip from his fingers, and there was a brief interval before the cap struck the soft earth when he knew for sure that it and the two bundles—everything—would go up, but nothing happened and he wasted another minute feeling around in the dirt for the slender copper tube, not finding it, his mouth moving in silent speaking sounds, terrified that he would step on it, finally giving up and whispering aloud in Spanish, "Oh, Jesus and Mary, be careful." So there was the extra cap to worry about, and finally after what seemed an endless time he got the bundles set against the wall, the wire wrapped around the bundles with its bare ends gently attached to the cap's terminals, the cap itself carefully inserted into the incised end of a stick, the whole rig as touchy as anything Deaguero could imagine, ready to blow with the slightest kick of a boot or yank of the wire, a bona fide infernal machine too delicate to even breath on, a very scary sort of bomb.

When he was satisfied that he'd wired it as best he could, he stepped with exaggerated care out from behind the hedges and started walking away from the building, looking over his shoulder to see if the windows were still dark, walking faster and looking back again, and then as he began to realize that he had gotten away with it, he began to trot and then to run, not caring about the sound of his boots, and if the sentry inside had been awake or had had a window opened a few inches he would have heard this, the sound of pounding feet, but again nothing happened except that Deaguero simply ran back to where Tixier waited, panting loudly now, the round belly bouncing up and down, finally collapsing beside Abilene, who looked at him with astonishment.

"What the hell's wrong with you? Goddamn, I could hear you sixty yards off—like a bull elephant on a rampage. For Christ's sake!"

"Lay off," Deaguero said. "Give me that bourbon." He took the bottle, drank, breathed deeply, and drank again. "I didn't think it was going to be that tough. I sure didn't. Abilene, I wouldn't do that again if you gave me ten thousand dollars."

"Were you scared?"

"Oh, God," Deaguero said. "Oh, Jesus." He drank again. "I dropped a damned cap and never did find it. I kept worrying I'd step on it. We'd have had that whole bunch down on us."

Tixier shook his head in disgust. "I ought to have my head examined, running around with a half-breed idiot like you. Dropping caps. It's a miracle you didn't blow yourself sky-high. Did you *wire* it right?"

"It'll be all right, I think."

Tixier said. "I hope so—I'm sure going to feel like one sadassed son of a bitch come six o'clock if I hit that detonator and nothing happens."

"It'll be okay, I think."

"Let's have another smoke," Tixier said. "We got an hour and a half to kill." He lit another cigarette and they passed it back and forth.

Forty-five minutes later the guard came out of the house and did another tour. By then it was five thirty, and they had taken the detonator out of its bag and connected it. In the east the sky was already turning blue.

BY FIVE MINUTES to six it was light enough to see. In the last hour a dew had come down that chilled the two men, working through the heavy jackets and stiffening their fingers. To their right a low mist hung over the Pecos River. Tixier blew on his numbed fingers.

Minutes earlier the guard, a tall, thin young trooper, had come out of the house again, yawning in the gray light, pausing in the gravel driveway to urinate before his last tour, and Willie had glanced at Abilene dumbly, as if mutely questioning whether the young Russian would notice the two thin strands leading away from the house. They waited, and the trooper walked off. The detonator was propped between Abilene's feet; their Winchesters were close by.

The guard reappeared, walking slowly toward the house, in no hurry. Abilene now had the detonator in his hands, Deaguero beside him, unmoving, one hand on his rifle. The trooper stepped back into the house, climbing the steps at the front door, pausing a second to knock caked dirt loose from his boot. After a moment, lights came on in one room. Then another window lit up, and they knew he was going through the house waking the others, and Willie said softly, "When I was in the army, they got us out at five sharp— these guys got it good."

Tixier murmured, "Couple of minutes, they ain't going to have it good." He was looking at his wristwatch now.

"Willie, you better turn around and face the other way."

He turned, too, and twisted the handle, the blast behind them coming with incredible swiftness, before he finished twisting the handle, the shock wave rolling across the flats and knocking them off balance, a terrific roar and flash; they turned to see what they had done, looking with astonishment at what was left of the house. The wall nearest the bundles was gone, most of the two walls adjoining it were demolished, too, along with practically all the roof —only the far wall had survived the blast. They had done what Vandenberg wanted, and then the first debris started thudding down around them, mortar and chunks of plaster, pieces of timber and roofing, some of it pretty large, twisting over as it descended through the thick pall of smoke and dust, and they got under the juniper as far as they could.

They lay there while the echoes of the explosion rolled back and forth across the valley. Tixier yelled, "Bet they heard that motherfucker in *Al*buquerque." He looked at Deaguero. "You should have been an electrician—you wired that okay."

"Your nose is bleeding," Willie said, and Tixier wiped the back of his hand across his face. "Concussion."

"Concussion, hell," Tixier said, getting up. "It was pure surprise—I never thought she'd go off. I swear, Willie, right up until I twisted the handle, I never thought it would really blow."

Deaguero stood up. "You think anybody's alive in that place?"

Tixier shook his head. He put his bottle of whiskey into the canvas carrying bag that had housed the detonator and slung it over his shoulder. They began walking across the open field, stepping over pieces of wreckage, rifles cocked now as they approached what was left of the house. A fire had started, probably the butane heating system, a soft, steady roar coming from somewhere in the wreckage, and already the wood-and-tar-paper roof was starting to ignite, thick streams of black smoke coiling and jetting up through the broken places in the decking.

Tixier picked up a Russian helmet that had been blown clear of the building and set it on his head, tucking his Stetson under one arm. "Nobody in there's going to bother us now, Willie."

They went through a section of twisted and torn chain link fence by the house, skirting the burning ruin, still alert, looking back over their shoulders as they walked into the parking field. In the stables they could hear the horses, frightened by the blast, kicking in their stalls and neighing, and then they had reached the weapons carrier, a low, heavy vehicle on partial Caterpillar tracks, its sides and front sheathed in sloping armorplate, the muzzle of the howitzer protruding through its port. Tixier said, "Get in and figure out how it works. I'll check the storage shed."

Deaguero climbed up the side of the half-track and untied the canvas tarpaulin covering the gun platform, while Tixier shot away the lock on the storage shed door. Deaguero stood up inside the carrier and yelled, "Quit shooting through that door, you damn fool —there's ammo inside."

Tixier said something indistinct that sounded like, "Now he tells me," and kicked open the door and went in. A moment later he came back out. "It's here, all right." Dust-covered and filthy, his upper lip smeared with blood, the helmet down over his eyes, he sat down beside the open door, got out his bottle and had a drink. He yelled, "You better hurry up—we ain't got all day."

Inside the half-track Deaguero was in an upside-down position in the cramped driver's cockpit, legs propped over the back of the bucket seat, head between the clutch and the gas pedals, trying to see up under the panel, finally losing patience and tearing loose a handful of wires that were connected to a lock-type ignition switch. There were six of them, each insulated with a different-colored plastic. He reached up with his pocketknife and stripped the ends clean one by one, then began touching one to another, trying combinations, getting a spark from two finally, looking for the ones that would activate the starter, and at last he found them, joining a black and a red, hearing the starter grind over slowly, and he said aloud, "Battery's low."

He disconnected the wires, wriggled out of the bucket seat, grunting and straining to get himself right side up, knocked his head against a steel bulwark once, cursed the pain, and then he was erect and sitting in the seat, checking the controls, talking aloud again, "She's got some kind of choke primer, like on a diesel. Hell, I wish it was a diesel." He pulled the choke out, pumped the gas pedal, and then carefully shunted the starter wires to the ignition. The motor turned slowly and then it coughed and took hold. He pumped the gas, revving the engine hard. The noise at full throttle was deafening. He eased the choke in halfway, still pumping gas, trying to get the feel of the engine, finally sitting back, relaxed now, finding the emergency brake, and then the transmission lever, a kind of automatic transmission, putting the half-track into low, then braking to a halt, then reversing, then forward again in low, peering through the driver's periscope. The heavy vehicle lurched forward toward Tixier, who was still sitting beside the shack.

Deaguero braked to a halt beside the shed and waited, while Abilene carried out rounds for the howitzer, stacking them on the top deck of the carrier. When he had eight of the heavy black cylindrical cartons aboard, he climbed onto the carrier, yelling over the noise of the engine, "Willie, you got this mechanical hermaphrodite figured out?"

Deaguero looked up from the driver's seat. "Hell, I'm operating it, ain't I?"

"Then let's move. Gene'll be losing his mind."

Willie said, "We'll get there." He put the carrier into low again and moved off toward the padlocked gate of the motor pool—the prow of the carrier struck it head on, tearing both sides of the gate from their hinges—shifting into high as he turned the vehicle onto the gravel driveway and then on up to where the road to Cowles began. Behind them the general store and the houses were silent, the windows dark. The people in the settlement had heard the explosion, but they knew better than to come out.

DURING THE LAST MOMENTS, Vandenberg admitted to himself that the compound wasn't enough, or Remington with his camera equipment. He thought, in forty-eight hours they'll have rounded up the inmates. They'll rebuild the camp, and if Claude does write up the story it won't be like in the old days, when Washington could send out an investigating committee to poke around. If they have to they can build a fence around the whole damned Pecos Wilderness to keep anyone from ever coming in, the way AEC did years ago with the sites at Los Alamos. They'll put the lid on this. Something like this may have already happened a dozen times in the past year—who'd know?

He looked down at his watch. It read thirty seconds past six. Close by, crouched on the sloping bank, Cipriano and Natividad were staring at him. Vandenberg made a sign of encouragement. Another minute passed.

He pointed toward their rifles and then nodded toward the camp. They went down into prone positions.

It seemed very light now. Birds were calling back and forth, and overhead the sky was clear and blue, growing brighter. He could see the guard in the gate tower, bundled in a jacket, standing erect, and then he slipped the safety off the Springfield and stretched out, a pasteboard carton of twenty rounds beside him, blinking to clear his eyes, then sighting through the scope, moving slightly until the cross hairs settled on the guard in the sentry box. Another thirty seconds passed. He began to wonder if the sound of the blast would carry that far. Then it came—a faint, far-off rumble, growing in volume until it was loud enough to be heard anywhere in the camp, and Vandenberg, his cheek against the comb of the stock, spoke in a clear, almost conversational tone, "Cipriano? Natividad? You ready?"

He heard the old man reply, but could not make out what it was he said.

"Shoot now, then." And at that moment, the figure centered in the cross hairs heard the rumble, too, and, as Vandenberg guessed he might, stood up, and he gently squeezed the trigger and felt the heavy jolt against his shoulder, his eardrums numbed by the report, hearing, too, Cipriano's Winchester on his left, the sound of both shots so close they seemed almost one, followed by the crack of Gabaldon's rifle.

He knew he had shot the guard, although with the kick of the rifle he had not actually seen the man go down. The window in the sentry box was empty. The sentry would be dying now. All this went through his mind in the space it took to operate the Springfield's bolt, and then the rifle was ready again, and he was settling the butt against his shoulder, aiming again, firing a second round through the wooden sentry box where he thought the man would be lying. Cipriano fired again.

He worked the bolt a third time and brought the cross hairs to rest on the front door of the main administration building with perfect timing, just as it opened and a man in breeches and an undershirt appeared, barefoot, blinking and staring around, and Vandenberg shot him too, high in the chest, and now he could hear firing from all around the compound, the deer rifles making flat, heavy thumping reports that were unmistakable, then a rapid sputtering that would be one of the submachine guns in the towers, and, reloaded, he put the cross hairs on the doorway again and saw the feet and lower legs of the man he had just killed sticking out

304

of the open doorway and down the steps, as though the man had been sitting there and had fallen backward.

In the scope he saw a faint movement from inside, someone moving in the shadows, and he fired, but the shot was a guess and he knew he had not hit anyone. He reloaded the magazine, squashing black-tipped cartridges in, one at a time, then glanced at Cipriano. The old man was not firing either, but was alert, stretched out on the bank of the ditch, his head low and thrust forward. Farther down the bank, Natividad let off a round. Vandenberg spoke loudly over the ringing in his ears. "You all right, Cip?"

"Okay." The old man looked at him. "I hit him—the one in the tower."

"Go light the fires. Hurry. They'll be trying to use the phone." From somewhere inside the building he heard several faint shouts.

The old man set down his rifle, backed down the bank, and then trotted past Vandenberg toward the poles they had mined. Vandenberg put the cross hairs on the main building again and fired four more rounds into the side of the wall, knowing he would probably not hit anyone. Inside he knew there would be those first minutes of confusion, with men struggling into their clothes and too many orders flying back and forth and no one really sure what was happening or what should be done next. He fired again, opened the bolt and refilled the magazine, and then, crouching low, he began moving toward the north side of the stock tank.

Gabaldon looked up at him as he trotted past. "What's wrong?"

"Nothing. The motor generator."

"What?"

"The auxiliary power plant," he said. "Keep firing."

He located the trailer-mounted unit in the motor pool, fired three rounds into it, and returned to his position on the bank. He fired into the building again, and then, as he was operating the bolt, he heard Cipriano's footsteps and he called out, "Did you get them started okay?" Before Cipriano could answer there was a thunderous crack, then a second, as the sticks went off, and he looked over his shoulder in time to see the severed poles tilt and sag heavily against the overhead lines, hold for a moment, and then go down. There was a brief crackling as the lines touched, then silence.

Gabaldon shouted to Cip, *"Bueno, amigo."*

Cipriano paused beside Vandenberg, panting. "Here is your hat." "Good."

Cip nodded and went back to his rifle. Vandenberg let off four more rounds and reloaded again. From the north flank of the camp, there was a heavy exchange of fire, the solid crack of a Winchester sounding steadily above long bursts of automatic fire, and Natividad called to him, "That's old Ben."

A clump of foliage near Cipriano's head suddenly fell, and with it there came the explosive crack of a bullet. The old man ducked and said, "Hey!"

The shot, Vandenberg knew, had come from a rifle, not a light automatic weapon. They would be passing out drums for the submachine guns and breaking open boxes of ammunition now, but he knew they had done all right so far—they had been lucky in having things go so well for them, the power lines, and the rest of it. So far it had gone all right. He fired two more rounds into the building that housed the officers and medical teams.

Just then Cipriano fired, and Vandenberg glanced at him. The old man raised himself up on one elbow to work the lever, and Vandenberg saw that he ought to warn him about exposing himself, but he didn't, because the old man was really doing better than he had hoped, considering the feelings Cip had had, and a bullet spun across the open space that separated them from the buildings, taking the old man flush in the forehead so that the entire top of his gray head lifted, as though hinged at the back, the Stetson flipping out into the trout pond, and with the heavy smack of the bullet striking there was a quick upward spray of red. Cipriano's head snapped back as though it had taken a heavy punch, and, with Vandenberg still watching, he fell forward against the bank of the stock tank.

ON THE WEST SLOPE Remington was busy with his cameras. Though the light was still tricky for color, he had loaded a reel into the big Bolex, and, shooting from a low-mounted tripod, panned back and forth across the compound, using the wide-angle lens on the turret. He shot most of the reel this way, trying different aperture stops and using a haze filter, and then switched to a long zoom just as the rumble from the Terrero blast echoed up the canyon. Talking to himself, he got good close-ups with the zoom, of Olguin, who was firing below him, and Vandenberg, Gabaldon, and Griego, and, by coincidence, he just happened to have the nearest watchtower in his viewfinder as the sentry inside went down.

He used a second reel in the Bolex, then took up the Nikon, which he had fitted with a 200-millimeter telephoto. The Nikon was loaded with fast black and white, and he was sure of getting good pictures with it. His position was relatively safe, but later, when the films were developed, it would seem as though he was right in the middle of it.

He used an entire roll in this fashion, then reloaded the Nikon and got ready to move to a better position, slinging his other still cameras around his neck. There was firing coming from the main building now. Remington started to move off, then stopped, remembering the automatic carbine. He set down the Nikon and picked up the gun. The four banana clips for it were in a canvas pouch beside the tripod. He opened the fastener on the pouch, took out a clip, stared at it, then slid it up under the trigger guard until it locked in place. He worked the bolt and took approximate aim at the main building.

Gabaldon had left the fire-selector on full automatic. The carbine went off with a deafening burst, bucking, the thirty rounds in the clip going out in a single burst. Remington had been aiming low when he depressed the trigger, but it was impossible to control the little gun, and by the time the magazine was empty, the muzzle was pointing skyward. Perhaps a dozen rounds had struck the building. Remington said, "My God." He stared at the smoking gun in his hands and then loaded another clip.

This time he gripped the carbine tightly, trying to keep the muzzle from climbing, and did better. The contents of the second clip sprayed into the side of the building. Two windows collapsed in a welter of shattered glass.

He loaded another clip and fired it into the building next to Administration, and used the last on the main building again. By then the wooden forearm of the carbine was smoking from the heat of the barrel. He put the gun down, tugged at an ear, made a face against the ringing in his head, and said, "Hell." He went back to the Nikon, and moved back among the trees on the bluff, searching for a vantage point that would enable him to continue taking pictures.

HIGH ABOVE TERRERO, near the Willow Creek cutoff, Tixier had Deaguero stop the half-track. He had stripped the tape off one of the cardboard cylinders protecting the rounds of ammunition and managed to load the howitzer. The shell was heavy. He finally got it into the breech, nearly losing several fingers as he shoved it in, not understanding that a sear automatically snapped the heavy steel block shut when the round had been inserted far enough. He found the traverse mechanism and cranked the weapon around until it pointed in the general direction of a high rock ledge to one side of the road. Warning Willie to cover his ears, he poked and fooled with various buttons and knobs that looked to him to have something to do with the firing device, but the howitzer would not go off.

"Worse'n a hay baler," Tixier said angrily. He went on twisting things, then noticed a lanyard, reached over and gave it a tug, and the howitzer roared. Willie had left his foot off the brake, and the recoil kicked the entire half-track back several feet, knocking Tixier to the floor. There was a second instantaneous explosion as the round struck the ledge of rocks, sending a geyser of boulders skyward.

Both were dazed by the concussion. Tixier crawled forward to the driver's cockpit, got the whiskey out of the canvas bag, drank, and then handed it to Deaguero. "Hey . . . how *about* that?"

Deaguero started laughing, as though this was the funniest thing he'd ever heard. He put the half-track in gear and began driving again. They had been drinking since three that morning.

Tixier got to his feet, staggering as the vehicle lurched over the bumpy road. He reloaded the howitzer, setting the time fuse at zero, then explored the interior of the firing platform, found, among other things, a battery-powered, hand-held loudspeaker, turned it on, and frightened Deaguero by pointing the bullhorn into the cockpit and bellowing, *"Com' está,* you-all?" He laughed delightedly, stood up, raised the horn, and spoke *sotto voce:* "Y'all better watch out."

The crackling whisper, amplified a thousand times, resounded from the steep slopes as Deaguero shifted into high.

CROUCHED AMONG THE BOULDERS the *viejo,* Olguin, was lost in a mist of bourbon-heightened reveries; past events, both real and phantasmagorical, drifted through his mind. He had been calm on the ride down, but gradually the tension built. Minutes earlier he had shot the sentry in the tower assigned him, and with this act had passed into a state of aberrant grace that would not lessen until the fighting was over.

Toward Vandenberg, who was obviously the band's *jefe*, he felt nothing. He was one more Anglo, and Anglos were known to be treacherous. He believed in very few things. Time and existence he did not worry about; there was nothing he could do to alter them. In the same way he had not been much interested in Cipriano's explanation of what they intended accomplishing here. He cared nothing about the Occupation, and he had asked to go with them for no reason other than that there was in him a streak of latent violence that was as much a part of him as his eyesight; he was not as crazy as Cip had made out, but in the last few years he had slipped further into the kind of restless senility that is marked by outbursts of senseless fury.

Stooping, he trotted to another boulder closer to the buildings. A rifle fired from one of them, and the bullet cracked overhead. He went down on hands and knees, crawled forward, pulled the hammer on the single-shot back, and fired a bullet through one of the windows. His temples throbbed visibly, and although it was chilly his face was shiny with sweat. His mouth hung open, and he spoke aloud in Spanish: "So, there are fighters inside." Without fear he stuck his head up, exposing himself like an inquisitive old gobbler. There was another shot, and he ducked. "Oh, Jesus, he is blind. Christ, such an eye." He exposed himself again, took aim at a window and fired quickly, the gun kicking hard. He got back down behind the boulder, and reloaded. "They like to shoot at poor old men." He laughed, bent over, then was caught in a paroxysm of coughing; a clot of phlegm rose from his throat and dangled from his grinning lips; he tried to catch it up, swallow it again, but it clung to his mouth and chin, a yellow string; he wiped it away with the back of his hand. A cold, icy chill started at the base of his skull, and then spread across his shoulders and down his back.

He spoke to the buildings. "Show yourself—you will see what an old man can do. Go ahead. In that tower is someone who showed himself to this old man. Go and ask him what it was like. I am right here. Don't be afraid—here I am." He laughed again, and heard in his mind an old chant, the wild flutes and drums sounding thinly, *las flautas y los tímpanos*. . . . Olguin listened, mouth open, eyes staring. They were there. He shook his head and smiled. No, not in his head—they were there, off in the trees on the high slopes somewhere, the lines of dancers dipping and swaying, the flutes sounding more loudly now, the drums a steady pulse.

In the small building nearest him he saw a man standing in a window, looking out. Olguin fired, sure of a hit. From somewhere up the slope behind him, an automatic rifle opened fire. He cowered —then understood that he was not the target, as a string of bullets stitched into the walls of the big building. Olguin laughed again. "See? You shoot at an old man, and sometimes he has a friend with a marvelous weapon, eh?" The automatic rifle went off again, sending a second burst into the building. "Now you have respect. Now you are not shooting at a poor old man. You are impressed, yes? I think you would like to be someplace else today, not where you are."

He squatted behind the rock, listening to the invisible instruments playing music that could not be heard. Another long burst of automatic rifle fire sounded on the slope.

IN THE SMALL BUILDING two lieutenants and the chief psychiatrist were crouched over the camp commandant, who lay sprawled beside a window. Colonel Brushnevesko was dressed in breeches and socks, and was naked from the waist up. A sprinkle of glass lay on the floor nearby. Beneath his right nipple, a thumb-sized hole pulsed blood, the opening bluish and swollen. His eyes were tightly shut, and his brows were contracted in an angry scowl; he had not spoken since being hit.

"What the devil was he doing at the window?" Dr. Orlov asked. He had his finger on the pulse, but he was not trying to time it.

"He was observing," one of the lieutenants said.

"Observing?"

"What else?"

"You mean, he went and stood in the window? Just stood there?"

"There was no firing from this side of the building," the young officer said. "It seemed safe. I myself was at the window. He told me to move aside."

"There was just one shot," the other officer said. "I saw it—it knocked him backward."

"How bad is he?" the first officer said.

"How bad?" the psychiatrist said. "Are you stupid? He's dying. Can't you see that?" The colonel's pulse had gone wild, faint for a moment, then strong, much too fast, missing beats. The breathing, too, was bad—ragged, stentorian gasps, as though the gray-haired man on the floor had run a long distance.

"There's nothing you can do?" the younger officer said.

"What do you want, a miracle?" the psychiatrist said. "If I had him on the operating table I'd open the chest, even though I'm not a surgeon. Or I could do it here, now, on the floor, but it wouldn't help."

"But in the chest, like that—I would think perhaps a lung, at the most—surely. . . ."

"A bullet strikes a rib, it goes anywhere," Dr. Orlov said. "Who knows where a bullet goes?"

The breathing of the man on the floor grew worse, and the psychiatrist set down the limp wrist. Suddenly a terrific spasm took hold of the colonel; his arms and legs grew rigid, trembled, shook; the head arched sharply back, the entire spine bent bowlike until the torso was clear of the floor; the mouth gaped in a frightening rictus, releasing a gush of bright arterial blood.

IN THE MAIN BUILDING the security detachment, in various stages of dress, was grouped together in and around the largest office, some of them in the corridors, others posted near windows or behind desks and file cabinets—thirty-five men, including medical clerks and orderlies. The senior noncommissioned officer of the group was a sergeant named Maximov, a tall, portly man who had assumed command when there was no answer from the telephone in the officers' billets. He was almost fully dressed, and had even got his tunic on, although he had not taken the time to button it.

Sprawled in the open doorway was another sergeant, a widening pool of blood soaking his undershirt and back. The first thing Sergeant Maximov had done was to forbid anyone to go near the dead man or approach the open door.

Inside the door was a clerk's desk, and Maximov had put a man there to operate the field phone lines that went to the towers. So far, only one had answered. Maximov himself had crawled over and spoken to the man in the tower, and from him had got an idea of how many men were attacking. The guard reported that he had seen firing on all sides of the camp, but that there was no great concentration of force. Maximov rightly concluded that the attackers were few, and went about supervising the distribution of rifles and automatic weapons.

He had put three men with rifles at the windows facing south, with orders to keep well back in the shadows. He knew that whoever was out there had high-powered rifles, and at least one of them was extremely powerful, because the bullets slammed completely through the building, except for several rounds that had ricocheted off desks and a steel chair. The shooter knew enough to aim low, guessing that most of them would be on the floor. None of the shots had come in over knee-high, and already three of Maximov's men had been hit. Two of the wounds were not serious, but the third was through the pelvis. The shooters out there were steady in their rate of fire, and he knew it would not take much more of this to demoralize his men. He himself had felt fear when the power lines blew up, afraid not so much of being cut off as of the attackers getting to the building with similar explosives.

He did not like having his men bunched together in the corridors and the main office, and he called again to the armorer to speed up the distribution of weapons. One of his men fired, and then shouted jubilantly, "I hit one. There's one gone."

The man on the line to the officers' billets called, and Maximov crawled over. One of the junior officers was at the other end. Sergeant Maximov gave a quick report, and the officer said, "How many do you estimate are out front?"

"Perhaps six or seven," Sergeant Maximov said.

"Sergeant, put men with automatic weapons at the windows. Have another dozen ready to go out the door. When you're ready, lay down a covering fire with the submachine guns—that will let you get your men out into the open."

"I was going to do that, sir," Maximov said. "We're almost ready."

"You can't do anything inside, you know. Once outside you can spread out and flank them. Have the men at the windows keep up a steady fire."

"Yes, sir."

"How many hurt?"

"One dead, sir. Sergeant Andreyevich. Three wounded." At that moment the commandant was shot, and the officer at the other end of the line dropped the phone and left Maximov on his own.

The sergeant got his men ready and talked to them. He was about to give the command to the gunners at the windows to open fire when a burst of automatic rifle fire tore through the far wall of the building, the burst rising until they heard the last rounds slapping into the corrugated steel roofing overhead.

"They've got automatic weapons," one of his men said.

"It's not out front," Maximov said. "It's up on that bluff somewhere."

Two more shots from the trout pond cracked through the building, and one of Sergeant Maximov's riflemen cried out and collapsed. He started to give the order to open fire again when the second long burst of automatic fire struck the building. This time it did not rise but was held in a tight cone of fire. Several windows on that side of the building went out, bullets tore through room partitions, ploughed gouges in the oak flooring and sent splinters flying. A good part of the burst went into the detachment he was readying to race out the door, and six or seven men went down. There were shouts, cries. Guns skidded across the floor. Stunned, he stood erect, ignoring the fire coming from the trout pond, and reversed his own orders, shouting at them, "Spread out, damn you—why must you bunch up?"

The medical orderlies were already busy among the wounded. Maximov heard several more bursts from the gun on the bluff.

The phone to the officers' billets rang, and Maximov himself answered; at the other end was the chief psychiatrist. "What's happening there, Sergeant?"

"We've been badly hit, sir," Maximov said.

"How many?" Dr. Orlov asked.

"I haven't counted, sir. It was from an automatic gun, not from out front. We were ready to go out the door. I don't know how many wounded we have."

"Listen to me, sergeant, the commandant is dead."

"Dead, sir?"

"I'm taking command," Dr. Orlov said.

"Yes, sir."

"What luck have you had with the radio?" Sergeant Maximov did not answer. "Damn it, can't you understand me? Have you contacted Santa Fe?"

"No, sir. We were going to rush them——"

"Is your signalman all right?"

Maximov called for the radio operator and heard a yell from the corridor: "He's all right, sir."

"Have him radio District Headquarters. Now."

"Sir—the power."

"Isn't there auxiliary power?"

Maximov paused. "Sir, let me check."

The psychiatrist said, "Get moving. Have your men keep firing. I'll wait here by the phone."

Maximov put down the receiver and crawled out to the corridor and found the signalman. "Are you in contact with District Headquarters?"

"I haven't tried."

"Let's go."

They crawled down a side corridor to the radio room. "There's no telephone connection," the signalman said, "and the regular power will be out too—I was watching from the window and saw the lines go down." He stood up and began flipping switches at a bank of equipment on a long table. "The remote is out, too, Sergeant. This switch, here, should actuate the auxiliary power plant in the motor pool, but, see for yourself—nothing happens."

"You can turn on the emergency power from here?"

"Yes, when its operating properly," the signalman said. "But maybe the plant has been damaged—there's enough bullets flying around."

"What else have we? A walkie-talkie?"

"Not over the mountains, Sergeant—it's too far."

"You mean there's nothing?"

"There's the mobile unit out in the scout car—in the motor pool. That might reach to Santa Fe," the signalman said. "It takes its power from the engine."

"You could contact District Headquarters with it?"

"Possibly—you'd want to use the emergency frequency. That crystal there is for Blue Alert." The signalman pointed to a small rectangular device, wafer-thin, that was plugged into the regular transmitter. "It would fit the mobile rig." The operator unplugged the crystal, and then stared at Sergeant Maximov. "But, listen, you don't want me to go out there?"

"I want you to contact District Headquarters," Maximov said.

"Sergeant Maximov, it must be forty meters to that scout car."

"You can do it," Maximov said. "Go out a back window and run fast. Once inside the car you get down on the floor, and they won't be able to reach you. You can operate the radio on the floor, can't you?"

"I don't think I can do that," the signalman said.

The signalman was young, still in his early twenties, and until this morning he had regarded his assignment with content. He was apart from the rest of the security detachment and did not pull guard duty. The radio schedule he had been given was routine, involving four report-ins daily. Although a good soldier, he feared a sprint such as Sergeant Maximov proposed, and was ready to argue further when the noncom said, "The Colonel is dead—he was shot. Major Orlov is in charge. You are to say nothing about this to the others, understand?" Maximov said this in such a way that the youthful signalman was left with the impression that he might be shot summarily if he protested. He considered this, and then said, "All right."

They crawled back to the other men. Several more shots crashed through the building, one striking the large, inverted bottle of a drinking fountain. Questions and demands were directed at Maximov, who said, pointing to the signalman, "The radios are out—he's going to try for the scout car. There's a transmitter in it."

"We stay?" somebody asked.

"Yes," he said; he noted the expressions of relief on their faces. "He'll go out a back window—we'll lay down a covering fire for him." He looked at the signalman. "Are you ready?" The young man stared at him for a moment, then turned and began crawling down the corridor to the rear windows.

He stopped, his face pale. "Sergeant Maximov—the key for the ignition? Is it in the car, do you think?"

Sergeant Maximov looked at the pegboard on the wall beside

the desk and saw that the key was there. Disgustedly he stood erect and strode over to the board, took down the key, and tossed it to the radio operator. "I'm glad you thought of it. It saved you an extra trip."

The signalman put the key in the pocket of his breeches and went on all fours to one of the windows. Maximov watched him; as he rose to climb through a shattered frame, he gave the order to fire.

OLGUIN WAS perhaps fifty yards from the motor pool. He heard the automatic weapons open fire, and raised his head in time to see a figure running along the back of the buildings; he slid the rifle forward, cocked the hammer, took aim, fired, and missed.

The running man put on more speed. Quite deliberately, Olguin reloaded, took aim again. The man was in among a line of vehicles now, not dodging or sidestepping, but sprinting in a straight line, his legs working like pistons. The old man fired again as the figure clambered into a car, and nodded, sure that the shot had been good.

THE YOUNG SIGNALMAN lay in a curled-up position, half on the floor of the scout car, half on the front bucket seat. He knew nothing about medicine, but he was convinced that the bullet that had torn off his kneecap would leave him a cripple. The wound bled freely, and he stripped off his belt as he'd been taught and tied it in a tourniquet above the knee. Mumbling to himself, he found neutral on the shift, pulled the choke, turned on the ignition, and got the motor started. Mounted behind the back seat was a medium-powered transceiver. He switched it on, waited a minute for it to warm up, and with difficulty got the emergency operating crystal from his breeches pocket and plugged it in. Luckily, the long whip antenna had not been lashed down, and as he adjusted the transmitter and tuned the receiver to the proper frequency, he wondered if the whip would put out enough juice to carry to District Headquarters in Santa Fe.

IN THE SMALL PARK Kevin and Luis waited, listening to the shooting. Luis had arrived about five with the horses. They had spoken little in the past hour.

Now Vialpando stood among the horses, looking in the direction of the compound. Kevin's expression was openly frightened. He said finally, "I wonder when it's going to stop?" Luis stared at him. "The shooting. Hear it?"

"I hear it."

"It's been going on for so long," Kevin said.

Luis did not reply.

"I just don't want him to be hurt."

"Who? Your father?"

Kevin nodded. The shooting seemed to increase rather than lessen.

He said, "Let's bring the horses out into the open."

Luis frowned. "Why?"

"If they're having trouble down there, they'll want to get away fast," Kevin said. "They're going to want the horses handy, not scattered all around in the trees."

Luis thought about this, and then nodded. "Okay."

They got a pair of horses and led them down to an open field. Luis rigged a stake rope, and when they had tethered the horses they went back up the slope for another pair.

BEN DEAGUERO joined them at the stock tank, crawling on all fours. He stopped near Cipriano's body, regarded it for a moment, and then took up a position on the sloping bank and began firing.

Vandenberg glanced at his watch. Almost six thirty. He wondered what had happened to Reuben Archuleta—the east side, where he'd stationed him, had been silent for some time.

AT DISTRICT HEADQUARTERS in the St. John's College complex, an Occupation officer wearing captain's pips was busy on a phone, trying to locate his colonel. An orderly finally found him at breakfast, gave a brief report, and then stepped aside as the colonel got up from his meal and hurried to the captain's desk.

He was handed two sheets of thin yellow paper. The captain said, "They came through Message Center about twenty minutes ago, Comrade—it has to be an attack."

The colonel glanced at the sheets. "Were these in code?"

"In the clear. Message Center—I checked myself, sir—reported that our operator here didn't think it was the regular transmitter, but that he recognized the man's style of sending."

"Was a challenge and countersign used?"

"Whoever sent the message had yesterday's."

The colonel read the second sheet again and glanced at the captain. "Has this been verified—the telephone?"

"We can't get through."

A major in CIC came in, read the message, and the colonel beckoned to him. "Any signs of partisan activity in that area?"

"None whatever."

"There are now," the colonel said. "They've mounted a full-scale raid."

"That far up in the mountains?"

The colonel did not answer, but went to a wall map of the northeast sector. He wrote down grid coordinates and then came back to the desk and told the captain, "Find General Durnet. I'm calling for an air strike."

"You're sure it's not a ruse of some sort?" the CIC major asked.

"Perhaps. I'll have them stand by until the general gets here." He picked up another phone, identified himself to the switchboard operator, and said, "Comrade, this is a Priority Blue Alert. Do you understand me? Put me through to Kirtland Air Force Base. The extension is three-nine-four-two—no, not my extension, theirs." He waited a minute, then identified himself again as the Kirtland duty officer came on the line. "Lieutenant, I have a Blue Alert here, and I'm calling for an air strike. Have you a pencil?" He gave the grid coordinates he had copied. "Please be good enough to get me your operations officer. Thank you."

There was another pause, and then the colonel began again. "This is Colonel Pavel, duty officer, Thirty-Second District, Santa Fe. I have a Blue Alert for you, Captain. Yes, it just came in. I want a strike readied but not released until General Durnet gets here. I've already given your duty officer the grid coordinates. Read them back to me, please." He listened, then nodded. "Very good. The target is a small training camp about eighteen miles due north of the town of Pecos. *Pay*-kos, yes. Actually, your target will be the force that is attacking it. No, Captain, the camp itself is not to be damaged. Yes, this is a real Blue Alert. If it's a practice alert I know nothing about it. No, there are no other buildings or communities nearby—there's no chance for confusion."

He sat on the edge of the desk, slipped one hand into his breeches pocket, got out matches, beckoned for the captain nearby to give him a cigarette. "Yes, so far as we can tell, it's a localized operation." He puffed at the cigarette, exhaled a cloud of smoke, listened, smiled. "No! Really? You mean you have them on stand-by there?" He listened, still smiling. "No, I don't feel that would be advisable. We have our own people available, don't we? Yes, of course. Go ahead. I'll have this line held open for you."

The colonel held the phone away from his ear and spoke to the major from Counter-intelligence. "He wanted to know if it was all right to use Americans. They have a couple of American Air National Guard pilots down there for two weeks' training. He wanted to tell them some sort of ridiculous story about vandals robbing a supply depot. I told him not to."

"I heard," the major said.

Seated on the edge of the desk, the colonel swung a booted leg back and forth. "Do you realize what this will mean, if Durnet gives a go-ahead?" The CIC major looked at him. "It will be the first incident in the Thirty-Second's area. For all we know it could be the first in the entire country."

"Do you really think so, Colonel?"

He shrugged. "Who knows. If it is, I want to have it handled properly, by our people—not by Americans."

OUTSIDE ALBUQUERQUE, at Kirtland, the scramble horns howled in the billets and hangers, and within minutes the wing commander was in preflight briefing. The two other pilots on alert that day gathered around their senior officers. They were young men, clean-shaven, with close-clipped hair and healthy, alert features. While the operations officer outlined the mission, the wing commander talked to Santa Fe. Further instructions were coming down.

On the flight line ground crews were already warming the aircraft. Slung in racks beneath the sweptback wings were banks of 90-millimeter rockets. Overhead, the sky was a clear, dazzling blue.

In the briefing room the operations officer was handed a report from the meteorological station. He read it aloud: "There's a cold front moving southeast from the Four Corners area near Farmington.

Low ceilings and intermittent snow through Colorado to Utah, but it won't reach us till late afternoon. You can expect perfect weather all the way."

IT HAD BEEN QUIET for some time now. Vandenberg glanced at his watch again. Six forty. He knew he would not be the only one almost out of ammunition.

There was a short burst of fire from the watchtower to the east—Reuben's—and he faintly heard the sound of whining ricochets. Hidden by the sloping bank, he moved to another position, closer to Ben Deaguero, and fired another round into the main building. He worked the bolt, listening. Miles down the valley there had been the explosion, over half an hour ago, and then, some time later, a fainter one, which he assumed must be Tixier trying to block the road behind them, but there had been nothing since.

And then, from far down the road, still out of sight, he heard it, the half-track, barely audible at first, the motor muffled by the woods, then growing louder, and he knew they'd be hearing it inside the buildings, too. They'd still be cautious, but would be feeling better now, convinced that the cavalry squad at Terrero had been alerted somehow and had sent up the half-track. He was counting on their accepting one of their own vehicles.

Without jubilation he called to Gabaldon and Ben Deaguero, ordering them to join him. They did so, running along the bank, doubled over, and he said, "How much ammunition have you?"

"About thirty rounds," Natividad said. He glanced at Cipriano's body nearby.

"Fifteen, sixteen shells," Ben replied.

"Start firing. Pin them down," he said. They spaced out, inched their way up to the top of the bank, and began shooting. The weapons carrier was very loud now. It came into view, the combat hatches swung shut and dogged down, the tall whip antennas untied and erect, swaying wildly as the vehicle rumbled up the road, red triangular Occupation pennants of cotton bunting fluttering bravely from their tips, and from where he was, Vandenberg caught a glimpse of someone inside the gun platform, a glint of a round steel helmet, and for one terrible moment he wondered if Tixier and Willie had been killed, and if the half-track was really manned by the troopers, his mind thinking ahead, figuring—or trying to figure—some kind of escape that would save some of them, and then the weapons carrier braked to a halt on the dirt road, less than forty yards from Vandenberg and Natividad and Ben Deaguero. The snoutlike muzzle of the howitzer swung toward the main building, and he knew they had been successful.

INSIDE THE MAIN BUILDING, Sergeant Maximov and his men watched the approach of the half-track and saw it stop. A man kneeling beside Maximov smiled. "He must have gotten the radio working."

"Everybody check their weapons," Maximov ordered. "When that half-track gets closer, we'll make a break for it. They'll finish this in a minute." He peered at the vehicle down the road. "What the hell are they up to. Why are they sitting there?"

He was about to speak again when the howitzer went off.

CLAUDE REMINGTON WAS on the slope with the Nikon when the howitzer fired. For a moment, there was a pause in which the sound of the half-track's motor could be heard idling, and then there came a heavy crack that seemed to rupture the silence of the morning, so thunderous that the previous small-arms fire was nothing, and he saw the shell strike the main building. There was a bright white flash and a puff of smoke, and then he heard the roar of the explosion, louder still than the howitzer, the concussion flattening the bushes and neatly mown lawn in front of the building as the round struck flush against the side and the sloping steel roof burst upward, large pieces of corrugated sheeting spinning end over end.

INSIDE THE CARRIER Tixier was laughing as he readied another shell. The strap on the steel helmet he was wearing was too loose, so that the helmet's rim came down over his eyes. The fifth of liquor he had brought was nearly gone. He got the round into the breech, taking care to keep his fingers out of the way as the block snapped shut. Both he and Deaguero were half deafened by the concussion of the big gun, and Tixier shouted, "Man, did you see that—did you see *that?*"

He began cranking the traverse mechanism to bring the muzzle to bear on the officers' billets, then stopped, stood erect on the firing platform, exposing himself, visible from the waist up, the portable bullhorn gripped in both hands, shouting, "Gene? Did you see that, Gene?" The voice from the speaker, metallic and amplified, boomed across the open fields. "Gene? Where're you hiding—hey, *G-E-N-E!*"

THE HELMETED PILOTS sat in their cockpits, marking off preflight checklists with pip marks. The bubble canopies were rolled back, and triangular chocks still held the wheels, but the planes were ready.

In the briefing room the operations officer was on the phone, waiting for a disposition order from Santa Fe. They were apparently having some difficulty locating the commanding general.

TIXIER, CAUGHT UP by the earsplitting havoc he was creating, loaded and fired, a third and fourth round landing in the already wrecked buildings outside the fences, the heavy shells whizzing into the frame structures to detonate deafeningly, until the ruins themselves were hidden in black haze. Flames shot up as gas lines ignited. A few yells were heard.

Vandenberg climbed now to the top of the bank, the Springfield under one arm. The heavy cloud of black smoke was settling and dispersing, spreading into the compound. He saw Tixier, working in the gun platform. The rancher swung the muzzle to the watchtower by the gate and fired; the framework burst apart and simply vanished. He heard Deaguero shout from the driver's seat, and the half-track moved forward, gaining speed, taking the main gate head on, tearing out steel uprights so that the hood of the vehicle was draped in a tangled cowl of wreckage and wire. He sat down on the top of the bank and lit a cigarette. Ben Deaguero and Natividad joined him.

They watched Claude Remington descending the west bluff, laden with cameras and gear, the carbine slung from one shoulder. He waved to them, then stopped to take another picture.

Olguin was out from behind his rocks, moving at a dogtrot across the open space that separated him from the buildings. He stopped for a moment among the vehicles in the motor pool. The radio operator he had winged was lying on the floorboards of the scout car, unconscious.

The motor of the car was still running. Olguin stared down at

322

him for a moment, then placed the muzzle of the .45-70 behind the young signalman's ear and pressed the trigger. The head bounced sharply against the steel floor. Olguin walked over to where Vandenberg and the others were waiting. They could see that the old man was excited. Gabaldon said in Spanish, "Did it go well, old-timer?"

Olguin nodded. "Very good." He looked around. "Is it over?"

"Yes."

"Good," Olguin said. He nodded toward Vandenberg. "Tell the Anglo that this old man knew how to do it." He laughed suddenly, struck the ground several times with the butt of his rifle, danced a step or two, sputtering. Then, as quickly, he snapped out of it. He saw Cipriano's body and looked at the others. *"Muerto?"*

"Sí," Vandenberg said. Olguin walked over and stared down at the body, then nudged it with the toe of his boot. He came back, and Ben Deaguero gave him a cigarette.

They saw someone moving toward them through the smoke—Reuben Archuleta. There was blood on his jacket, and he had tied a dirty hankerchief around one arm. Vandenberg went up to him. "Let's have a look."

"The guard in that tower could really use a gun," Reuben said. "I was behind a big tree—I didn't think any of me was showing."

Ben Deaguero laughed. "He was waving hello to the guard, that's what. Little Reuben, he was hiding behind a tree and he put his hand out to wave hello, and that damned Russian said hello right back."

"Did you get him?" Vandenberg asked.

"Yes. I think so."

Vandenberg unwrapped the handkerchief and cut open the sleeve of the jacket. The bullet had made a small, neat hole halfway between the wrist and elbow, but the exit hole on the underside was raised and opened almost like a chancre, with nodules of flesh protruding. Archuleta regarded this. "Every time I moved, he shot at me. I bet he let off two hundred rounds. Finally I lay quiet, and then I saw him stand up. What happened to Cipriano?"

"He didn't stay down," Vandenberg said. "Someone inside spotted him, and was ready the next time he stuck his head up."

"Too bad," Reuben said.

"Yes."

"We better dig him a grave," Natividad said.

"There's no time for that," Vandenberg said.

"You just want to leave him here?" Gabaldon demanded.

"Yes. Let the Russians bury him."

Natividad gave him a hard look, and it wasn't just show; he meant it.

"You want a grave, make it big enough for both of you," Vandenberg said. "Personally, I'm going to be gone from here in about ten minutes. They'll have troops all over this place in no time."

Gabaldon glared at him for another moment, then looked to the others. Vandenberg walked off. The others followed. Claude Remington was kneeling on the ground near the front gate, shooting one Kodacolor after another with the Rolleiflex as the group of filthy, exhausted men walked through the black haze.

"AIR FORCE one-eight-three-seven . . . Kirtland Tower." The voice of the Russian tower operator crackled in the headsets of the men waiting in the planes.

"Go ahead, tower."

"You are clear for Flight One, Priority Blue Alert, according to preflight briefings. Repeat, you are cleared for Priority Blue Alert."

"Acknowledged."

The flight leader waved an arm. The wheel chocks were jerked loose, and the ground crews dashed to one side as the jets taxied out of the flight line onto a concrete apron. The bubble canopies eased shut.

"Kirtland Tower here," the voice in the headsets said. "You are clear for runway two-zero. Wind is from the west, at one-seven knots. Altimeter is five-four-three-nine."

"Am I clear for take-off?" the flight leader asked.

"Clear for take-off."

The three silvery jets swung out onto one of the main runways, the roar of their engines building. They picked up speed; the concrete runway, scarred by the marks of thousands of wheels, flashed by beneath the wings, and then they were airborne. At two hundred and fifty kilometers an hour they banked and rose sharply, and in another minute were clear of the flight pattern.

The wingmen held a close formation. They looked at one another, waved greetings, and then the flight leader spoke into the microphone. "Kirtland, this is Air Force one-eight-three-seven. We are clear of flight pattern. The destination is Pecos, New Mexico. Estimated flight time, twelve minutes, ETA zero-six-five-eight."

The tower acknowledged this, and the flight leader spoke to his wingmen. "Course is zero-two-eight degrees."

The wingmen dipped their wings in reply, and, still maintaining the tight formation, the flight altered course slightly. At full throttle now, they were approaching the sound barrier. Seventy miles to the north the Sangre de Cristos were clearly visible, a series of broken-backed spurs rising above the dull-green plains. Far beneath them a thin ribbon of concrete, U.S. 85, stretched off in the same direction, arrow-straight, seeming almost a guideline to their destination.

INSIDE THE COMPOUND the smoke and stinking haze from the burning buildings had still not cleared. Vandenberg and the others walked up to the half-track and saw Tixier atop the gun platform, one leg crossed over the other, the enlisted man's steel helmet still on his head.

Vandenberg stared up at him. "How'd you get so stoned?"

Tixier smiled grandly. "Ah, Gene . . ."

Deaguero appeared on the gun platform, too, and Vandenberg said, "You two did a real job."

"Where's Cipriano?" Tixier asked.

"Dead."

The rancher said nothing.

"He was shot during the first few minutes," Vandenberg said. "Give me that loudspeaker you were yelling into."

Abilene handed down the bullhorn and Vandenberg fiddled with the switch on the battery pack, blowing into the mouthpiece until he got it to work. He climbed up on the gun platform and pointed it toward the dorms. "Listen to me. All of you. Come out."

His voice, rasping from the speaker, rolling across the smoke-hazed field, went on: "Come out. Do you hear me?" He turned the switch off, watched the buildings, and then glanced at Abilene. "We may have to go in and lead them out by the hand." He raised the bullhorn again and shouted, "Come out—that's an order. Leave your dorms and assemble here on the drill field immediately."

The doors of the dormitories opened and the inmates began filing out, slowly at first, then with increasing speed until finally they were jostling and shoving at one another in their eagerness to obey the bullhorn.

Confused, they gathered in front of the dorms. The routine of their day had been destroyed. Dressed in clean, neatly pressed fatigues, their faces and hands burned brown by the sun, healthy, well fed, they were immeasurably better-looking than the filthy group with Vandenberg. Tixier and the others regarded the inmates. The old rancher said, "You know, they sort of remind me of one of those health clubs."

"What did you expect," Vandenberg said. "A battalion of Green Berets?"

"Somehow, seeing them, I don't feel so hot," Tixier said, slurring the words. He took off the steel helmet and replaced it with his Stetson. The formations of inmates waited.

"One thing for sure," Tixier said. "We can't say you didn't warn us, Gene. They're every bit what you said they'd be."

Vandenberg raised the bullhorn. "Listen to me. We don't have much time. M.G. will be up here quickly."

He paused, and then went on. "Something you must understand. You've been on drugs. It's in the diet—"

One of the trainees, perhaps a dorm captain, stepped forward and called, "What is it you're telling us to do?"

Quite clearly he saw how useless this was. He spoke to them without conviction. "I want you to try and escape. Some of you will be caught right away. Others may make it back to their homes. The drugs will wear off in three or four days." He paused, then spoke again with the patient tones of a schoolteacher leading a class of children across a street. "All right, let's move out. Quickly, now. All of you. See how far you can get. Try to stay hidden. Good luck."

They did not move.

Vandenberg waited, then spoke into the speaker again. "Everybody move out on the double. The gate is open. Let's go. We're going to blow up the rest of the buildings."

Alarmed by the last statement, a few started across the field toward the smashed gate. Others joined them.

Vandenberg shouted into the horn. *"Move!"*

They broke into a shuffling trot, picked up speed; at last all of them were running, their work shoes thudding on the packed dirt of the field. Claude Remington was taking pictures.

Vandenberg put down the horn, and Abilene looked at him disgustedly. "You mean, that's all you wanted to tell them?"

Vandenberg did not reply for a moment; he jumped to the ground, and then said, "That's all I wanted to tell them."

Tixier climbed off the half-track with him. "You think you accomplished anything with all that?"

"No."

"You sounded worse'n a goddamned Baptist preacher."

"Tell me about it later," he said. "Let's get moving. Reuben is wounded."

"I saw that," Tixier said angrily. He turned to Archuleta. "How is it?"

"It hurts."

Tixier and Reuben and the others began walking away from the half-track. A pall of smoke still hung over the compound, obscuring the sky. Claude Remington was down on one knee, operating the Nikon.

Vandenberg paused beside him. "Did you get your pictures?"

Remington grinned. "Gene, we're asshole deep in photos. I must have gotten three hundred. And two reels in the Bolex."

"Fine," he said.

"I got a couple of great ones of you. Offhand, I'd say some of these shots may fall into the category of unforgettable."

"We better get moving."

"I'm with you—give me a hand."

Vandenberg took the empty carbine and Remington's leather camera bag while Remington shouldered the tripod-mounted Bolex. They broke into a trot until they had caught up with the others. Tixier and Reuben Archuleta were at the rear. Tixier had taken Archuleta's lever-action and had an arm around the young man, who looked sick. Vandenberg looked behind him toward the compound and saw Olguin standing near the gate. He stopped, and shouted, *"Olguin!"* The old man turned and waved. *"Olguin— ándale. Vámonos—muy pronto!"*

"Sí—" the old man called. He began following.

Vandenberg caught up with Remington again.

"Gene—what now?"

"Now we get out of here," he said. "A long way. Split up. I hope those boys have the horses waiting."

"And then? Afterward?"

"You've got some film to develop and print. And a story to write. And a press run. And a circulation problem that, by ordinary standards, would be very discouraging."

"And after that?" Remington asked.

"We've got a printing machine. The next thing is a transmitter." He was puffing for breath. "To talk to Ivan."

Remington stopped. "From up here? They'll find us in minutes."

"They haven't caught me yet," said Vandenberg. "Hurry your ass up."

"You son of a bitch, you're crazy—you're looking to be a martyr."

"Maybe so. But we're going to make ourselves heard."

They were on the old trail north of the compound now, climbing the last of the slopes that had been cleared of trees. The compound was still burning.

Abilene Tixier slowed his pace, looking over his shoulder frowning. "Gene, where do you think you can find a radio?"

"If you were able to swipe a printing press, I'll find a transmitter," he said.

"Listen, we ain't going to draw attention to ourselves with any radio," Tixier said. "We're in enough trouble—"

"Let's talk about it later—there's no time now," Vandenberg said.

Up front Natividad let out a yell as he spotted the horses gathered in the park. The men quickened their pace. Minutes later Gabaldon and Willie Deaguero had reached their horses and mounted, turning the animals and waiting for the others.

Kevin and Luis Vialpando had also mounted. Reuben had trouble getting into his saddle, and Vandenberg and Abilene took a moment to help him.

Kevin called out, "Daddy—we brought the horses down here. Was that all right?"

Vandenberg grinned and waved to his son across the clearing. "You did just fine."

Then he saw the look on Luis' face as the boy realized his grandfather was not with them. He started toward Luis.

COMING UP the narrow valley to Cowles, the bright silver jets broke out of their arrow-shaped formation and dropped one behind the other. Several miles down the valley the flight leader sighted the pall of black smoke above the compound. He glanced quickly at the grid coordinates blocked off on his flight map and then spoke over the radio. "There it is."

Seconds later he made a pass over the compound, banking sharply, and again his voice came over the radio, immensely calm. "I have a target. Half a kilometer north of the smoke cloud. They're in a little valley. Men and horses."

IN THE PARK Vandenberg and the others stared up for a second as the jet fighters streaked overhead. Then he shouted above their echoing thunder, "Get out of here!"

They spurred their horses as the jets parted in a mushroom breakaway, the second banking right, the third arcing left in a tight turn that would bring them in again on the park. The flight leader had already completed his 360-degree turn, and now he came in low and fast, almost at treetop level, catching in his aiming indicator for a fleeting moment before he pressed the firing button a fragmentary image of mounted men, seven or eight hundred yards ahead of him, galloping wildly. His salvo fired, he pulled back hard on the control stick, noting the serpentine smoke trails of the rockets spiraling into the valley. Less than a minute later the left wingman made his pass, followed by his partner. The flight leader was circling overhead; he called over the radio, "Cease firing."

"How did you do?" the left wingman called back.

"All right," the flight leader replied. "Most of mine were short, but I saw the last one go directly into four or five of them. They were bunched together."

They circled for several minutes longer above the burning valley. The open, grassy meadow of the park was no longer identifiable. Up and down the steep slopes, tall spruces, blown loose from their roots, lay at crazy angles, splintered and burning; the valley itself was almost obscured by a haze of brown dust and smoke.

LATE THAT AFTERNOON, clouds built up and it began snowing. Advance cavalry units from the Glorieta Assembly garrison had already reached the compound and had taken charge of the trainees who had stayed in the vicinity. The road above Terrero was still blocked by a rockslide, and the trainees were formed into a column and marched on foot to Terrero, where trailer vans waited to transport them elsewhere.

Shortly before sunset two squads of mounted troopers walked their horses up to the valley that had sustained the rocket attack. The troopers had been supplied with a full combat issue of ammunition and grenades. They had been impressed by what they had seen at the compound, and they moved cautiously.

Light snow was falling, covering the trees and underbrush, muffling the sound of the horses' hooves. Most of the scattered fires had burned themselves out, but there was still a strong smell of smoke, charred wood, and cordite.

As the light faded and they saw that there was nothing to fear, the troopers moved more quickly, spreading out, searching. The lieutenant in charge dismounted, going from one group of soldiers to another to see what they had found. Half an hour later he returned to his mount, which had a transceiver strapped to the saddle, and radioed the main detachment at Cowles. He gave his report quickly: "There must have been ten or twelve of them."

"How does it look?"

"For once, the Air Force wasn't exaggerating."

"No tracks leading out?"

"Impossible to tell," the lieutenant said. "Not only the snow—everything's a ruin up here."

"No bodies?"

"The biggest thing we've found so far was the head of a horse."

"Very good." There was a pause, then, "Would you rather camp there or return?"

"It's almost dark," the lieutenant said. "We'll camp here."

"All right," the voice at the other end replied. "Tomorrow morning, CIC will want a look."

"Yes, they'll be interested—one of my men found a piece of what looks like a movie camera."

They spoke for another few minutes, and then the lieutenant signed off and went about his duties, overseeing his men as they erected tents and built cooking fires for tea and evening meal. They were tired, but they worked willingly, and soon several small fires were visible in the twilight. It snowed for most of the night. By morning there was more than a foot of dry, white powder on the ground.

COMMUNICATIONS

Special:
To: AP, UPI and the *Santa Fe Journal News.*

FREAK EXPLOSION KILLS TWELVE

Pecos, N.M.—A faulty butane connection is believed to have been the cause of an explosion early this morning that resulted in the deaths of 12 Occupation personnel at Terrero, north of Pecos, N.M.

According to the Public Information Officer of the Thirty-Second District, a preliminary investigation revealed that a wall heater control valve was . . .

If they won't listen, then demonstrated violence is necessary.

Military Government might prefer me dead, but it would not be stupid enough to regard me as either a criminal or an eccentric if I were able to mount a full-scale demonstration. They'd have to listen to me then.

—The Journals.

THE VIEJO OLGUIN lay on the floor of the cabin. Lagging behind the others, he had been the last to reach the park. When the rockets began exploding he'd crouched behind a boulder, drooling with terror, and had looked up just as a heavy branch spun through the air. It had caught him full in the mouth, knocking him unconscious. By the time he came around, the planes were gone and the valley was silent except for the crackle of burning fires. He saw that he was the only one left, and slowly got up. Staring around, he inserted a finger into his shattered mouth and gingerly pried out pieces of teeth and fragments of bone that protruded through the gums. He found his rifle, remembering vaguely that there were eight rounds of ammunition left for it. Using the gun as a staff he began walking.

Later that day it began to snow. Sometime in the middle of the night he found the cabin, forced the small door, and, safe inside, curled up and slept until the middle of the following day. When he finally wakened he crawled to the door and looked out, happy to see the deep fall of snow.

He found a blanket, wrapped it around himself, curled up, and slept again. He was wakened hours later by hunger. Searching the small room, he came upon a store of *carne seca* and broke off small pieces, which he forced between his split and swollen lips. The tough meat was impossible to chew; instead he sucked at it, his damaged mouth filling with saliva, warming and softening the meat until he could taste the juices.

Stronger now, he searched the place, ransacking cans and boxes. Just before dusk he found matches and candles, and then a quarter-full bottle of whiskey, which he drank in tiny, birdlike sips, crying out as the alcohol burned the open flesh inside his mouth. His mind was already functioning automatically in terms of firewood, water, more food. He went outside and gathered an armload of thin branches and brought them back to the fireplace.

The branches were snow-covered. Searching for paper, he came upon a stack of cardboard-covered notebooks and used these, tearing out the pages one by one, crumpling them into loose balls that he shoved beneath the branches in the fireplace. He got the fire going finally and knelt in front of it, warming his hands and the front of his body as the heat got to him.

The branches lasted for an hour, and at the end of that time the old man felt better, but he was too weak to gather more wood. Methodically he kept the tiny blaze going, feeding it pages from

332

the notebooks, holding his hands cupped to the warm flames. When all the pages were gone from one notebook, he threw in the cardboard cover and began tearing pages from another.

The pages were filled with a small, tight script. Once, out of curiosity, he held a page up, so that the light of the fire glanced across its surface. Olguin studied the script carefully, as if by inspecting it closely he might in some way learn the meaning contained in the few lines. Then, blinking, he tossed the sheet into the fire.

—